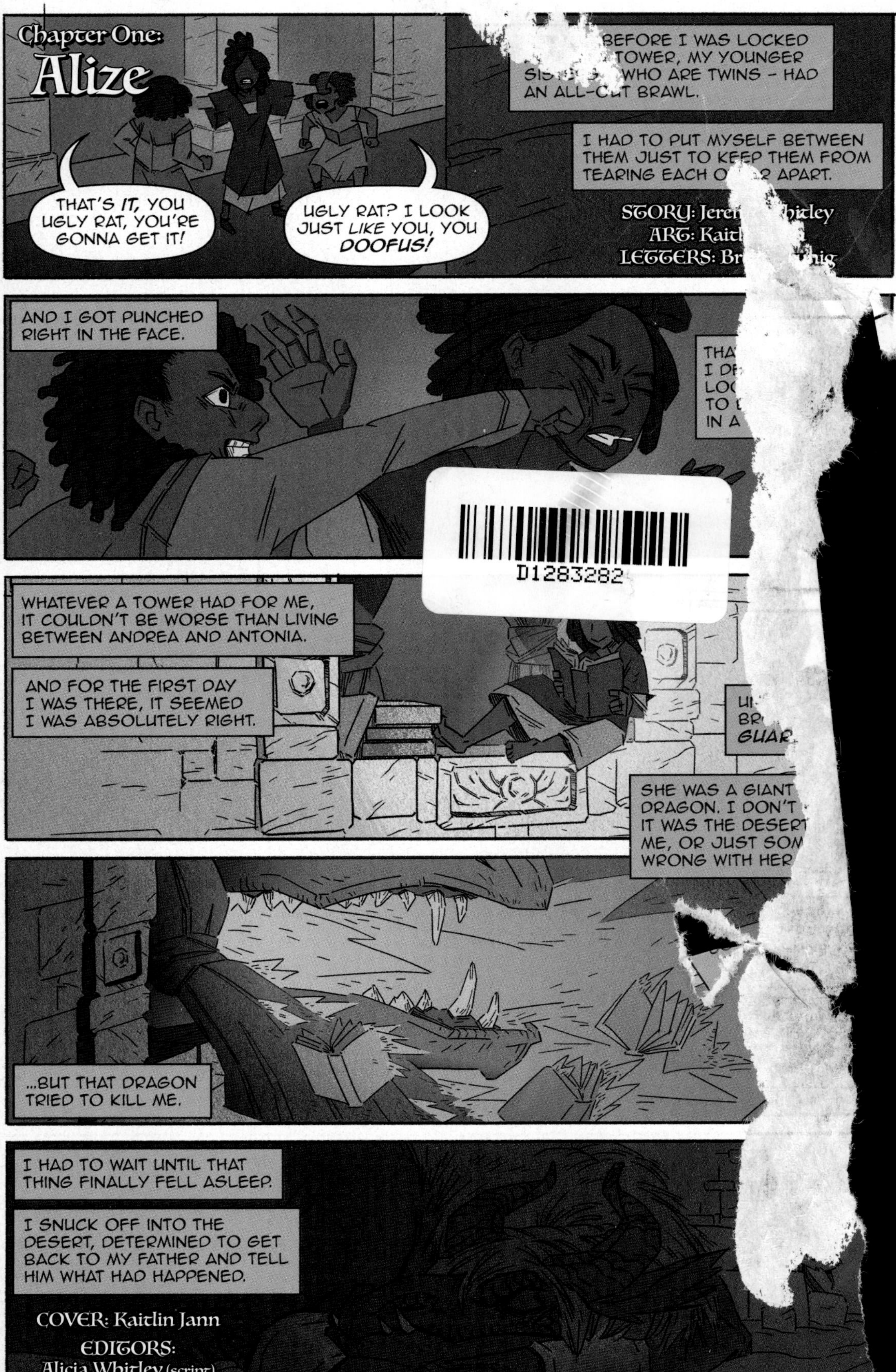
Chapter One:
Alize
BEFORE I WAS LOCKED
TOWER, MY YOUNGER
WHO ARE TWINS – HAD
AN ALL-OUT BRAWL.
I HAD TO PUT MYSELF BETWEEN THEM JUST TO KEEP THEM FROM TEARING EACH O APART.
THAT'S IT, YOU UGLY RAT, YOU'RE GONNA GET IT!
UGLY RAT? I LOOK JUST LIKE YOU, YOU DOOFUS!
STORY: Jere hitley
ART: Kait
LETTERS: Br nig
AND I GOT PUNCHED RIGHT IN THE FACE.
THA
I DE
LOC
TO
IN A
WHATEVER A TOWER HAD FOR ME, IT COULDN'T BE WORSE THAN LIVING BETWEEN ANDREA AND ANTONIA.
AND FOR THE FIRST DAY I WAS THERE, IT SEEMED I WAS ABSOLUTELY RIGHT.
UN
BR
GUAR
SHE WAS A GIANT
DRAGON. I DON'T
IT WAS THE DESERT
ME, OR JUST SOM
WRONG WITH HER
...BUT THAT DRAGON TRIED TO KILL ME.
I HAD TO WAIT UNTIL THAT THING FINALLY FELL ASLEEP.
I SNUCK OFF INTO THE DESERT, DETERMINED TO GET BACK TO MY FATHER AND TELL HIM WHAT HAD HAPPENED.
COVER: Kaitlin Jann
EDITORS:
Alicia Whitley (script)
Nicole D'Andria (comic)

Bryan Seaton: Publisher/ CEO • Shawn Gabborin: Editor In Chief • Jason Martin: Publisher-Danger Zone • Nicole D'Andria: Marketing Director/Editor
Jessica Lowrie: Social Media Czar • Danielle Davison: Executive Administrator • Chad Cicconi: Still Waiting For His Princess • Shawn Pryor: President of Creator Relations
PRINCELESS Vol. 8: PRINCESSES #1, April 2019. Copyright Jeremy Whitley, 2015. Published by Action Lab Comics.

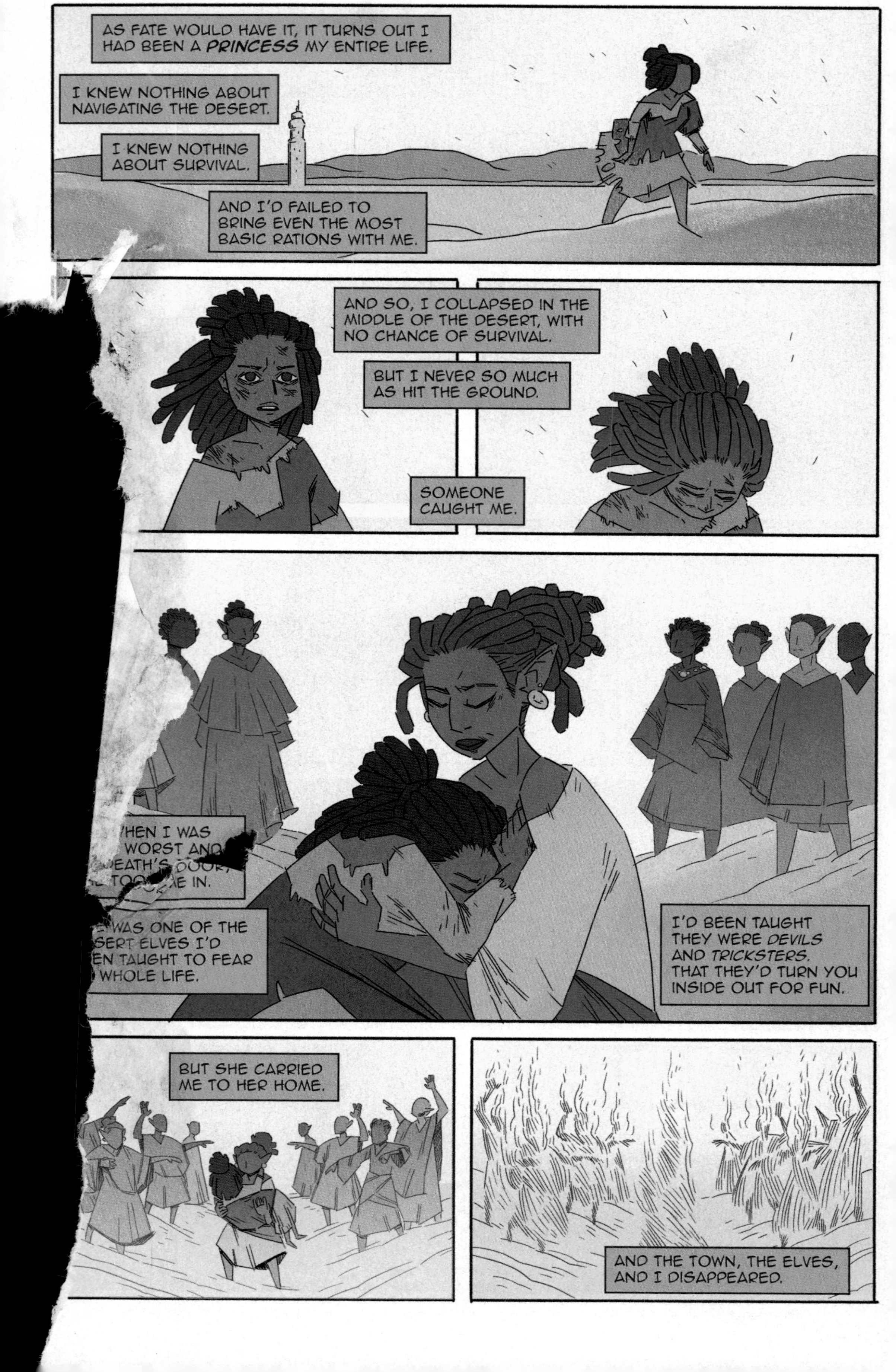
AS FATE WOULD HAVE IT, IT TURNS OUT I HAD BEEN A *PRINCESS* MY ENTIRE LIFE.
I KNEW NOTHING ABOUT NAVIGATING THE DESERT.
I KNEW NOTHING ABOUT SURVIVAL.
AND I'D FAILED TO BRING EVEN THE MOST BASIC RATIONS WITH ME.
AND SO, I COLLAPSED IN THE MIDDLE OF THE DESERT, WITH NO CHANCE OF SURVIVAL.
BUT I NEVER SO MUCH AS HIT THE GROUND.
SOMEONE CAUGHT ME.
HEN I WAS WORST AND EATH'S DOOR, IN.
E WAS ONE OF THE SERT ELVES I'D EN TAUGHT TO FEAR WHOLE LIFE.
I'D BEEN TAUGHT THEY WERE *DEVILS* AND *TRICKSTERS*. THAT THEY'D TURN YOU INSIDE OUT FOR FUN.
BUT SHE CARRIED ME TO HER HOME.
AND THE TOWN, THE ELVES, AND I DISAPPEARED.

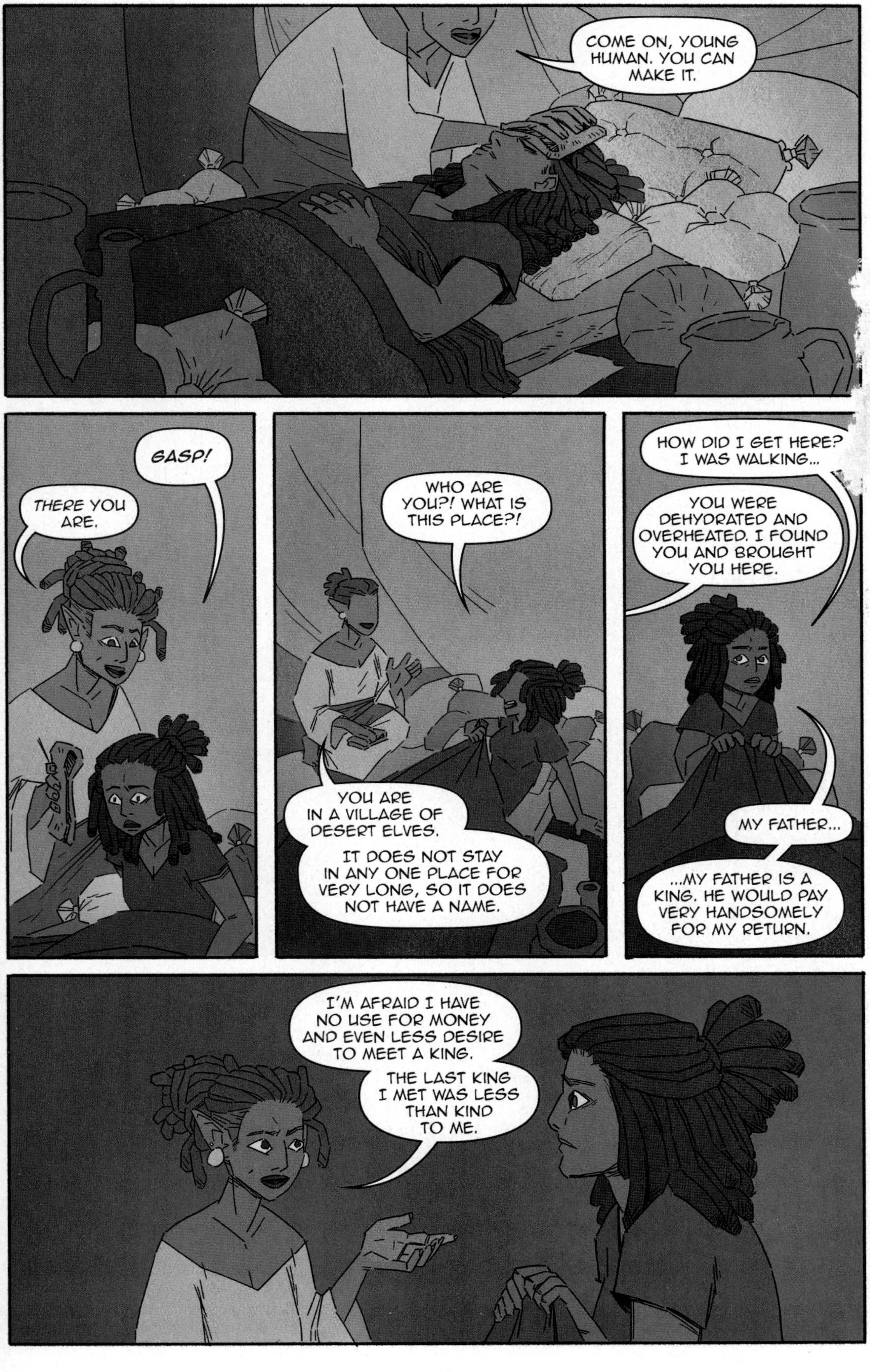
COME ON, YOUNG HUMAN. YOU CAN MAKE IT.
GASP!
THERE YOU ARE.
WHO ARE YOU?! WHAT IS THIS PLACE?!
YOU ARE IN A VILLAGE OF DESERT ELVES.
IT DOES NOT STAY IN ANY ONE PLACE FOR VERY LONG, SO IT DOES NOT HAVE A NAME.
HOW DID I GET HERE? I WAS WALKING...
YOU WERE DEHYDRATED AND OVERHEATED. I FOUND YOU AND BROUGHT YOU HERE.
MY FATHER...
...MY FATHER IS A KING. HE WOULD PAY VERY HANDSOMELY FOR MY RETURN.
I'M AFRAID I HAVE NO USE FOR MONEY AND EVEN LESS DESIRE TO MEET A KING.
THE LAST KING I MET WAS LESS THAN KIND TO ME.

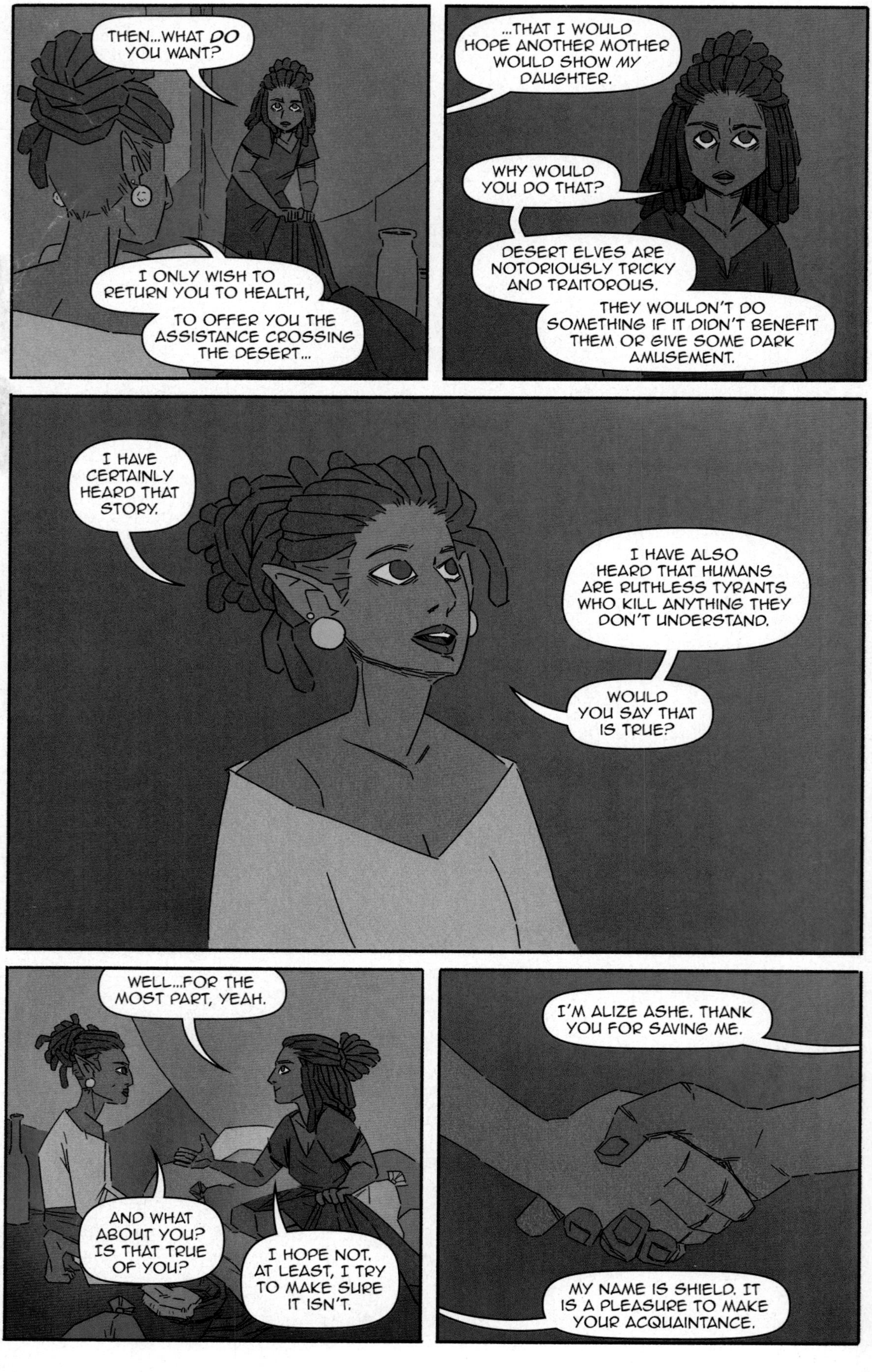
THEN...WHAT *DO* YOU WANT?
I ONLY WISH TO RETURN YOU TO HEALTH,
TO OFFER YOU THE ASSISTANCE CROSSING THE DESERT...
...THAT I WOULD HOPE ANOTHER MOTHER WOULD SHOW MY DAUGHTER.
WHY WOULD YOU DO THAT?
DESERT ELVES ARE NOTORIOUSLY TRICKY AND TRAITOROUS.
THEY WOULDN'T DO SOMETHING IF IT DIDN'T BENEFIT THEM OR GIVE SOME DARK AMUSEMENT.
I HAVE CERTAINLY HEARD THAT STORY.
I HAVE ALSO HEARD THAT HUMANS ARE RUTHLESS TYRANTS WHO KILL ANYTHING THEY DON'T UNDERSTAND.
WOULD YOU SAY THAT IS TRUE?
WELL...FOR THE MOST PART, YEAH.
AND WHAT ABOUT YOU? IS THAT TRUE OF YOU?
I HOPE NOT. AT LEAST, I TRY TO MAKE SURE IT ISN'T.
I'M ALIZE ASHE. THANK YOU FOR SAVING ME.
MY NAME IS SHIELD. IT IS A PLEASURE TO MAKE YOUR ACQUAINTANCE.

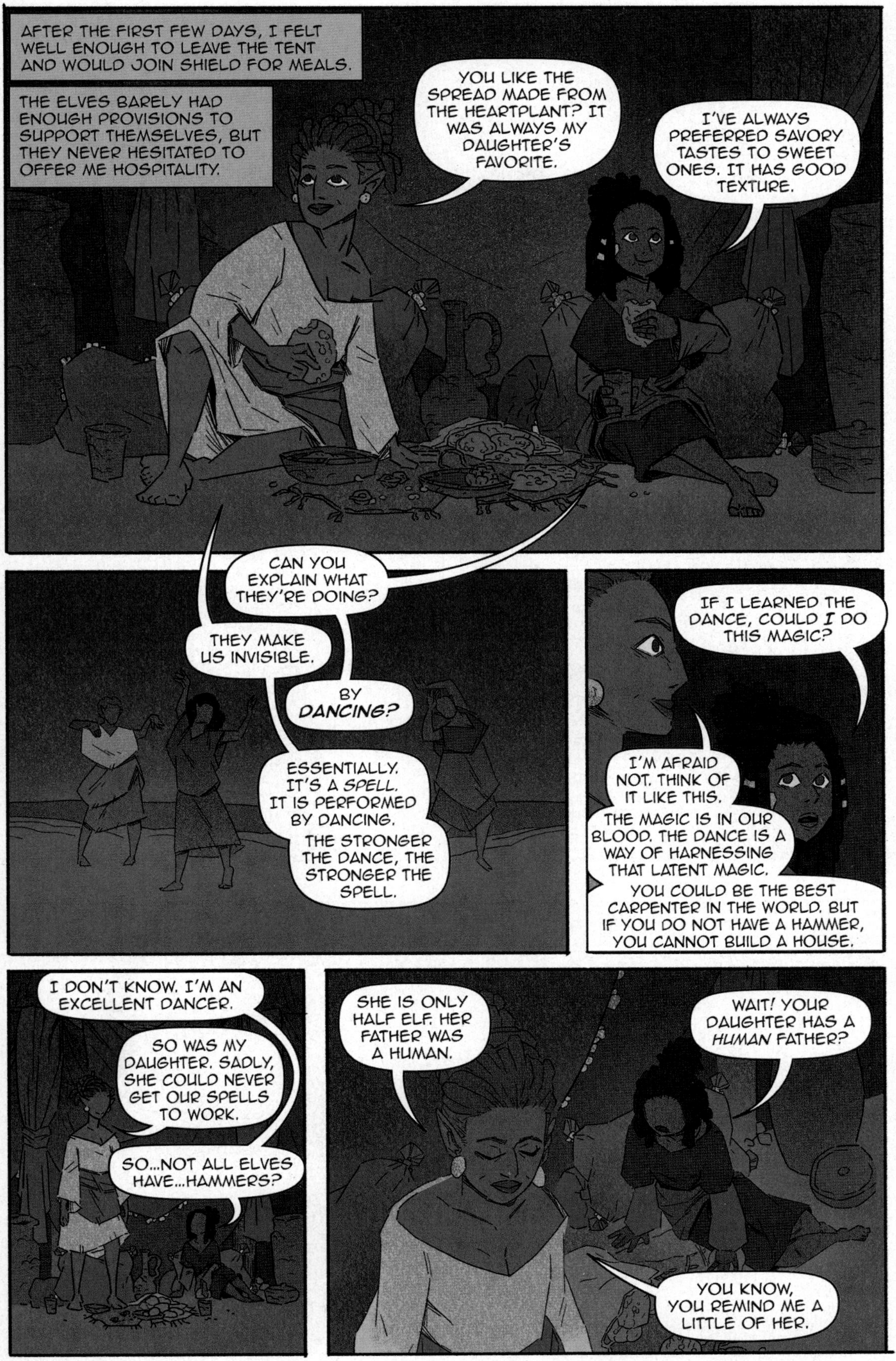
AFTER THE FIRST FEW DAYS, I FELT WELL ENOUGH TO LEAVE THE TENT AND WOULD JOIN SHIELD FOR MEALS.
THE ELVES BARELY HAD ENOUGH PROVISIONS TO SUPPORT THEMSELVES, BUT THEY NEVER HESITATED TO OFFER ME HOSPITALITY.
YOU LIKE THE SPREAD MADE FROM THE HEARTPLANT? IT WAS ALWAYS MY DAUGHTER'S FAVORITE.
I'VE ALWAYS PREFERRED SAVORY TASTES TO SWEET ONES. IT HAS GOOD TEXTURE.
CAN YOU EXPLAIN WHAT THEY'RE DOING?
THEY MAKE US INVISIBLE.
BY *DANCING?*
ESSENTIALLY. IT'S A *SPELL*. IT IS PERFORMED BY DANCING.
THE STRONGER THE DANCE, THE STRONGER THE SPELL.
IF I LEARNED THE DANCE, COULD *I* DO THIS MAGIC?
I'M AFRAID NOT. THINK OF IT LIKE THIS.
THE MAGIC IS IN OUR BLOOD. THE DANCE IS A WAY OF HARNESSING THAT LATENT MAGIC.
YOU COULD BE THE BEST CARPENTER IN THE WORLD. BUT IF YOU DO NOT HAVE A HAMMER, YOU CANNOT BUILD A HOUSE.
I DON'T KNOW. I'M AN EXCELLENT DANCER.
SO WAS MY DAUGHTER. SADLY, SHE COULD NEVER GET OUR SPELLS TO WORK.
SO...NOT ALL ELVES HAVE...HAMMERS?
SHE IS ONLY HALF ELF. HER FATHER WAS A HUMAN.
WAIT! YOUR DAUGHTER HAS A *HUMAN* FATHER?
YOU KNOW, YOU REMIND ME A LITTLE OF HER.

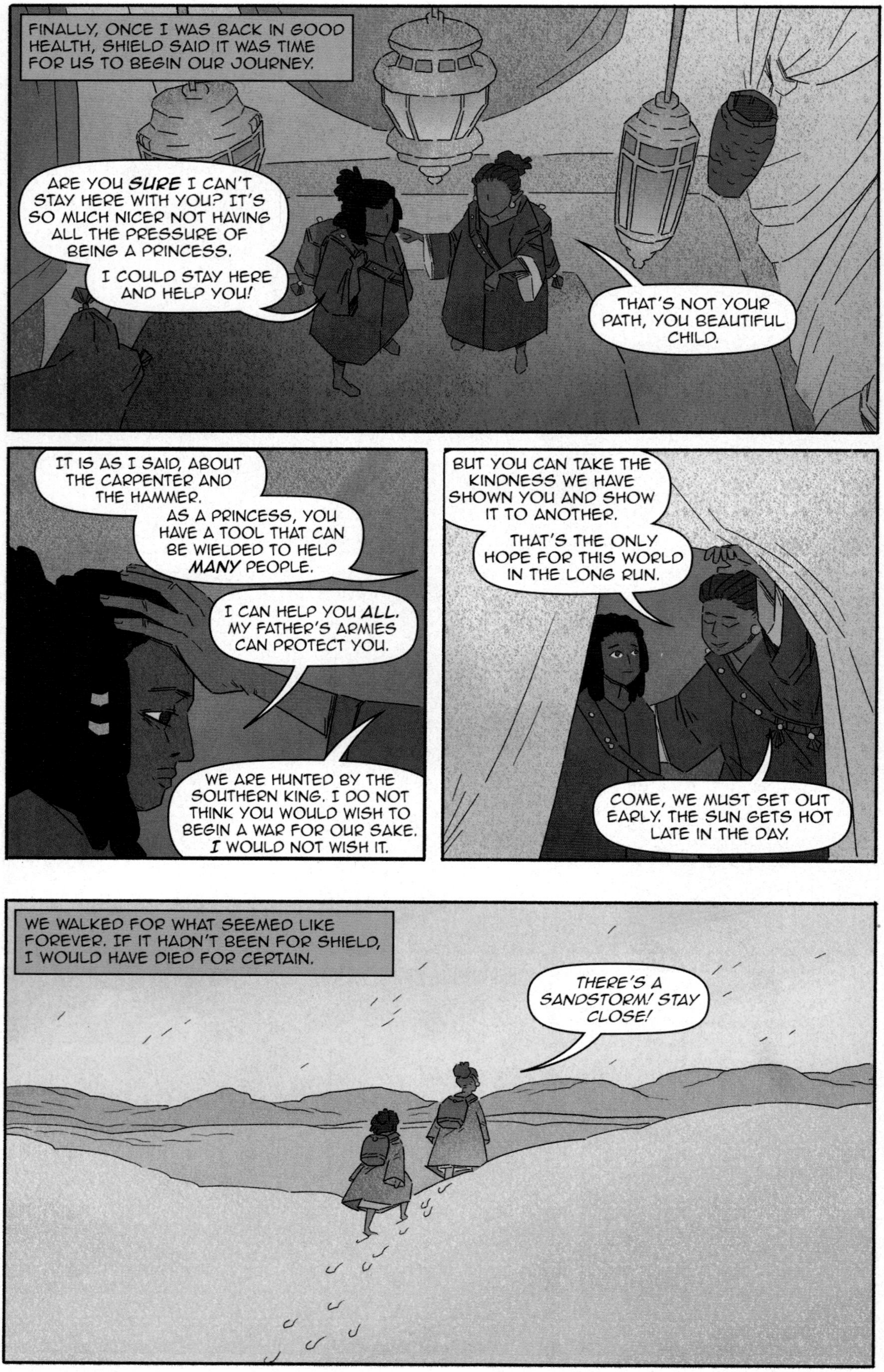
FINALLY, ONCE I WAS BACK IN GOOD HEALTH, SHIELD SAID IT WAS TIME FOR US TO BEGIN OUR JOURNEY.
ARE YOU SURE I CAN'T STAY HERE WITH YOU? IT'S SO MUCH NICER NOT HAVING ALL THE PRESSURE OF BEING A PRINCESS.
I COULD STAY HERE AND HELP YOU!
THAT'S NOT YOUR PATH, YOU BEAUTIFUL CHILD.
IT IS AS I SAID, ABOUT THE CARPENTER AND THE HAMMER.
AS A PRINCESS, YOU HAVE A TOOL THAT CAN BE WIELDED TO HELP MANY PEOPLE.
I CAN HELP YOU ALL. MY FATHER'S ARMIES CAN PROTECT YOU.
WE ARE HUNTED BY THE SOUTHERN KING. I DO NOT THINK YOU WOULD WISH TO BEGIN A WAR FOR OUR SAKE. I WOULD NOT WISH IT.
BUT YOU CAN TAKE THE KINDNESS WE HAVE SHOWN YOU AND SHOW IT TO ANOTHER.
THAT'S THE ONLY HOPE FOR THIS WORLD IN THE LONG RUN.
COME, WE MUST SET OUT EARLY. THE SUN GETS HOT LATE IN THE DAY.
WE WALKED FOR WHAT SEEMED LIKE FOREVER. IF IT HADN'T BEEN FOR SHIELD, I WOULD HAVE DIED FOR CERTAIN.
THERE'S A SANDSTORM! STAY CLOSE!

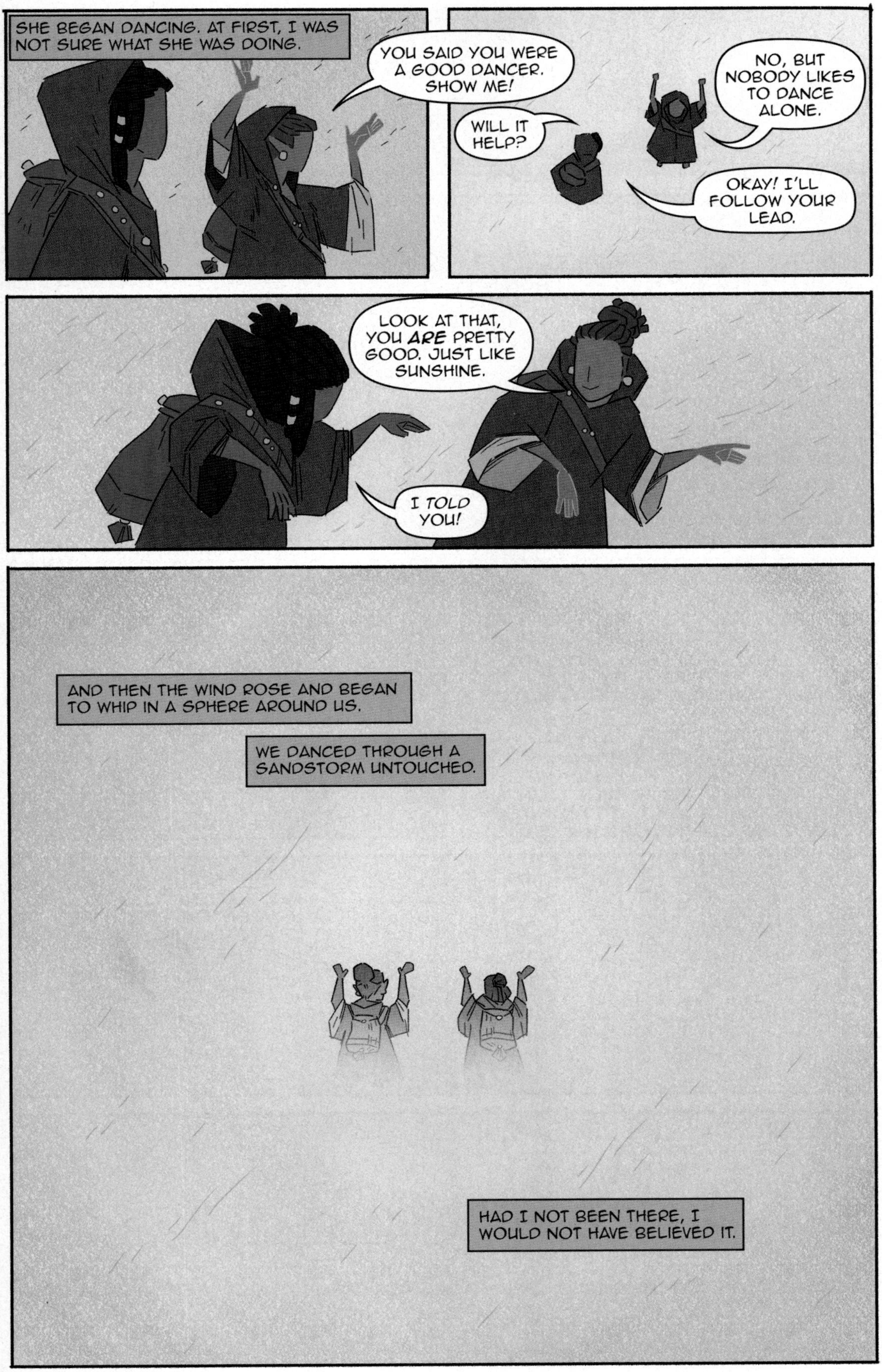

SHE BEGAN DANCING. AT FIRST, I WAS NOT SURE WHAT SHE WAS DOING.
YOU SAID YOU WERE A GOOD DANCER. SHOW ME!
WILL IT HELP?
NO, BUT NOBODY LIKES TO DANCE ALONE.
OKAY! I'LL FOLLOW YOUR LEAD.
LOOK AT THAT, YOU ARE PRETTY GOOD. JUST LIKE SUNSHINE.
I TOLD YOU!
AND THEN THE WIND ROSE AND BEGAN TO WHIP IN A SPHERE AROUND US.
WE DANCED THROUGH A SANDSTORM UNTOUCHED.
HAD I NOT BEEN THERE, I WOULD NOT HAVE BELIEVED IT.

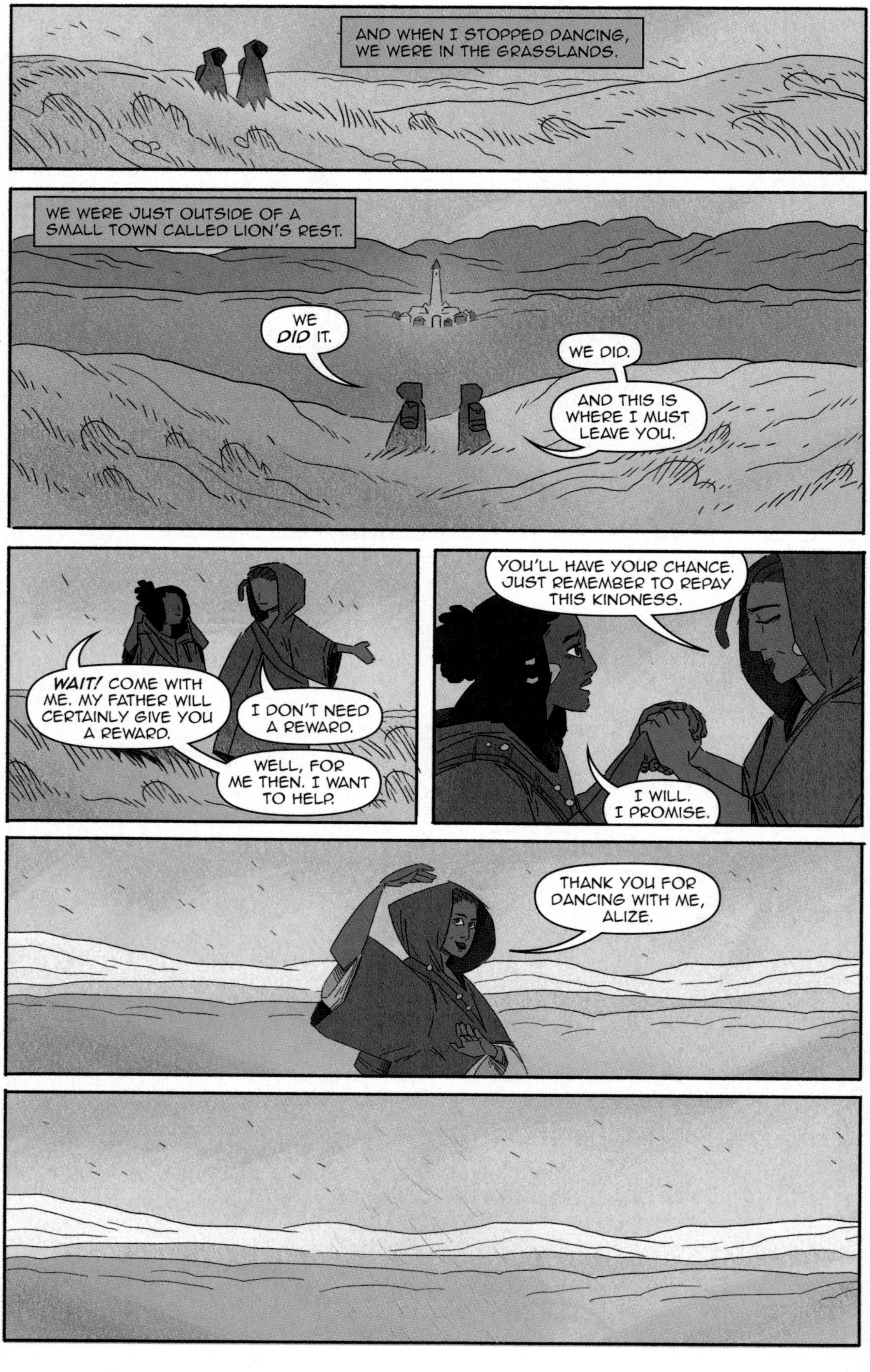
AND WHEN I STOPPED DANCING, WE WERE IN THE GRASSLANDS.
WE WERE JUST OUTSIDE OF A SMALL TOWN CALLED LION'S REST.
WE DID IT.
WE DID.
AND THIS IS WHERE I MUST LEAVE YOU.
WAIT! COME WITH ME. MY FATHER WILL CERTAINLY GIVE YOU A REWARD.
I DON'T NEED A REWARD.
WELL, FOR ME THEN. I WANT TO HELP.
YOU'LL HAVE YOUR CHANCE. JUST REMEMBER TO REPAY THIS KINDNESS.
I WILL. I PROMISE.
THANK YOU FOR DANCING WITH ME, ALIZE.

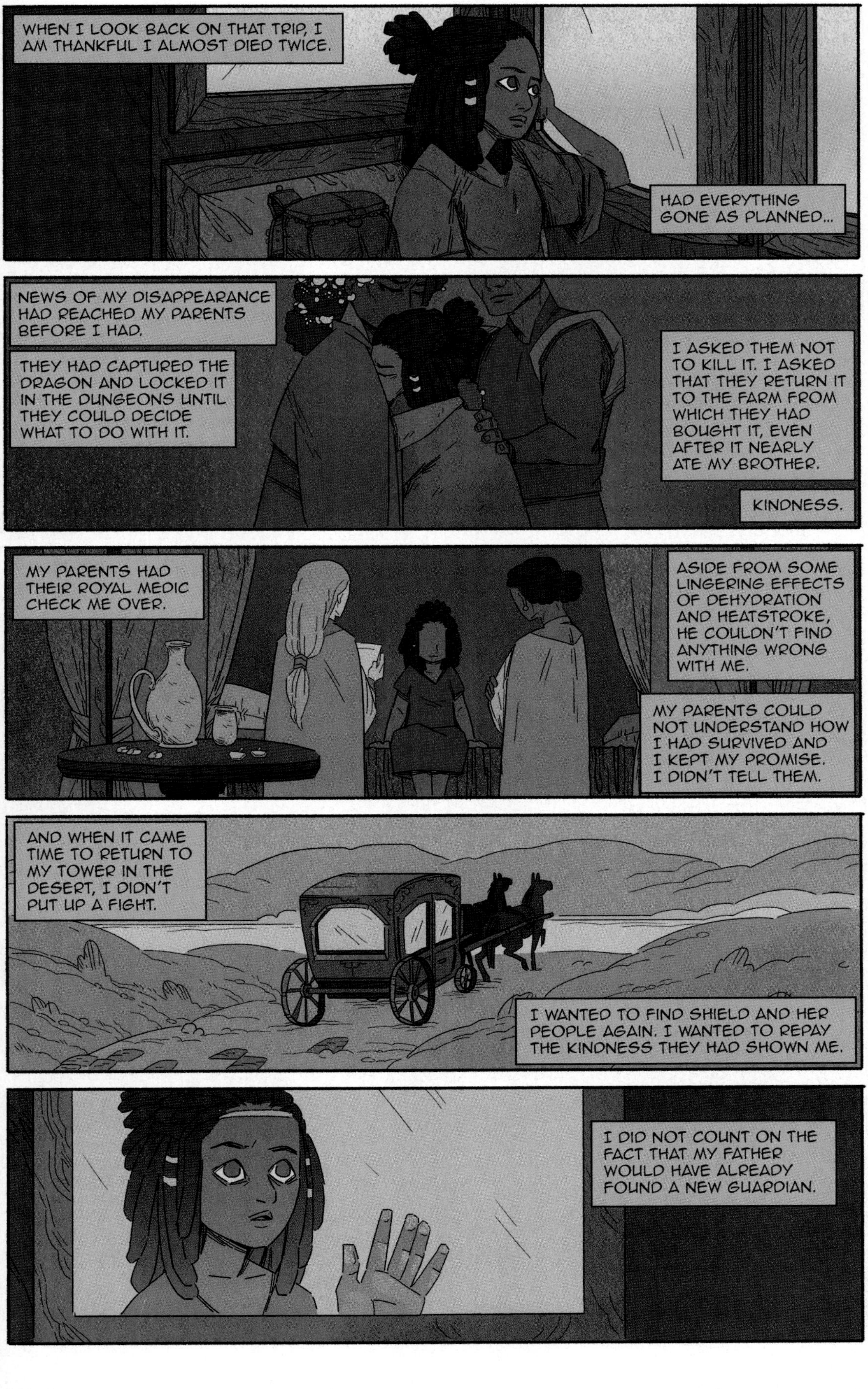
WHEN I LOOK BACK ON THAT TRIP, I AM THANKFUL I ALMOST DIED TWICE.
HAD EVERYTHING GONE AS PLANNED...
NEWS OF MY DISAPPEARANCE HAD REACHED MY PARENTS BEFORE I HAD.
THEY HAD CAPTURED THE DRAGON AND LOCKED IT IN THE DUNGEONS UNTIL THEY COULD DECIDE WHAT TO DO WITH IT.
I ASKED THEM NOT TO KILL IT. I ASKED THAT THEY RETURN IT TO THE FARM FROM WHICH THEY HAD BOUGHT IT, EVEN AFTER IT NEARLY ATE MY BROTHER.
KINDNESS.
MY PARENTS HAD THEIR ROYAL MEDIC CHECK ME OVER.
ASIDE FROM SOME LINGERING EFFECTS OF DEHYDRATION AND HEATSTROKE, HE COULDN'T FIND ANYTHING WRONG WITH ME.
MY PARENTS COULD NOT UNDERSTAND HOW I HAD SURVIVED AND I KEPT MY PROMISE. I DIDN'T TELL THEM.
AND WHEN IT CAME TIME TO RETURN TO MY TOWER IN THE DESERT, I DIDN'T PUT UP A FIGHT.
I WANTED TO FIND SHIELD AND HER PEOPLE AGAIN. I WANTED TO REPAY THE KINDNESS THEY HAD SHOWN ME.
I DID NOT COUNT ON THE FACT THAT MY FATHER WOULD HAVE ALREADY FOUND A NEW GUARDIAN.

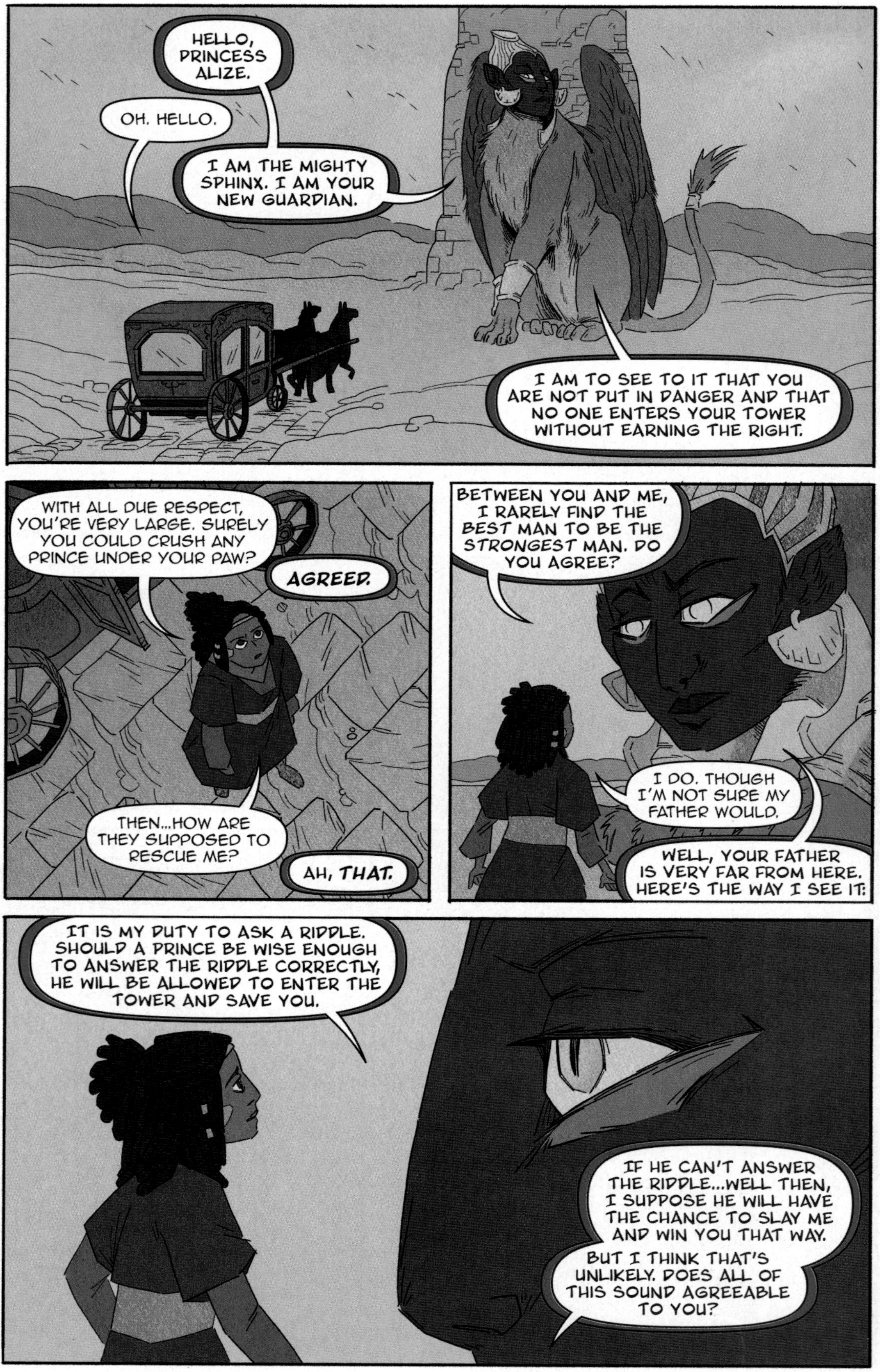
HELLO, PRINCESS ALIZE.
OH. HELLO.
I AM THE MIGHTY SPHINX. I AM YOUR NEW GUARDIAN.
I AM TO SEE TO IT THAT YOU ARE NOT PUT IN DANGER AND THAT NO ONE ENTERS YOUR TOWER WITHOUT EARNING THE RIGHT.
WITH ALL DUE RESPECT, YOU'RE VERY LARGE. SURELY YOU COULD CRUSH ANY PRINCE UNDER YOUR PAW?
AGREED.
THEN...HOW ARE THEY SUPPOSED TO RESCUE ME?
AH, THAT.
BETWEEN YOU AND ME, I RARELY FIND THE BEST MAN TO BE THE STRONGEST MAN. DO YOU AGREE?
I DO. THOUGH I'M NOT SURE MY FATHER WOULD.
WELL, YOUR FATHER IS VERY FAR FROM HERE. HERE'S THE WAY I SEE IT:
IT IS MY DUTY TO ASK A RIDDLE. SHOULD A PRINCE BE WISE ENOUGH TO ANSWER THE RIDDLE CORRECTLY, HE WILL BE ALLOWED TO ENTER THE TOWER AND SAVE YOU.
IF HE CAN'T ANSWER THE RIDDLE...WELL THEN, I SUPPOSE HE WILL HAVE THE CHANCE TO SLAY ME AND WIN YOU THAT WAY.
BUT I THINK THAT'S UNLIKELY. DOES ALL OF THIS SOUND AGREEABLE TO YOU?

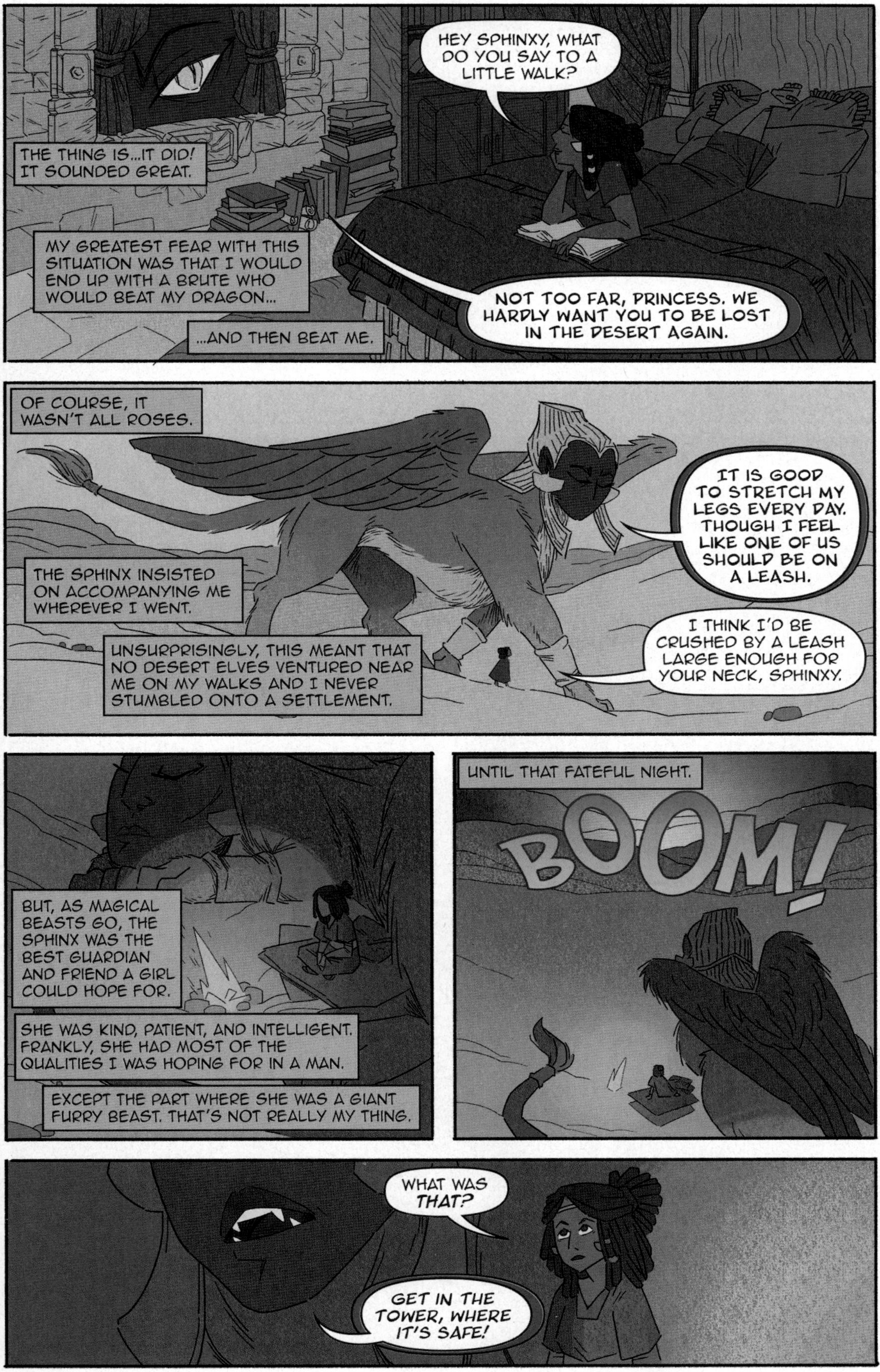
HEY SPHINXY, WHAT DO YOU SAY TO A LITTLE WALK?
THE THING IS...IT DID! IT SOUNDED GREAT.
MY GREATEST FEAR WITH THIS SITUATION WAS THAT I WOULD END UP WITH A BRUTE WHO WOULD BEAT MY DRAGON...
...AND THEN BEAT ME.
NOT TOO FAR, PRINCESS. WE HARDLY WANT YOU TO BE LOST IN THE DESERT AGAIN.
OF COURSE, IT WASN'T ALL ROSES.
THE SPHINX INSISTED ON ACCOMPANYING ME WHEREVER I WENT.
UNSURPRISINGLY, THIS MEANT THAT NO DESERT ELVES VENTURED NEAR ME ON MY WALKS AND I NEVER STUMBLED ONTO A SETTLEMENT.
IT IS GOOD TO STRETCH MY LEGS EVERY DAY. THOUGH I FEEL LIKE ONE OF US SHOULD BE ON A LEASH.
I THINK I'D BE CRUSHED BY A LEASH LARGE ENOUGH FOR YOUR NECK, SPHINXY.
BUT, AS MAGICAL BEASTS GO, THE SPHINX WAS THE BEST GUARDIAN AND FRIEND A GIRL COULD HOPE FOR.
SHE WAS KIND, PATIENT, AND INTELLIGENT. FRANKLY, SHE HAD MOST OF THE QUALITIES I WAS HOPING FOR IN A MAN.
EXCEPT THE PART WHERE SHE WAS A GIANT FURRY BEAST. THAT'S NOT REALLY MY THING.
UNTIL THAT FATEFUL NIGHT.
BOOM!
WHAT WAS *THAT?*
GET IN THE TOWER, WHERE IT'S SAFE!

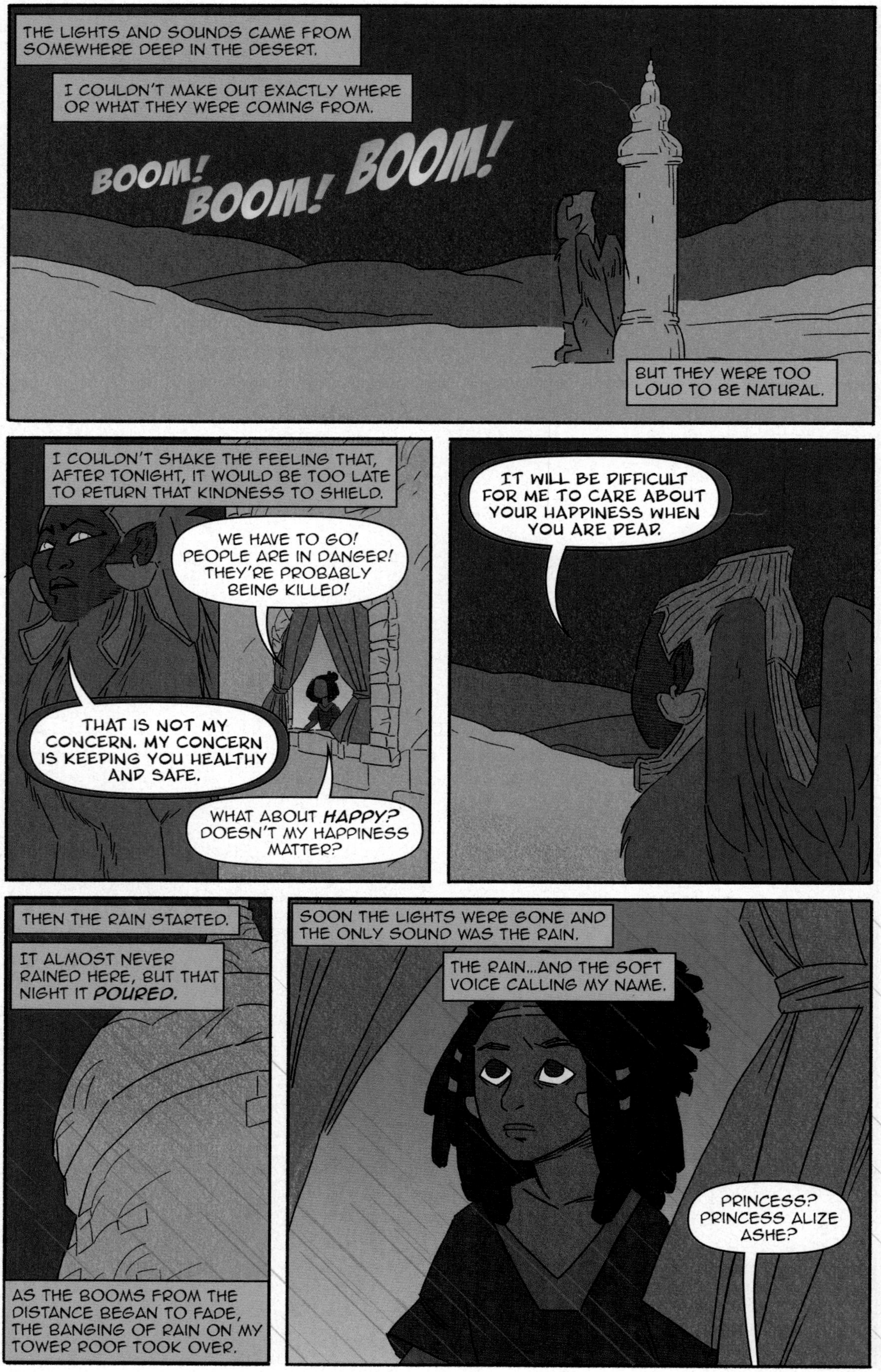
THE LIGHTS AND SOUNDS CAME FROM SOMEWHERE DEEP IN THE DESERT.
I COULDN'T MAKE OUT EXACTLY WHERE OR WHAT THEY WERE COMING FROM.
BOOM! BOOM! BOOM!
BUT THEY WERE TOO LOUD TO BE NATURAL.
I COULDN'T SHAKE THE FEELING THAT, AFTER TONIGHT, IT WOULD BE TOO LATE TO RETURN THAT KINDNESS TO SHIELD.
WE HAVE TO GO! PEOPLE ARE IN DANGER! THEY'RE PROBABLY BEING KILLED!
THAT IS NOT MY CONCERN. MY CONCERN IS KEEPING YOU HEALTHY AND SAFE.
WHAT ABOUT *HAPPY?* DOESN'T MY HAPPINESS MATTER?
IT WILL BE DIFFICULT FOR ME TO CARE ABOUT YOUR HAPPINESS WHEN YOU ARE DEAD.
THEN THE RAIN STARTED.
IT ALMOST NEVER RAINED HERE, BUT THAT NIGHT IT *POURED.*
AS THE BOOMS FROM THE DISTANCE BEGAN TO FADE, THE BANGING OF RAIN ON MY TOWER ROOF TOOK OVER.
SOON THE LIGHTS WERE GONE AND THE ONLY SOUND WAS THE RAIN.
THE RAIN...AND THE SOFT VOICE CALLING MY NAME.
PRINCESS? PRINCESS ALIZE ASHE?

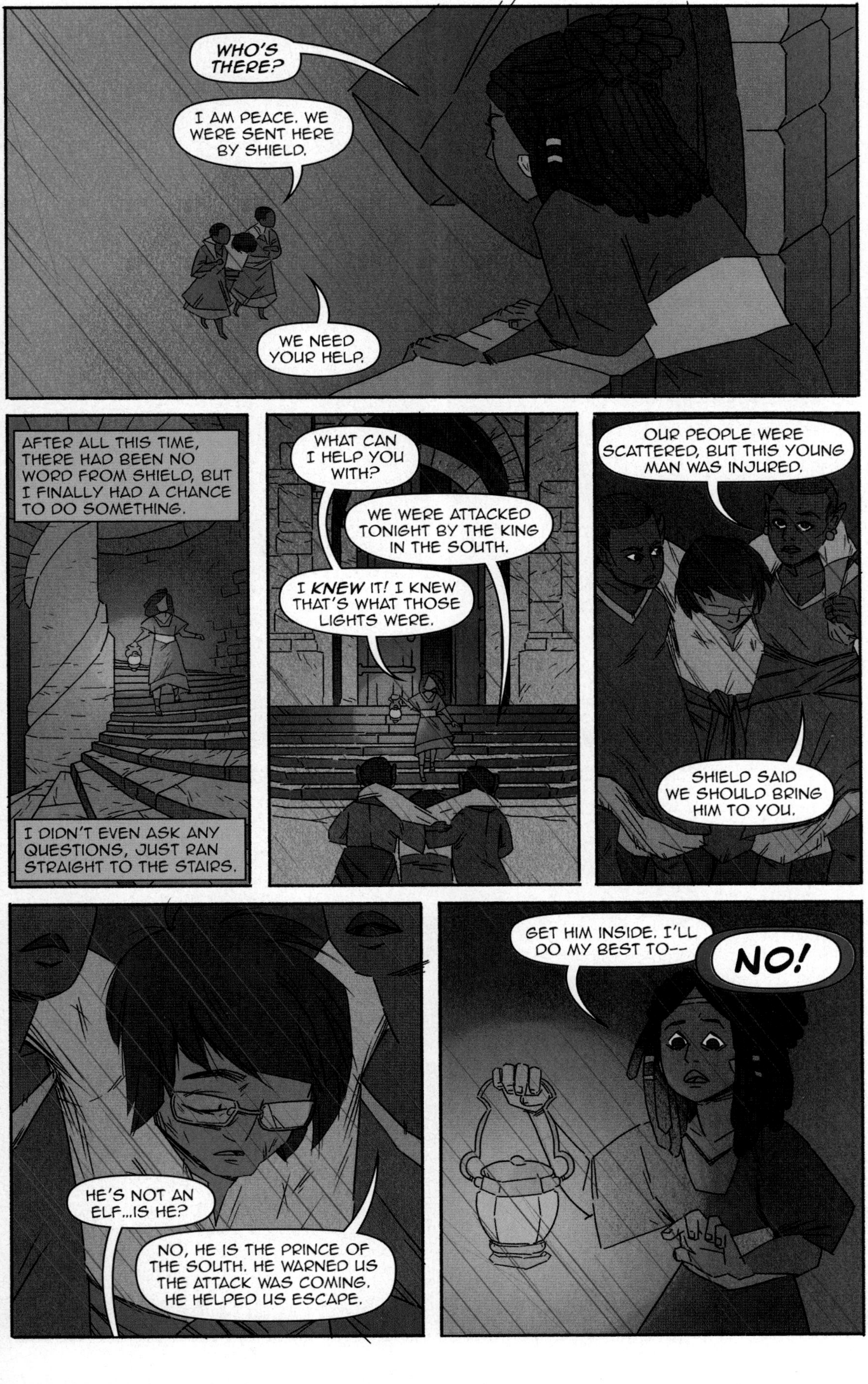
WHO'S THERE?
I AM PEACE. WE WERE SENT HERE BY SHIELD.
WE NEED YOUR HELP.
AFTER ALL THIS TIME, THERE HAD BEEN NO WORD FROM SHIELD, BUT I FINALLY HAD A CHANCE TO DO SOMETHING.
I DIDN'T EVEN ASK ANY QUESTIONS, JUST RAN STRAIGHT TO THE STAIRS.
WHAT CAN I HELP YOU WITH?
WE WERE ATTACKED TONIGHT BY THE KING IN THE SOUTH.
I KNEW IT! I KNEW THAT'S WHAT THOSE LIGHTS WERE.
OUR PEOPLE WERE SCATTERED, BUT THIS YOUNG MAN WAS INJURED.
SHIELD SAID WE SHOULD BRING HIM TO YOU.
HE'S NOT AN ELF...IS HE?
NO, HE IS THE PRINCE OF THE SOUTH. HE WARNED US THE ATTACK WAS COMING. HE HELPED US ESCAPE.
GET HIM INSIDE. I'LL DO MY BEST TO--
NO!

SPHINX, WHAT ARE YOU DOING?

MY DUTY, PRINCESS.

HE'S INJURED.

HE'S A PRINCE.

ONLY ONE PRINCE MAY ENTER THIS TOWER AND HE MUST PROVE HIMSELF FIRST.

PROVE HIMSELF? HE'S UNCONSCIOUS! HOW SHOULD HE PROVE HIMSELF?

WAKING UP WOULD BE A GOOD START.

NOW? NOW YOU FINALLY GROW A SENSE OF HUMOR?

THERE IS NOTHING FUNNY ABOUT THIS. IF THEY ATTEMPT TO CARRY HIM PAST THIS THRESHOLD, I WILL BE FORCED TO ATTACK THEM.

OH REALLY? YOU'RE JUST GOING TO CRUSH INNOCENT PEOPLE FOR TRYING TO HELP SOMEONE NOW?

I WILL DO MY DUTY. MY DUTY IS TO PROTECT YOU.

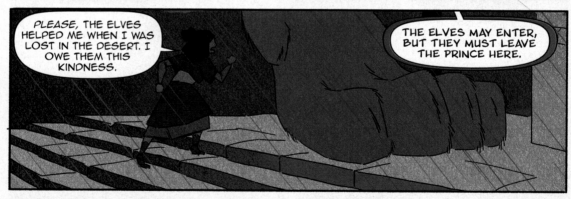

PLEASE, THE ELVES HELPED ME WHEN I WAS LOST IN THE DESERT. I OWE THEM THIS KINDNESS.

THE ELVES MAY ENTER, BUT THEY MUST LEAVE THE PRINCE HERE.

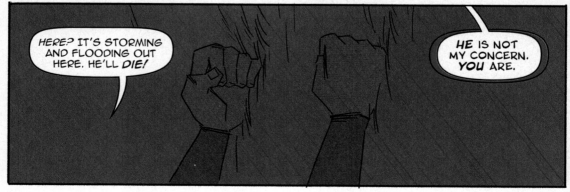

HERE? IT'S STORMING AND FLOODING OUT HERE. HE'LL DIE!

HE IS NOT MY CONCERN. YOU ARE.

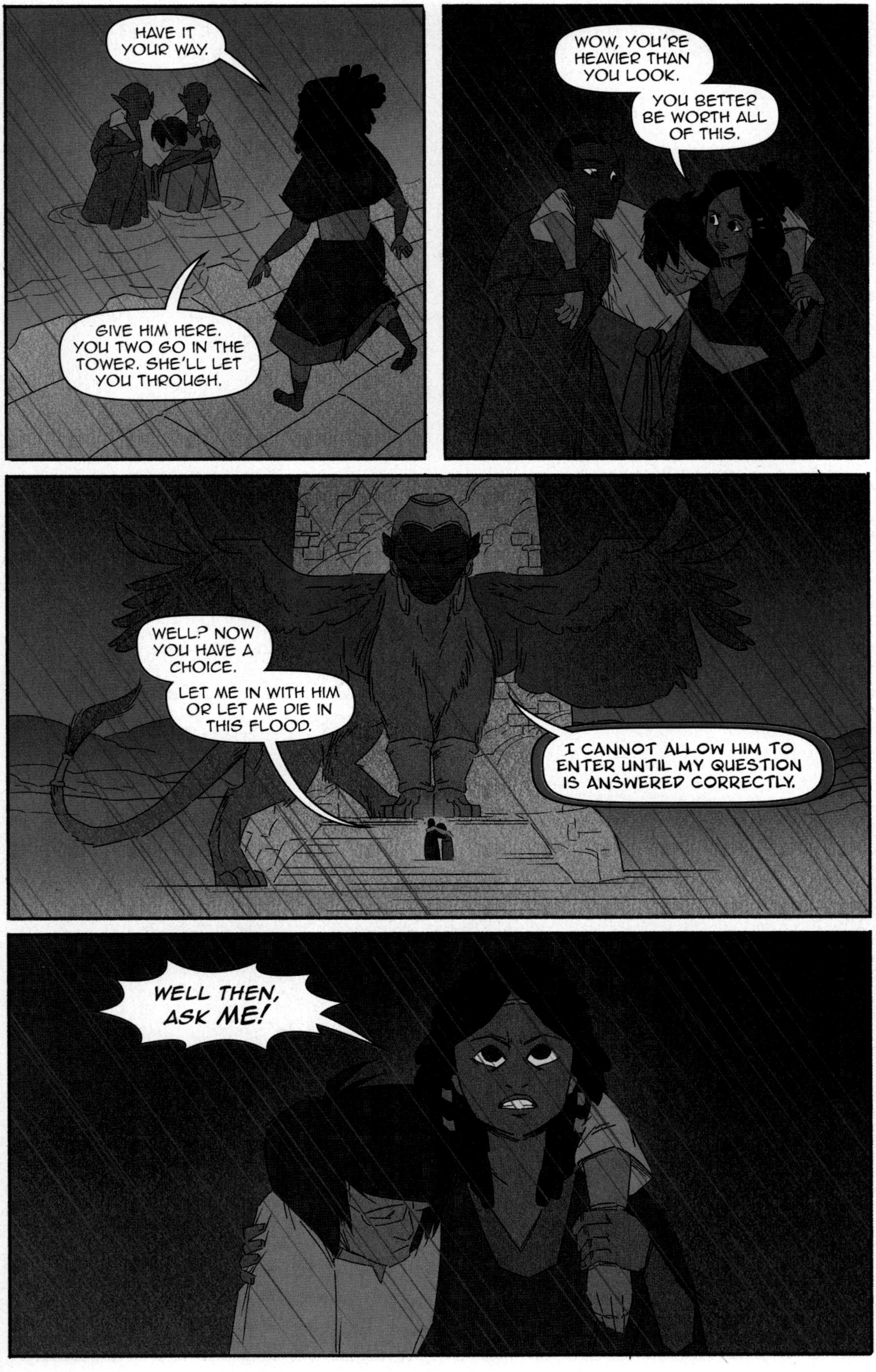
HAVE IT YOUR WAY.
GIVE HIM HERE. YOU TWO GO IN THE TOWER. SHE'LL LET YOU THROUGH.
WOW, YOU'RE HEAVIER THAN YOU LOOK.
YOU BETTER BE WORTH ALL OF THIS.
WELL? NOW YOU HAVE A CHOICE.
LET ME IN WITH HIM OR LET ME DIE IN THIS FLOOD.
I CANNOT ALLOW HIM TO ENTER UNTIL MY QUESTION IS ANSWERED CORRECTLY.
WELL THEN, ASK ME!

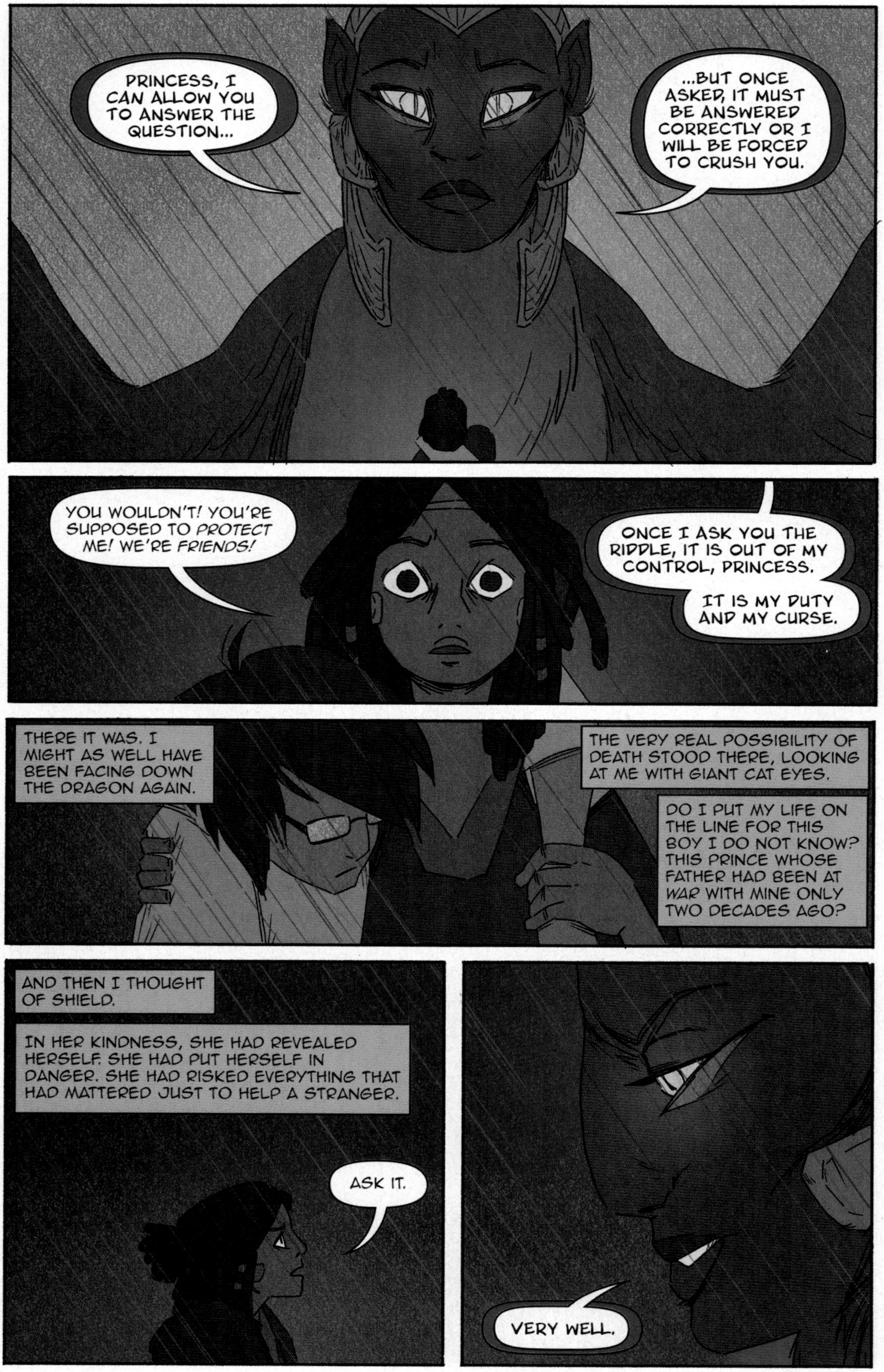
PRINCESS, I CAN ALLOW YOU TO ANSWER THE QUESTION...
...BUT ONCE ASKED, IT MUST BE ANSWERED CORRECTLY OR I WILL BE FORCED TO CRUSH YOU.
YOU WOULDN'T! YOU'RE SUPPOSED TO *PROTECT* ME! WE'RE *FRIENDS!*
ONCE I ASK YOU THE RIDDLE, IT IS OUT OF MY CONTROL, PRINCESS.
IT IS MY DUTY AND MY CURSE.
THERE IT WAS. I MIGHT AS WELL HAVE BEEN FACING DOWN THE DRAGON AGAIN.
THE VERY REAL POSSIBILITY OF DEATH STOOD THERE, LOOKING AT ME WITH GIANT CAT EYES.
DO I PUT MY LIFE ON THE LINE FOR THIS BOY I DO NOT KNOW? THIS PRINCE WHOSE FATHER HAD BEEN AT *WAR* WITH MINE ONLY TWO DECADES AGO?
AND THEN I THOUGHT OF SHIELD.
IN HER KINDNESS, SHE HAD REVEALED HERSELF. SHE HAD PUT HERSELF IN DANGER. SHE HAD RISKED EVERYTHING THAT HAD MATTERED JUST TO HELP A STRANGER.
ASK IT.
VERY WELL.

I AM THE WEAPON OF THOSE WHO WISH NOT TO FIGHT. I AM A PRIZE WON BY THOSE WHO LOSE.

I AM NEEDED FOR VICTORY, BUT INVISIBLE FROM SIGHT. I AM ENEMY OF IGNORANCE AND DESTROYER OF RUSE.

WHAT AM I?

IN THAT MOMENT, I PANICKED.

I HAD NEVER STOPPED TO CONSIDER IT MIGHT NOT BE SOMETHING I WOULD KNOW.

I READ CONSTANTLY, AFTER ALL. MY BRAIN WAS PACKED TO THE BRIM WITH KNOWLEDGE.

BUT, OF COURSE, READING ABOUT A THING AND ACTUALLY *DOING* A THING ARE TWO DIFFERENT THINGS.

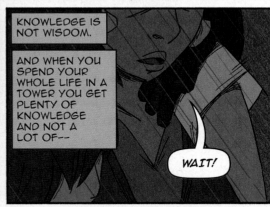

KNOWLEDGE IS NOT WISDOM.

AND WHEN YOU SPEND YOUR WHOLE LIFE IN A TOWER YOU GET PLENTY OF KNOWLEDGE AND NOT A LOT OF--

WAIT!

IT'S WISDOM, ISN'T IT?

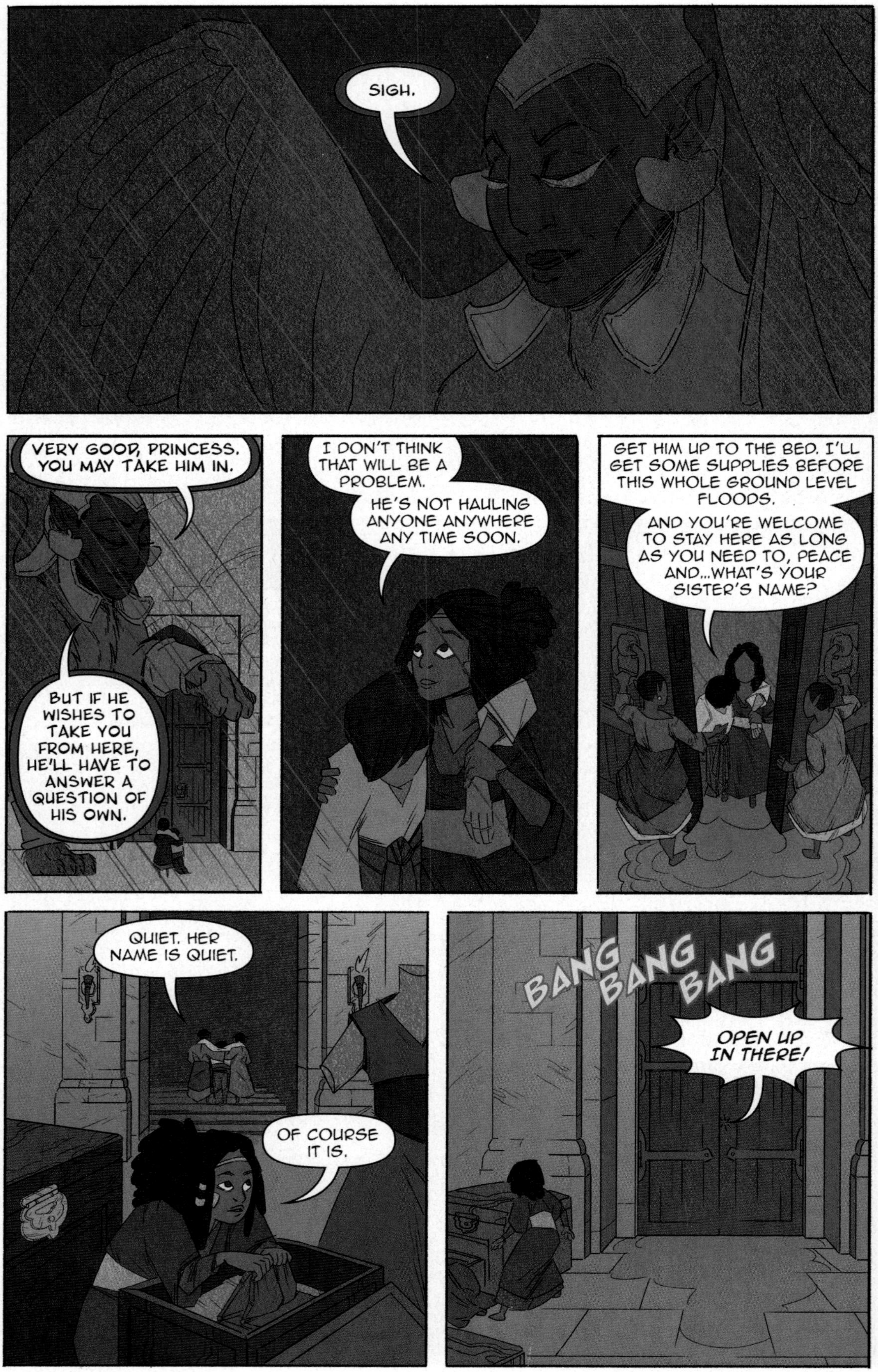
SIGH.
VERY GOOD, PRINCESS. YOU MAY TAKE HIM IN.
BUT IF HE WISHES TO TAKE YOU FROM HERE, HE'LL HAVE TO ANSWER A QUESTION OF HIS OWN.
I DON'T THINK THAT WILL BE A PROBLEM.
HE'S NOT HAULING ANYONE ANYWHERE ANY TIME SOON.
GET HIM UP TO THE BED. I'LL GET SOME SUPPLIES BEFORE THIS WHOLE GROUND LEVEL FLOODS.
AND YOU'RE WELCOME TO STAY HERE AS LONG AS YOU NEED TO, PEACE AND...WHAT'S YOUR SISTER'S NAME?
QUIET. HER NAME IS QUIET.
OF COURSE IT IS.
BANG BANG BANG
OPEN UP IN THERE!

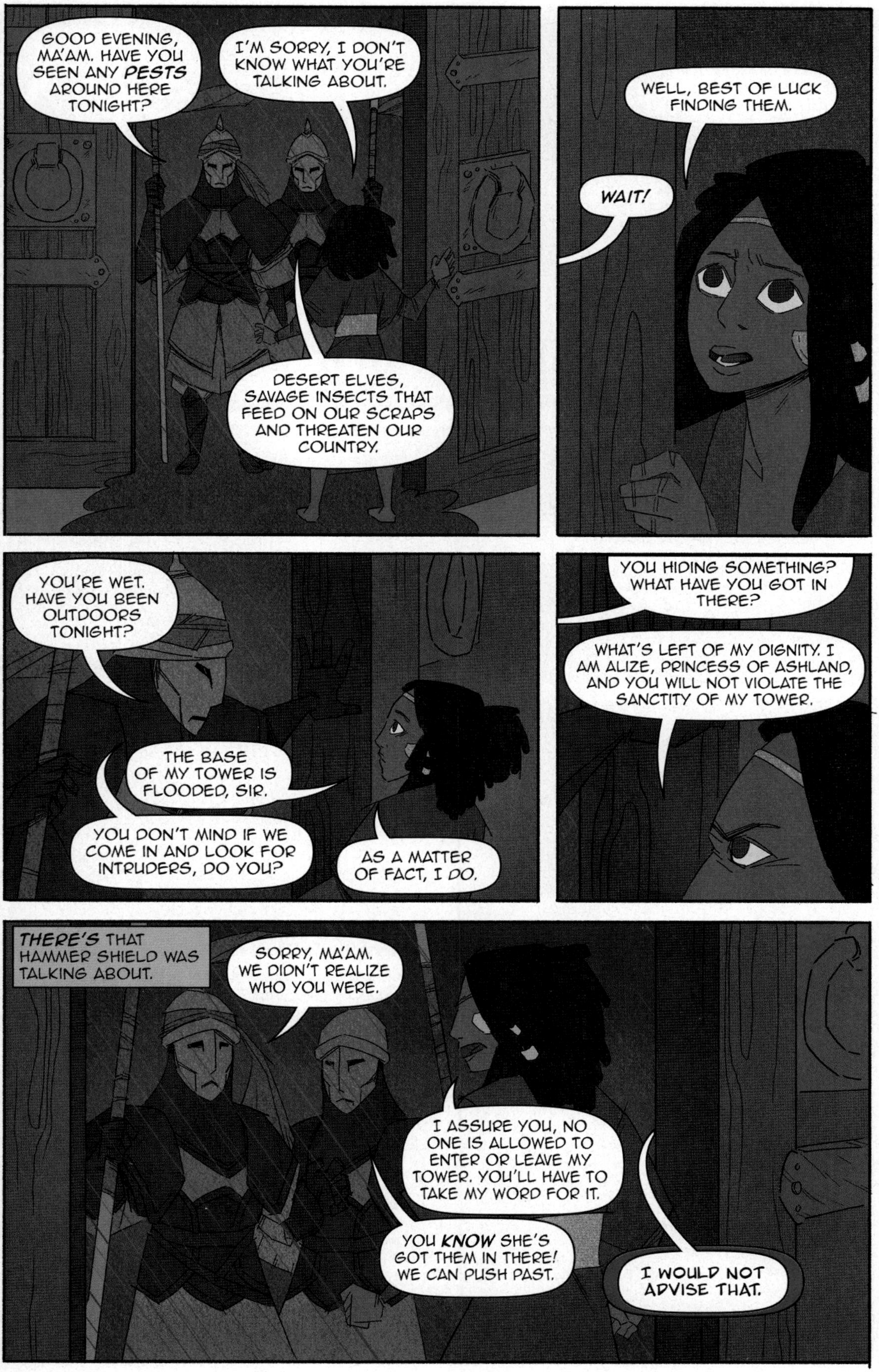
GOOD EVENING, MA'AM. HAVE YOU SEEN ANY PESTS AROUND HERE TONIGHT?
I'M SORRY, I DON'T KNOW WHAT YOU'RE TALKING ABOUT.
DESERT ELVES, SAVAGE INSECTS THAT FEED ON OUR SCRAPS AND THREATEN OUR COUNTRY.
WELL, BEST OF LUCK FINDING THEM.
WAIT!
YOU'RE WET. HAVE YOU BEEN OUTDOORS TONIGHT?
THE BASE OF MY TOWER IS FLOODED, SIR.
YOU DON'T MIND IF WE COME IN AND LOOK FOR INTRUDERS, DO YOU?
AS A MATTER OF FACT, I DO.
YOU HIDING SOMETHING? WHAT HAVE YOU GOT IN THERE?
WHAT'S LEFT OF MY DIGNITY. I AM ALIZE, PRINCESS OF ASHLAND, AND YOU WILL NOT VIOLATE THE SANCTITY OF MY TOWER.
THERE'S THAT HAMMER SHIELD WAS TALKING ABOUT.
SORRY, MA'AM. WE DIDN'T REALIZE WHO YOU WERE.
I ASSURE YOU, NO ONE IS ALLOWED TO ENTER OR LEAVE MY TOWER. YOU'LL HAVE TO TAKE MY WORD FOR IT.
YOU KNOW SHE'S GOT THEM IN THERE! WE CAN PUSH PAST.
I WOULD NOT ADVISE THAT.

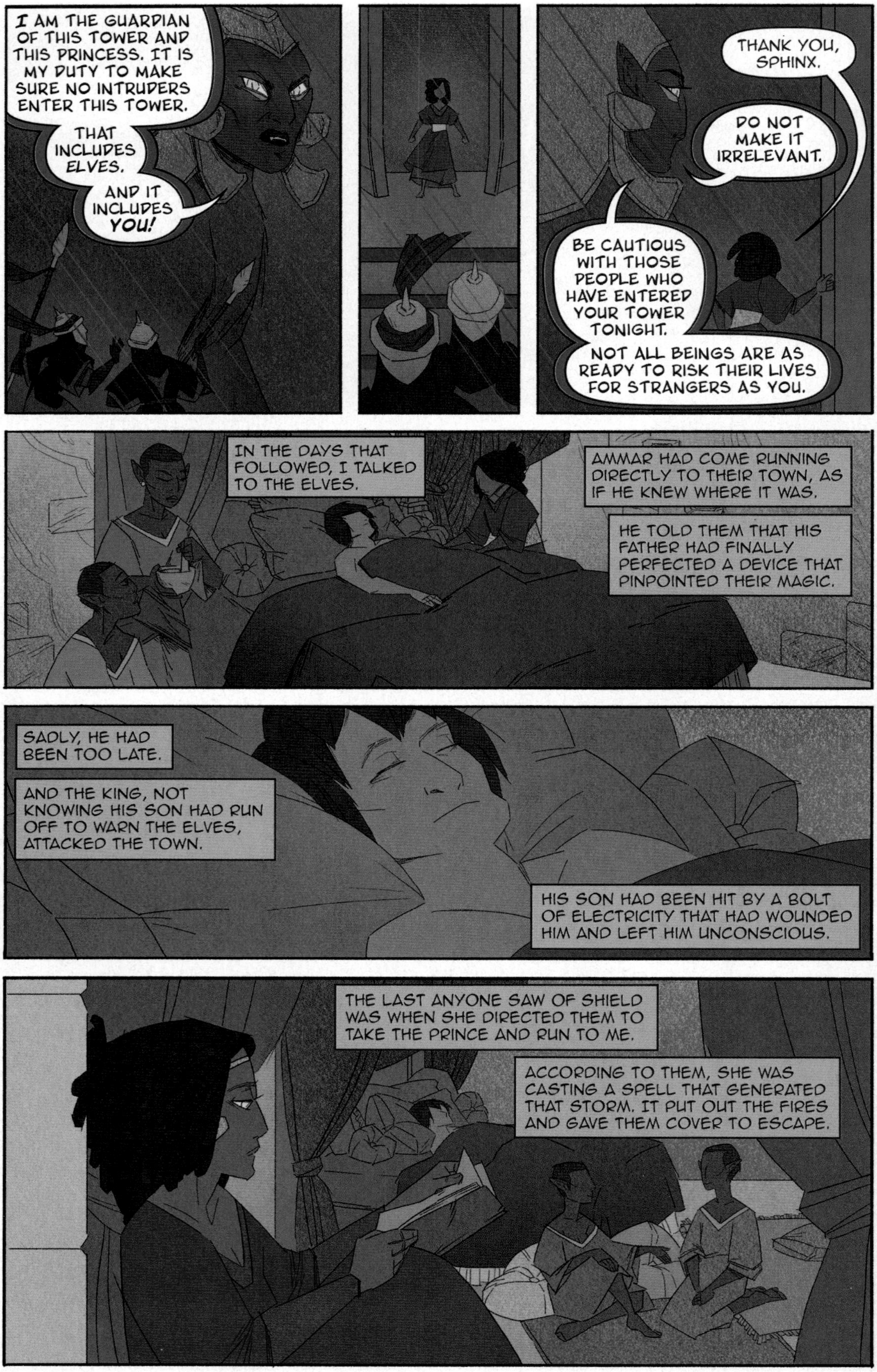
I AM THE GUARDIAN OF THIS TOWER AND THIS PRINCESS. IT IS MY DUTY TO MAKE SURE NO INTRUDERS ENTER THIS TOWER.
THAT INCLUDES ELVES.
AND IT INCLUDES YOU!
THANK YOU, SPHINX.
DO NOT MAKE IT IRRELEVANT.
BE CAUTIOUS WITH THOSE PEOPLE WHO HAVE ENTERED YOUR TOWER TONIGHT.
NOT ALL BEINGS ARE AS READY TO RISK THEIR LIVES FOR STRANGERS AS YOU.
IN THE DAYS THAT FOLLOWED, I TALKED TO THE ELVES.
AMMAR HAD COME RUNNING DIRECTLY TO THEIR TOWN, AS IF HE KNEW WHERE IT WAS.
HE TOLD THEM THAT HIS FATHER HAD FINALLY PERFECTED A DEVICE THAT PINPOINTED THEIR MAGIC.
SADLY, HE HAD BEEN TOO LATE.
AND THE KING, NOT KNOWING HIS SON HAD RUN OFF TO WARN THE ELVES, ATTACKED THE TOWN.
HIS SON HAD BEEN HIT BY A BOLT OF ELECTRICITY THAT HAD WOUNDED HIM AND LEFT HIM UNCONSCIOUS.
THE LAST ANYONE SAW OF SHIELD WAS WHEN SHE DIRECTED THEM TO TAKE THE PRINCE AND RUN TO ME.
ACCORDING TO THEM, SHE WAS CASTING A SPELL THAT GENERATED THAT STORM. IT PUT OUT THE FIRES AND GAVE THEM COVER TO ESCAPE.

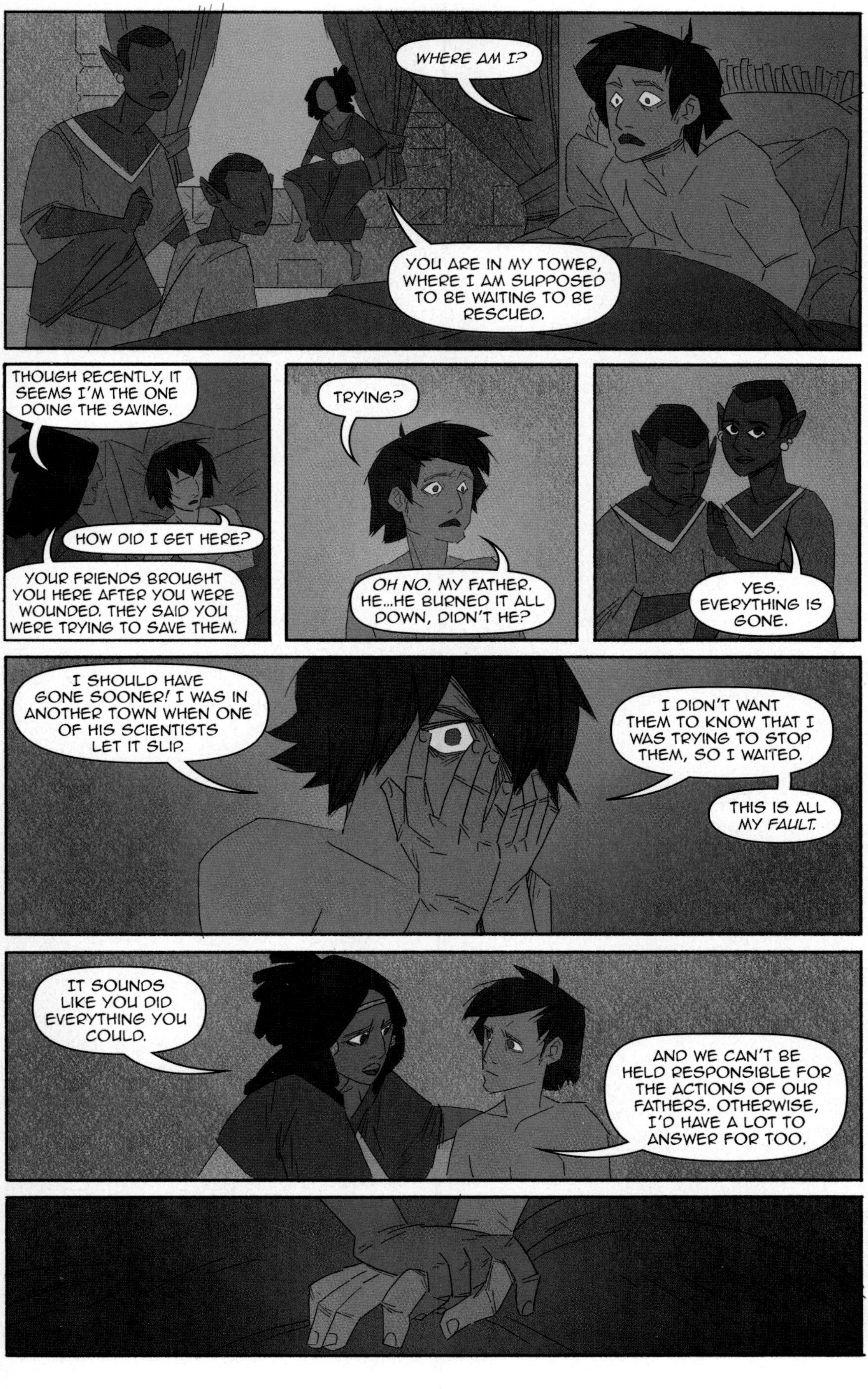
WHERE AM I?
YOU ARE IN MY TOWER, WHERE I AM SUPPOSED TO BE WAITING TO BE RESCUED.
THOUGH RECENTLY, IT SEEMS I'M THE ONE DOING THE SAVING.
HOW DID I GET HERE?
YOUR FRIENDS BROUGHT YOU HERE AFTER YOU WERE WOUNDED. THEY SAID YOU WERE TRYING TO SAVE THEM.
TRYING?
OH NO. MY FATHER. HE...HE BURNED IT ALL DOWN, DIDN'T HE?
YES. EVERYTHING IS GONE.
I SHOULD HAVE GONE SOONER! I WAS IN ANOTHER TOWN WHEN ONE OF HIS SCIENTISTS LET IT SLIP.
I DIDN'T WANT THEM TO KNOW THAT I WAS TRYING TO STOP THEM, SO I WAITED.
THIS IS ALL MY FAULT.
IT SOUNDS LIKE YOU DID EVERYTHING YOU COULD.
AND WE CAN'T BE HELD RESPONSIBLE FOR THE ACTIONS OF OUR FATHERS. OTHERWISE, I'D HAVE A LOT TO ANSWER FOR TOO.

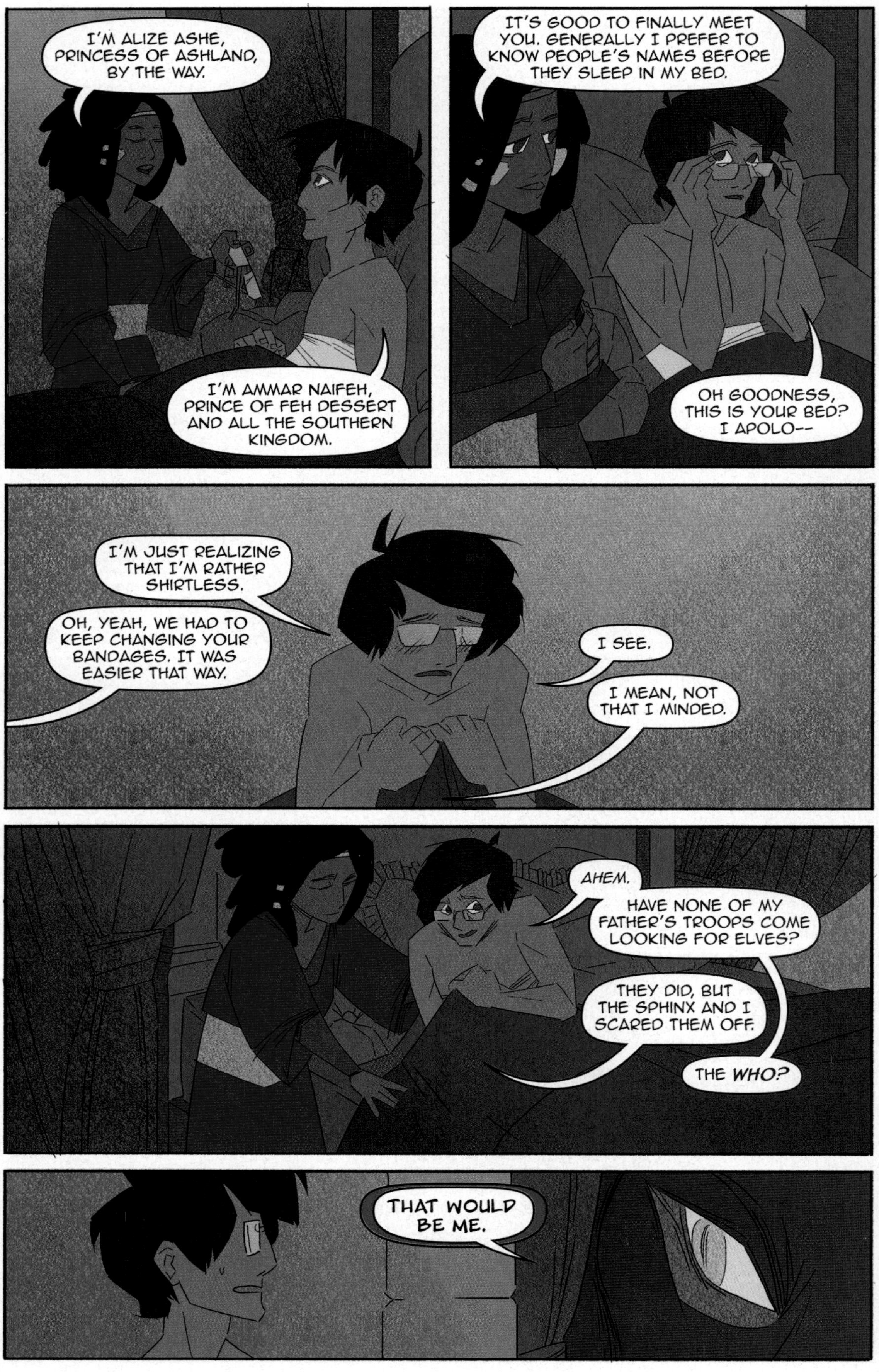
I'M ALIZE ASHE, PRINCESS OF ASHLAND, BY THE WAY.
I'M AMMAR NAIFEH, PRINCE OF FEH DESSERT AND ALL THE SOUTHERN KINGDOM.
IT'S GOOD TO FINALLY MEET YOU. GENERALLY I PREFER TO KNOW PEOPLE'S NAMES BEFORE THEY SLEEP IN MY BED.
OH GOODNESS, THIS IS YOUR BED? I APOLO--
I'M JUST REALIZING THAT I'M RATHER SHIRTLESS.
OH, YEAH, WE HAD TO KEEP CHANGING YOUR BANDAGES. IT WAS EASIER THAT WAY.
I SEE.
I MEAN, NOT THAT I MINDED.
AHEM.
HAVE NONE OF MY FATHER'S TROOPS COME LOOKING FOR ELVES?
THEY DID, BUT THE SPHINX AND I SCARED THEM OFF.
THE *WHO?*
THAT WOULD BE ME.

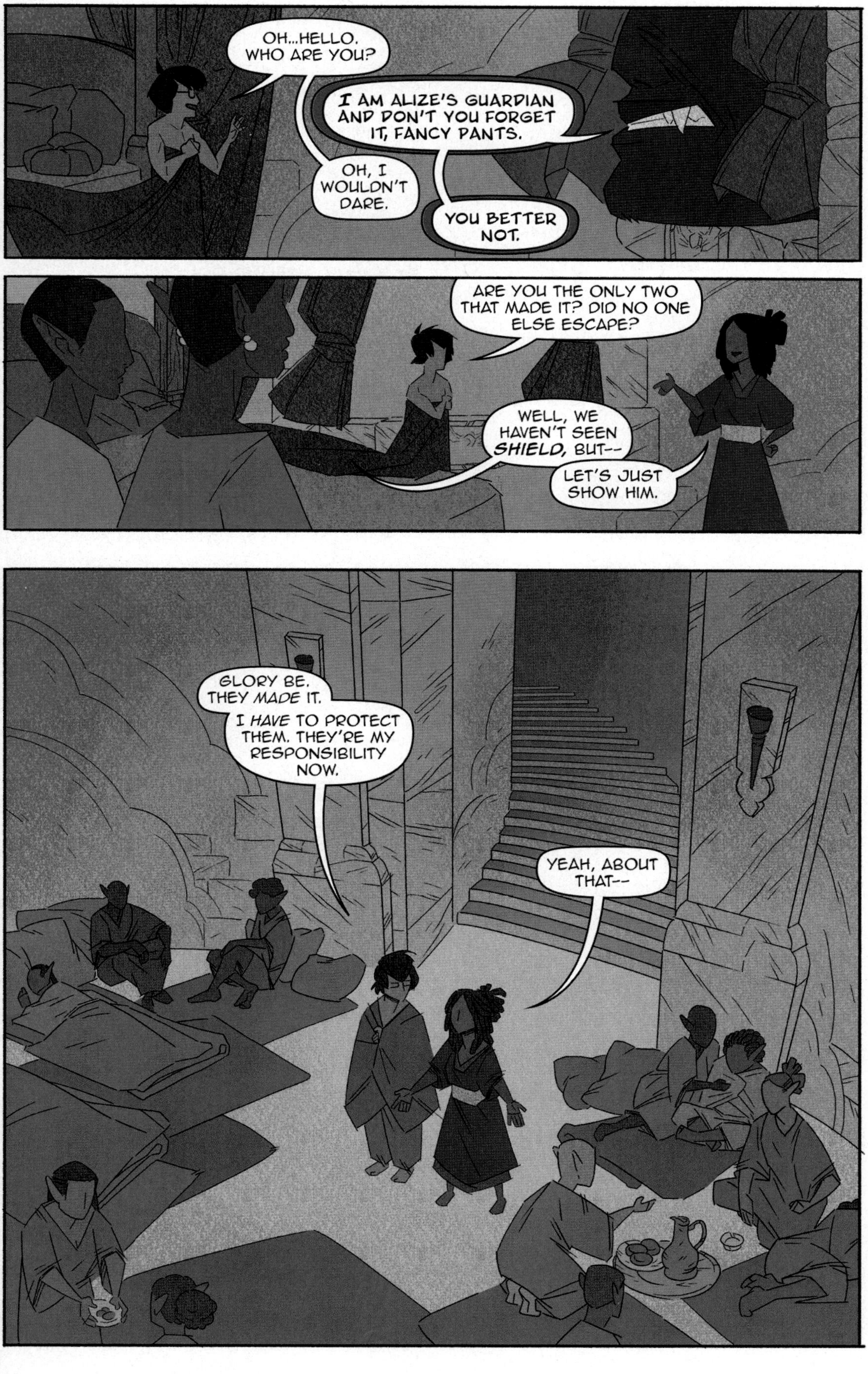
OH...HELLO. WHO ARE YOU?
I AM ALIZE'S GUARDIAN AND DON'T YOU FORGET IT, FANCY PANTS.
OH, I WOULDN'T DARE.
YOU BETTER NOT.
ARE YOU THE ONLY TWO THAT MADE IT? DID NO ONE ELSE ESCAPE?
WELL, WE HAVEN'T SEEN *SHIELD,* BUT--
LET'S JUST SHOW HIM.
GLORY BE. THEY *MADE* IT.
I *HAVE* TO PROTECT THEM. THEY'RE MY RESPONSIBILITY NOW.
YEAH, ABOUT THAT--

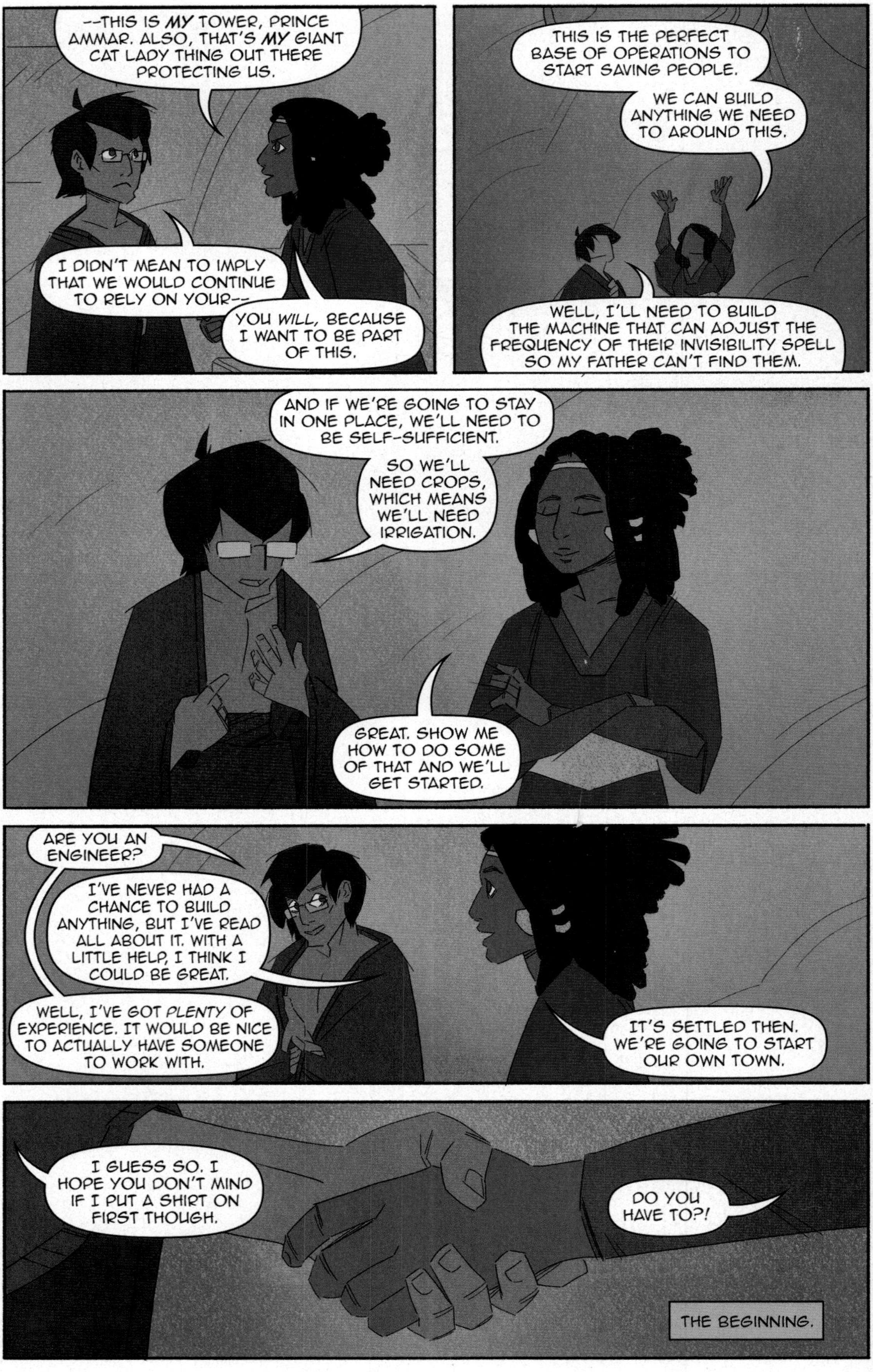
--THIS IS *MY* TOWER, PRINCE AMMAR. ALSO, THAT'S *MY* GIANT CAT LADY THING OUT THERE PROTECTING US.
I DIDN'T MEAN TO IMPLY THAT WE WOULD CONTINUE TO RELY ON YOUR--
YOU *WILL*, BECAUSE I WANT TO BE PART OF THIS.
THIS IS THE PERFECT BASE OF OPERATIONS TO START SAVING PEOPLE.
WE CAN BUILD ANYTHING WE NEED TO AROUND THIS.
WELL, I'LL NEED TO BUILD THE MACHINE THAT CAN ADJUST THE FREQUENCY OF THEIR INVISIBILITY SPELL SO MY FATHER CAN'T FIND THEM.
AND IF WE'RE GOING TO STAY IN ONE PLACE, WE'LL NEED TO BE SELF-SUFFICIENT.
SO WE'LL NEED CROPS, WHICH MEANS WE'LL NEED IRRIGATION.
GREAT. SHOW ME HOW TO DO SOME OF THAT AND WE'LL GET STARTED.
ARE YOU AN ENGINEER?
I'VE NEVER HAD A CHANCE TO BUILD ANYTHING, BUT I'VE READ ALL ABOUT IT. WITH A LITTLE HELP, I THINK I COULD BE GREAT.
WELL, I'VE GOT *PLENTY* OF EXPERIENCE. IT WOULD BE NICE TO ACTUALLY HAVE SOMEONE TO WORK WITH.
IT'S SETTLED THEN. WE'RE GOING TO START OUR OWN TOWN.
I GUESS SO. I HOPE YOU DON'T MIND IF I PUT A SHIRT ON FIRST THOUGH.
DO YOU HAVE TO?!
THE BEGINNING.

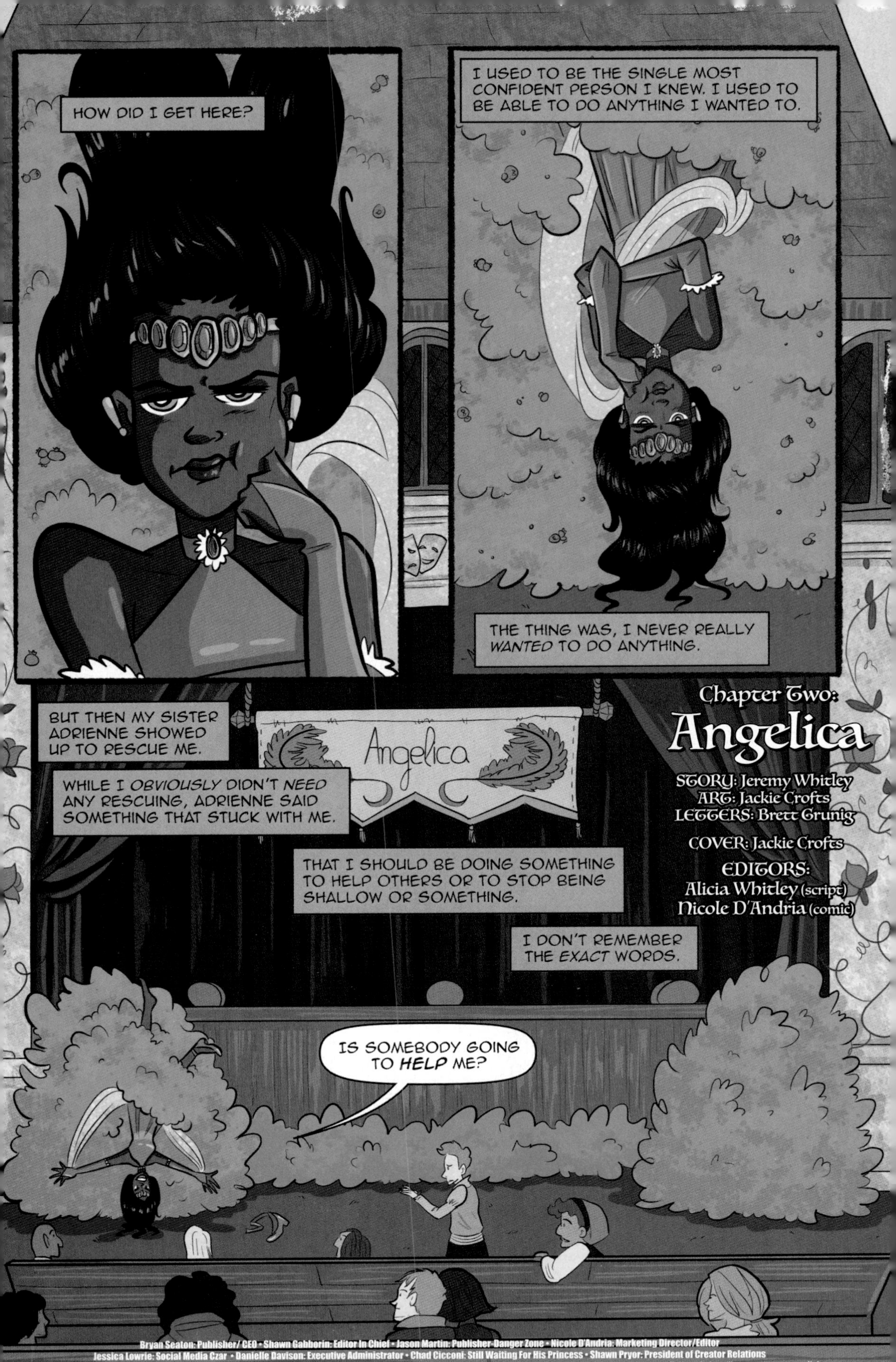
HOW DID I GET HERE?
I USED TO BE THE SINGLE MOST CONFIDENT PERSON I KNEW. I USED TO BE ABLE TO DO ANYTHING I WANTED TO.
THE THING WAS, I NEVER REALLY *WANTED* TO DO ANYTHING.
BUT THEN MY SISTER ADRIENNE SHOWED UP TO RESCUE ME.
Angelica
WHILE I *OBVIOUSLY* DIDN'T *NEED* ANY RESCUING, ADRIENNE SAID SOMETHING THAT STUCK WITH ME.
THAT I SHOULD BE DOING SOMETHING TO HELP OTHERS OR TO STOP BEING SHALLOW OR SOMETHING.
I DON'T REMEMBER THE *EXACT* WORDS.
IS SOMEBODY GOING TO *HELP* ME?
Chapter Two:
Angelica
STORY: Jeremy Whitley
ART: Jackie Crofts
LETTERS: Brett Grunig
COVER: Jackie Crofts
EDITORS:
Alicia Whitley (script)
Nicole D'Andria (comic)

**Bryan Seaton: Publisher/ CEO • Shawn Gabborin: Editor In Chief • Jason Martin: Publisher-Danger Zone • Nicole D'Andria: Marketing Director/Editor**
**Jessica Lowrie: Social Media Czar • Danielle Davison: Executive Administrator • Chad Cicconi: Still Waiting For His Princess • Shawn Pryor: President of Creator Relations**
PRINCELESS Vol. 8: PRINCESSES #2, April 2019. Copyright Jeremy Whitley, 2015. Published by Action Lab Comics.

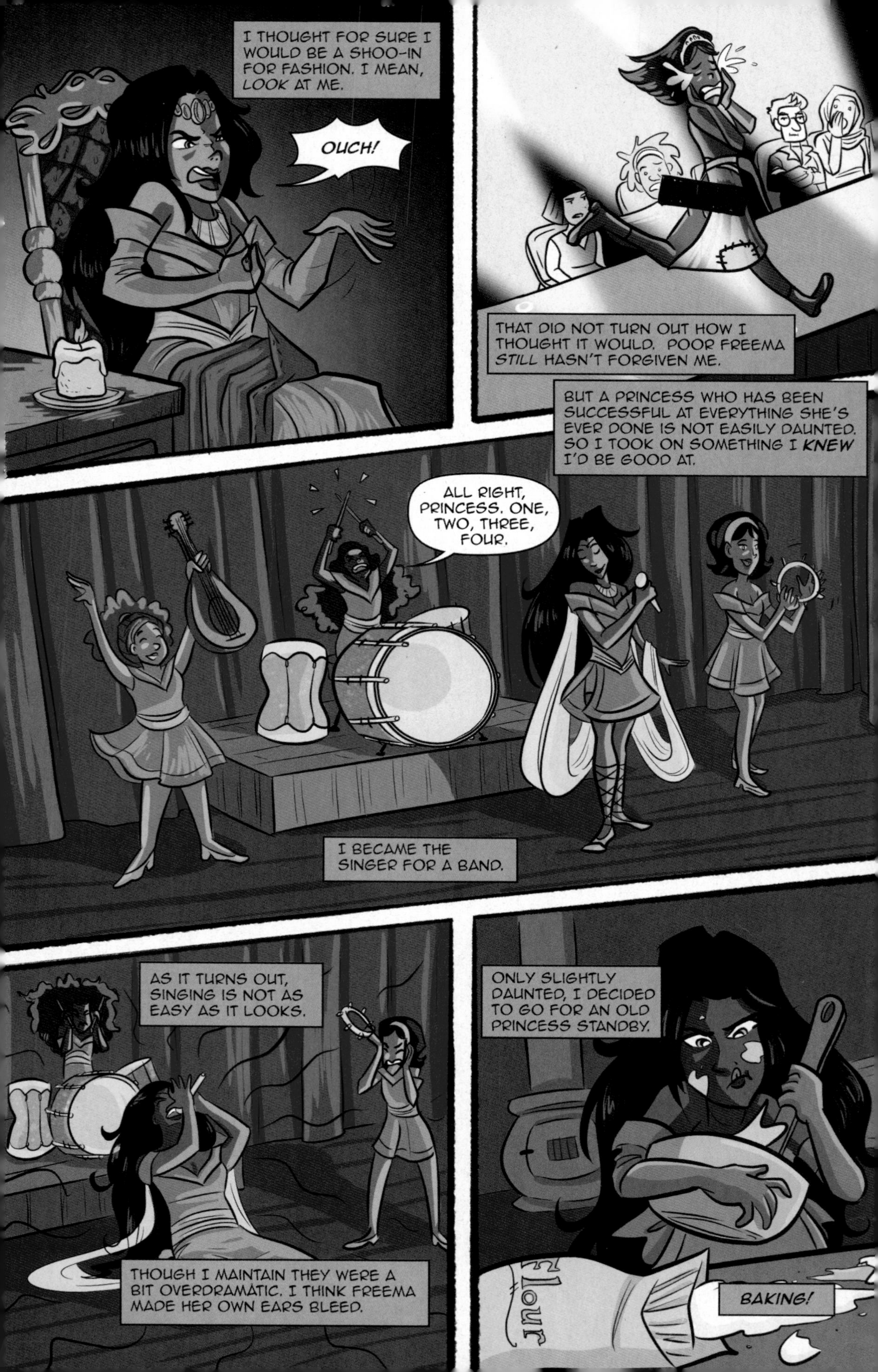
I THOUGHT FOR SURE I WOULD BE A SHOO-IN FOR FASHION. I MEAN, *LOOK* AT ME.
OUCH!
THAT DID NOT TURN OUT HOW I THOUGHT IT WOULD. POOR FREEMA *STILL* HASN'T FORGIVEN ME.
BUT A PRINCESS WHO HAS BEEN SUCCESSFUL AT EVERYTHING SHE'S EVER DONE IS NOT EASILY DAUNTED. SO I TOOK ON SOMETHING I ***KNEW*** I'D BE GOOD AT.
ALL RIGHT, PRINCESS. ONE, TWO, THREE, FOUR.
I BECAME THE SINGER FOR A BAND.
AS IT TURNS OUT, SINGING IS NOT AS EASY AS IT LOOKS.
THOUGH I MAINTAIN THEY WERE A BIT OVERDRAMATIC. I THINK FREEMA MADE HER OWN EARS BLEED.
ONLY SLIGHTLY DAUNTED, I DECIDED TO GO FOR AN OLD PRINCESS STANDBY.
Flour
BAKING!

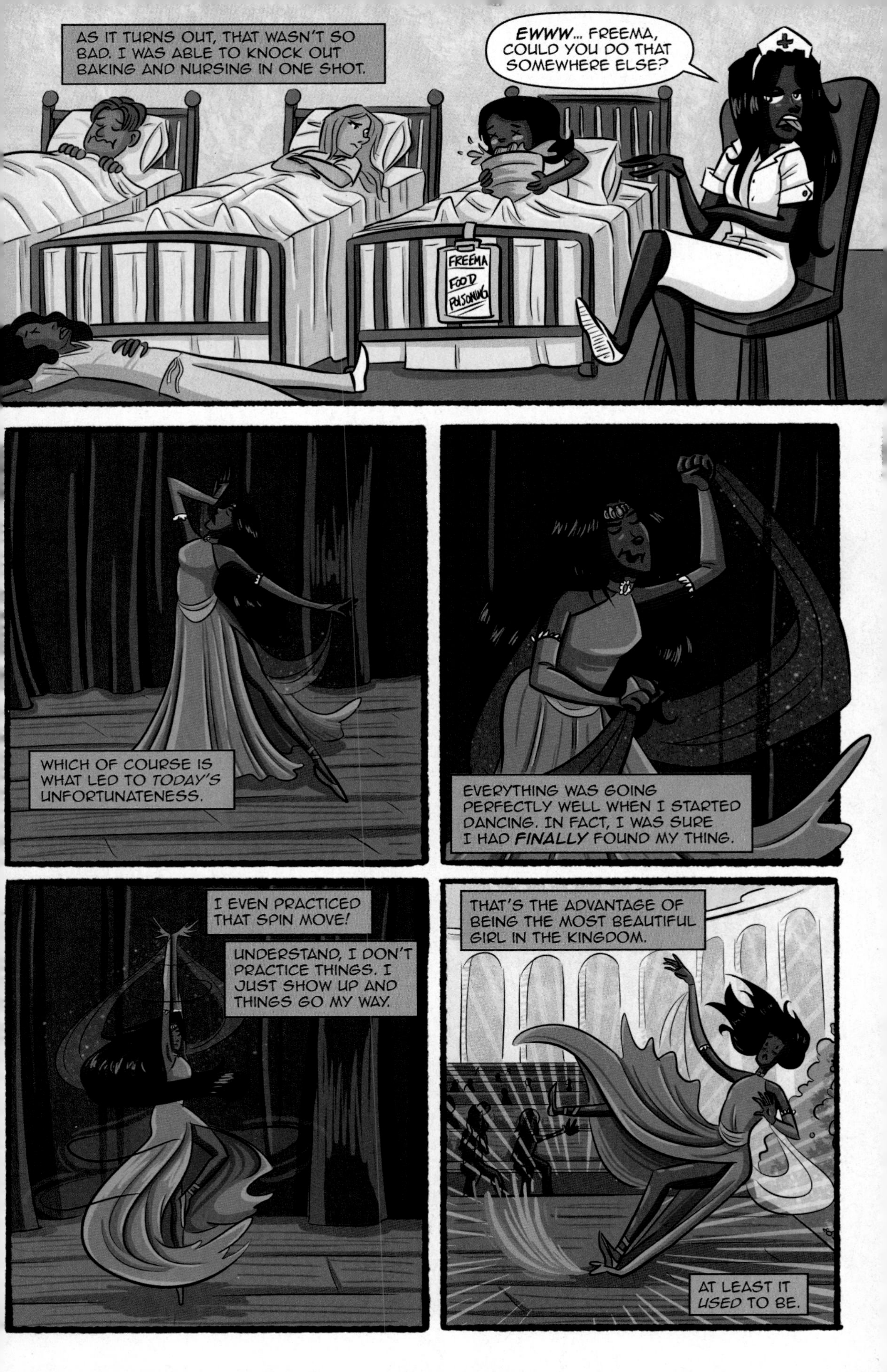
AS IT TURNS OUT, THAT WASN'T SO BAD. I WAS ABLE TO KNOCK OUT BAKING AND NURSING IN ONE SHOT.
EWWW... FREEMA, COULD YOU DO THAT SOMEWHERE ELSE?
FREEMA FOOD POISONING
WHICH OF COURSE IS WHAT LED TO TODAY'S UNFORTUNATENESS.
EVERYTHING WAS GOING PERFECTLY WELL WHEN I STARTED DANCING. IN FACT, I WAS SURE I HAD FINALLY FOUND MY THING.
I EVEN PRACTICED THAT SPIN MOVE!
UNDERSTAND, I DON'T PRACTICE THINGS. I JUST SHOW UP AND THINGS GO MY WAY.
THAT'S THE ADVANTAGE OF BEING THE MOST BEAUTIFUL GIRL IN THE KINGDOM.
AT LEAST IT USED TO BE.

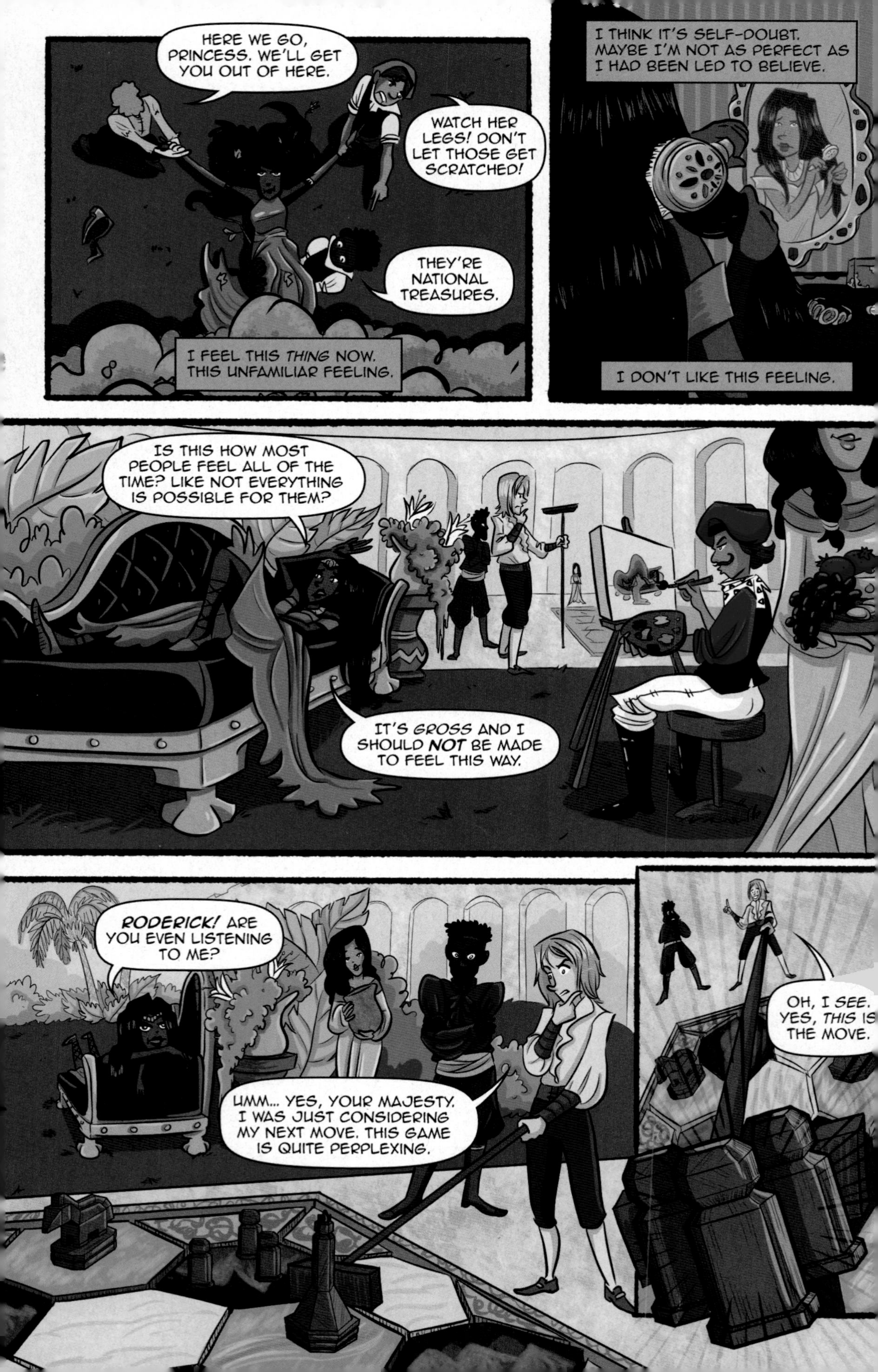
HERE WE GO, PRINCESS. WE'LL GET YOU OUT OF HERE.
WATCH HER LEGS! DON'T LET THOSE GET SCRATCHED!
THEY'RE NATIONAL TREASURES.
I FEEL THIS THING NOW. THIS UNFAMILIAR FEELING.
I THINK IT'S SELF-DOUBT. MAYBE I'M NOT AS PERFECT AS I HAD BEEN LED TO BELIEVE.
I DON'T LIKE THIS FEELING.
IS THIS HOW MOST PEOPLE FEEL ALL OF THE TIME? LIKE NOT EVERYTHING IS POSSIBLE FOR THEM?
IT'S GROSS AND I SHOULD NOT BE MADE TO FEEL THIS WAY.
RODERICK! ARE YOU EVEN LISTENING TO ME?
UMM... YES, YOUR MAJESTY. I WAS JUST CONSIDERING MY NEXT MOVE. THIS GAME IS QUITE PERPLEXING.
OH, I SEE. YES, THIS IS THE MOVE.

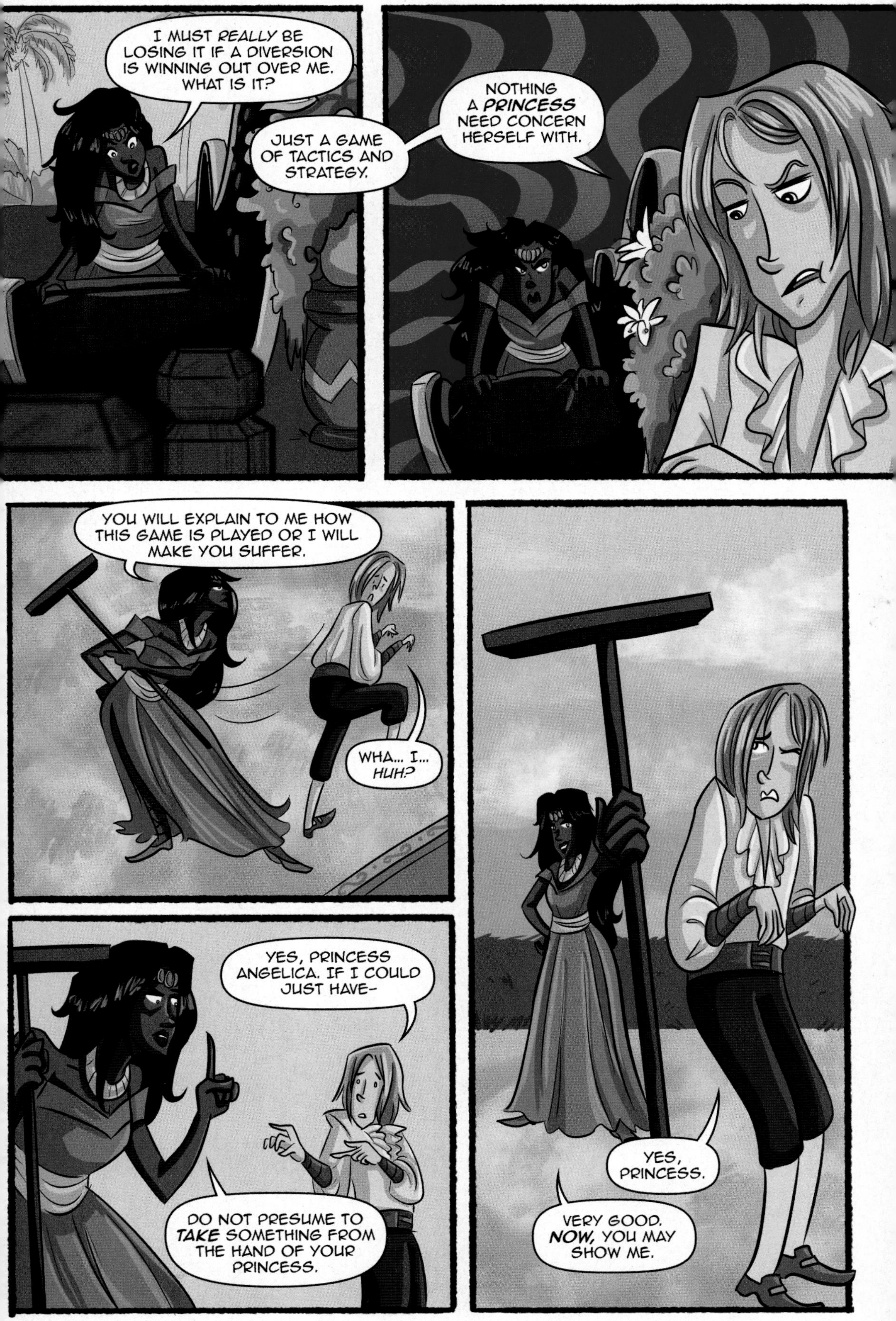
I MUST *REALLY* BE LOSING IT IF A DIVERSION IS WINNING OUT OVER ME. WHAT IS IT?
JUST A GAME OF TACTICS AND STRATEGY.
NOTHING A ***PRINCESS*** NEED CONCERN HERSELF WITH.
YOU WILL EXPLAIN TO ME HOW THIS GAME IS PLAYED OR I WILL MAKE YOU SUFFER.
WHA... I... *HUH?*
YES, PRINCESS ANGELICA. IF I COULD JUST HAVE-
DO NOT PRESUME TO ***TAKE*** SOMETHING FROM THE HAND OF YOUR PRINCESS.
YES, PRINCESS.
VERY GOOD. ***NOW,*** YOU MAY SHOW ME.

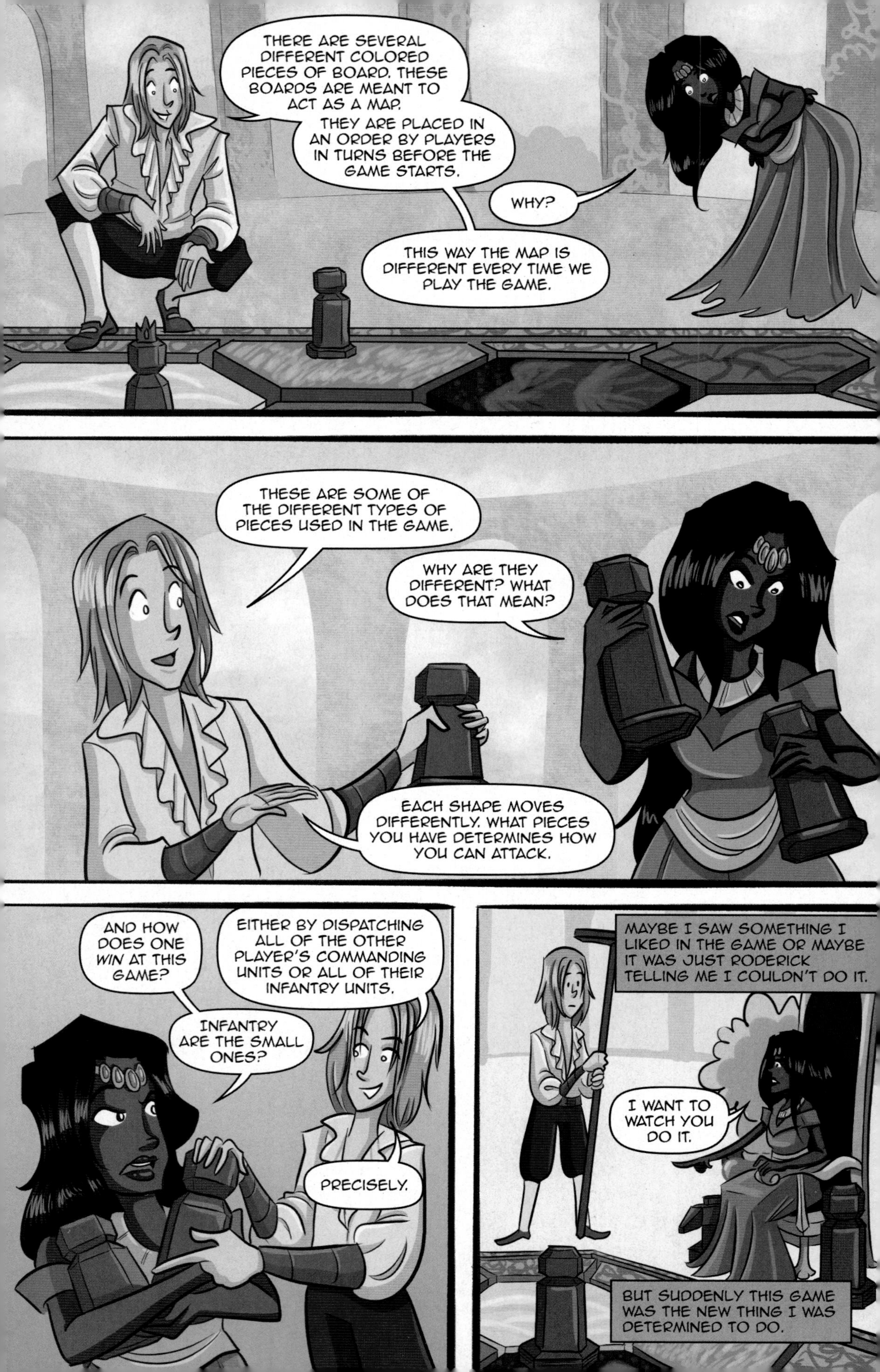
THERE ARE SEVERAL DIFFERENT COLORED PIECES OF BOARD. THESE BOARDS ARE MEANT TO ACT AS A MAP.
THEY ARE PLACED IN AN ORDER BY PLAYERS IN TURNS BEFORE THE GAME STARTS.
WHY?
THIS WAY THE MAP IS DIFFERENT EVERY TIME WE PLAY THE GAME.
THESE ARE SOME OF THE DIFFERENT TYPES OF PIECES USED IN THE GAME.
WHY ARE THEY DIFFERENT? WHAT DOES THAT MEAN?
EACH SHAPE MOVES DIFFERENTLY. WHAT PIECES YOU HAVE DETERMINES HOW YOU CAN ATTACK.
AND HOW DOES ONE WIN AT THIS GAME?
EITHER BY DISPATCHING ALL OF THE OTHER PLAYER'S COMMANDING UNITS OR ALL OF THEIR INFANTRY UNITS.
INFANTRY ARE THE SMALL ONES?
PRECISELY.
MAYBE I SAW SOMETHING I LIKED IN THE GAME OR MAYBE IT WAS JUST RODERICK TELLING ME I COULDN'T DO IT.
I WANT TO WATCH YOU DO IT.
BUT SUDDENLY THIS GAME WAS THE NEW THING I WAS DETERMINED TO DO.

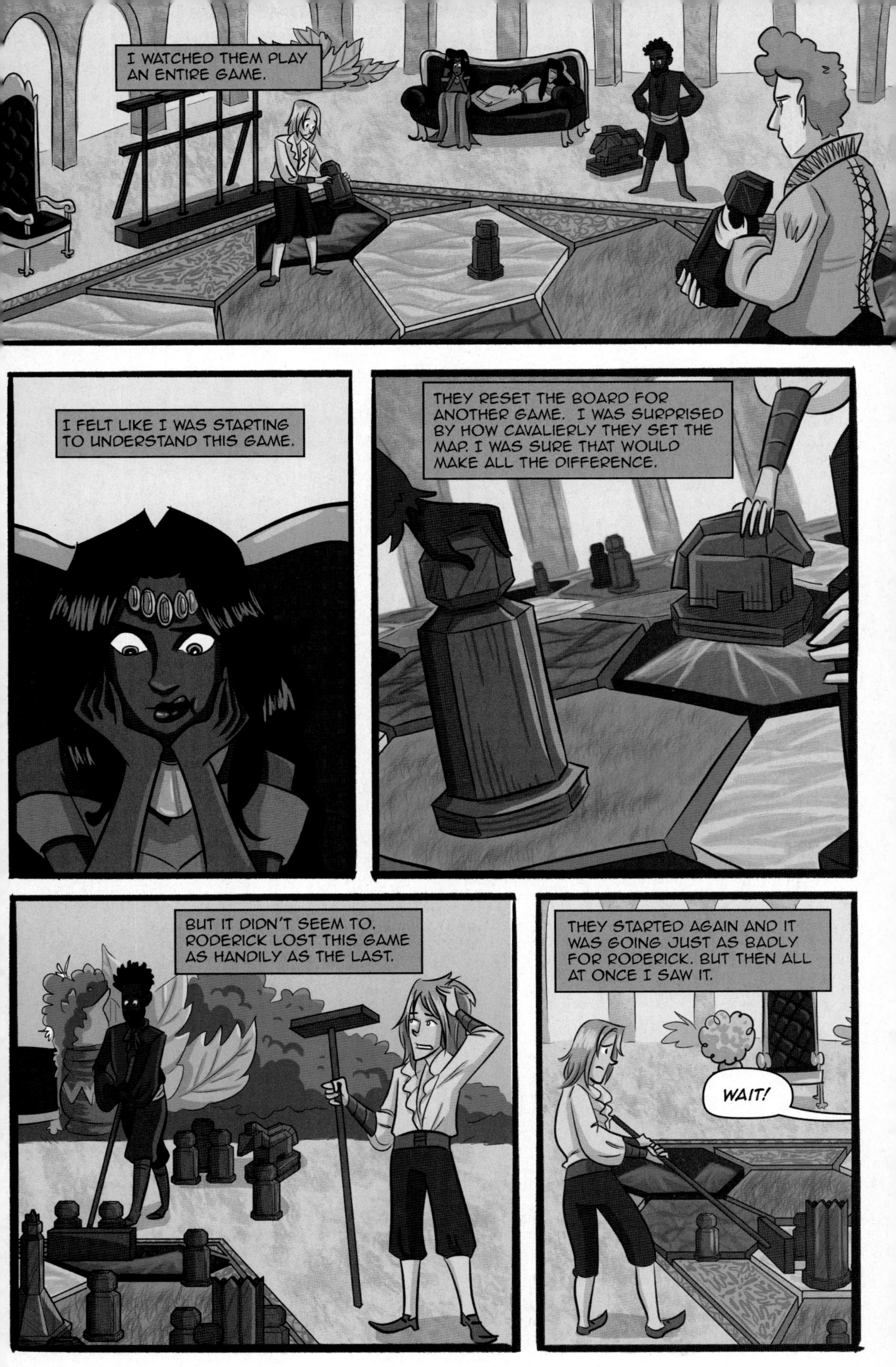
I WATCHED THEM PLAY AN ENTIRE GAME.
I FELT LIKE I WAS STARTING TO UNDERSTAND THIS GAME.
THEY RESET THE BOARD FOR ANOTHER GAME. I WAS SURPRISED BY HOW CAVALIERLY THEY SET THE MAP. I WAS SURE THAT WOULD MAKE ALL THE DIFFERENCE.
BUT IT DIDN'T SEEM TO. RODERICK LOST THIS GAME AS HANDILY AS THE LAST.
THEY STARTED AGAIN AND IT WAS GOING JUST AS BADLY FOR RODERICK. BUT THEN ALL AT ONCE I SAW IT.
WAIT!

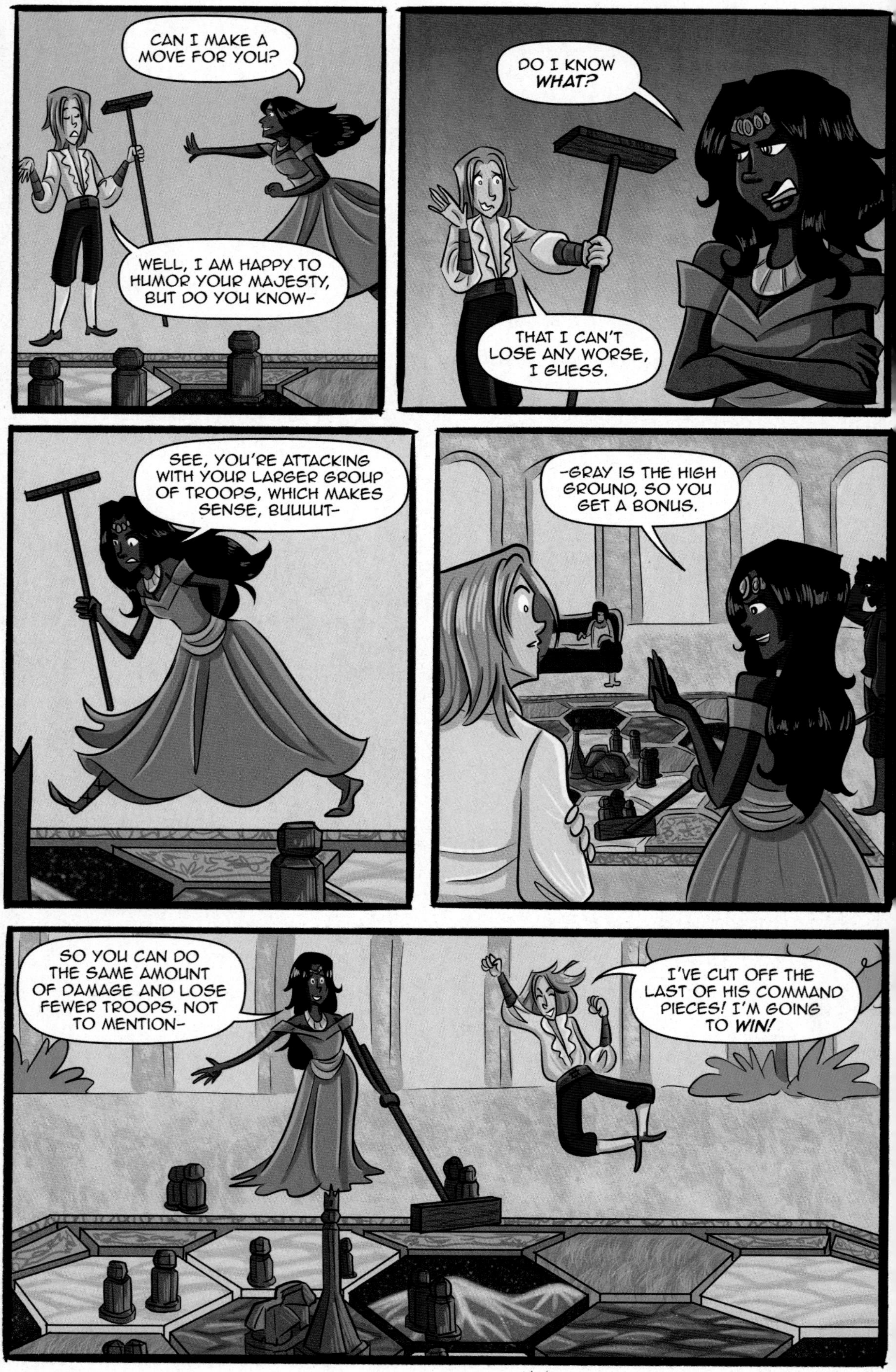
CAN I MAKE A MOVE FOR YOU?
WELL, I AM HAPPY TO HUMOR YOUR MAJESTY, BUT DO YOU KNOW-
DO I KNOW *WHAT?*
THAT I CAN'T LOSE ANY WORSE, I GUESS.
SEE, YOU'RE ATTACKING WITH YOUR LARGER GROUP OF TROOPS, WHICH MAKES SENSE, BUUUUT-
-GRAY IS THE HIGH GROUND, SO YOU GET A BONUS.
SO YOU CAN DO THE SAME AMOUNT OF DAMAGE AND LOSE FEWER TROOPS. NOT TO MENTION-
I'VE CUT OFF THE LAST OF HIS COMMAND PIECES! I'M GOING TO *WIN!*

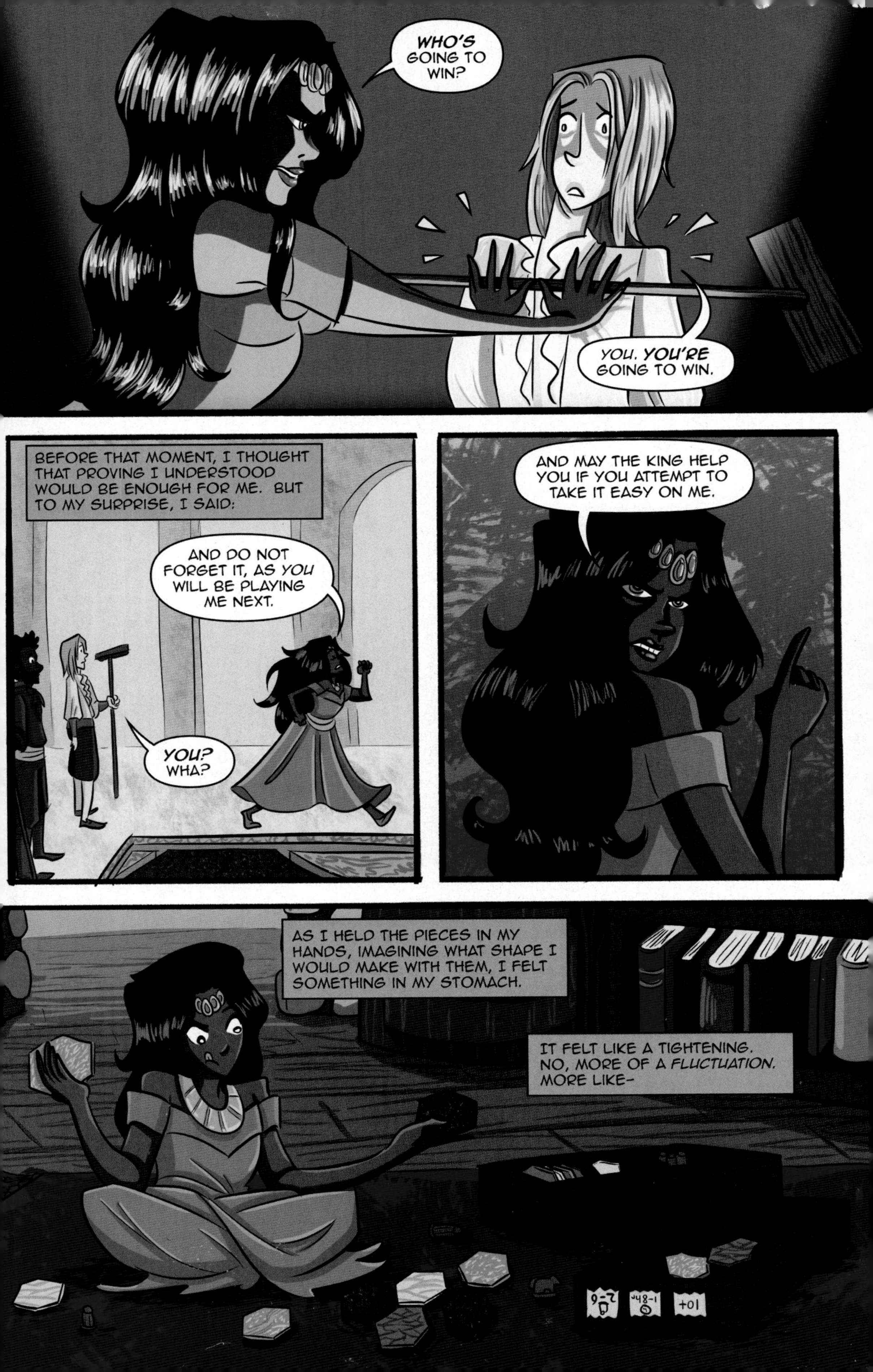
WHO'S GOING TO WIN?
YOU. YOU'RE GOING TO WIN.
BEFORE THAT MOMENT, I THOUGHT THAT PROVING I UNDERSTOOD WOULD BE ENOUGH FOR ME. BUT TO MY SURPRISE, I SAID:
AND DO NOT FORGET IT, AS YOU WILL BE PLAYING ME NEXT.
YOU? WHA?
AND MAY THE KING HELP YOU IF YOU ATTEMPT TO TAKE IT EASY ON ME.
AS I HELD THE PIECES IN MY HANDS, IMAGINING WHAT SHAPE I WOULD MAKE WITH THEM, I FELT SOMETHING IN MY STOMACH.
IT FELT LIKE A TIGHTENING. NO, MORE OF A FLUCTUATION. MORE LIKE-

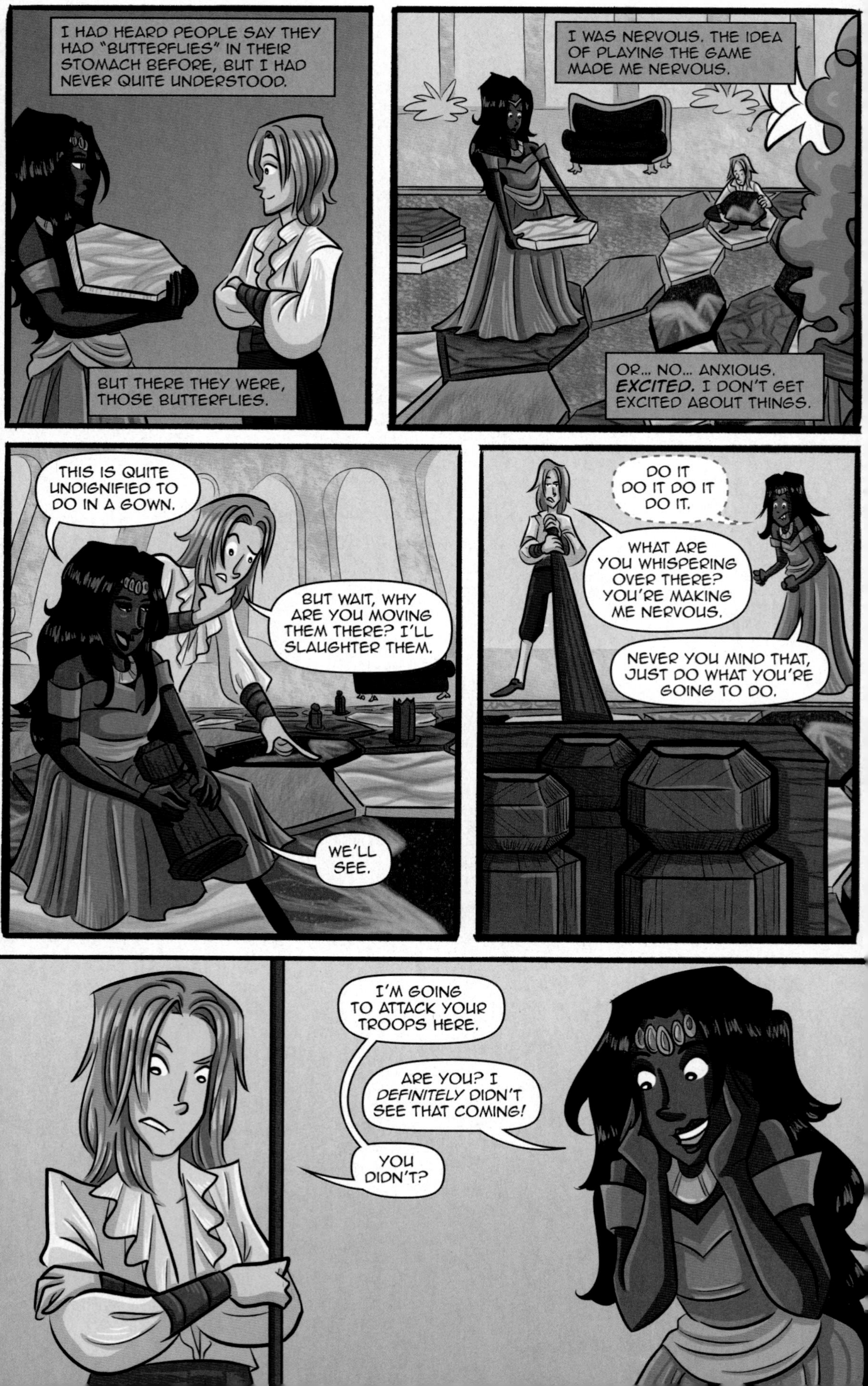
I HAD HEARD PEOPLE SAY THEY HAD "BUTTERFLIES" IN THEIR STOMACH BEFORE, BUT I HAD NEVER QUITE UNDERSTOOD.
BUT THERE THEY WERE, THOSE BUTTERFLIES.
I WAS NERVOUS. THE IDEA OF PLAYING THE GAME MADE ME NERVOUS.
OR... NO... ANXIOUS. EXCITED. I DON'T GET EXCITED ABOUT THINGS.
THIS IS QUITE UNDIGNIFIED TO DO IN A GOWN.
BUT WAIT, WHY ARE YOU MOVING THEM THERE? I'LL SLAUGHTER THEM.
WE'LL SEE.
DO IT DO IT DO IT DO IT.
WHAT ARE YOU WHISPERING OVER THERE? YOU'RE MAKING ME NERVOUS.
NEVER YOU MIND THAT, JUST DO WHAT YOU'RE GOING TO DO.
I'M GOING TO ATTACK YOUR TROOPS HERE.
ARE YOU? I DEFINITELY DIDN'T SEE THAT COMING!
YOU DIDN'T?

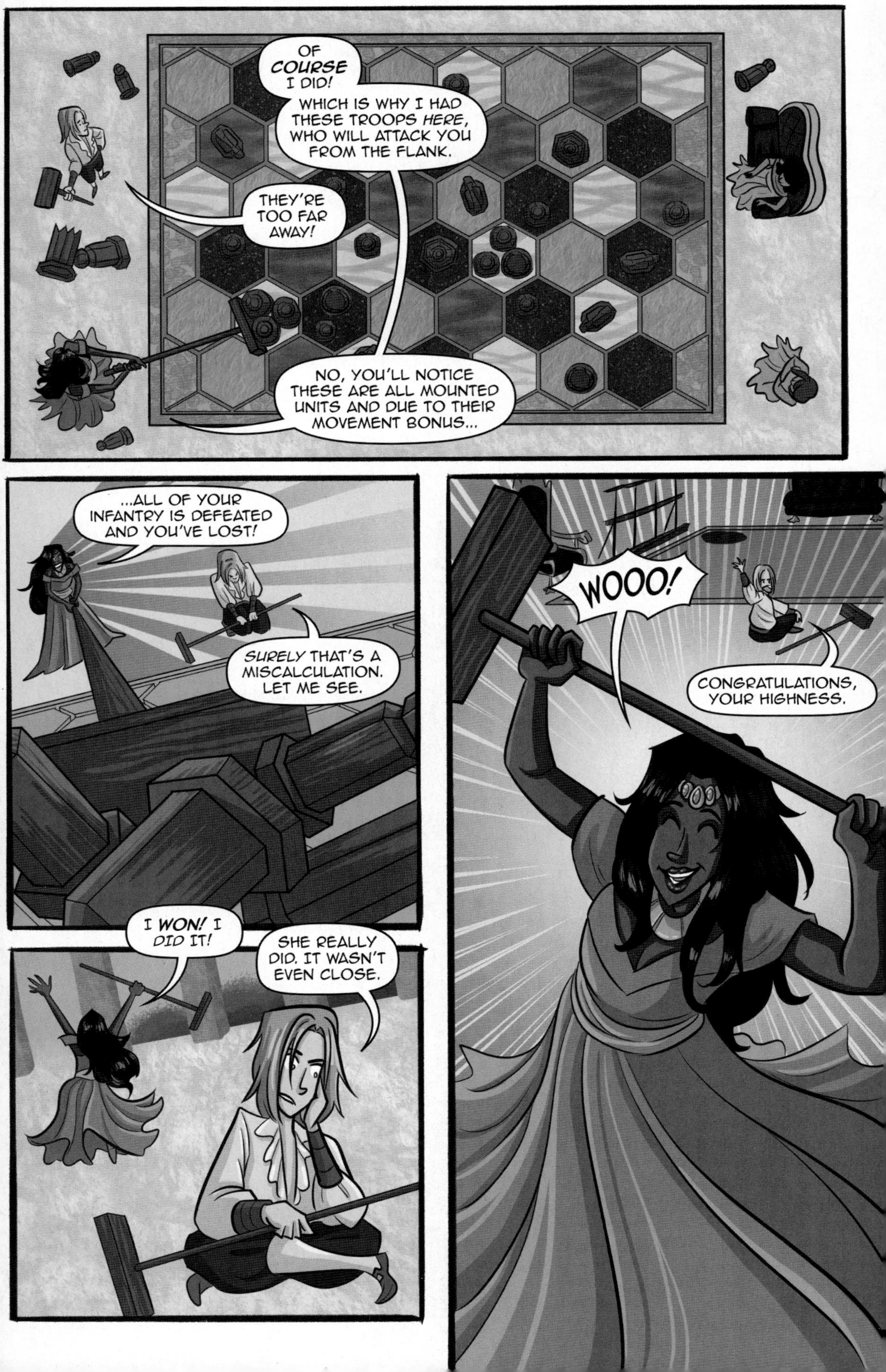
OF COURSE I DID!
WHICH IS WHY I HAD THESE TROOPS HERE, WHO WILL ATTACK YOU FROM THE FLANK.
THEY'RE TOO FAR AWAY!
NO, YOU'LL NOTICE THESE ARE ALL MOUNTED UNITS AND DUE TO THEIR MOVEMENT BONUS...
...ALL OF YOUR INFANTRY IS DEFEATED AND YOU'VE LOST!
SURELY THAT'S A MISCALCULATION. LET ME SEE.
I WON! I DID IT!
SHE REALLY DID. IT WASN'T EVEN CLOSE.
WOOO!
CONGRATULATIONS, YOUR HIGHNESS.

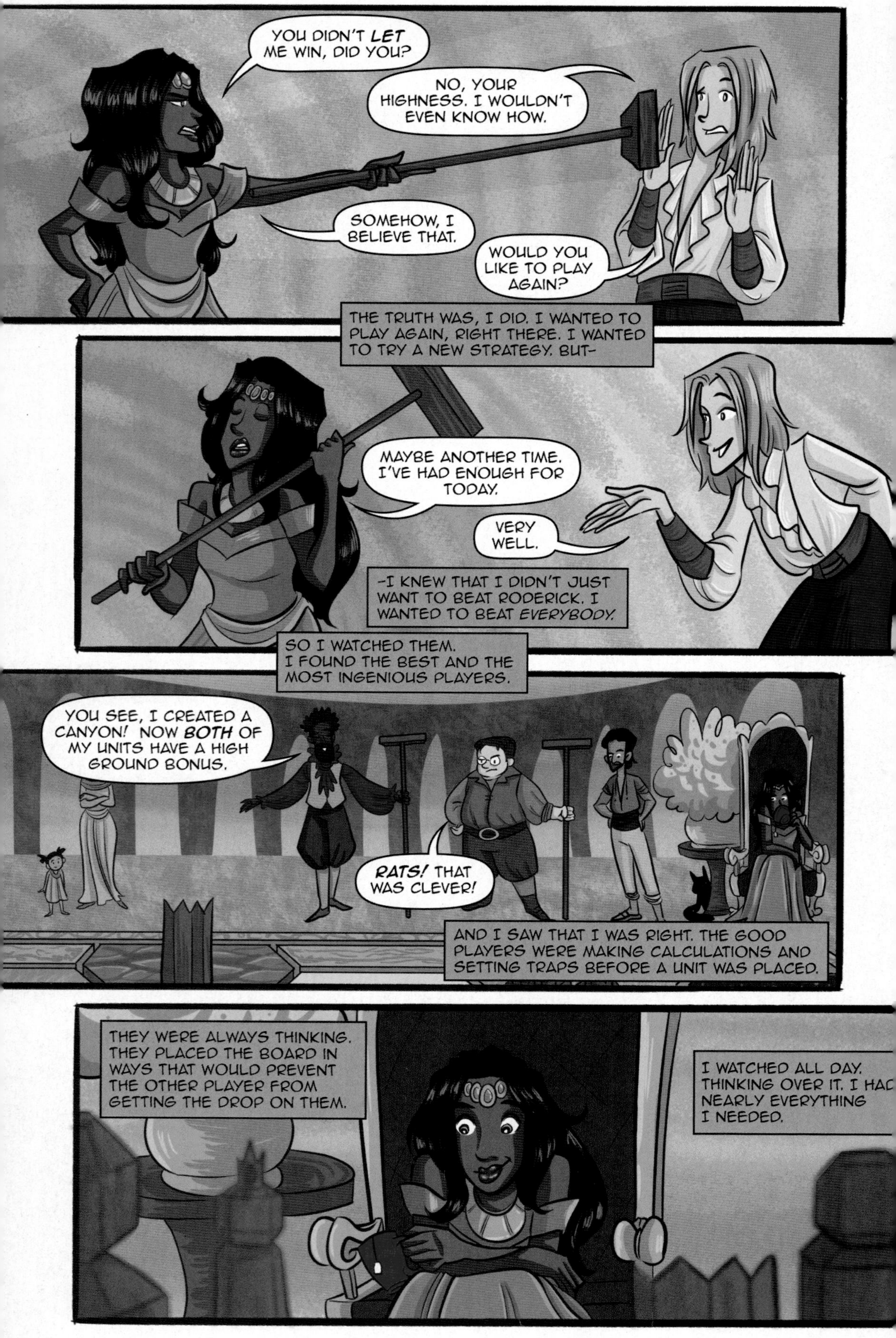
YOU DIDN'T *LET* ME WIN, DID YOU?
NO, YOUR HIGHNESS. I WOULDN'T EVEN KNOW HOW.
SOMEHOW, I BELIEVE THAT.
WOULD YOU LIKE TO PLAY AGAIN?
THE TRUTH WAS, I DID. I WANTED TO PLAY AGAIN, RIGHT THERE. I WANTED TO TRY A NEW STRATEGY. BUT-
MAYBE ANOTHER TIME. I'VE HAD ENOUGH FOR TODAY.
VERY WELL.
-I KNEW THAT I DIDN'T JUST WANT TO BEAT RODERICK. I WANTED TO BEAT *EVERYBODY.*
SO I WATCHED THEM. I FOUND THE BEST AND THE MOST INGENIOUS PLAYERS.
YOU SEE, I CREATED A CANYON! NOW *BOTH* OF MY UNITS HAVE A HIGH GROUND BONUS.
*RATS!* THAT WAS CLEVER!
AND I SAW THAT I WAS RIGHT. THE GOOD PLAYERS WERE MAKING CALCULATIONS AND SETTING TRAPS BEFORE A UNIT WAS PLACED.
THEY WERE ALWAYS THINKING. THEY PLACED THE BOARD IN WAYS THAT WOULD PREVENT THE OTHER PLAYER FROM GETTING THE DROP ON THEM.
I WATCHED ALL DAY. THINKING OVER IT. I HAD NEARLY EVERYTHING I NEEDED.

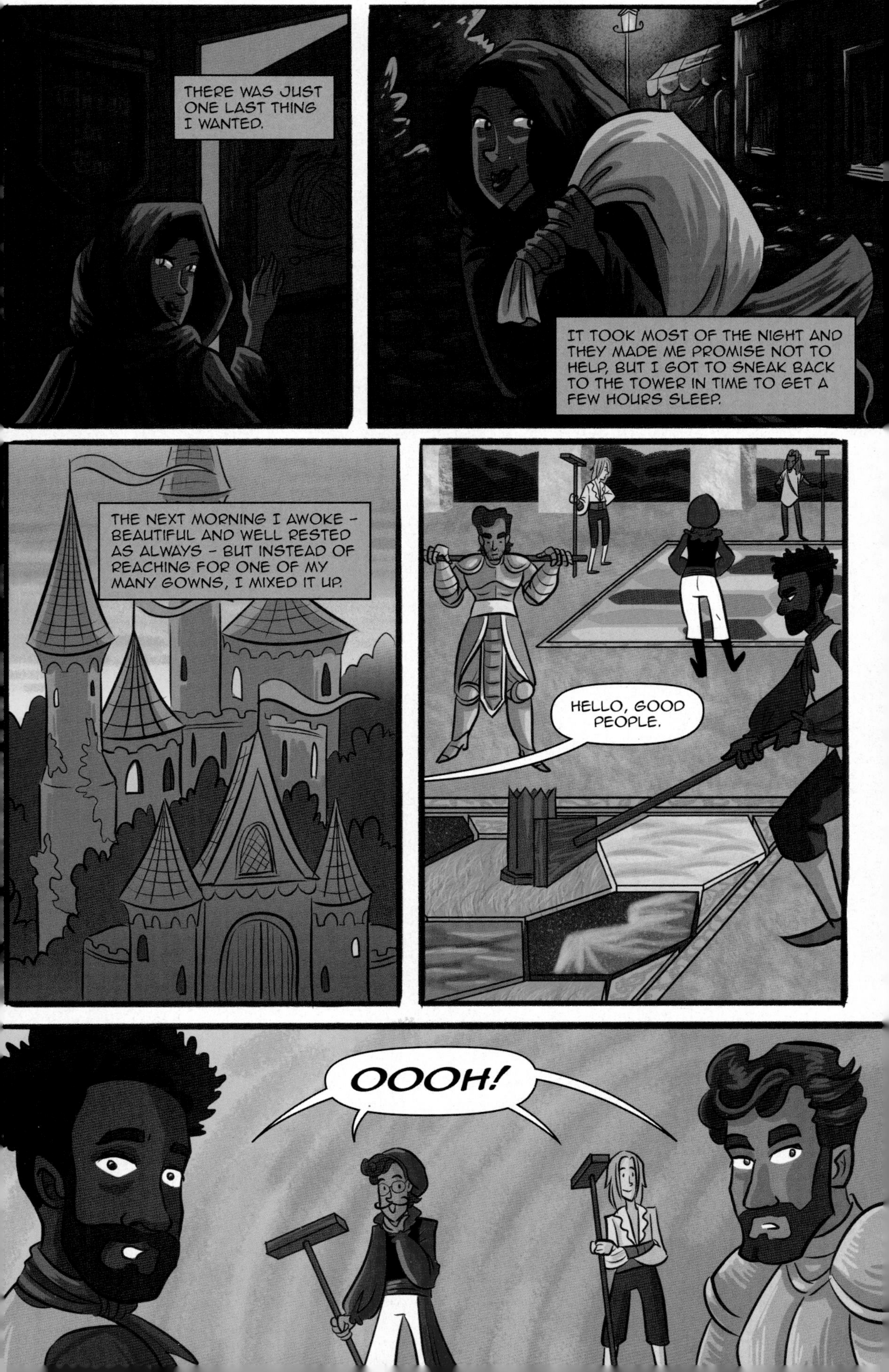
THERE WAS JUST ONE LAST THING I WANTED.
IT TOOK MOST OF THE NIGHT AND THEY MADE ME PROMISE NOT TO HELP, BUT I GOT TO SNEAK BACK TO THE TOWER IN TIME TO GET A FEW HOURS SLEEP.
THE NEXT MORNING I AWOKE - BEAUTIFUL AND WELL RESTED AS ALWAYS - BUT INSTEAD OF REACHING FOR ONE OF MY MANY GOWNS, I MIXED IT UP.
HELLO, GOOD PEOPLE.
OOOH!

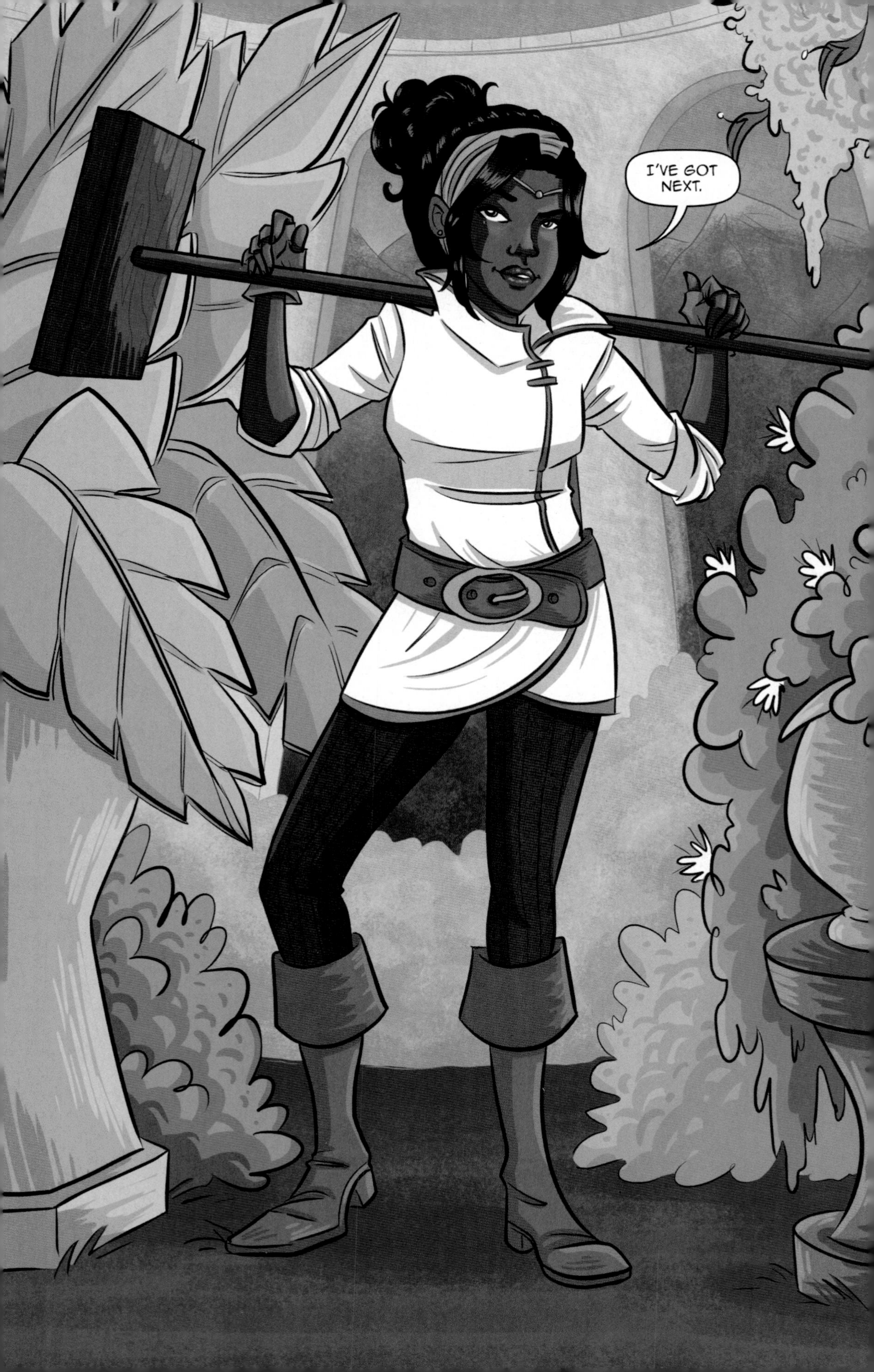
I'VE GOT NEXT.

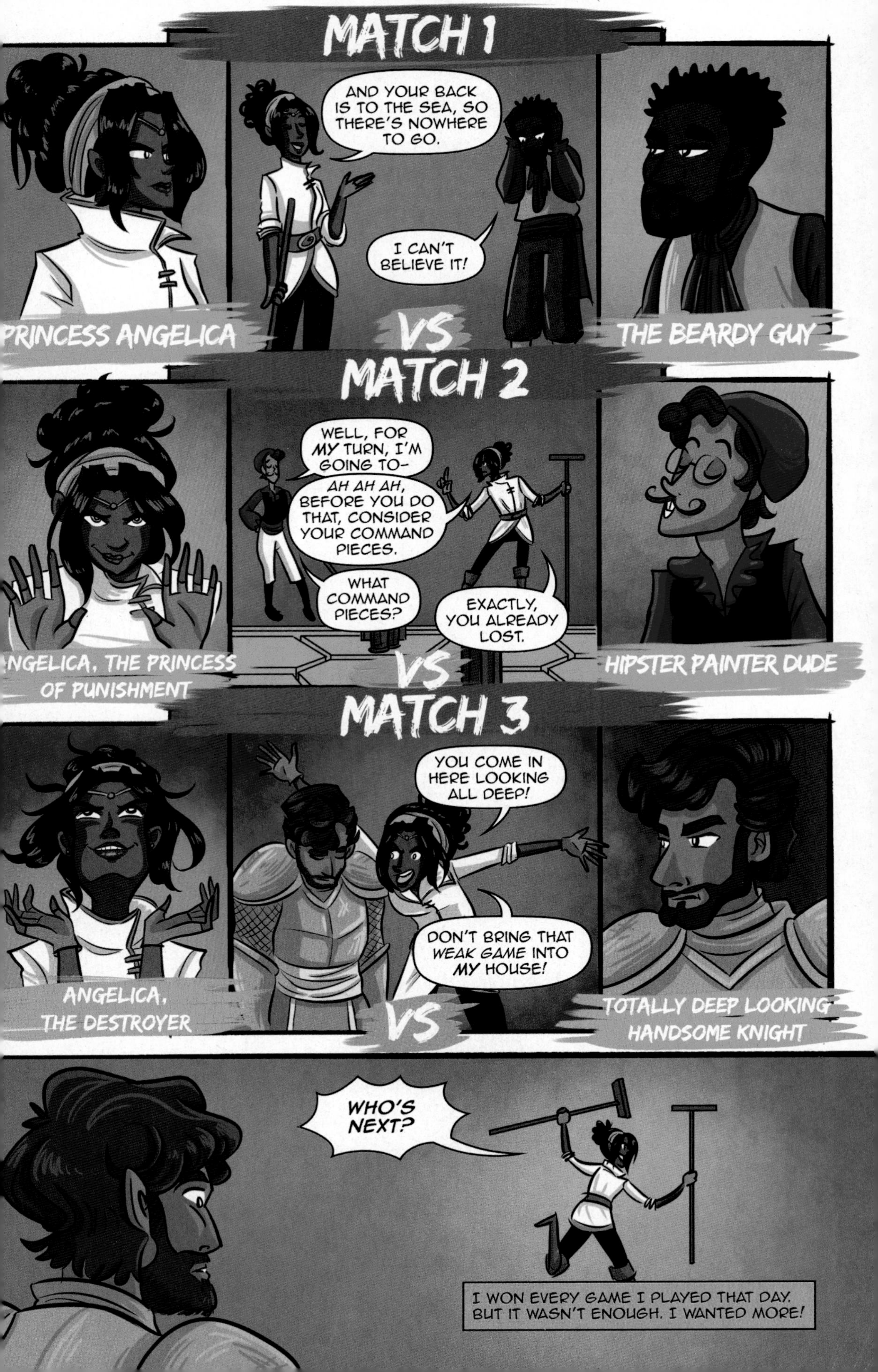
MATCH 1
AND YOUR BACK IS TO THE SEA, SO THERE'S NOWHERE TO GO.
I CAN'T BELIEVE IT!
PRINCESS ANGELICA
VS
THE BEARDY GUY
MATCH 2
WELL, FOR MY TURN, I'M GOING TO-
AH AH AH, BEFORE YOU DO THAT, CONSIDER YOUR COMMAND PIECES.
WHAT COMMAND PIECES?
EXACTLY, YOU ALREADY LOST.
NGELICA, THE PRINCESS OF PUNISHMENT
VS
HIPSTER PAINTER DUDE
MATCH 3
YOU COME IN HERE LOOKING ALL DEEP!
DON'T BRING THAT WEAK GAME INTO MY HOUSE!
ANGELICA, THE DESTROYER
VS
TOTALLY DEEP LOOKING HANDSOME KNIGHT
WHO'S NEXT?
I WON EVERY GAME I PLAYED THAT DAY. BUT IT WASN'T ENOUGH. I WANTED MORE!

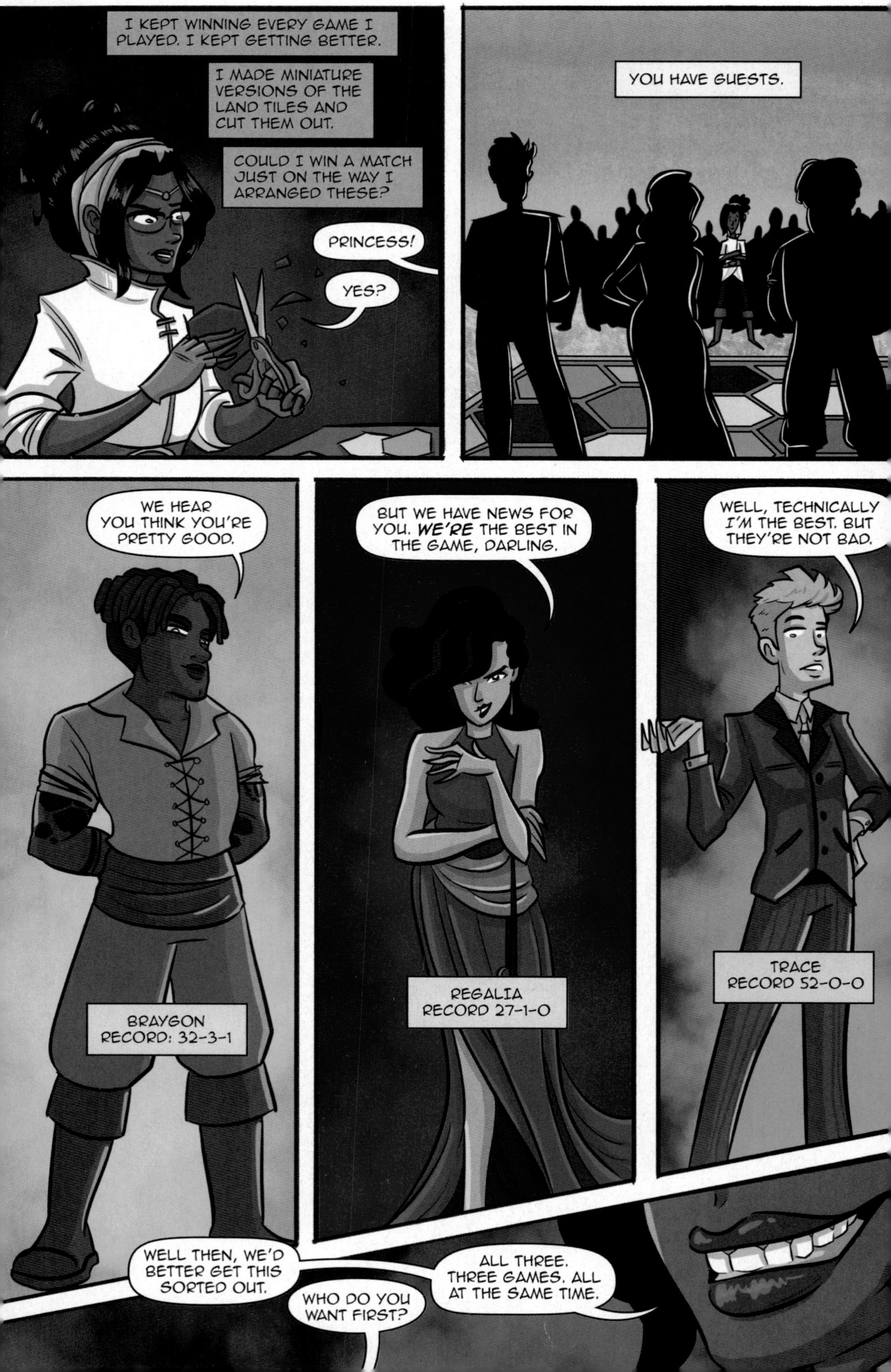

I KEPT WINNING EVERY GAME I PLAYED. I KEPT GETTING BETTER.
I MADE MINIATURE VERSIONS OF THE LAND TILES AND CUT THEM OUT.
COULD I WIN A MATCH JUST ON THE WAY I ARRANGED THESE?
PRINCESS!
YES?
YOU HAVE GUESTS.
WE HEAR YOU THINK YOU'RE PRETTY GOOD.
BRAYGON RECORD: 32-3-1
BUT WE HAVE NEWS FOR YOU. *WE'RE* THE BEST IN THE GAME, DARLING.
REGALIA RECORD 27-1-0
WELL, TECHNICALLY *I'M* THE BEST. BUT THEY'RE NOT BAD.
TRACE RECORD 52-0-0
WELL THEN, WE'D BETTER GET THIS SORTED OUT.
WHO DO YOU WANT FIRST?
ALL THREE. THREE GAMES. ALL AT THE SAME TIME.

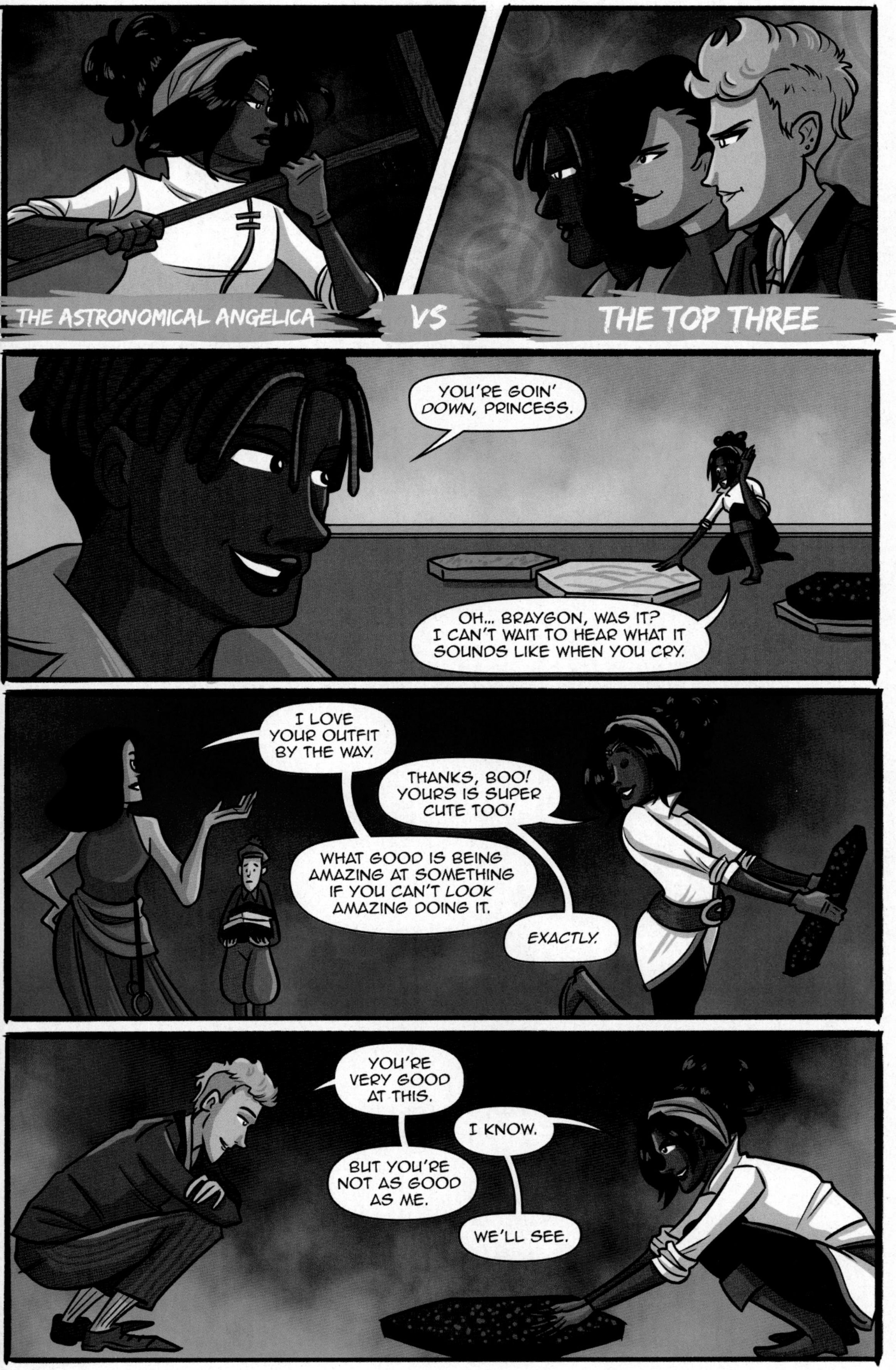
THE ASTRONOMICAL ANGELICA
VS
THE TOP THREE
YOU'RE GOIN' *DOWN*, PRINCESS.
OH... BRAYGON, WAS IT? I CAN'T WAIT TO HEAR WHAT IT SOUNDS LIKE WHEN YOU CRY.
I LOVE YOUR OUTFIT BY THE WAY.
THANKS, BOO! YOURS IS SUPER CUTE TOO!
WHAT GOOD IS BEING AMAZING AT SOMETHING IF YOU CAN'T *LOOK* AMAZING DOING IT.
*EXACTLY.*
YOU'RE VERY GOOD AT THIS.
I KNOW.
BUT YOU'RE NOT AS GOOD AS ME.
WE'LL SEE.

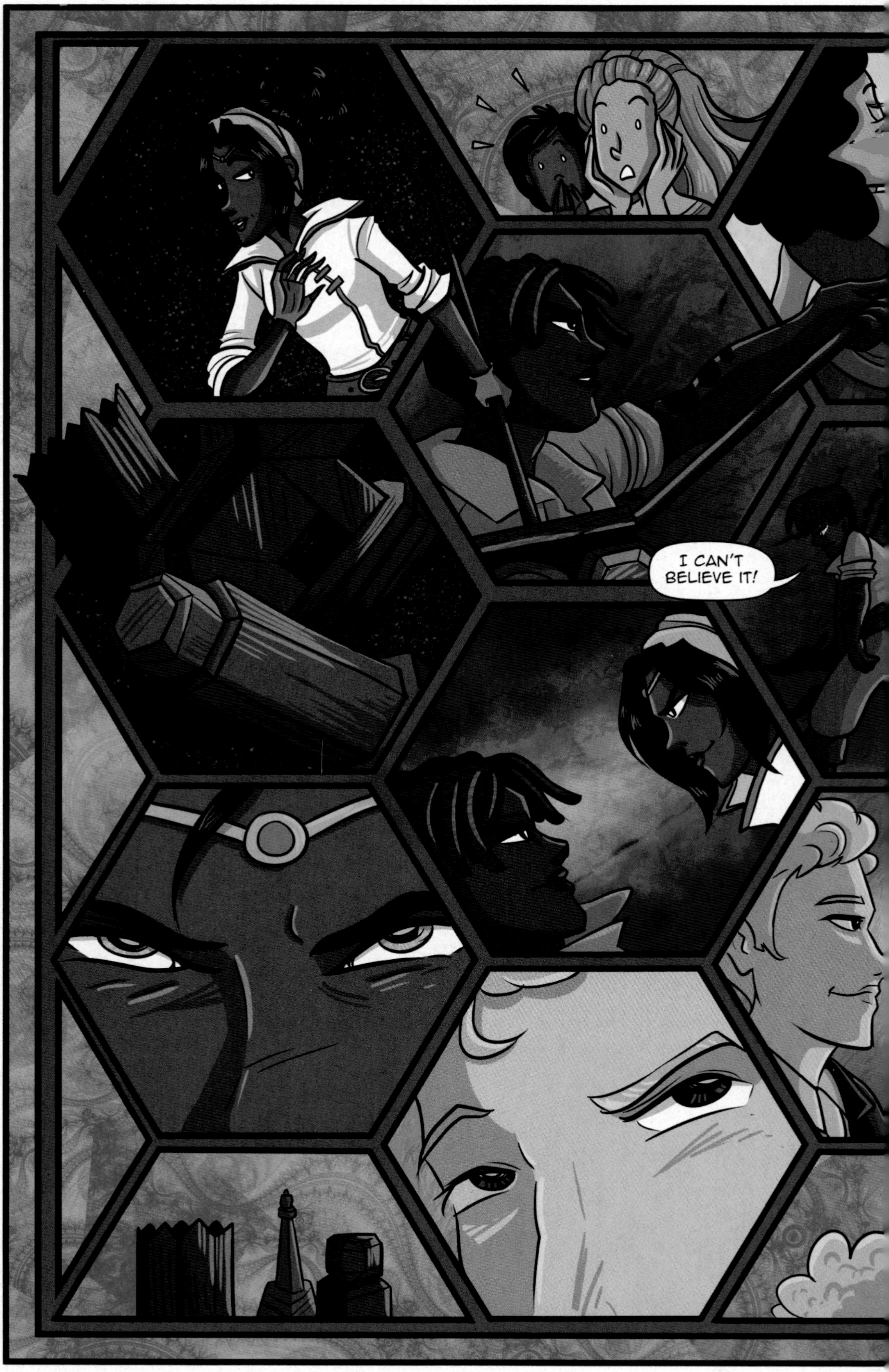
I CAN'T BELIEVE IT!

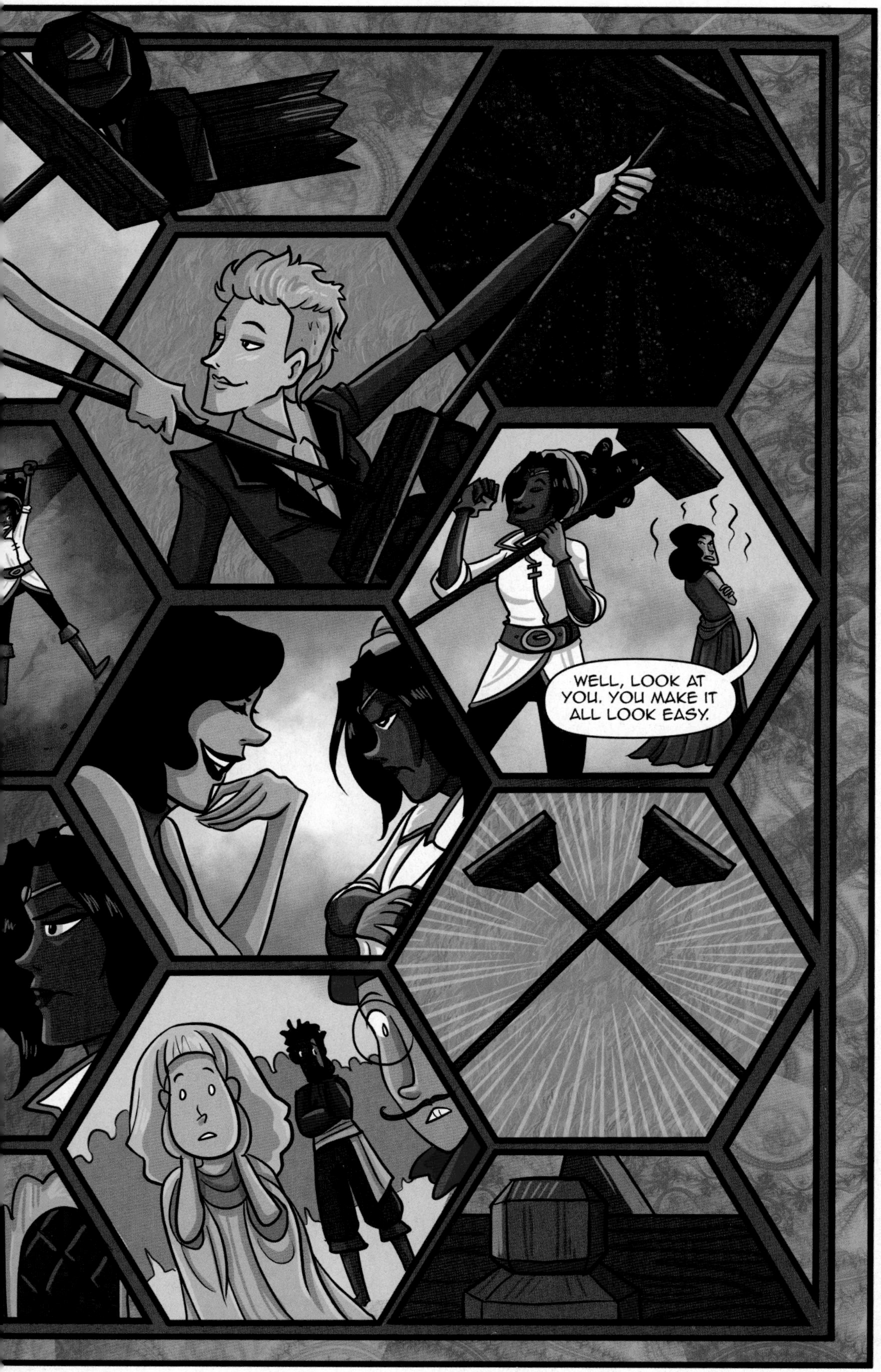
WELL, LOOK AT YOU. YOU MAKE IT ALL LOOK EASY.

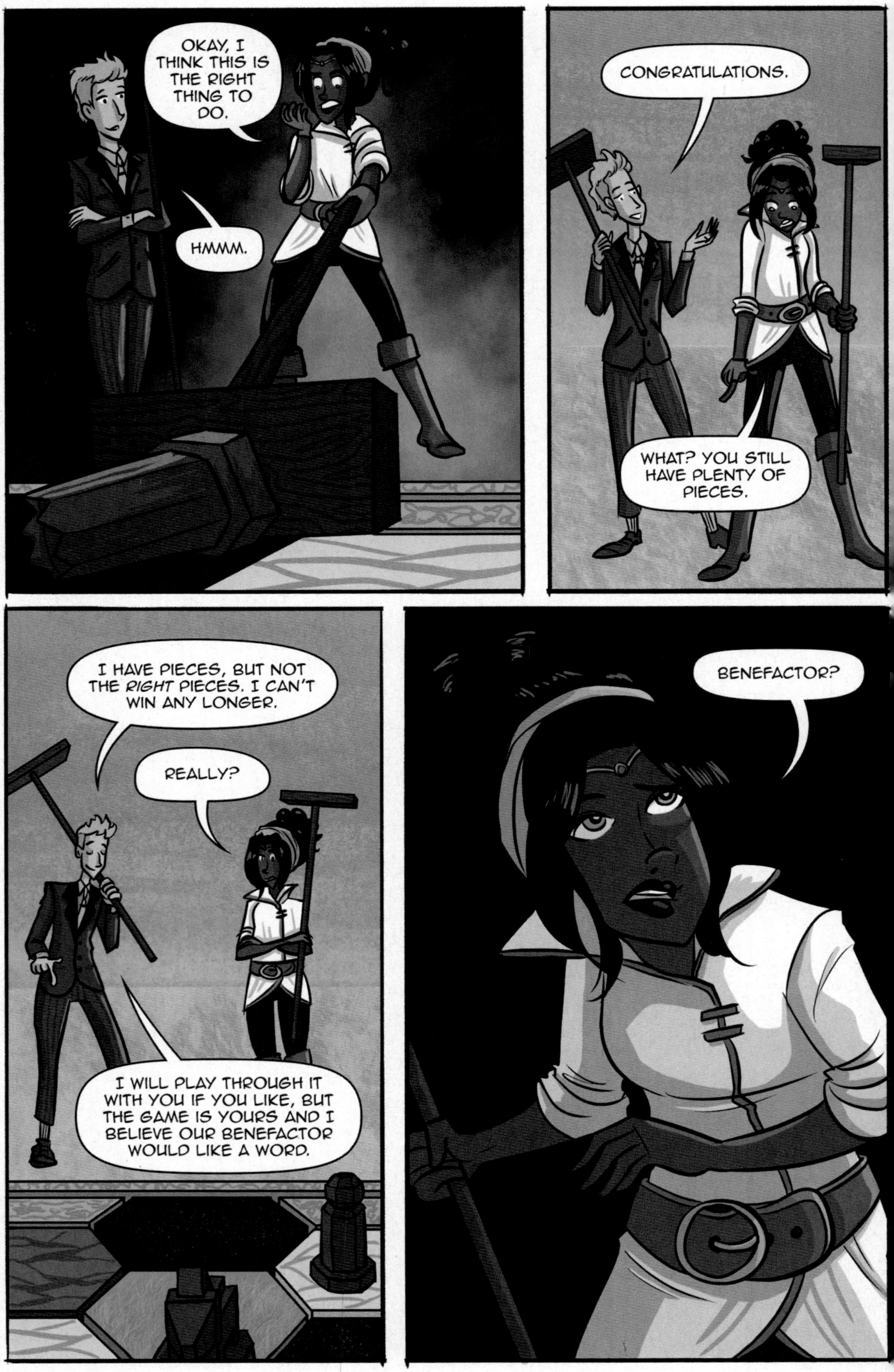
OKAY, I THINK THIS IS THE RIGHT THING TO DO.
HMMM.
CONGRATULATIONS.
WHAT? YOU STILL HAVE PLENTY OF PIECES.
I HAVE PIECES, BUT NOT THE *RIGHT* PIECES. I CAN'T WIN ANY LONGER.
REALLY?
I WILL PLAY THROUGH IT WITH YOU IF YOU LIKE, BUT THE GAME IS YOURS AND I BELIEVE OUR BENEFACTOR WOULD LIKE A WORD.
BENEFACTOR?

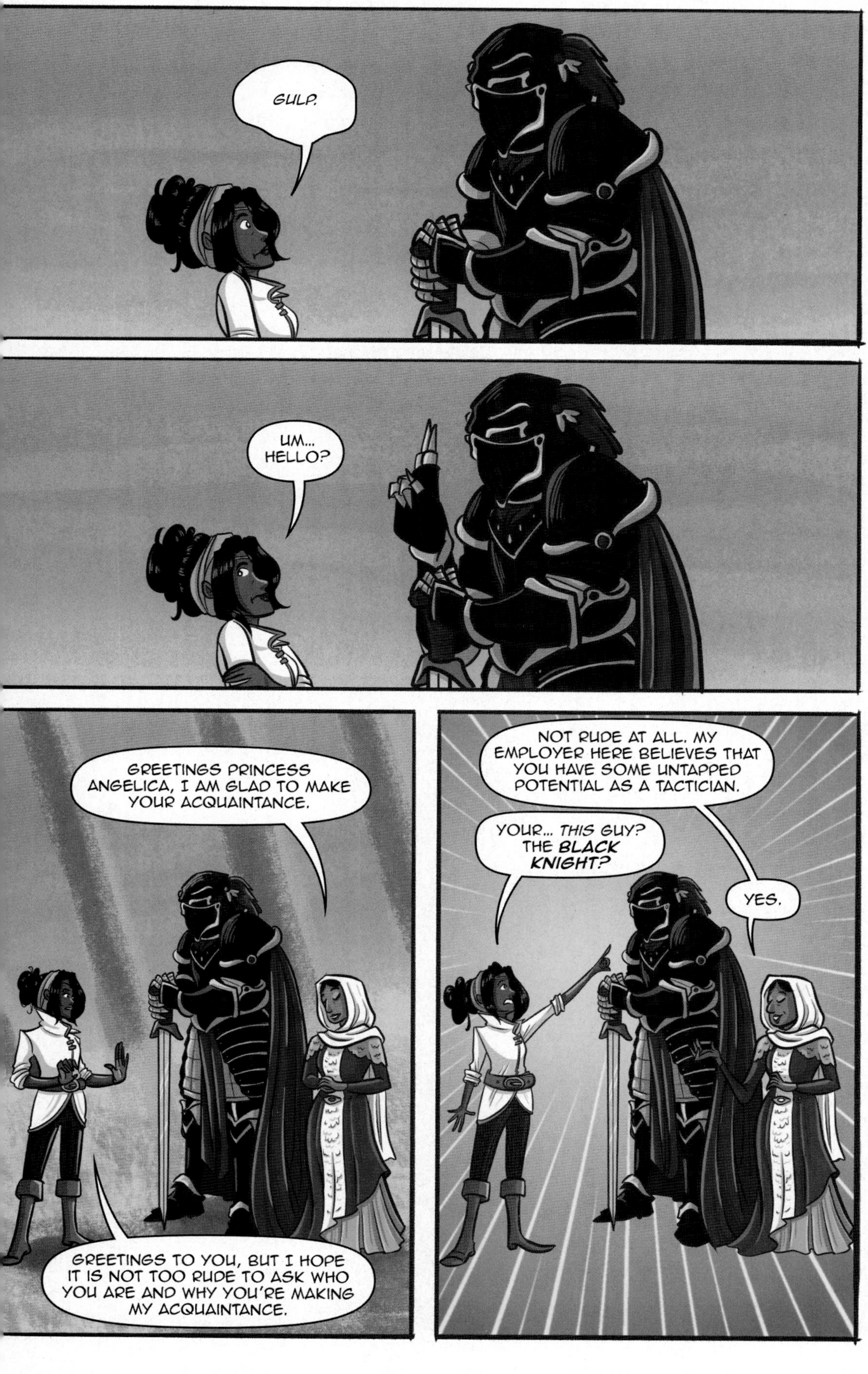
GULP.
UM... HELLO?
GREETINGS PRINCESS ANGELICA, I AM GLAD TO MAKE YOUR ACQUAINTANCE.
GREETINGS TO YOU, BUT I HOPE IT IS NOT TOO RUDE TO ASK WHO YOU ARE AND WHY YOU'RE MAKING MY ACQUAINTANCE.
NOT RUDE AT ALL. MY EMPLOYER HERE BELIEVES THAT YOU HAVE SOME UNTAPPED POTENTIAL AS A TACTICIAN.
YOUR... *THIS GUY?* THE ***BLACK KNIGHT?***
YES.

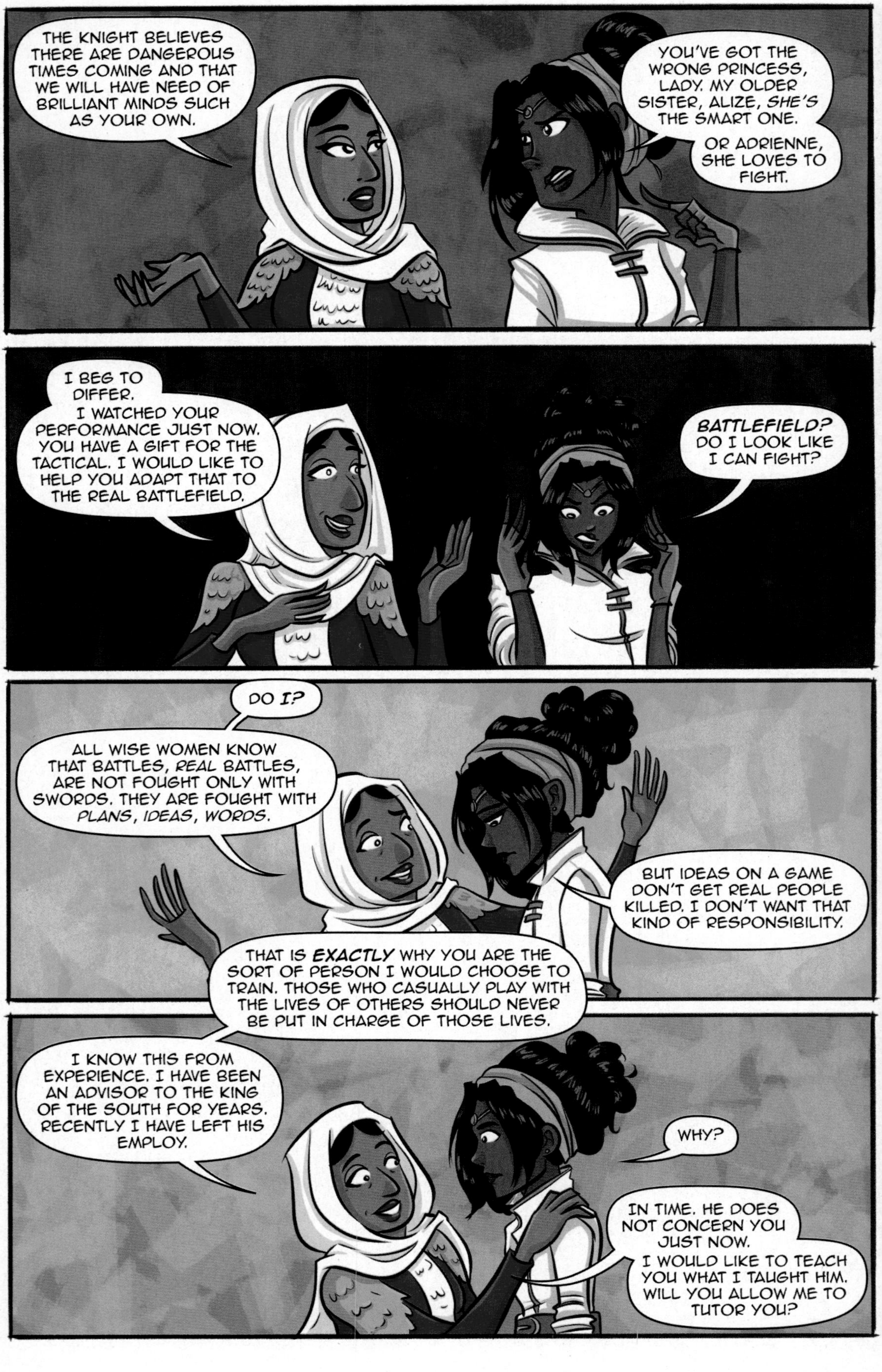
THE KNIGHT BELIEVES THERE ARE DANGEROUS TIMES COMING AND THAT WE WILL HAVE NEED OF BRILLIANT MINDS SUCH AS YOUR OWN.
YOU'VE GOT THE WRONG PRINCESS, LADY. MY OLDER SISTER, ALIZE, *SHE'S* THE SMART ONE.
OR ADRIENNE, SHE LOVES TO FIGHT.
I BEG TO DIFFER.
I WATCHED YOUR PERFORMANCE JUST NOW. YOU HAVE A GIFT FOR THE TACTICAL. I WOULD LIKE TO HELP YOU ADAPT THAT TO THE REAL BATTLEFIELD.
*BATTLEFIELD?* DO I LOOK LIKE I CAN FIGHT?
DO *I?*
ALL WISE WOMEN KNOW THAT BATTLES, *REAL* BATTLES, ARE NOT FOUGHT ONLY WITH SWORDS. THEY ARE FOUGHT WITH *PLANS*, *IDEAS*, *WORDS*.
BUT IDEAS ON A GAME DON'T GET REAL PEOPLE KILLED. I DON'T WANT THAT KIND OF RESPONSIBILITY.
THAT IS ***EXACTLY*** WHY YOU ARE THE SORT OF PERSON I WOULD CHOOSE TO TRAIN. THOSE WHO CASUALLY PLAY WITH THE LIVES OF OTHERS SHOULD NEVER BE PUT IN CHARGE OF THOSE LIVES.
I KNOW THIS FROM EXPERIENCE. I HAVE BEEN AN ADVISOR TO THE KING OF THE SOUTH FOR YEARS. RECENTLY I HAVE LEFT HIS EMPLOY.
WHY?
IN TIME. HE DOES NOT CONCERN YOU JUST NOW.
I WOULD LIKE TO TEACH YOU WHAT I TAUGHT HIM. WILL YOU ALLOW ME TO TUTOR YOU?

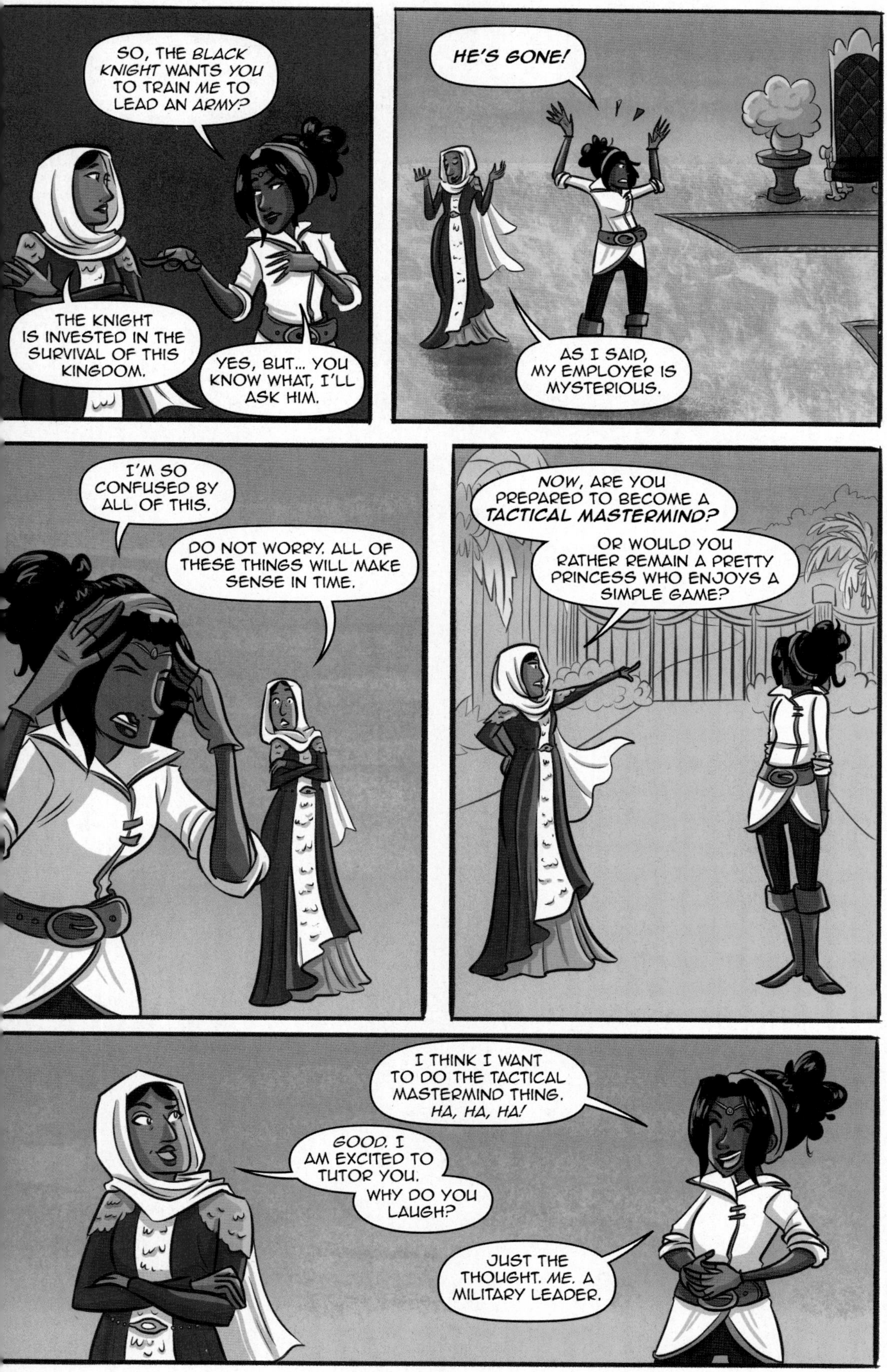
SO, THE BLACK KNIGHT WANTS YOU TO TRAIN ME TO LEAD AN ARMY?
THE KNIGHT IS INVESTED IN THE SURVIVAL OF THIS KINGDOM.
YES, BUT... YOU KNOW WHAT, I'LL ASK HIM.
HE'S GONE!
AS I SAID, MY EMPLOYER IS MYSTERIOUS.
I'M SO CONFUSED BY ALL OF THIS.
DO NOT WORRY. ALL OF THESE THINGS WILL MAKE SENSE IN TIME.
NOW, ARE YOU PREPARED TO BECOME A TACTICAL MASTERMIND?
OR WOULD YOU RATHER REMAIN A PRETTY PRINCESS WHO ENJOYS A SIMPLE GAME?
I THINK I WANT TO DO THE TACTICAL MASTERMIND THING. HA, HA, HA!
GOOD. I AM EXCITED TO TUTOR YOU.
WHY DO YOU LAUGH?
JUST THE THOUGHT. ME. A MILITARY LEADER.

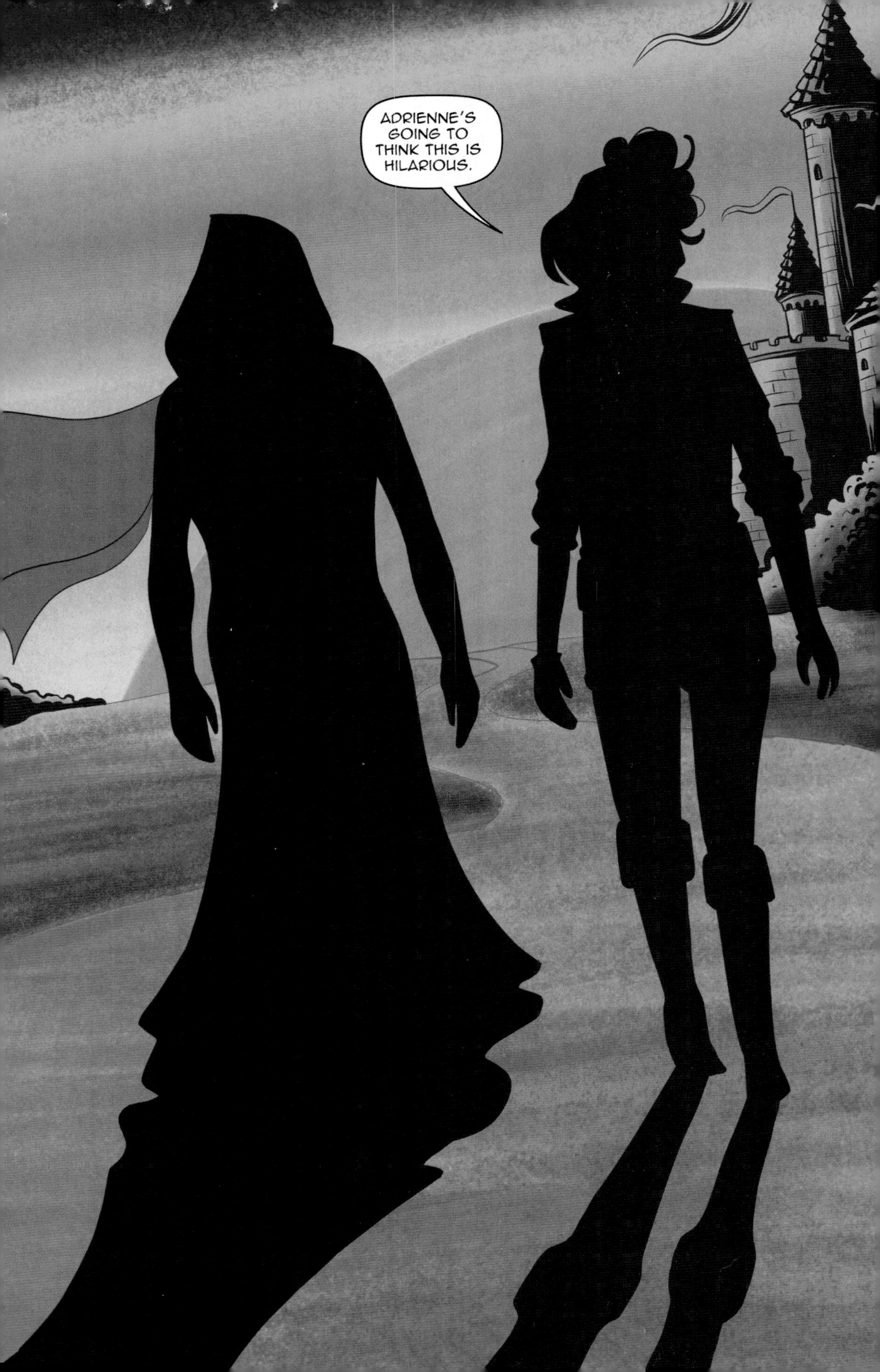
ADRIENNE'S GOING TO THINK THIS IS HILARIOUS.

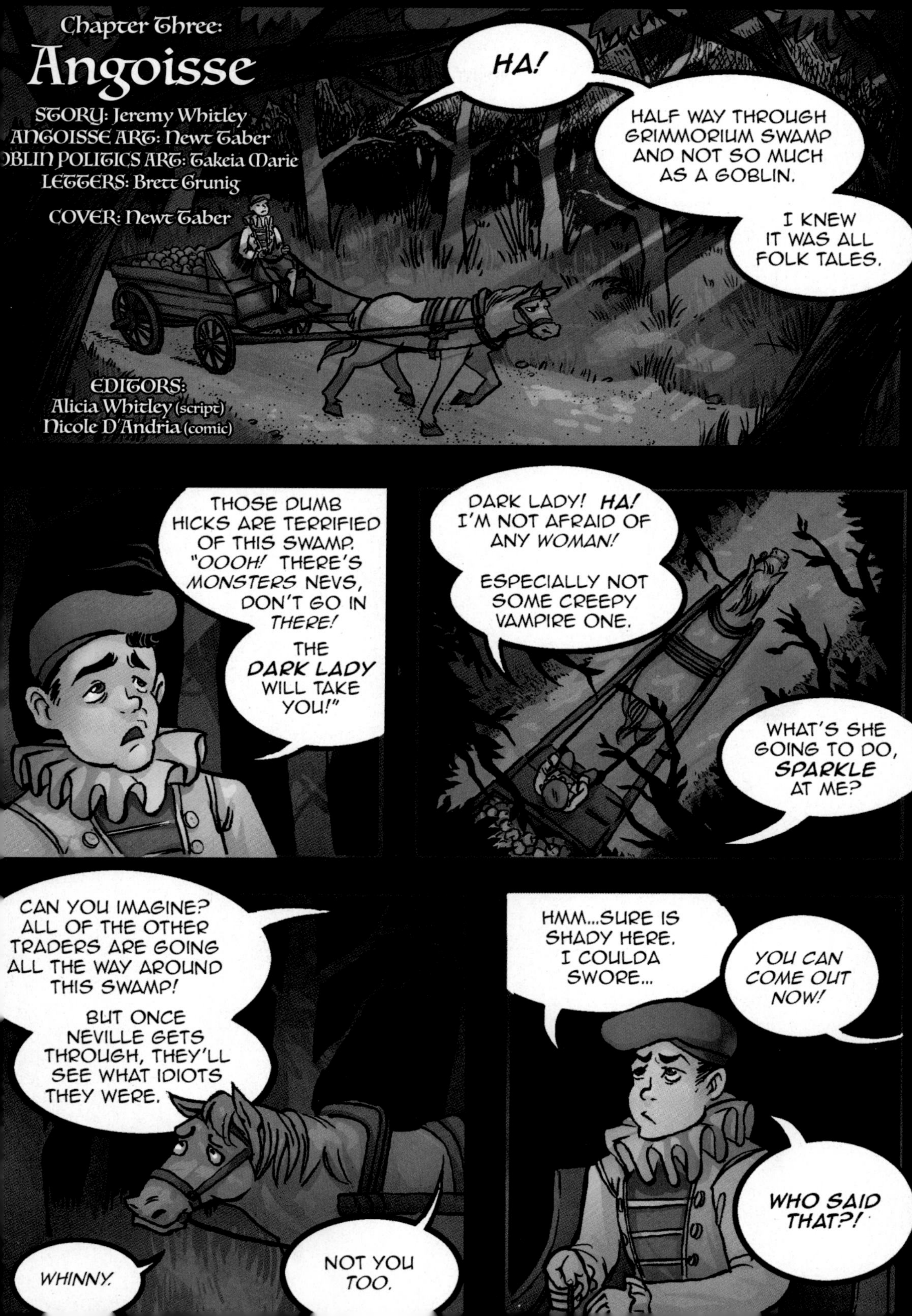
Chapter Three:
Angoisse
STORY: Jeremy Whitley
ANGOISSE ART: Newt Taber
GOBLIN POLITICS ART: Takeia Marie
LETTERS: Brett Grunig
COVER: Newt Taber
EDITORS:
Alicia Whitley (script)
Nicole D'Andria (comic)
HA!
HALF WAY THROUGH GRIMMORIUM SWAMP AND NOT SO MUCH AS A GOBLIN.
I KNEW IT WAS ALL FOLK TALES.
THOSE DUMB HICKS ARE TERRIFIED OF THIS SWAMP. "OOOH! THERE'S MONSTERS NEVS, DON'T GO IN THERE!
THE DARK LADY WILL TAKE YOU!"
DARK LADY! HA! I'M NOT AFRAID OF ANY WOMAN!
ESPECIALLY NOT SOME CREEPY VAMPIRE ONE.
WHAT'S SHE GOING TO DO, SPARKLE AT ME?
CAN YOU IMAGINE? ALL OF THE OTHER TRADERS ARE GOING ALL THE WAY AROUND THIS SWAMP!
BUT ONCE NEVILLE GETS THROUGH, THEY'LL SEE WHAT IDIOTS THEY WERE.
WHINNY.
NOT YOU TOO.
HMM...SURE IS SHADY HERE. I COULDA SWORE...
YOU CAN COME OUT NOW!
WHO SAID THAT?!

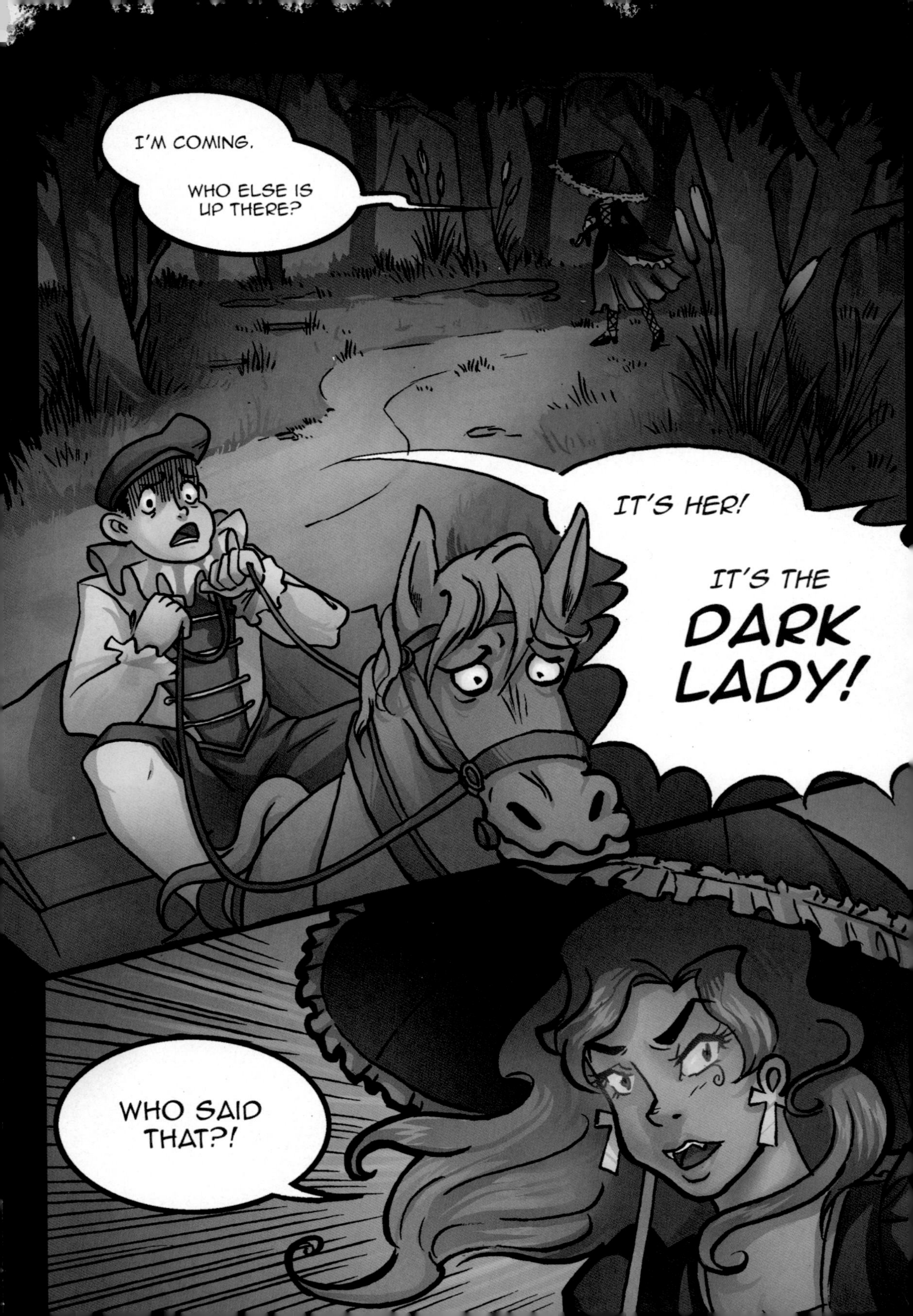
I'M COMING.
WHO ELSE IS UP THERE?
IT'S HER!
IT'S THE DARK LADY!
WHO SAID THAT?!

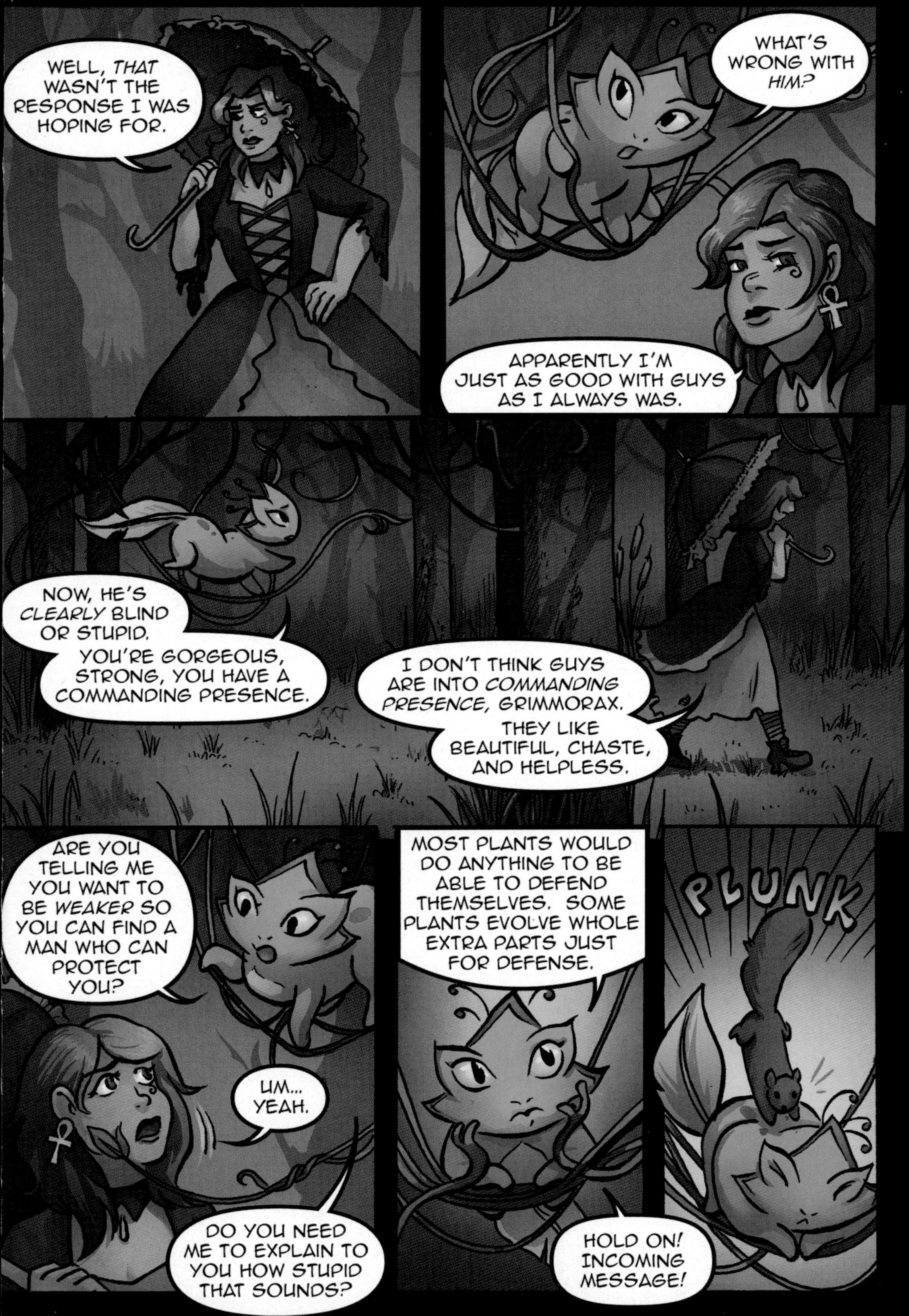
WELL, *THAT* WASN'T THE RESPONSE I WAS HOPING FOR.
WHAT'S WRONG WITH *HIM?*
APPARENTLY I'M JUST AS GOOD WITH GUYS AS I ALWAYS WAS.
NOW, HE'S *CLEARLY* BLIND OR STUPID.
YOU'RE GORGEOUS, STRONG, YOU HAVE A COMMANDING PRESENCE.
I DON'T THINK GUYS ARE INTO *COMMANDING PRESENCE*, GRIMMORAX.
THEY LIKE BEAUTIFUL, CHASTE, AND HELPLESS.
ARE YOU TELLING ME YOU WANT TO BE *WEAKER* SO YOU CAN FIND A MAN WHO CAN PROTECT YOU?
UM... YEAH.
DO YOU NEED ME TO EXPLAIN TO YOU HOW STUPID THAT SOUNDS?
MOST PLANTS WOULD DO ANYTHING TO BE ABLE TO DEFEND THEMSELVES. SOME PLANTS EVOLVE WHOLE EXTRA PARTS JUST FOR DEFENSE.
PLUNK
HOLD ON! INCOMING MESSAGE!

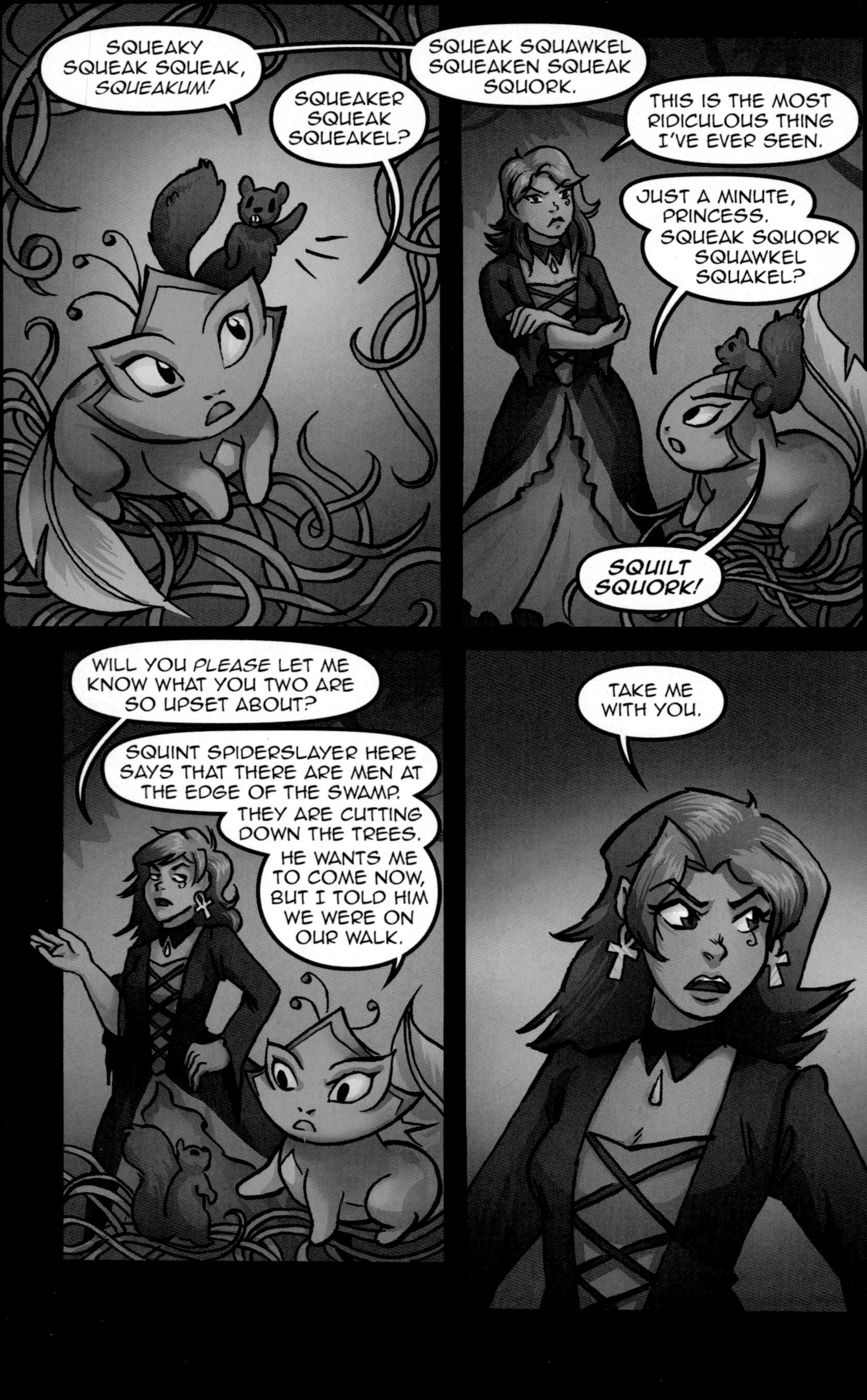
SQUEAKY SQUEAK SQUEAK, *SQUEAKUM!*
SQUEAK SQUAWKEL SQUEAKEN SQUEAK SQUORK.
SQUEAKER SQUEAK SQUEAKEL?
THIS IS THE MOST RIDICULOUS THING I'VE EVER SEEN.
JUST A MINUTE, PRINCESS. SQUEAK SQUORK SQUAWKEL SQUAKEL?
*SQUILT SQUORK!*
WILL YOU *PLEASE* LET ME KNOW WHAT YOU TWO ARE SO UPSET ABOUT?
SQUINT SPIDERSLAYER HERE SAYS THAT THERE ARE MEN AT THE EDGE OF THE SWAMP.
THEY ARE CUTTING DOWN THE TREES.
HE WANTS ME TO COME NOW, BUT I TOLD HIM WE WERE ON OUR WALK.
TAKE ME WITH YOU.

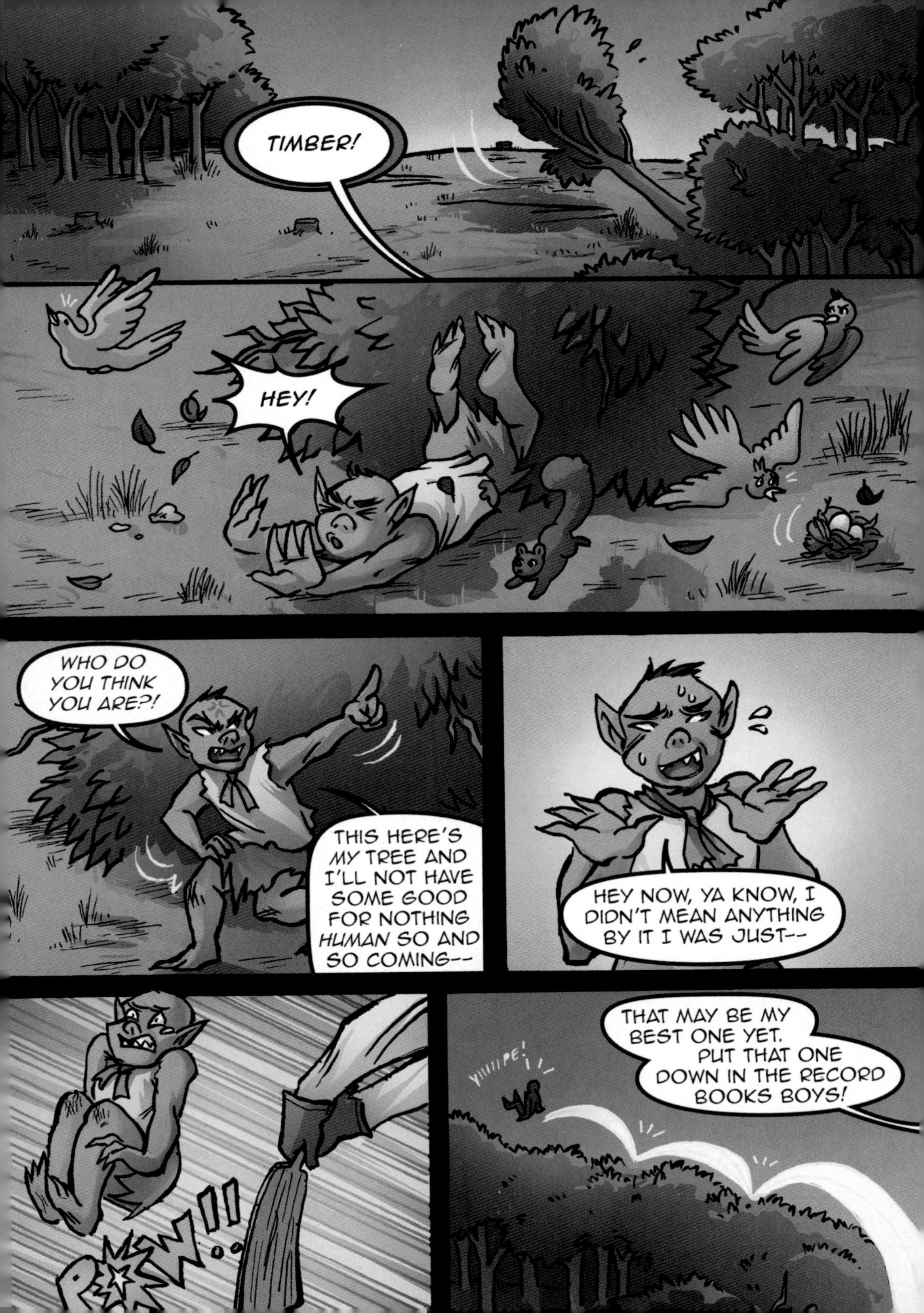
TIMBER!
HEY!
WHO DO YOU THINK YOU ARE?!
THIS HERE'S MY TREE AND I'LL NOT HAVE SOME GOOD FOR NOTHING *HUMAN* SO AND SO COMING--
HEY NOW, YA KNOW, I DIDN'T MEAN ANYTHING BY IT I WAS JUST--
POW!!
YIIIIIPE!
THAT MAY BE MY BEST ONE YET. PUT THAT ONE DOWN IN THE RECORD BOOKS BOYS!

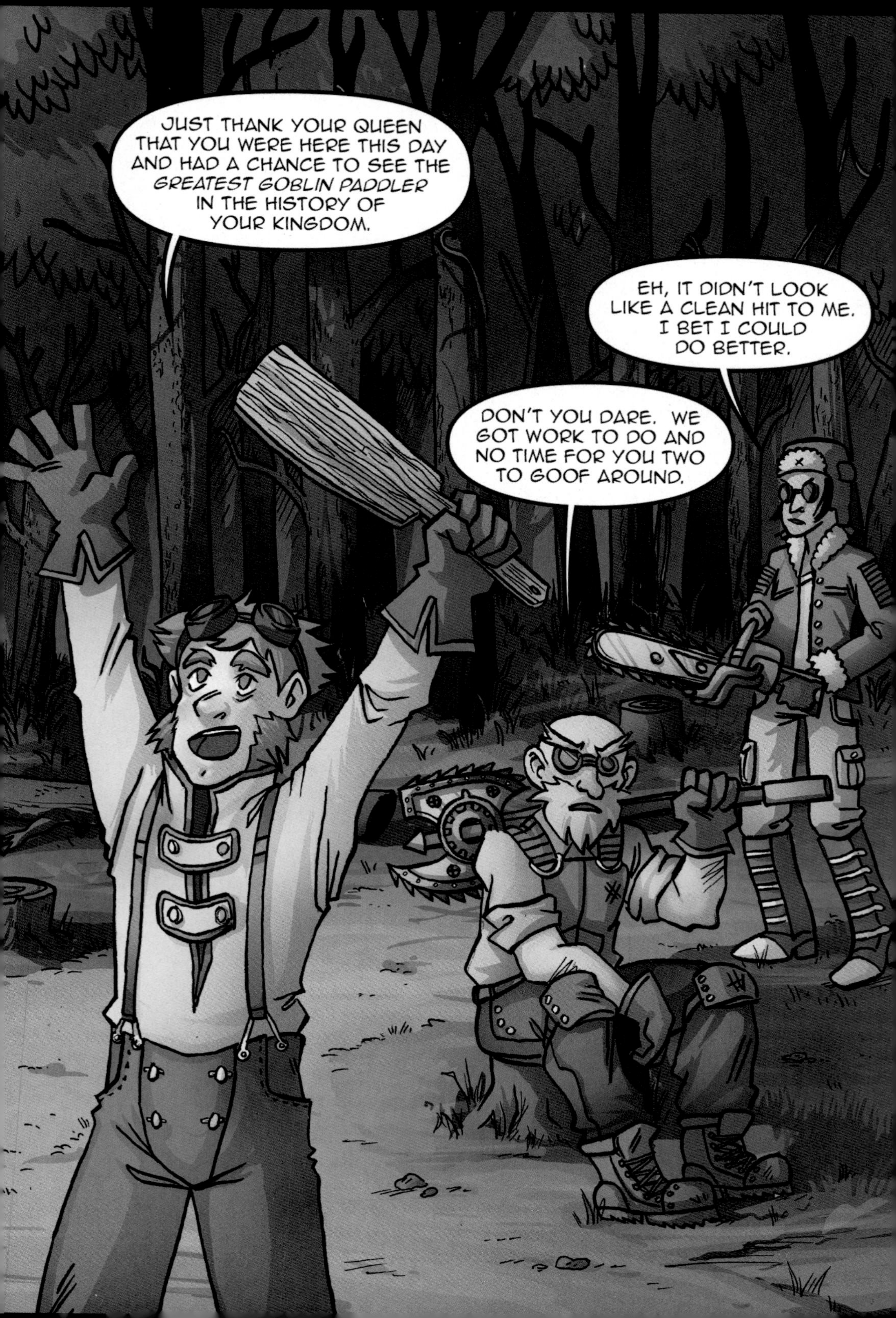
JUST THANK YOUR QUEEN THAT YOU WERE HERE THIS DAY AND HAD A CHANCE TO SEE THE *GREATEST GOBLIN PADDLER* IN THE HISTORY OF YOUR KINGDOM.
EH, IT DIDN'T LOOK LIKE A CLEAN HIT TO ME. I BET I COULD DO BETTER.
DON'T YOU DARE. WE GOT WORK TO DO AND NO TIME FOR YOU TWO TO GOOF AROUND.

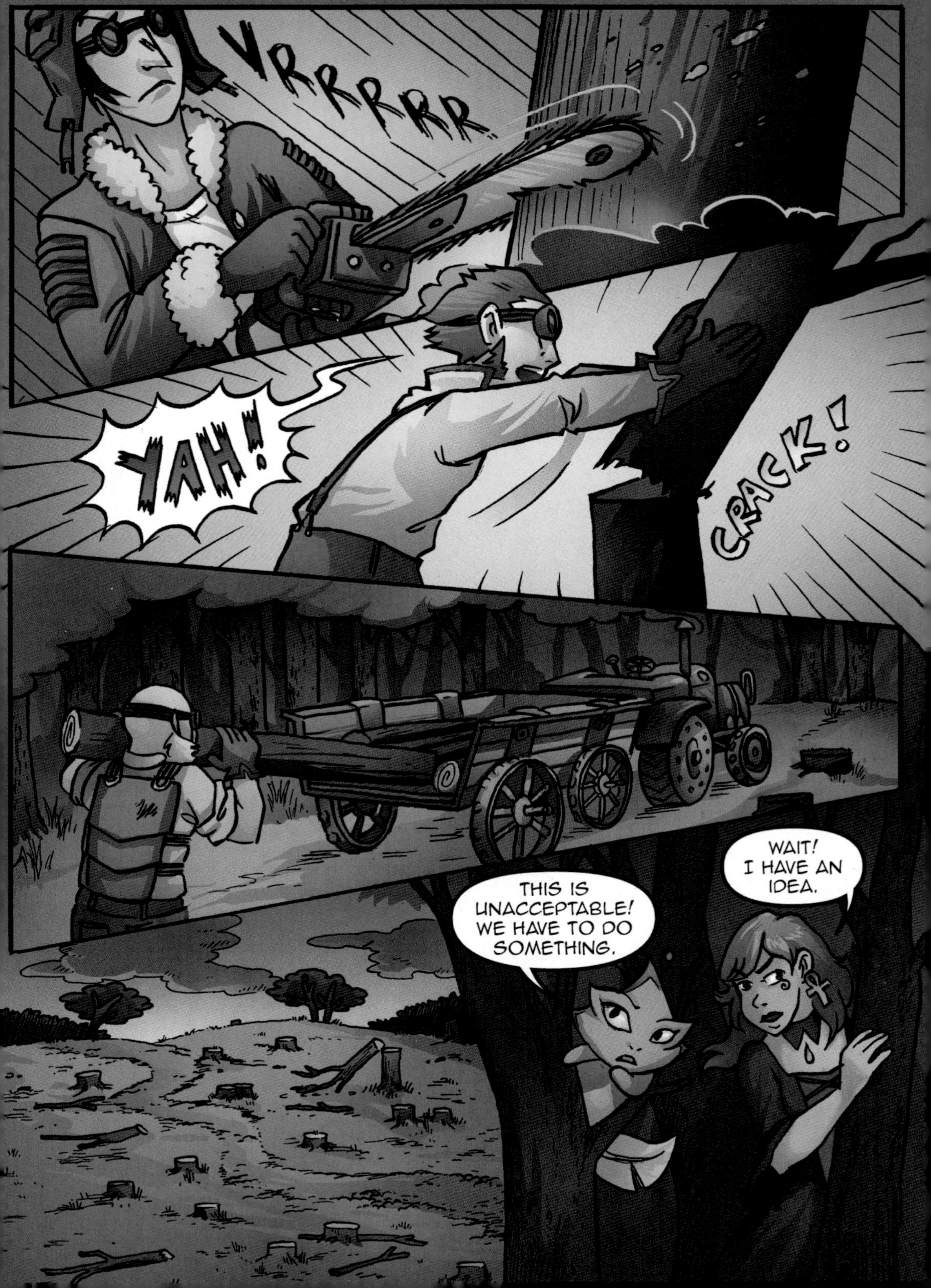
VRRRRRR
YAH!
CRACK!
THIS IS UNACCEPTABLE! WE HAVE TO DO SOMETHING.
WAIT! I HAVE AN IDEA.

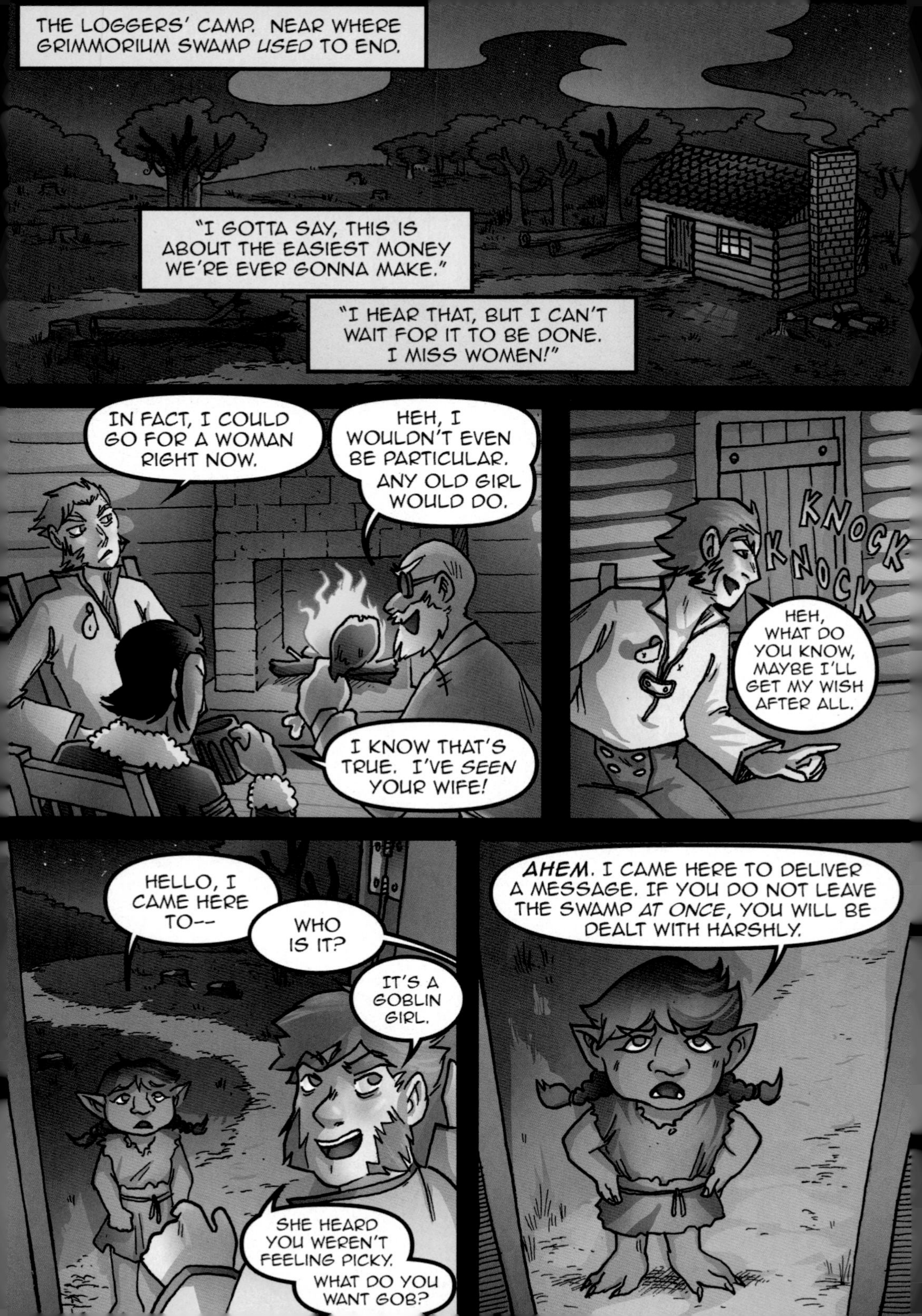
THE LOGGERS' CAMP. NEAR WHERE GRIMMORIUM SWAMP *USED* TO END.
"I GOTTA SAY, THIS IS ABOUT THE EASIEST MONEY WE'RE EVER GONNA MAKE."
"I HEAR THAT, BUT I CAN'T WAIT FOR IT TO BE DONE. I MISS WOMEN!"
IN FACT, I COULD GO FOR A WOMAN RIGHT NOW.
HEH, I WOULDN'T EVEN BE PARTICULAR. ANY OLD GIRL WOULD DO.
I KNOW THAT'S TRUE. I'VE *SEEN* YOUR WIFE!
KNOCK KNOCK
HEH, WHAT DO YOU KNOW, MAYBE I'LL GET MY WISH AFTER ALL.
HELLO, I CAME HERE TO--
WHO IS IT?
IT'S A GOBLIN GIRL.
SHE HEARD YOU WEREN'T FEELING PICKY.
WHAT DO YOU WANT GOB?
***AHEM***. I CAME HERE TO DELIVER A MESSAGE. IF YOU DO NOT LEAVE THE SWAMP *AT ONCE*, YOU WILL BE DEALT WITH HARSHLY.

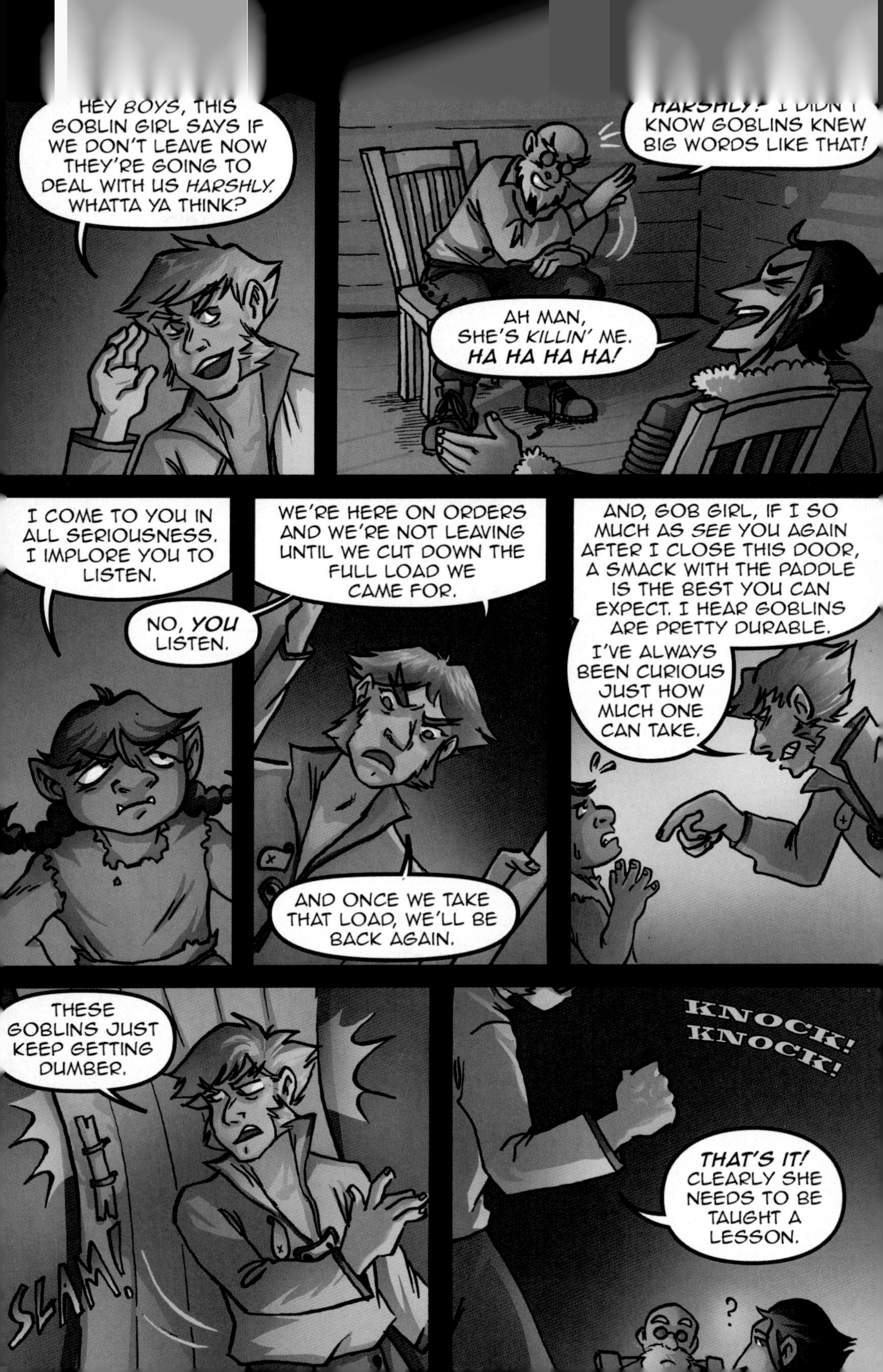
HEY BOYS, THIS GOBLIN GIRL SAYS IF WE DON'T LEAVE NOW THEY'RE GOING TO DEAL WITH US HARSHLY. WHATTA YA THINK?
KNOW GOBLINS KNEW BIG WORDS LIKE THAT!
AH MAN, SHE'S KILLIN' ME. HA HA HA HA!
I COME TO YOU IN ALL SERIOUSNESS. I IMPLORE YOU TO LISTEN.
NO, YOU LISTEN.
WE'RE HERE ON ORDERS AND WE'RE NOT LEAVING UNTIL WE CUT DOWN THE FULL LOAD WE CAME FOR.
AND ONCE WE TAKE THAT LOAD, WE'LL BE BACK AGAIN.
AND, GOB GIRL, IF I SO MUCH AS SEE YOU AGAIN AFTER I CLOSE THIS DOOR, A SMACK WITH THE PADDLE IS THE BEST YOU CAN EXPECT. I HEAR GOBLINS ARE PRETTY DURABLE.
I'VE ALWAYS BEEN CURIOUS JUST HOW MUCH ONE CAN TAKE.
THESE GOBLINS JUST KEEP GETTING DUMBER.
SLAM!
KNOCK! KNOCK!
THAT'S IT! CLEARLY SHE NEEDS TO BE TAUGHT A LESSON.
?

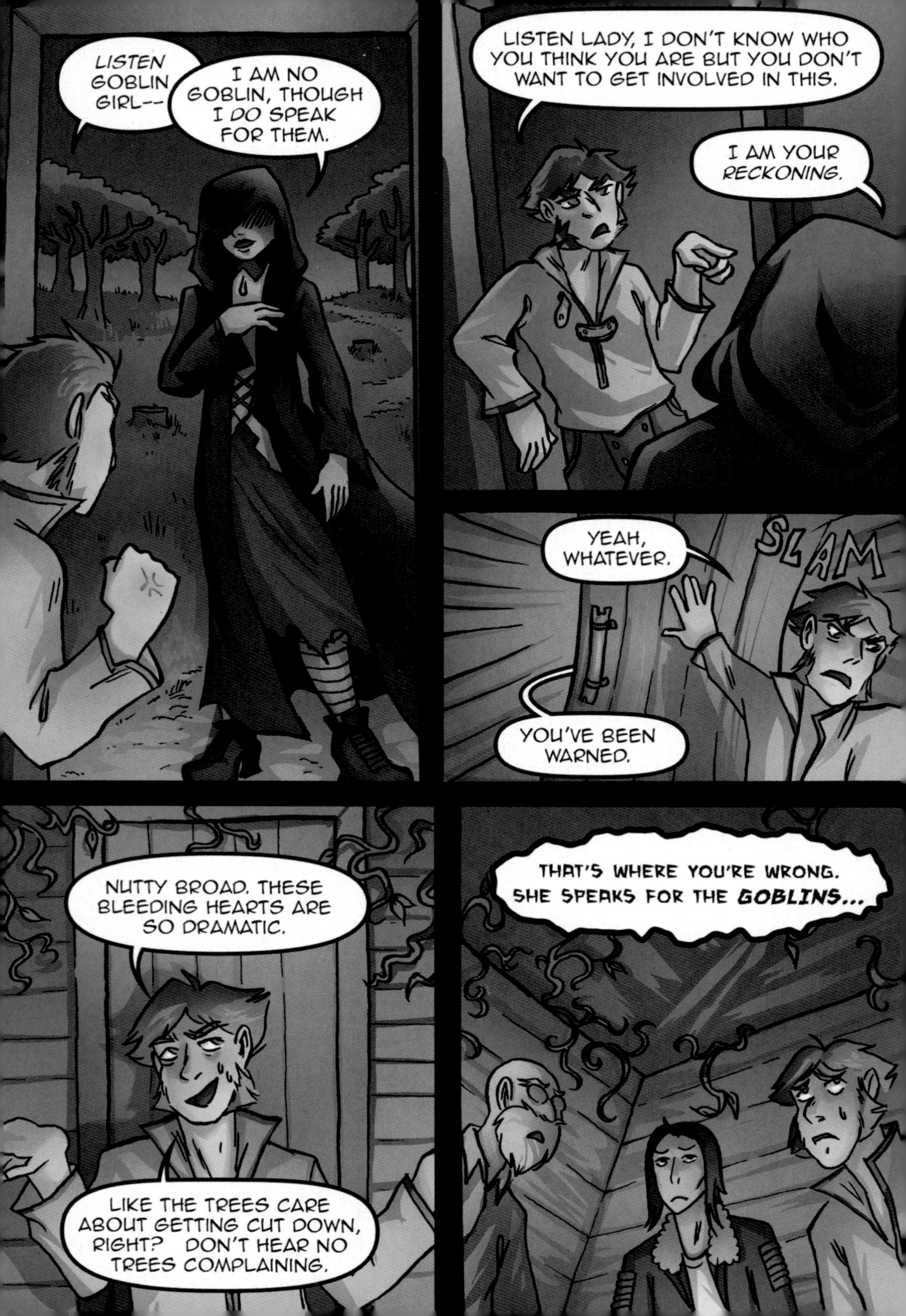
LISTEN GOBLIN GIRL--
I AM NO GOBLIN, THOUGH I *DO* SPEAK FOR THEM.
LISTEN LADY, I DON'T KNOW WHO YOU THINK YOU ARE BUT YOU DON'T WANT TO GET INVOLVED IN THIS.
I AM YOUR *RECKONING.*
YEAH, WHATEVER.
SLAM
YOU'VE BEEN WARNED.
NUTTY BROAD. THESE BLEEDING HEARTS ARE SO DRAMATIC.
LIKE THE TREES CARE ABOUT GETTING CUT DOWN, RIGHT? DON'T HEAR NO TREES COMPLAINING.
THAT'S WHERE YOU'RE WRONG. SHE SPEAKS FOR THE ***GOBLINS...***

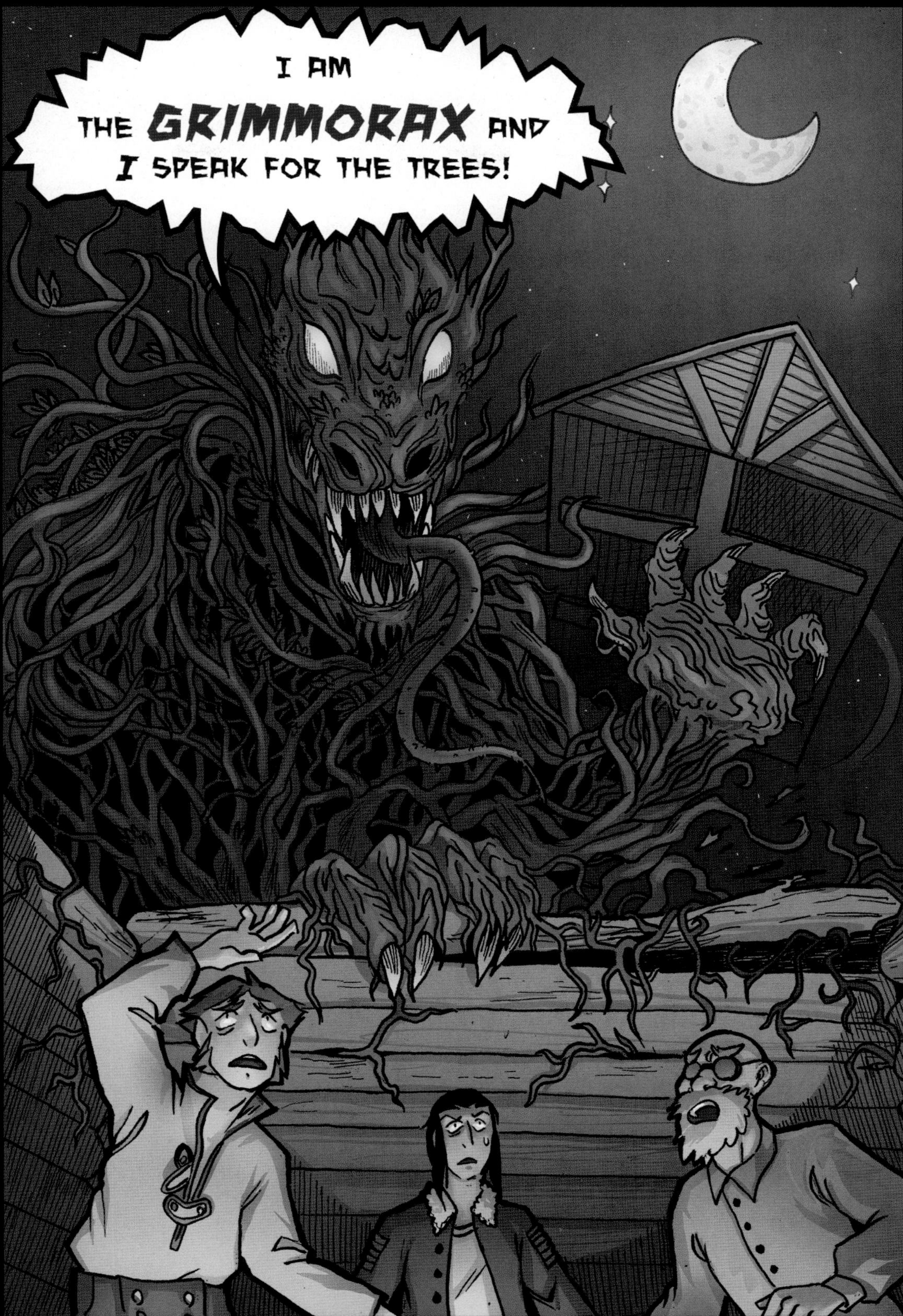
I AM THE GRIMMORAX AND I SPEAK FOR THE TREES!

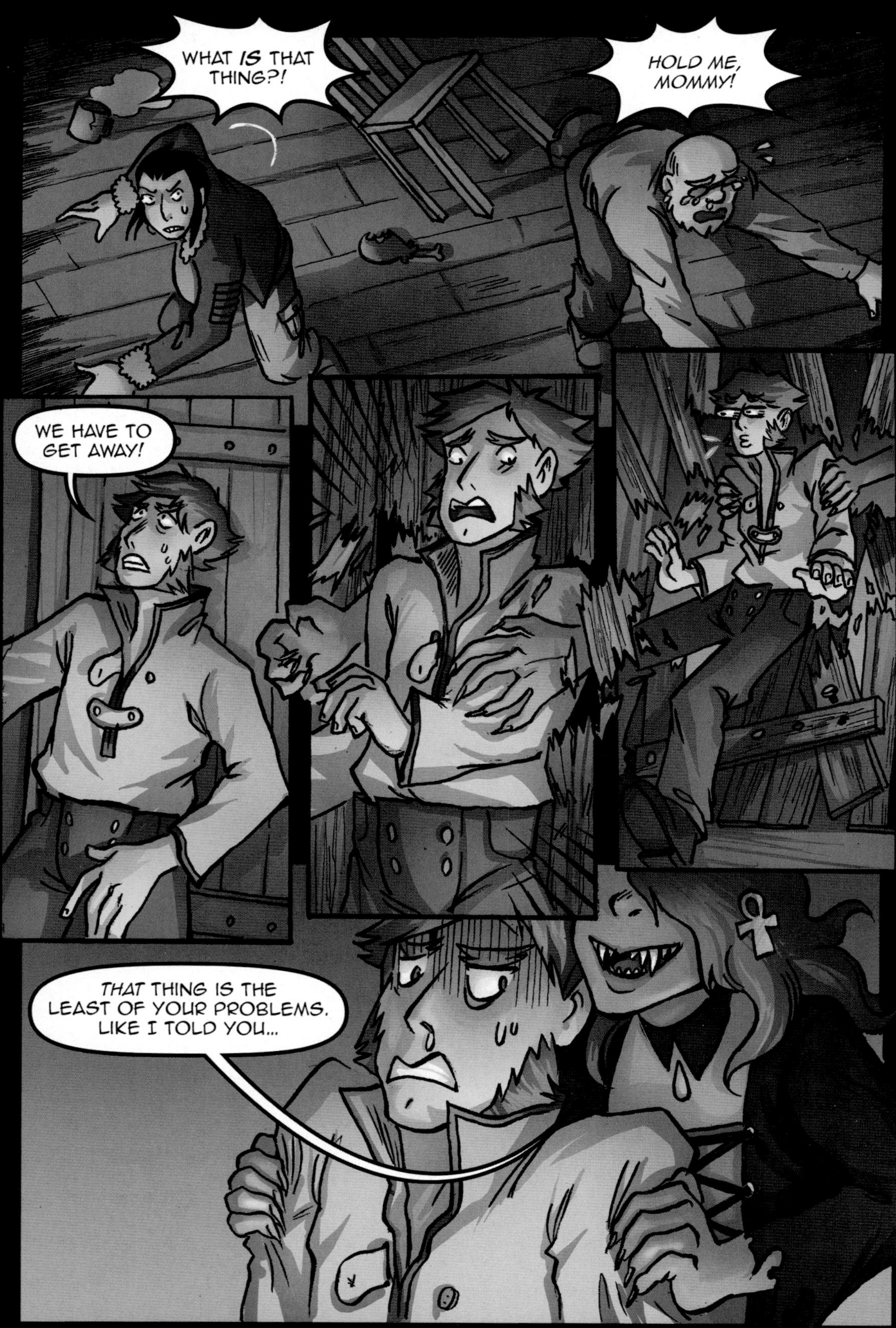
WHAT *IS* THAT THING?!
HOLD ME, MOMMY!
WE HAVE TO GET AWAY!
*THAT* THING IS THE LEAST OF YOUR PROBLEMS. LIKE I TOLD YOU...

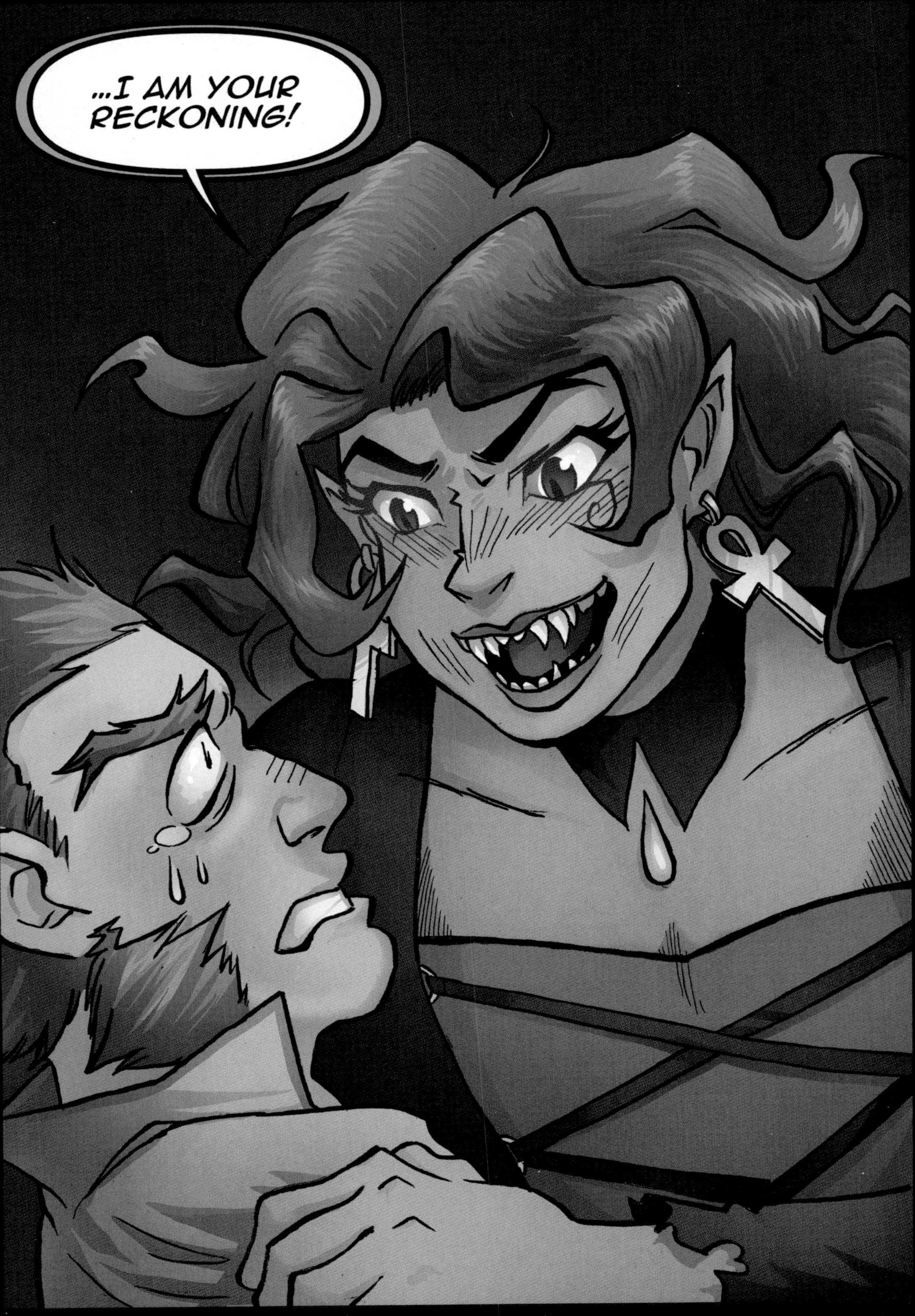
...I AM YOUR RECKONING!

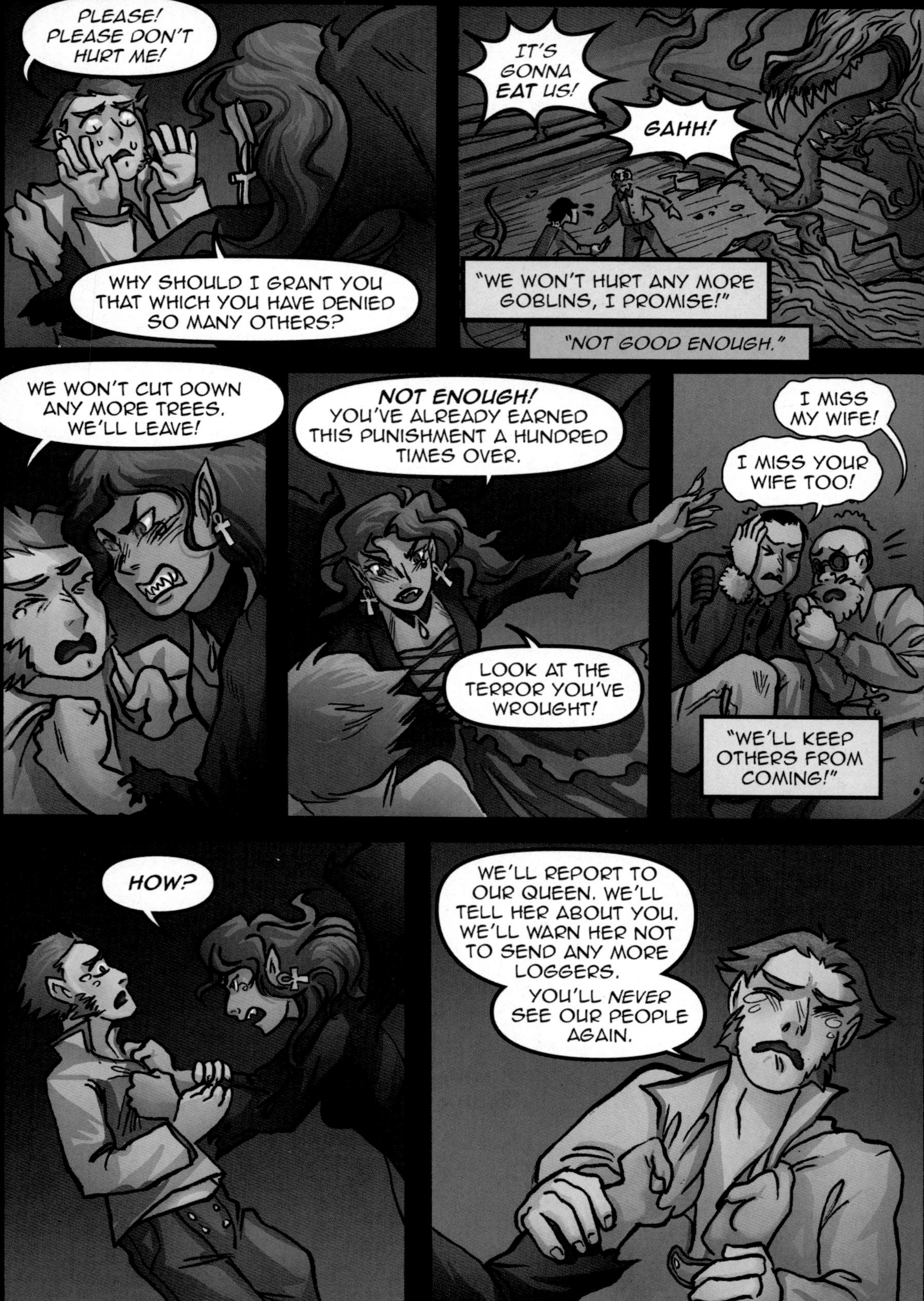
PLEASE! PLEASE DON'T HURT ME!
WHY SHOULD I GRANT YOU THAT WHICH YOU HAVE DENIED SO MANY OTHERS?
IT'S GONNA EAT US!
GAHH!
"WE WON'T HURT ANY MORE GOBLINS, I PROMISE!"
"NOT GOOD ENOUGH."
WE WON'T CUT DOWN ANY MORE TREES. WE'LL LEAVE!
NOT ENOUGH! YOU'VE ALREADY EARNED THIS PUNISHMENT A HUNDRED TIMES OVER.
LOOK AT THE TERROR YOU'VE WROUGHT!
I MISS MY WIFE!
I MISS YOUR WIFE TOO!
"WE'LL KEEP OTHERS FROM COMING!"
HOW?
WE'LL REPORT TO OUR QUEEN. WE'LL TELL HER ABOUT YOU. WE'LL WARN HER NOT TO SEND ANY MORE LOGGERS.
YOU'LL NEVER SEE OUR PEOPLE AGAIN.

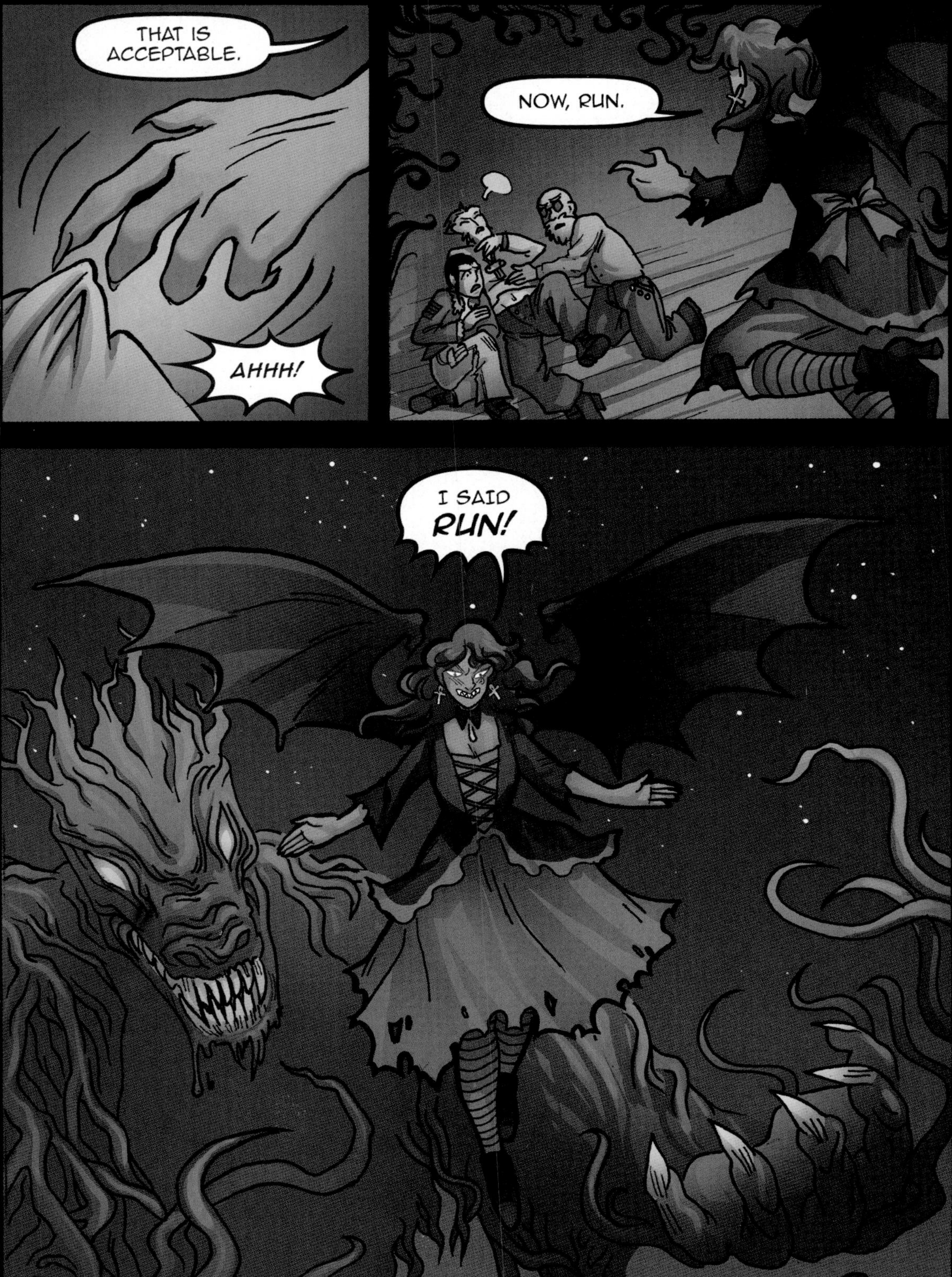
THAT IS ACCEPTABLE.
AHHH!
NOW, RUN.
I SAID RUN!

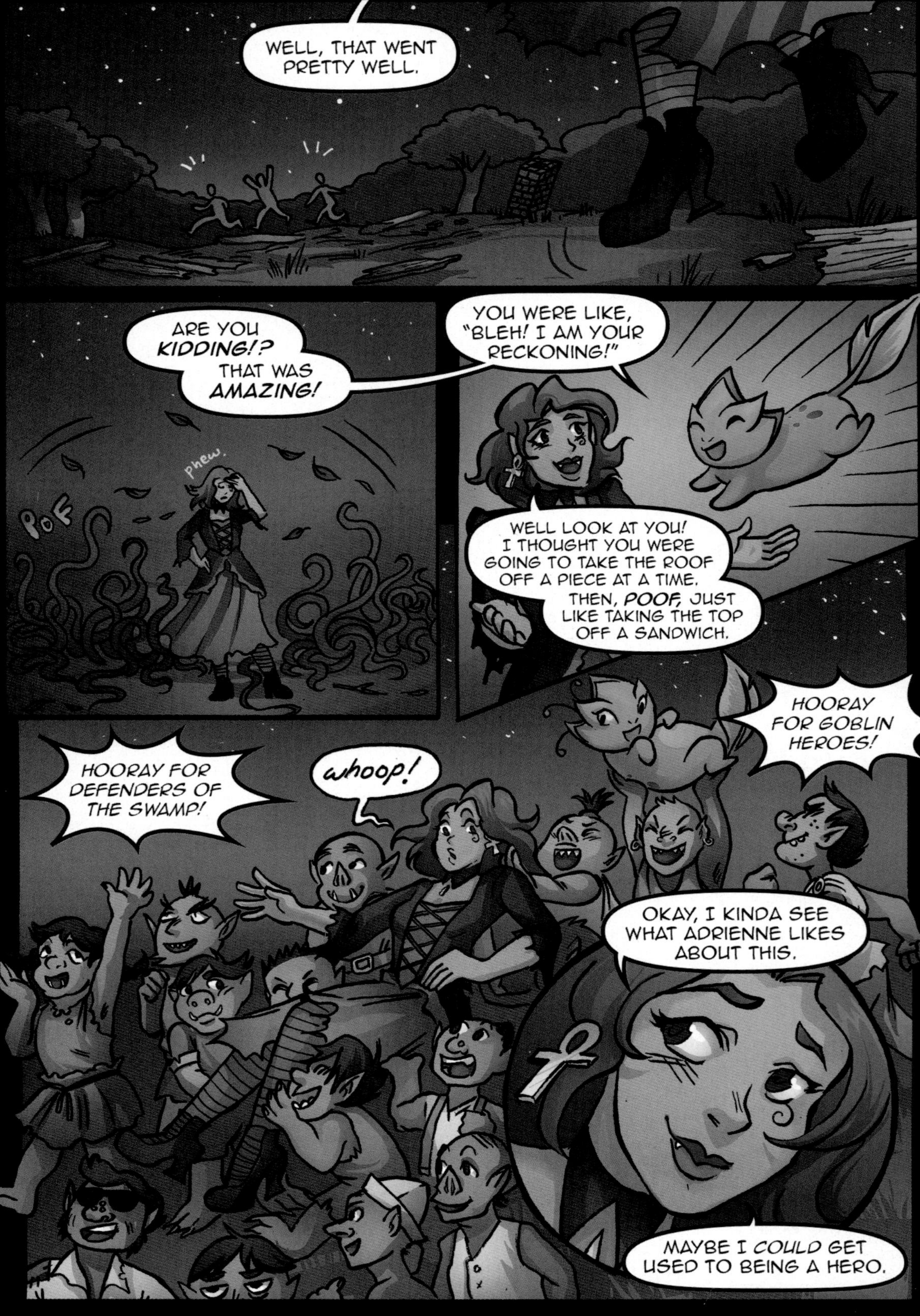
WELL, THAT WENT PRETTY WELL.
ARE YOU *KIDDING!?* THAT WAS *AMAZING!*
phew.
POF
YOU WERE LIKE, "BLEH! I AM YOUR RECKONING!"
WELL LOOK AT YOU! I THOUGHT YOU WERE GOING TO TAKE THE ROOF OFF A PIECE AT A TIME.
THEN, *POOF,* JUST LIKE TAKING THE TOP OFF A SANDWICH.
HOORAY FOR DEFENDERS OF THE SWAMP!
whoop!
HOORAY FOR GOBLIN HEROES!
OKAY, I KINDA SEE WHAT ADRIENNE LIKES ABOUT THIS.
MAYBE I *COULD* GET USED TO BEING A HERO.

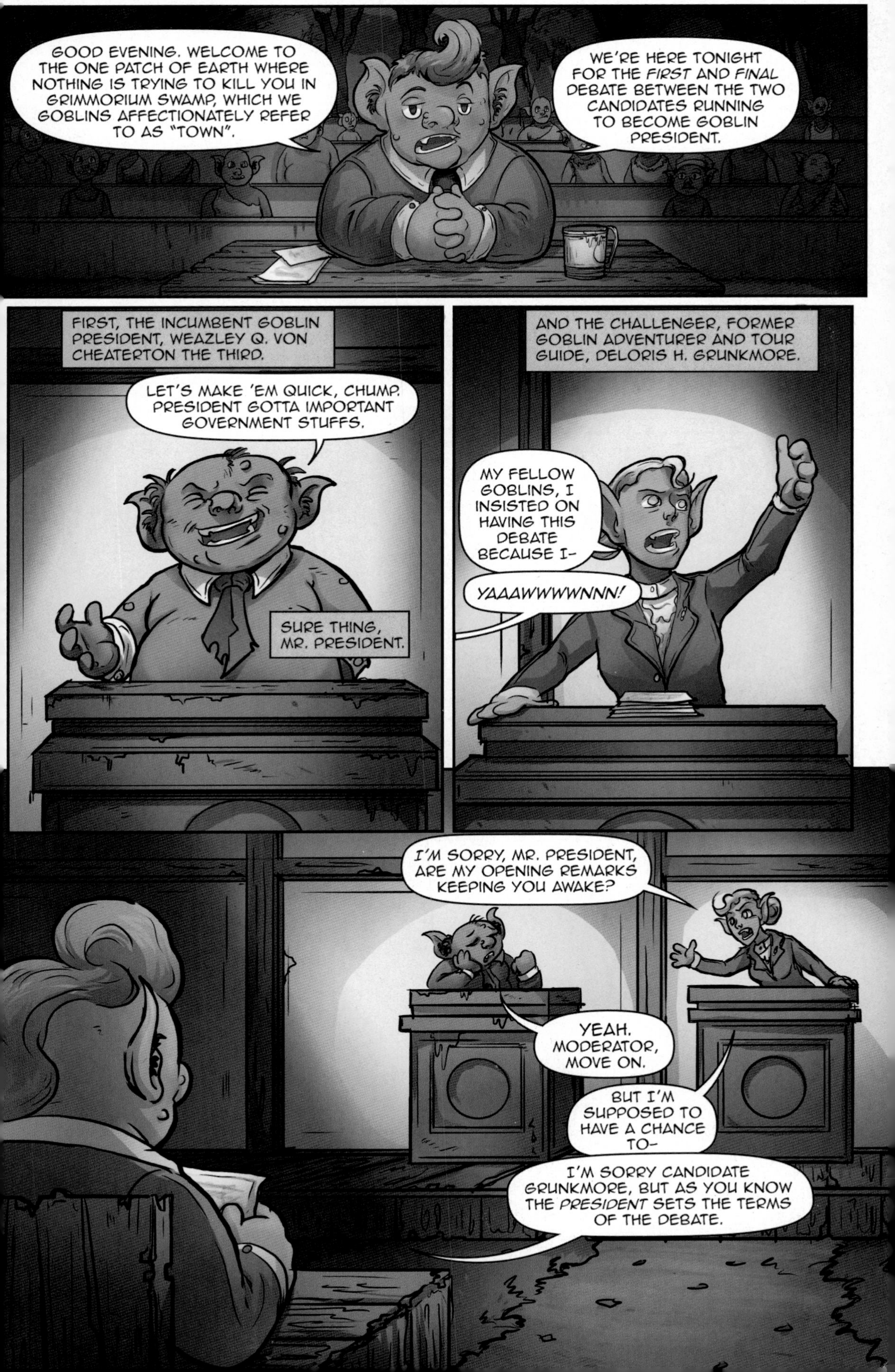
GOOD EVENING. WELCOME TO THE ONE PATCH OF EARTH WHERE NOTHING IS TRYING TO KILL YOU IN GRIMMORIUM SWAMP, WHICH WE GOBLINS AFFECTIONATELY REFER TO AS "TOWN".
WE'RE HERE TONIGHT FOR THE *FIRST* AND *FINAL* DEBATE BETWEEN THE TWO CANDIDATES RUNNING TO BECOME GOBLIN PRESIDENT.
FIRST, THE INCUMBENT GOBLIN PRESIDENT, WEAZLEY Q. VON CHEATERTON THE THIRD.
LET'S MAKE 'EM QUICK, CHUMP. PRESIDENT GOTTA IMPORTANT GOVERNMENT STUFFS.
SURE THING, MR. PRESIDENT.
AND THE CHALLENGER, FORMER GOBLIN ADVENTURER AND TOUR GUIDE, DELORIS H. GRUNKMORE.
MY FELLOW GOBLINS, I INSISTED ON HAVING THIS DEBATE BECAUSE I-
*YAAAWWWWNNN!*
I'M SORRY, MR. PRESIDENT, ARE MY OPENING REMARKS KEEPING YOU AWAKE?
YEAH. MODERATOR, MOVE ON.
BUT I'M SUPPOSED TO HAVE A CHANCE TO-
I'M SORRY CANDIDATE GRUNKMORE, BUT AS YOU KNOW THE *PRESIDENT* SETS THE TERMS OF THE DEBATE.

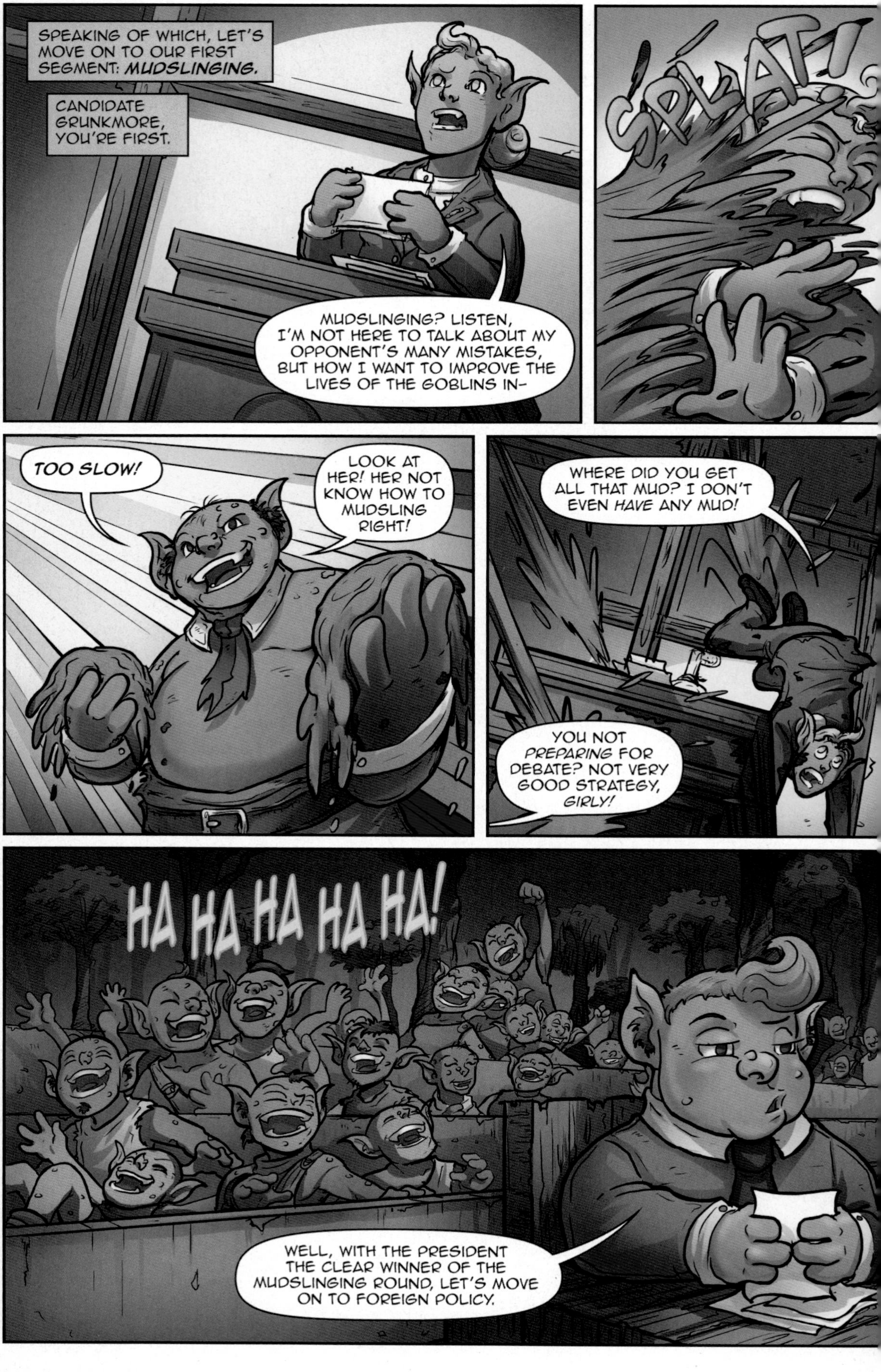
SPEAKING OF WHICH, LET'S MOVE ON TO OUR FIRST SEGMENT: MUDSLINGING.
CANDIDATE GRUNKMORE, YOU'RE FIRST.
MUDSLINGING? LISTEN, I'M NOT HERE TO TALK ABOUT MY OPPONENT'S MANY MISTAKES, BUT HOW I WANT TO IMPROVE THE LIVES OF THE GOBLINS IN-
SPLAT!
TOO SLOW!
LOOK AT HER! HER NOT KNOW HOW TO MUDSLING RIGHT!
WHERE DID YOU GET ALL THAT MUD? I DON'T EVEN HAVE ANY MUD!
YOU NOT PREPARING FOR DEBATE? NOT VERY GOOD STRATEGY, GIRLY!
HA HA HA HA HA!
WELL, WITH THE PRESIDENT THE CLEAR WINNER OF THE MUDSLINGING ROUND, LET'S MOVE ON TO FOREIGN POLICY.

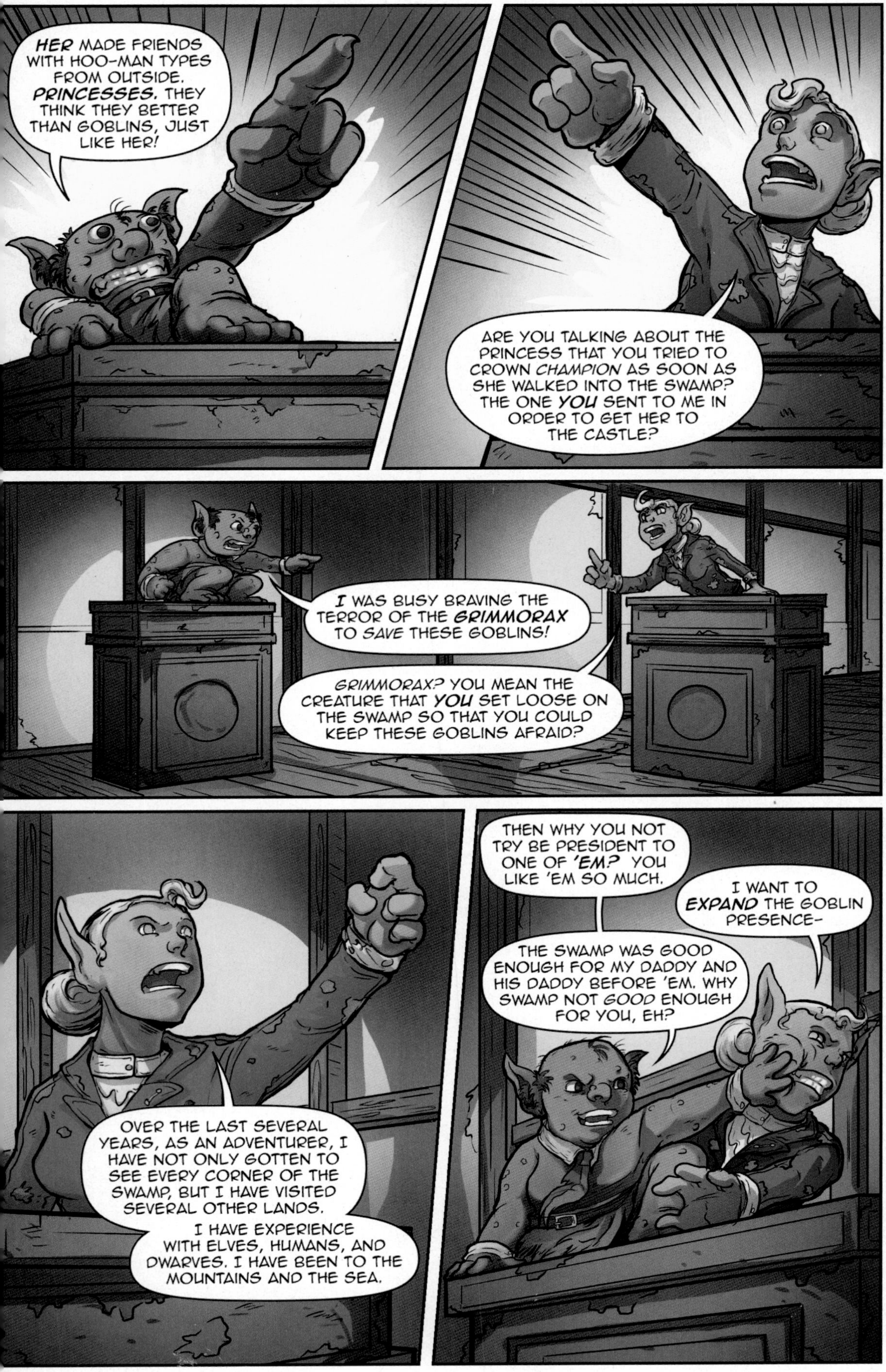
HER MADE FRIENDS WITH HOO-MAN TYPES FROM OUTSIDE. PRINCESSES. THEY THINK THEY BETTER THAN GOBLINS, JUST LIKE HER!
ARE YOU TALKING ABOUT THE PRINCESS THAT YOU TRIED TO CROWN CHAMPION AS SOON AS SHE WALKED INTO THE SWAMP? THE ONE YOU SENT TO ME IN ORDER TO GET HER TO THE CASTLE?
I WAS BUSY BRAVING THE TERROR OF THE GRIMMORAX TO SAVE THESE GOBLINS!
GRIMMORAX? YOU MEAN THE CREATURE THAT YOU SET LOOSE ON THE SWAMP SO THAT YOU COULD KEEP THESE GOBLINS AFRAID?
OVER THE LAST SEVERAL YEARS, AS AN ADVENTURER, I HAVE NOT ONLY GOTTEN TO SEE EVERY CORNER OF THE SWAMP, BUT I HAVE VISITED SEVERAL OTHER LANDS.
I HAVE EXPERIENCE WITH ELVES, HUMANS, AND DWARVES. I HAVE BEEN TO THE MOUNTAINS AND THE SEA.
THEN WHY YOU NOT TRY BE PRESIDENT TO ONE OF 'EM? YOU LIKE 'EM SO MUCH.
I WANT TO EXPAND THE GOBLIN PRESENCE-
THE SWAMP WAS GOOD ENOUGH FOR MY DADDY AND HIS DADDY BEFORE 'EM. WHY SWAMP NOT GOOD ENOUGH FOR YOU, EH?

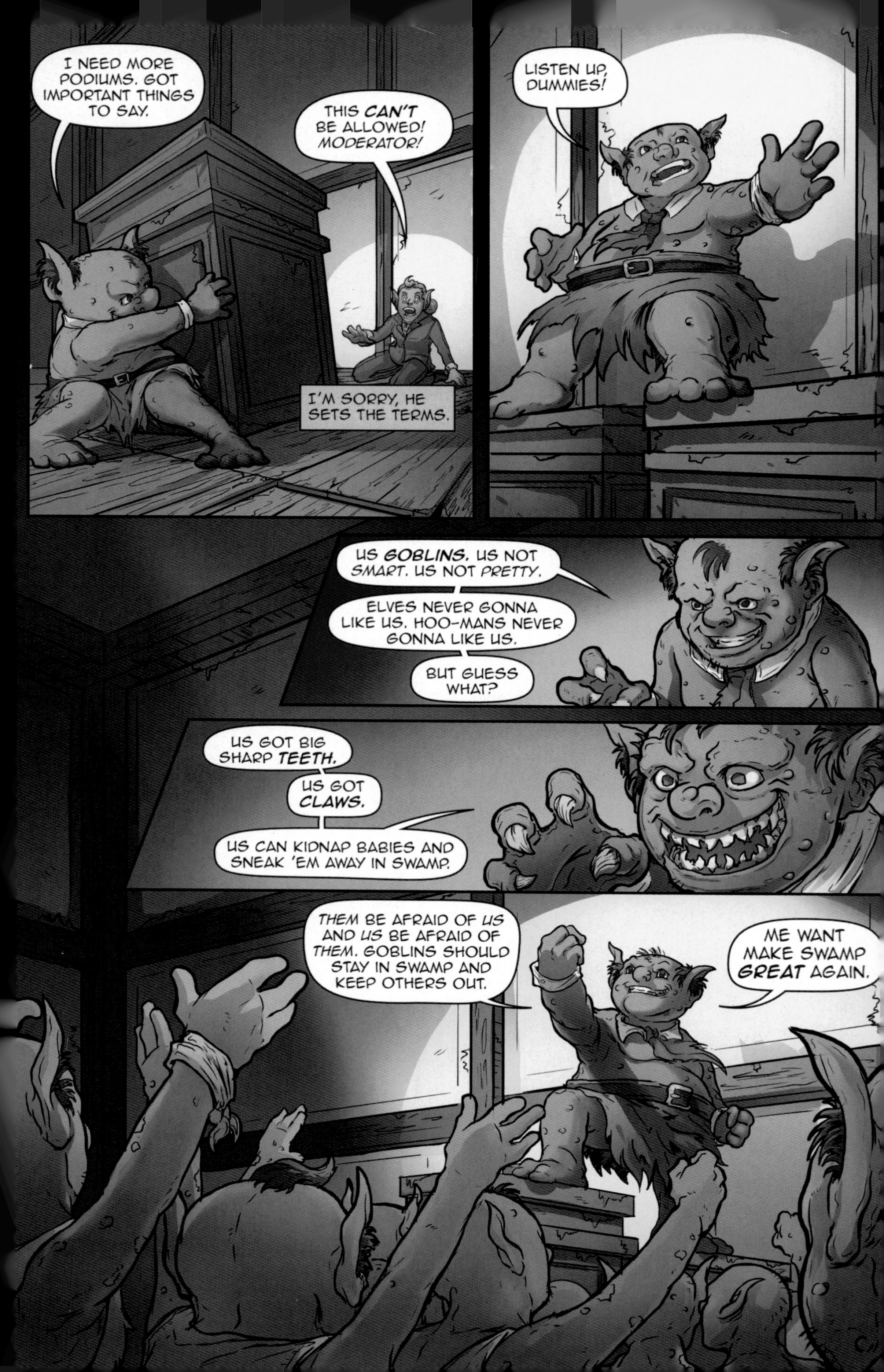
I NEED MORE PODIUMS. GOT IMPORTANT THINGS TO SAY.
THIS *CAN'T* BE ALLOWED! *MODERATOR!*
I'M SORRY, HE SETS THE TERMS.
LISTEN UP, DUMMIES!
US *GOBLINS.* US NOT *SMART*. US NOT *PRETTY*.
ELVES NEVER GONNA LIKE US. HOO-MANS NEVER GONNA LIKE US.
BUT GUESS WHAT?
US GOT BIG SHARP *TEETH.*
US GOT *CLAWS.*
US CAN KIDNAP BABIES AND SNEAK 'EM AWAY IN SWAMP.
*THEM* BE AFRAID OF *US* AND *US* BE AFRAID OF *THEM*. GOBLINS SHOULD STAY IN SWAMP AND KEEP OTHERS OUT.
ME WANT MAKE SWAMP *GREAT* AGAIN.

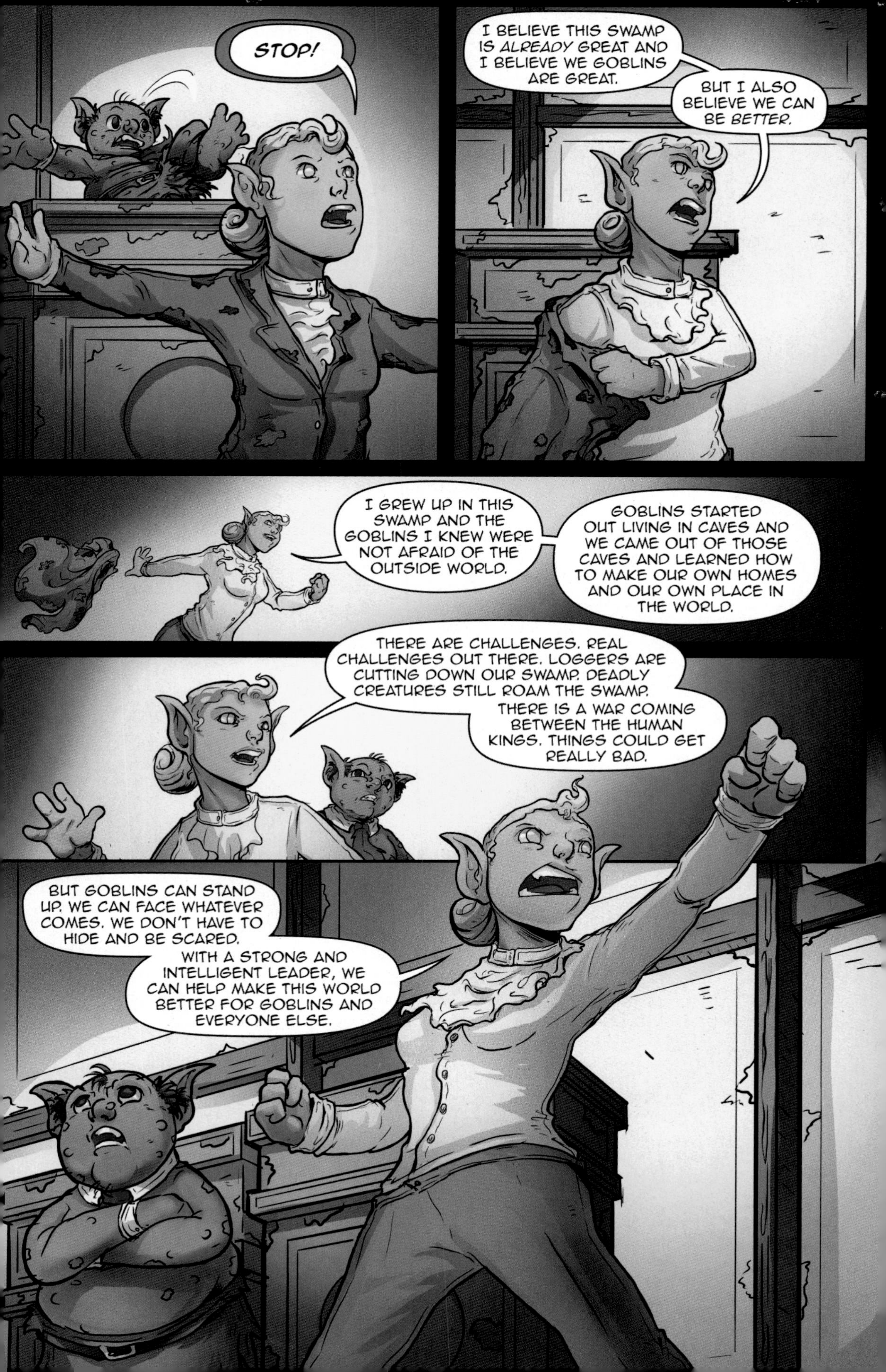
STOP!
I BELIEVE THIS SWAMP IS *ALREADY* GREAT AND I BELIEVE WE GOBLINS ARE GREAT.
BUT I ALSO BELIEVE WE CAN BE *BETTER*.
I GREW UP IN THIS SWAMP AND THE GOBLINS I KNEW WERE NOT AFRAID OF THE OUTSIDE WORLD.
GOBLINS STARTED OUT LIVING IN CAVES AND WE CAME OUT OF THOSE CAVES AND LEARNED HOW TO MAKE OUR OWN HOMES AND OUR OWN PLACE IN THE WORLD.
THERE ARE CHALLENGES. REAL CHALLENGES OUT THERE. LOGGERS ARE CUTTING DOWN OUR SWAMP. DEADLY CREATURES STILL ROAM THE SWAMP.
THERE IS A WAR COMING BETWEEN THE HUMAN KINGS. THINGS COULD GET REALLY BAD.
BUT GOBLINS CAN STAND UP. WE CAN FACE WHATEVER COMES. WE DON'T HAVE TO HIDE AND BE SCARED.
WITH A STRONG AND INTELLIGENT LEADER, WE CAN HELP MAKE THIS WORLD BETTER FOR GOBLINS AND EVERYONE ELSE.

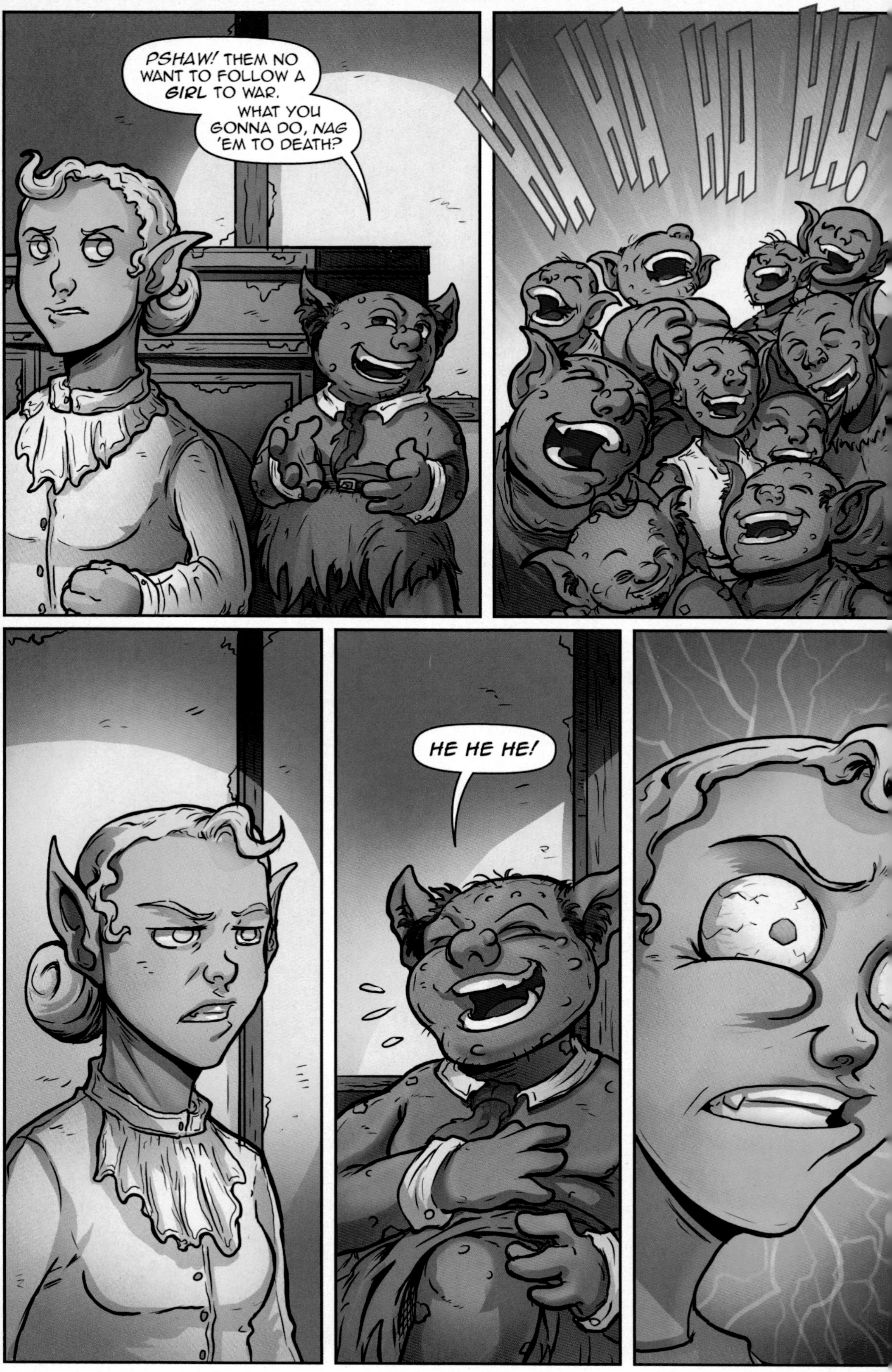
PSHAW! THEM NO WANT TO FOLLOW A GIRL TO WAR.
WHAT YOU GONNA DO, NAG 'EM TO DEATH?
HA HA HA HA!
HE HE HE!

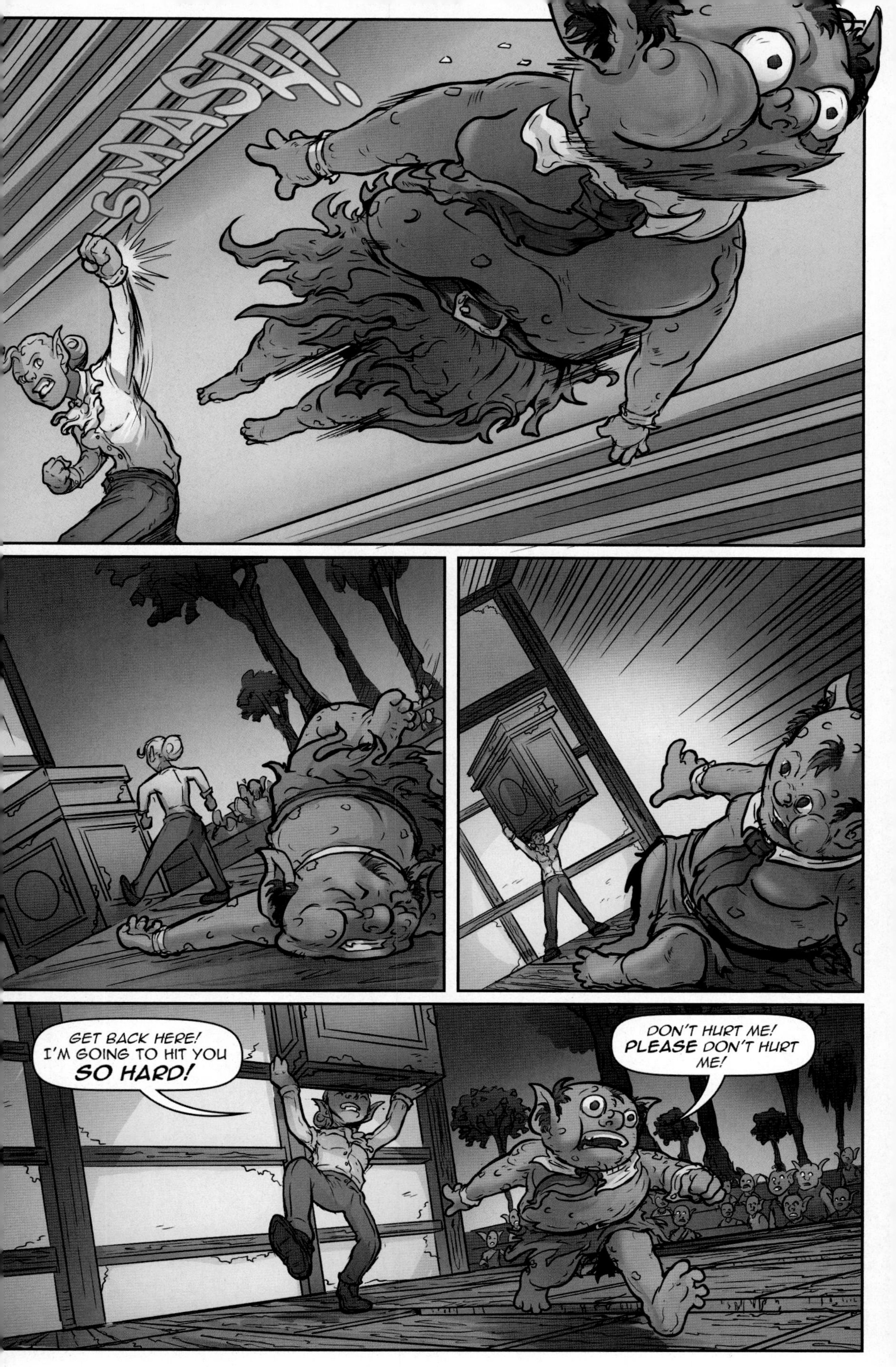
SMASH!
GET BACK HERE! I'M GOING TO HIT YOU SO HARD!
DON'T HURT ME! PLEASE DON'T HURT ME!

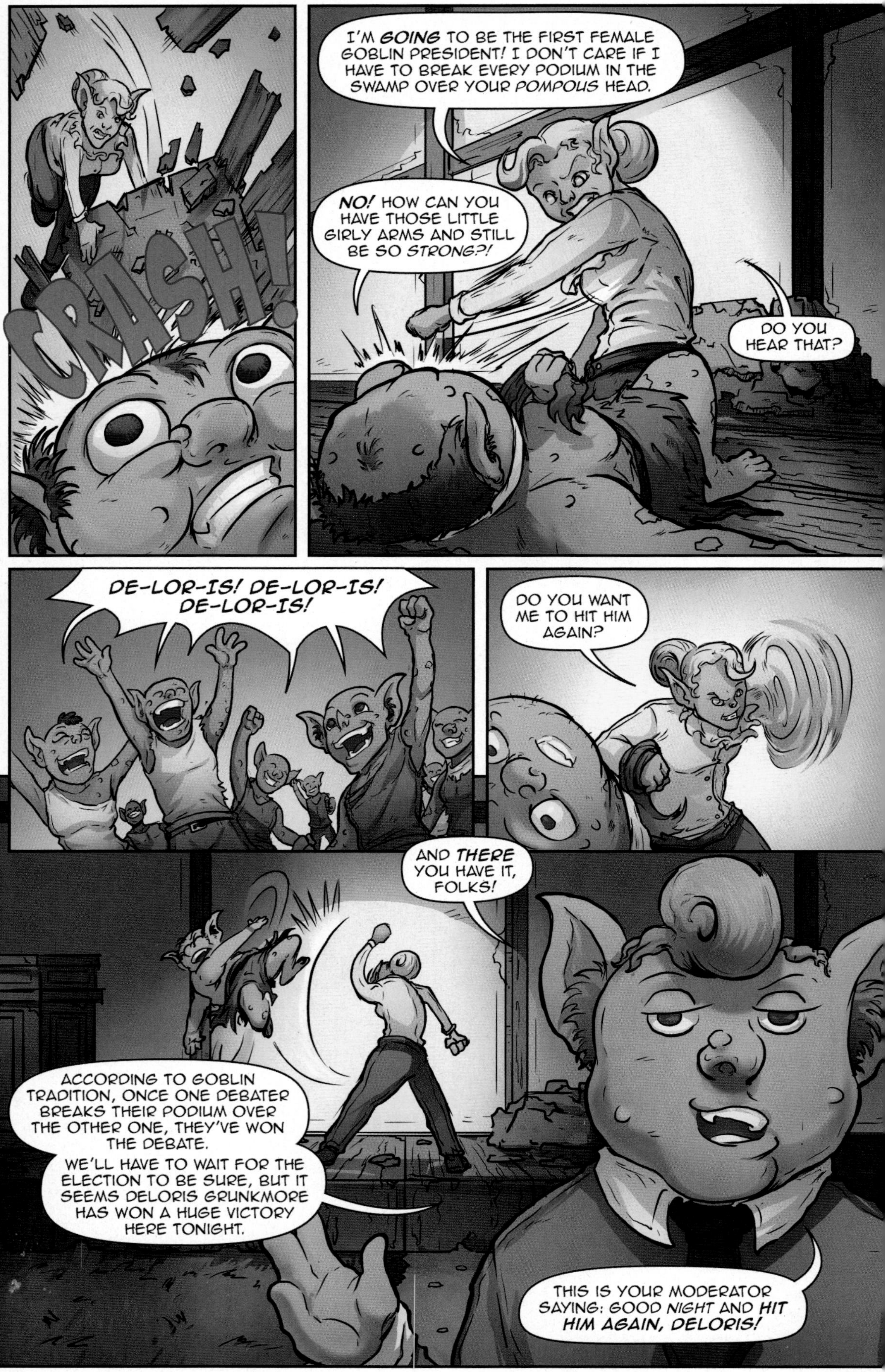
CRASH!
I'M GOING TO BE THE FIRST FEMALE GOBLIN PRESIDENT! I DON'T CARE IF I HAVE TO BREAK EVERY PODIUM IN THE SWAMP OVER YOUR POMPOUS HEAD.
NO! HOW CAN YOU HAVE THOSE LITTLE GIRLY ARMS AND STILL BE SO STRONG?!
DO YOU HEAR THAT?
DE-LOR-IS! DE-LOR-IS! DE-LOR-IS!
DO YOU WANT ME TO HIT HIM AGAIN?
AND THERE YOU HAVE IT, FOLKS!
ACCORDING TO GOBLIN TRADITION, ONCE ONE DEBATER BREAKS THEIR PODIUM OVER THE OTHER ONE, THEY'VE WON THE DEBATE.
WE'LL HAVE TO WAIT FOR THE ELECTION TO BE SURE, BUT IT SEEMS DELORIS GRUNKMORE HAS WON A HUGE VICTORY HERE TONIGHT.
THIS IS YOUR MODERATOR SAYING: GOOD NIGHT AND HIT HIM AGAIN, DELORIS!

# Chapter Four: Antonia & Andrea

**STORY:** Jeremy Whitley
**ART:** Robin Kaplan
**LETTERS:** Brett Grunig

**COVER:** Robin Kaplan

**EDITORS:**
Alicia Whitley (script)
Nicole D'Andria (comic)

ANDREA, TIME TO WAKE UP.

I DON'T *WANNA* GET UP, ANTONIA. IT'S COMFORTABLE HERE.

ANDREA ASHE. ONE OF THE TWIN ASHE PRINCESSES. THROWS FIREBALLS AND OTHER MAGIC.

COME ON NOW, DARLING SISTER. REMEMBER THAT WE HAVE A GREATER CALLING NOW. WE HAVE TO FIND PEOPLE TO HELP WITH OUR MAGIC.

ANTONIA ASHE. ANDREA'S TWIN SISTER. THROWS ICE BOLTS AND OTHER MAGIC.

LATER. I'LL HELP PEOPLE IN THE AFTERNOON.

NOPE, WE NEED TO GET UP AND HELP NOW.

JUST FIVE MORE MINUTES.

Bryan Seaton: Publisher/ CEO • Shawn Gabborin: Editor in Chief • Jason Martin: Publisher-Danger Zone • Nicole D'Andria: Marketing Director/Editor
Jessica Lowrie: Social Media Czar • Danielle Davison: Executive Administrator • Chad Cicconi: Still Waiting For His Princess • Shawn Pryor: President of Creator Relations

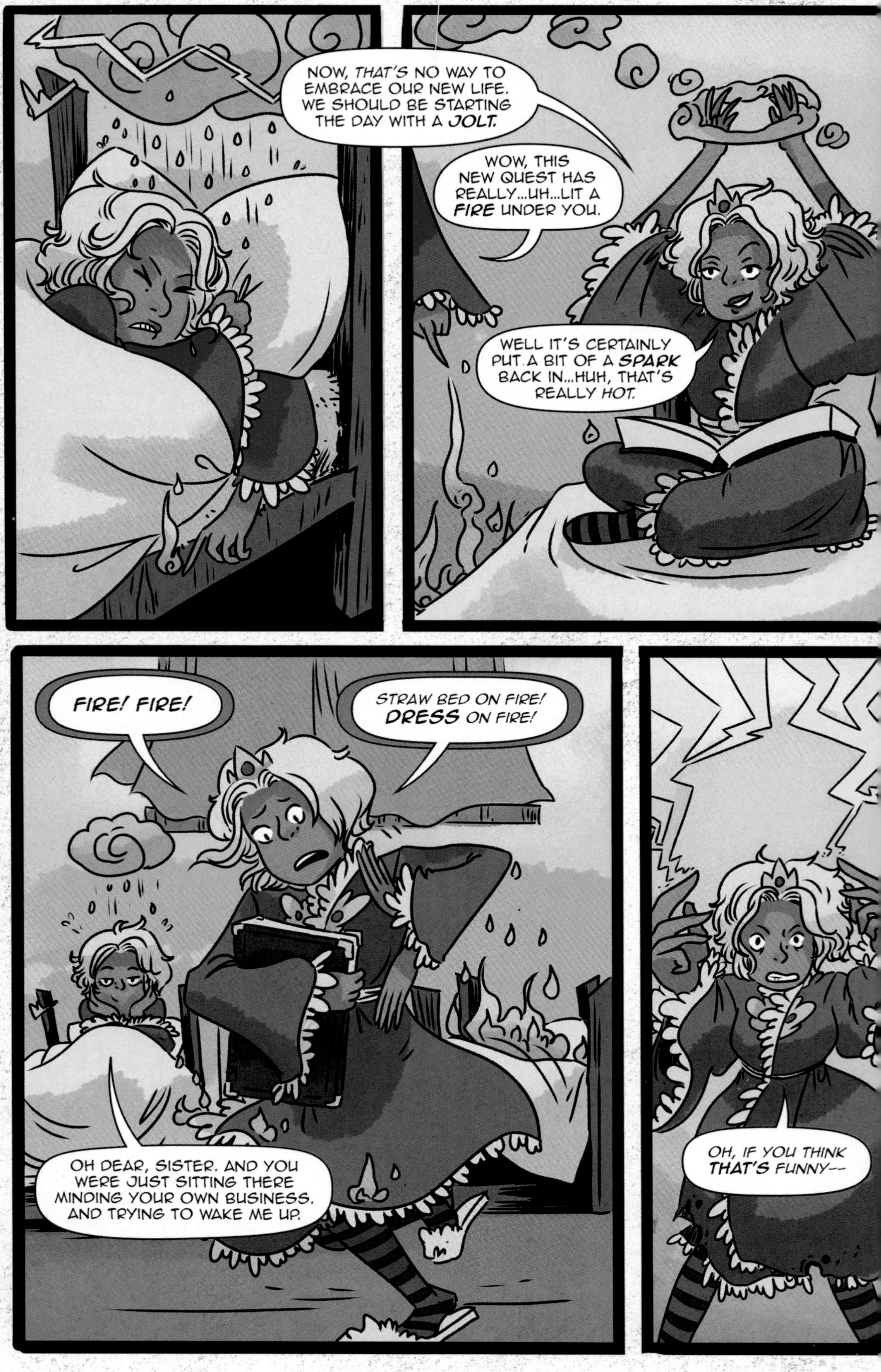
NOW, *THAT'S* NO WAY TO EMBRACE OUR NEW LIFE. WE SHOULD BE STARTING THE DAY WITH A *JOLT.*
WOW, THIS NEW QUEST HAS REALLY...UH...LIT A *FIRE* UNDER YOU.
WELL IT'S CERTAINLY PUT A BIT OF A *SPARK* BACK IN...HUH, THAT'S REALLY *HOT.*
*FIRE! FIRE!*
*STRAW BED ON FIRE!* ***DRESS*** *ON FIRE!*
OH DEAR, SISTER. AND YOU WERE JUST SITTING THERE MINDING YOUR OWN BUSINESS. AND TRYING TO WAKE ME UP.
*OH, IF YOU THINK* ***THAT'S*** *FUNNY--*

--THIS'LL *REALLY* SHOCK YOU!

ZOT!

YOUCH!

HOW DO *YOU* LIKE IT?!

DON'T PRETEND LIKE YOU DIDN'T START THIS, YOU SLY *CAT!*

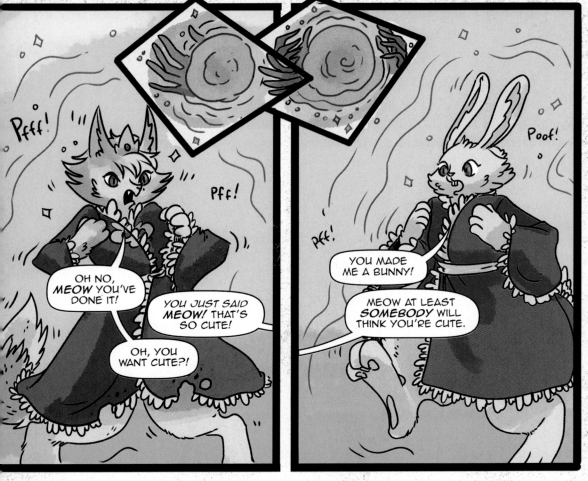

Pfff!

Pff!

Pff!

Poof!

OH NO, *MEOW* YOU'VE DONE IT!

YOU JUST SAID *MEOW!* THAT'S SO CUTE!

OH, YOU WANT CUTE?!

YOU MADE ME A BUNNY!

*MEOW* AT LEAST *SOMEBODY* WILL THINK YOU'RE CUTE.

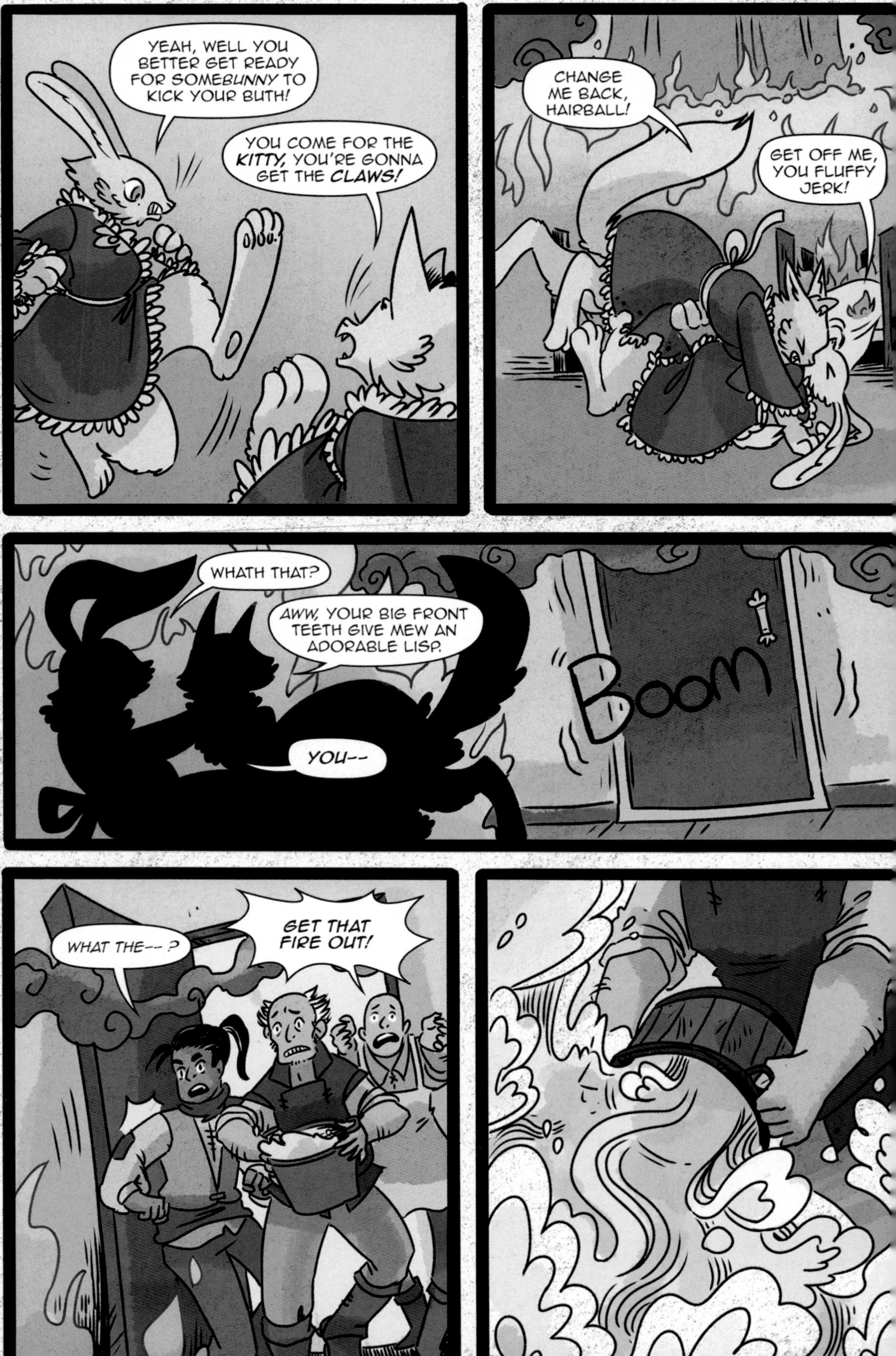
YEAH, WELL YOU BETTER GET READY FOR SOMEBUNNY TO KICK YOUR BUTH!
YOU COME FOR THE KITTY, YOU'RE GONNA GET THE CLAWS!
CHANGE ME BACK, HAIRBALL!
GET OFF ME, YOU FLUFFY JERK!
WHATH THAT?
AWW, YOUR BIG FRONT TEETH GIVE MEW AN ADORABLE LISP.
YOU--
Boom!
WHAT THE-- ?
GET THAT FIRE OUT!

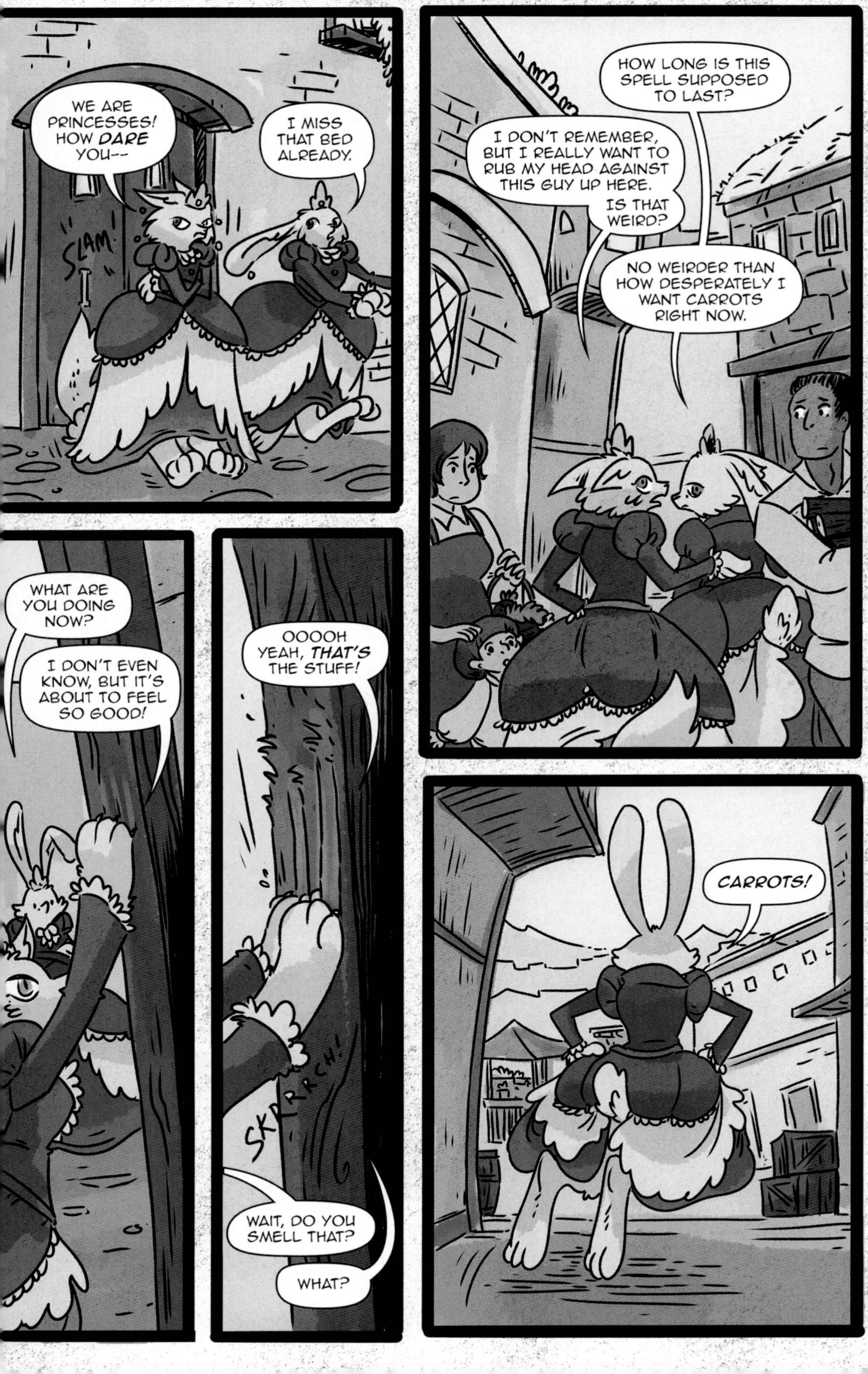
WE ARE PRINCESSES! HOW DARE YOU--
SLAM!
I MISS THAT BED ALREADY.
HOW LONG IS THIS SPELL SUPPOSED TO LAST?
I DON'T REMEMBER, BUT I REALLY WANT TO RUB MY HEAD AGAINST THIS GUY UP HERE.
IS THAT WEIRD?
NO WEIRDER THAN HOW DESPERATELY I WANT CARROTS RIGHT NOW.
WHAT ARE YOU DOING NOW?
I DON'T EVEN KNOW, BUT IT'S ABOUT TO FEEL SO GOOD!
OOOOH YEAH, THAT'S THE STUFF!
SKRRRCH!
WAIT, DO YOU SMELL THAT?
WHAT?
CARROTS!

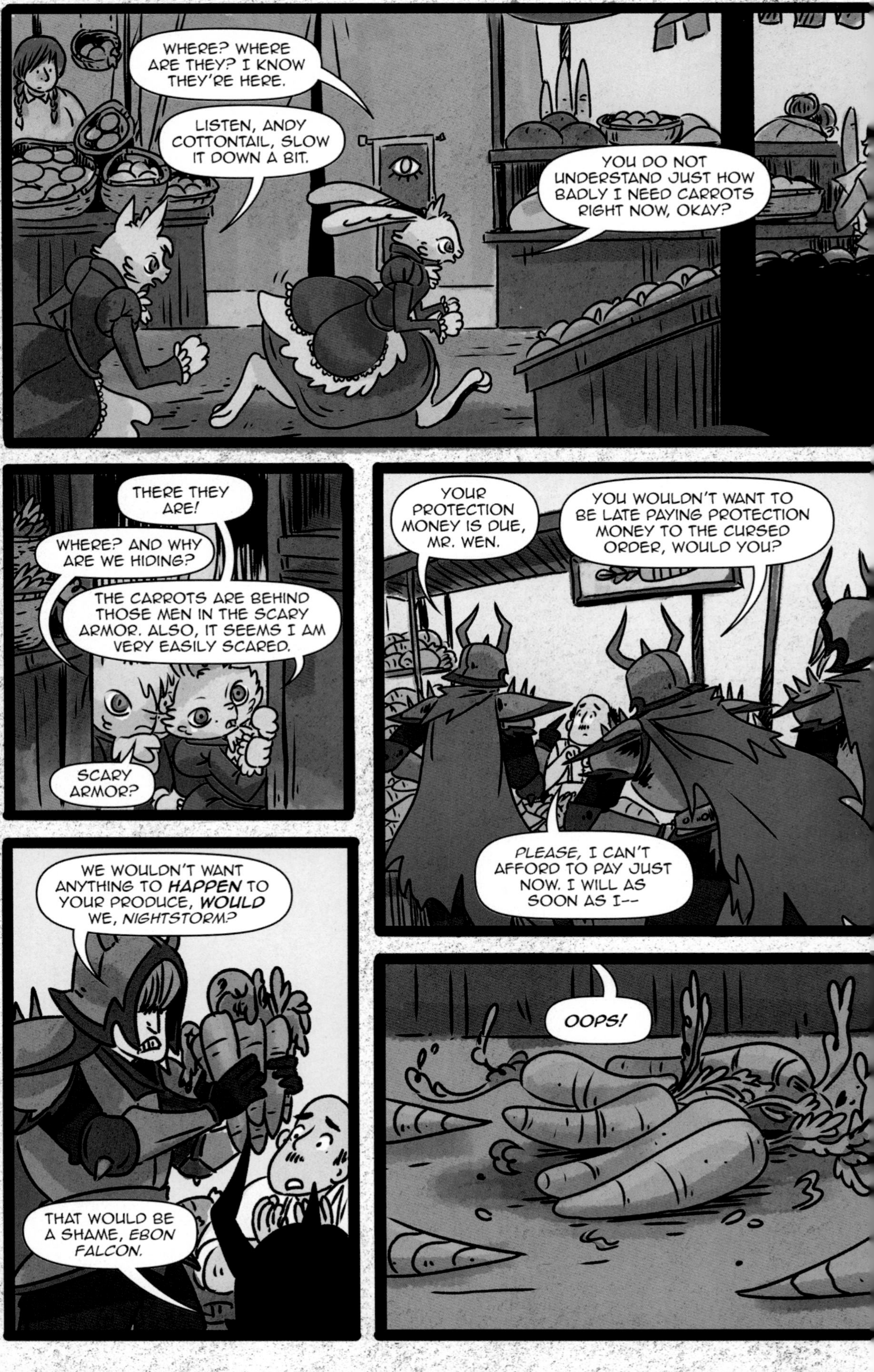
WHERE? WHERE ARE THEY? I KNOW THEY'RE HERE.
LISTEN, ANDY COTTONTAIL, SLOW IT DOWN A BIT.
YOU DO NOT UNDERSTAND JUST HOW BADLY I NEED CARROTS RIGHT NOW, OKAY?
THERE THEY ARE!
WHERE? AND WHY ARE WE HIDING?
THE CARROTS ARE BEHIND THOSE MEN IN THE SCARY ARMOR. ALSO, IT SEEMS I AM VERY EASILY SCARED.
SCARY ARMOR?
YOUR PROTECTION MONEY IS DUE, MR. WEN.
YOU WOULDN'T WANT TO BE LATE PAYING PROTECTION MONEY TO THE CURSED ORDER, WOULD YOU?
*PLEASE*, I CAN'T AFFORD TO PAY JUST NOW. I WILL AS SOON AS I--
WE WOULDN'T WANT ANYTHING TO ***HAPPEN*** TO YOUR PRODUCE, ***WOULD*** WE, *NIGHTSTORM*?
THAT WOULD BE A SHAME, *EBON FALCON*.
*OOPS!*

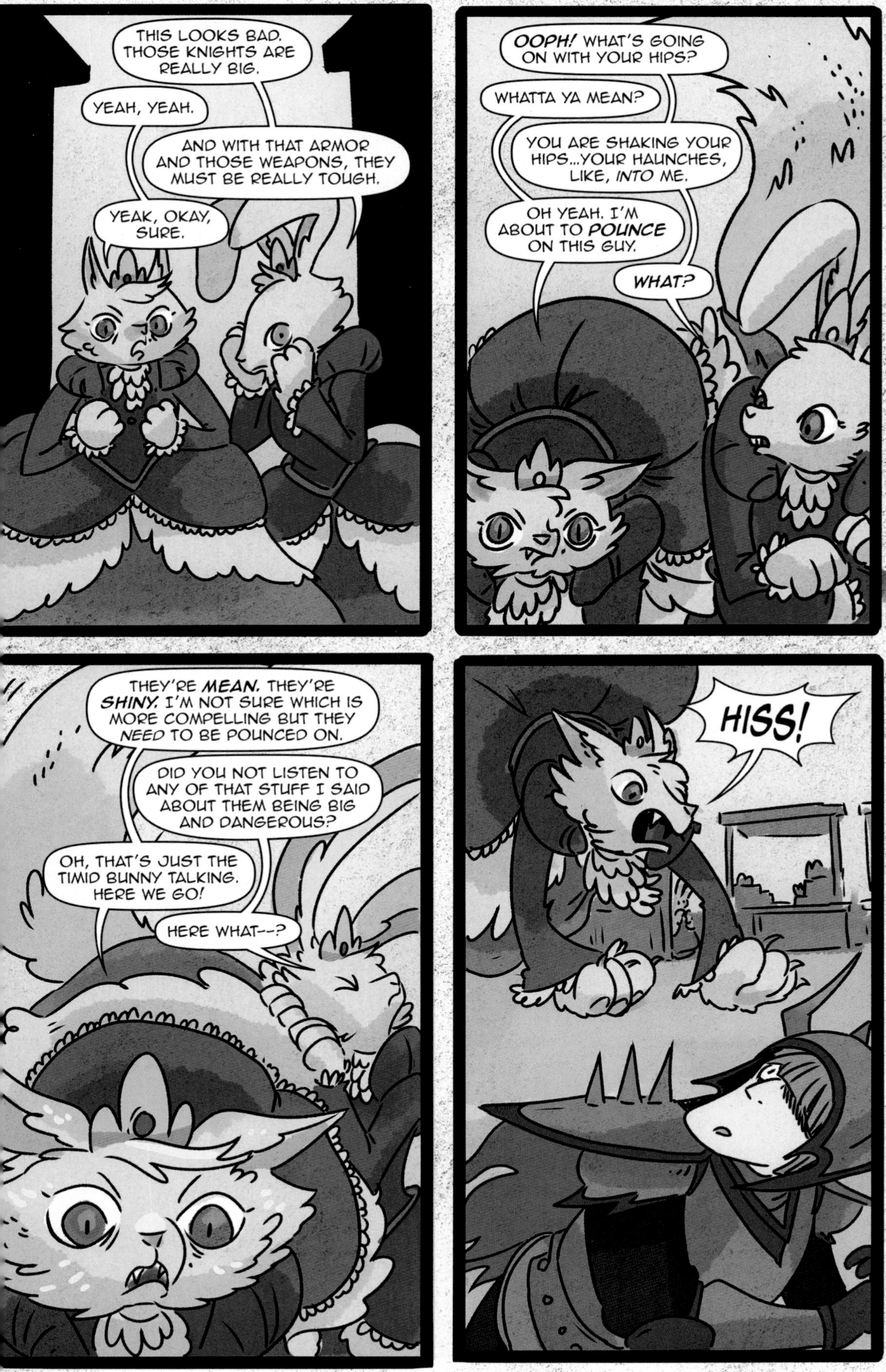

THIS LOOKS BAD. THOSE KNIGHTS ARE REALLY BIG.
YEAH, YEAH.
AND WITH THAT ARMOR AND THOSE WEAPONS, THEY MUST BE REALLY TOUGH.
YEAK, OKAY, SURE.
OOPH! WHAT'S GOING ON WITH YOUR HIPS?
WHATTA YA MEAN?
YOU ARE SHAKING YOUR HIPS...YOUR HAUNCHES, LIKE, INTO ME.
OH YEAH. I'M ABOUT TO POUNCE ON THIS GUY.
WHAT?
THEY'RE MEAN. THEY'RE SHINY. I'M NOT SURE WHICH IS MORE COMPELLING BUT THEY NEED TO BE POUNCED ON.
DID YOU NOT LISTEN TO ANY OF THAT STUFF I SAID ABOUT THEM BEING BIG AND DANGEROUS?
OH, THAT'S JUST THE TIMID BUNNY TALKING. HERE WE GO!
HERE WHAT--?
HISS!

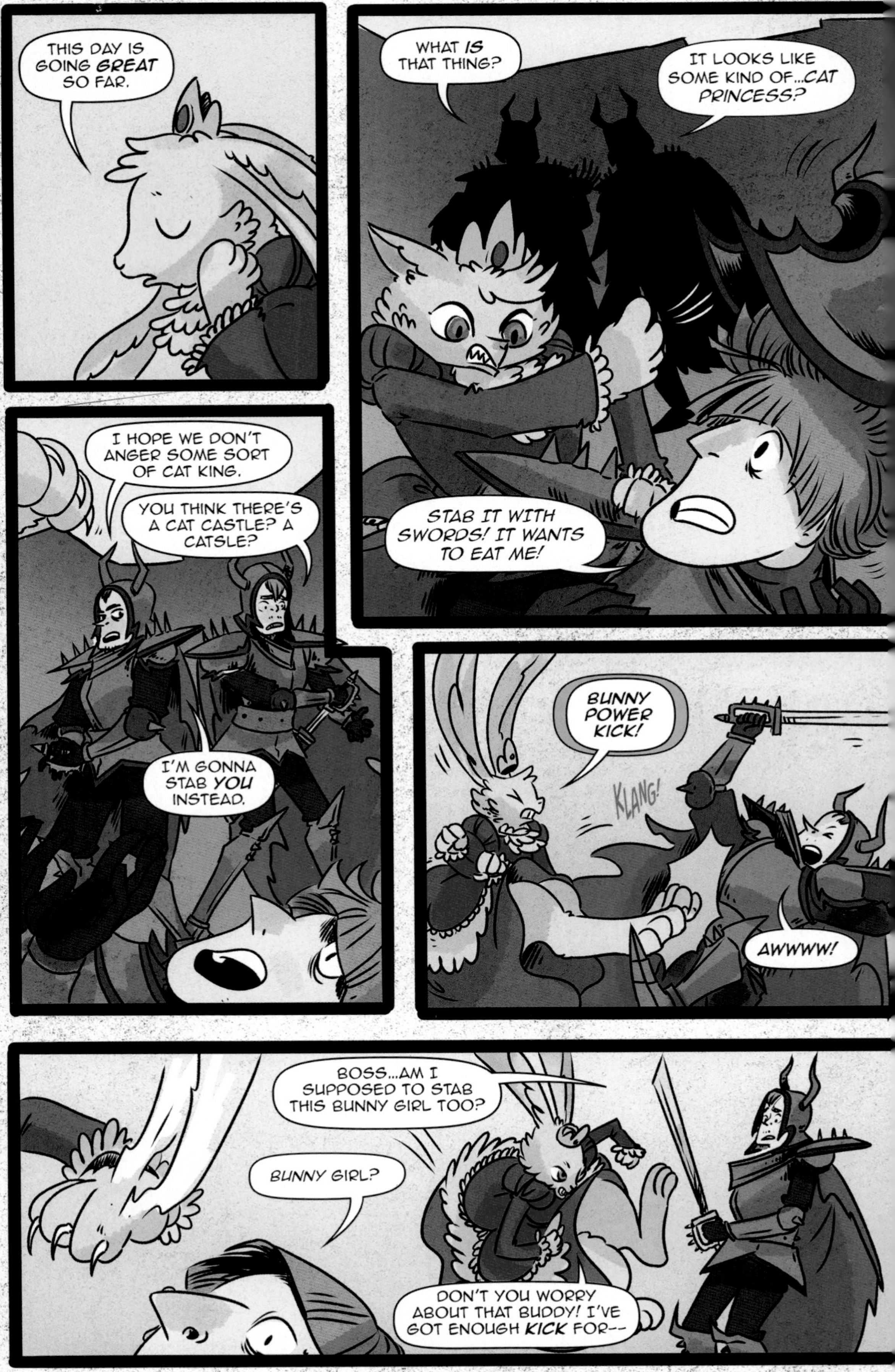
THIS DAY IS GOING GREAT SO FAR.
WHAT IS THAT THING?
IT LOOKS LIKE SOME KIND OF...CAT PRINCESS?
STAB IT WITH SWORDS! IT WANTS TO EAT ME!
I HOPE WE DON'T ANGER SOME SORT OF CAT KING.
YOU THINK THERE'S A CAT CASTLE? A CATSLE?
I'M GONNA STAB YOU INSTEAD.
BUNNY POWER KICK!
KLANG!
AWWWW!
BOSS...AM I SUPPOSED TO STAB THIS BUNNY GIRL TOO?
BUNNY GIRL?
DON'T YOU WORRY ABOUT THAT BUDDY! I'VE GOT ENOUGH KICK FOR--

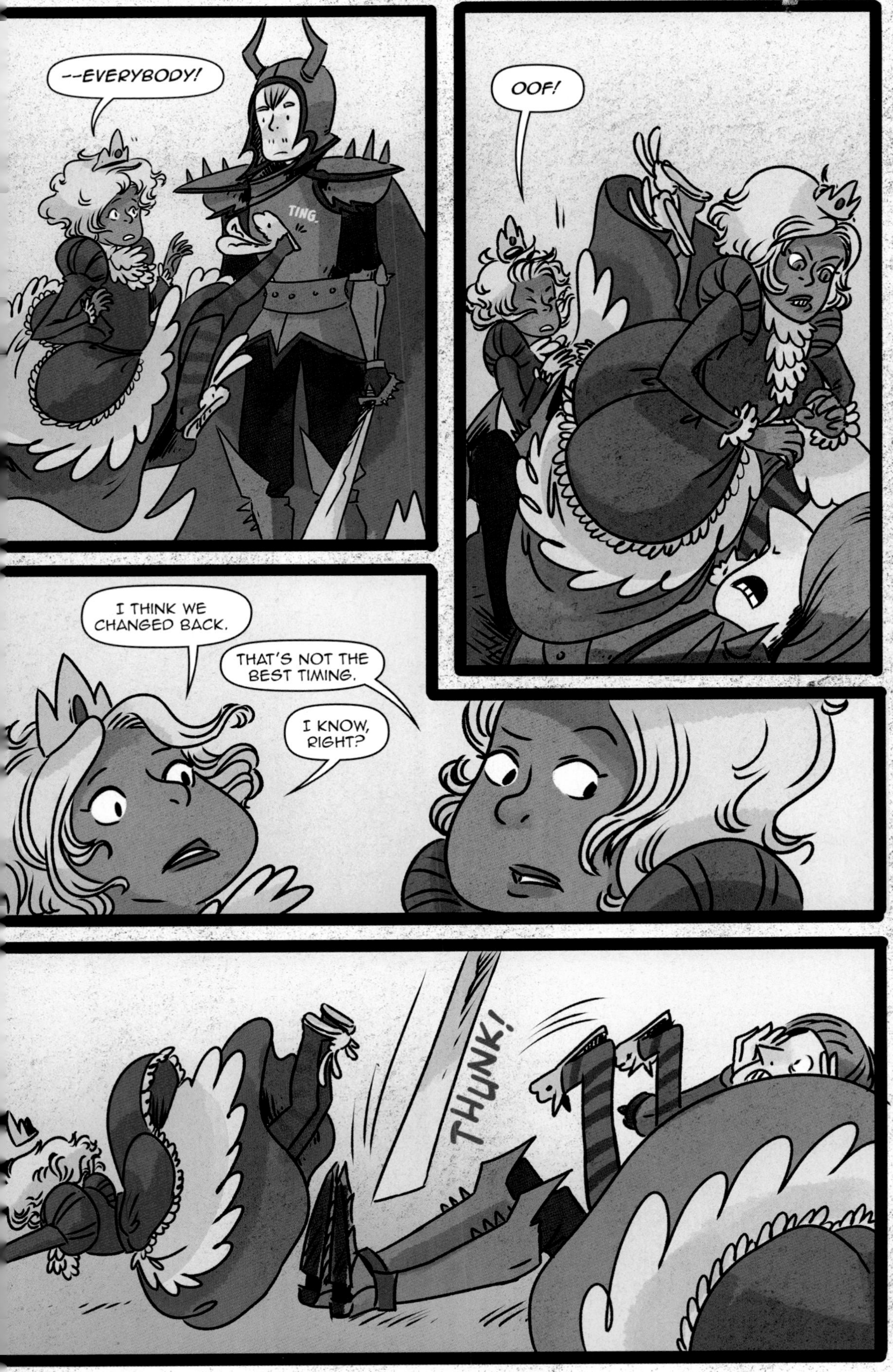
--EVERYBODY!
TING.
OOF!
I THINK WE CHANGED BACK.
THAT'S NOT THE BEST TIMING.
I KNOW, RIGHT?
THUNK!

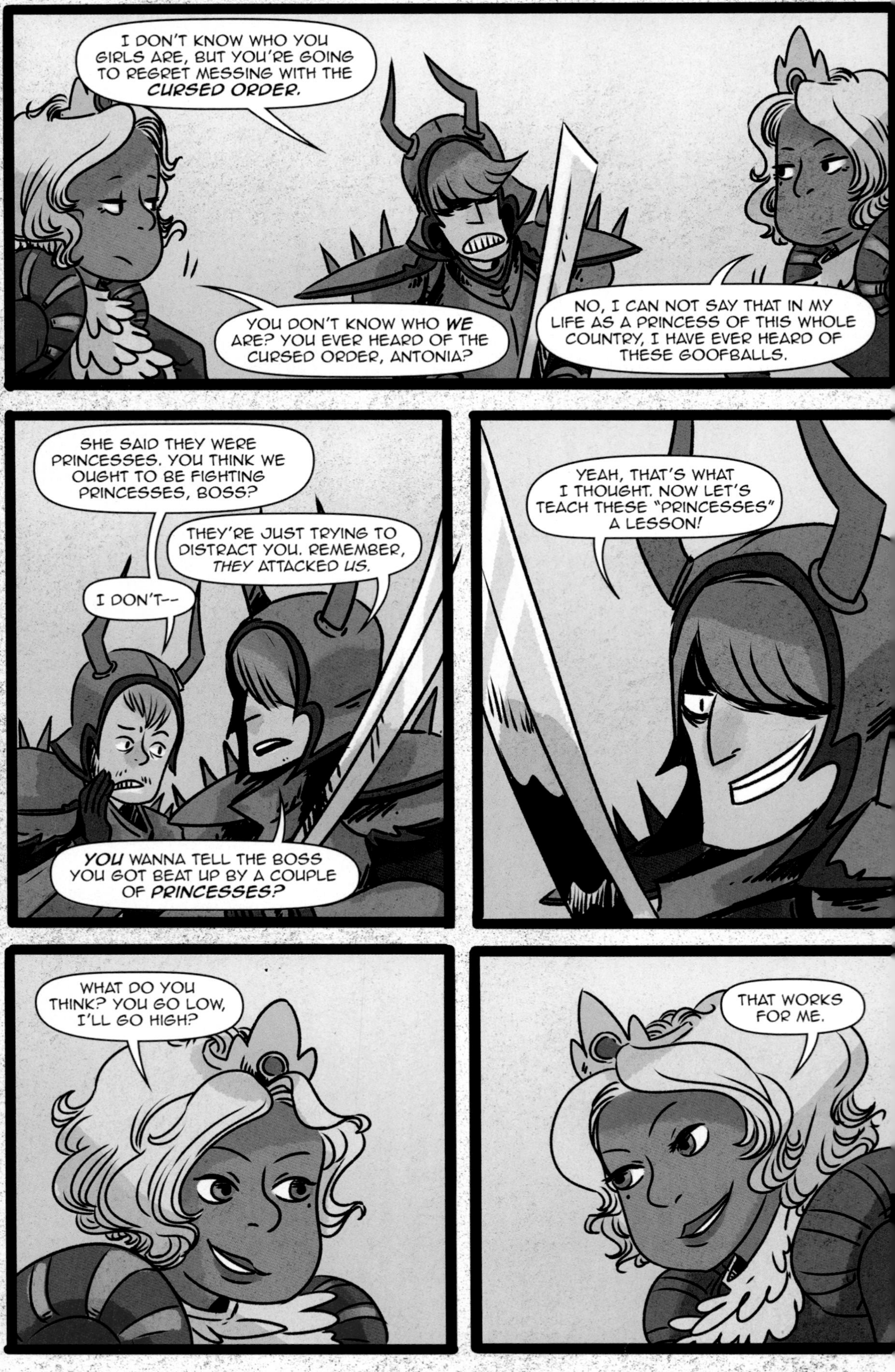
I DON'T KNOW WHO YOU GIRLS ARE, BUT YOU'RE GOING TO REGRET MESSING WITH THE *CURSED ORDER.*
YOU DON'T KNOW WHO *WE* ARE? YOU EVER HEARD OF THE CURSED ORDER, ANTONIA?
NO, I CAN NOT SAY THAT IN MY LIFE AS A PRINCESS OF THIS WHOLE COUNTRY, I HAVE EVER HEARD OF THESE GOOFBALLS.
SHE SAID THEY WERE PRINCESSES. YOU THINK WE OUGHT TO BE FIGHTING PRINCESSES, BOSS?
THEY'RE JUST TRYING TO DISTRACT YOU. REMEMBER, *THEY* ATTACKED *US.*
I DON'T--
*YOU* WANNA TELL THE BOSS YOU GOT BEAT UP BY A COUPLE OF *PRINCESSES?*
YEAH, THAT'S WHAT I THOUGHT. NOW LET'S TEACH THESE "PRINCESSES" A LESSON!
WHAT DO YOU THINK? YOU GO LOW, I'LL GO HIGH?
THAT WORKS FOR ME.

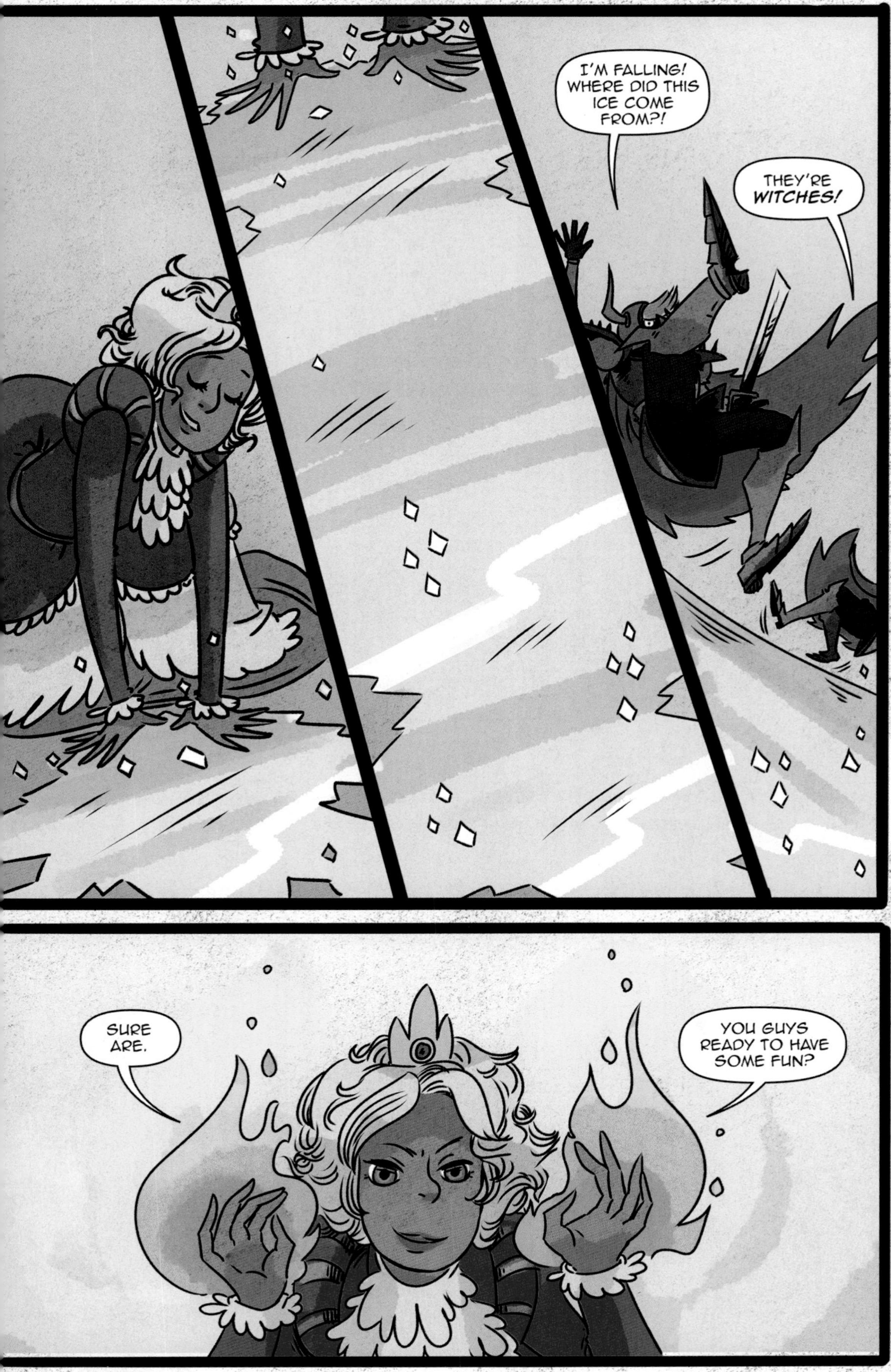
I'M FALLING! WHERE DID THIS ICE COME FROM?!
THEY'RE *WITCHES!*
SURE ARE.
YOU GUYS READY TO HAVE SOME FUN?

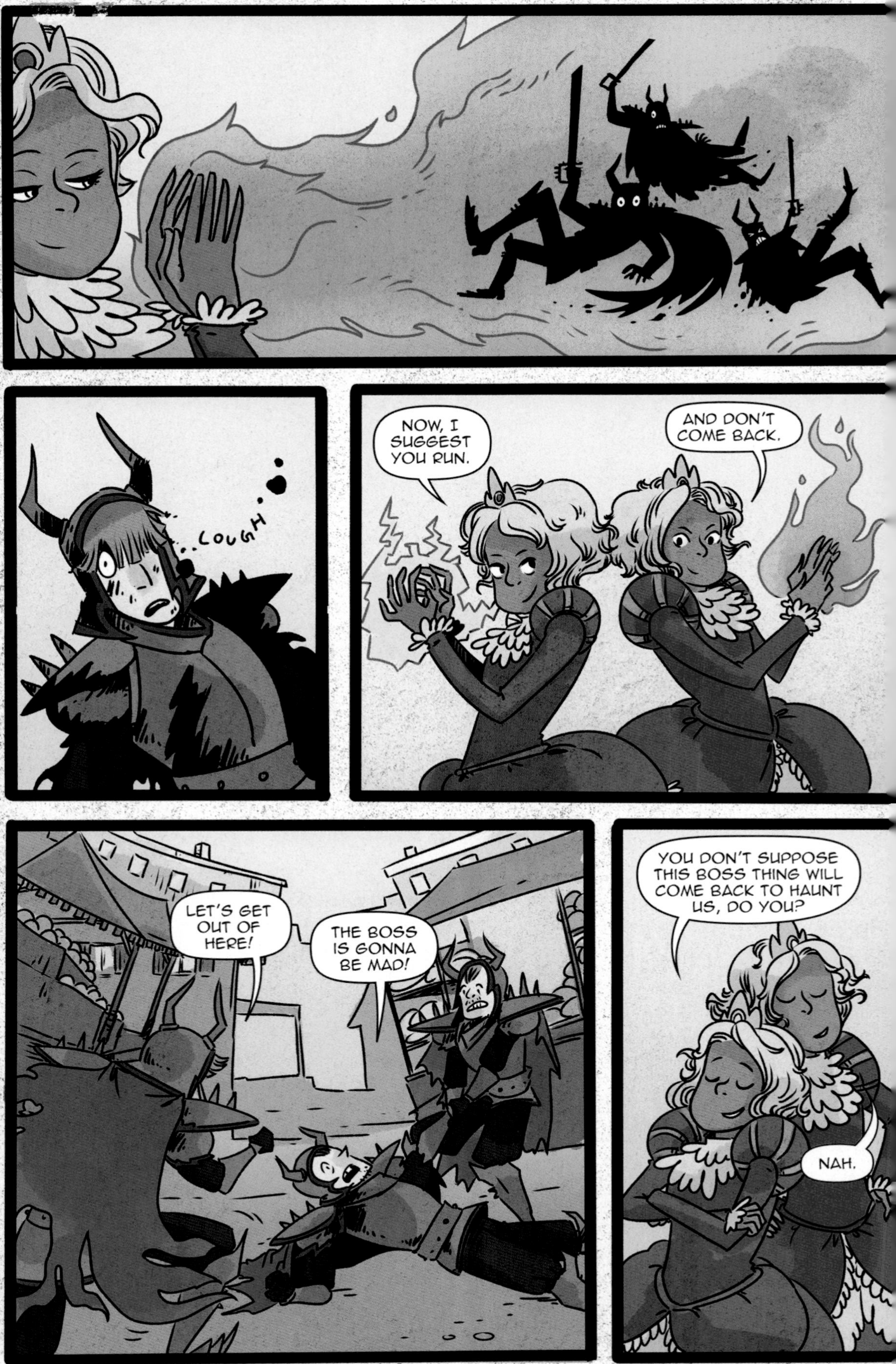
...COUGH
NOW, I SUGGEST YOU RUN.
AND DON'T COME BACK.
LET'S GET OUT OF HERE!
THE BOSS IS GONNA BE MAD!
YOU DON'T SUPPOSE THIS BOSS THING WILL COME BACK TO HAUNT US, DO YOU?
NAH.

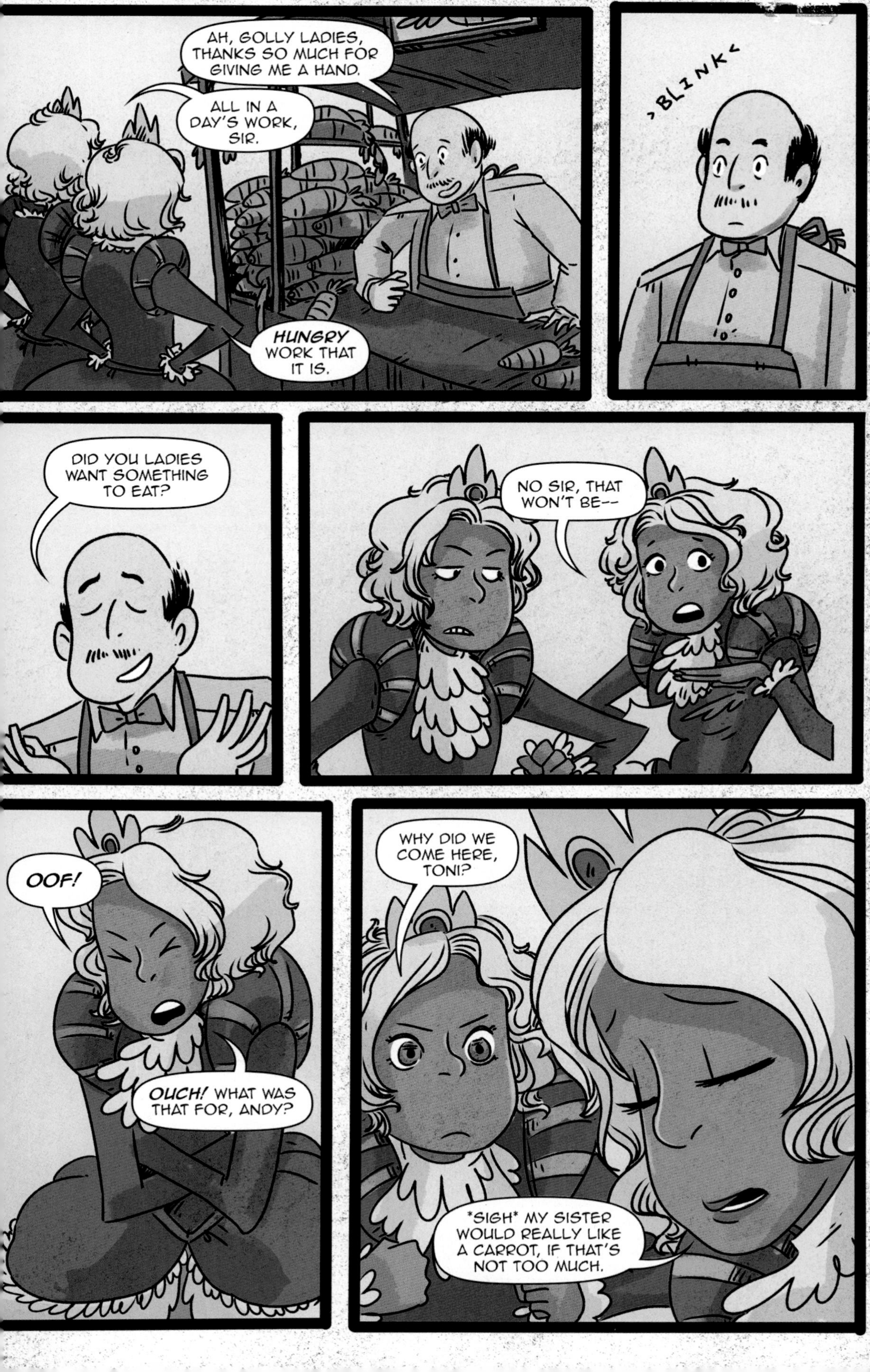
AH, GOLLY LADIES, THANKS SO MUCH FOR GIVING ME A HAND.
ALL IN A DAY'S WORK, SIR.
HUNGRY WORK THAT IT IS.
BLINK
DID YOU LADIES WANT SOMETHING TO EAT?
NO SIR, THAT WON'T BE--
OOF!
OUCH! WHAT WAS THAT FOR, ANDY?
WHY DID WE COME HERE, TONI?
*SIGH* MY SISTER WOULD REALLY LIKE A CARROT, IF THAT'S NOT TOO MUCH.

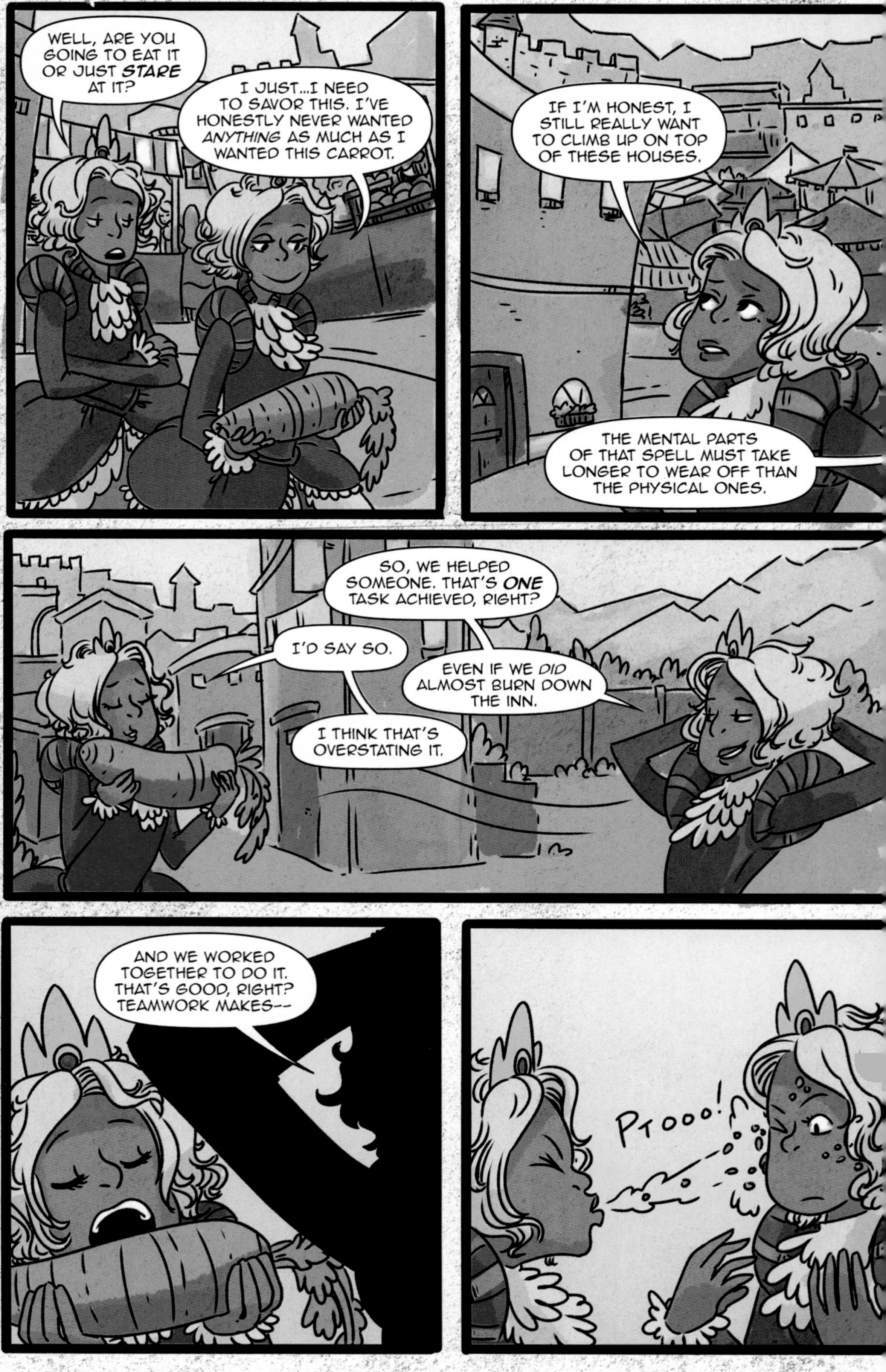
WELL, ARE YOU GOING TO EAT IT OR JUST *STARE* AT IT?
I JUST...I NEED TO SAVOR THIS. I'VE HONESTLY NEVER WANTED *ANYTHING* AS MUCH AS I WANTED THIS CARROT.
IF I'M HONEST, I STILL REALLY WANT TO CLIMB UP ON TOP OF THESE HOUSES.
THE MENTAL PARTS OF THAT SPELL MUST TAKE LONGER TO WEAR OFF THAN THE PHYSICAL ONES.
SO, WE HELPED SOMEONE. THAT'S *ONE* TASK ACHIEVED, RIGHT?
I'D SAY SO.
EVEN IF WE *DID* ALMOST BURN DOWN THE INN.
I THINK THAT'S OVERSTATING IT.
AND WE WORKED TOGETHER TO DO IT. THAT'S GOOD, RIGHT? TEAMWORK MAKES--
PTOOO!

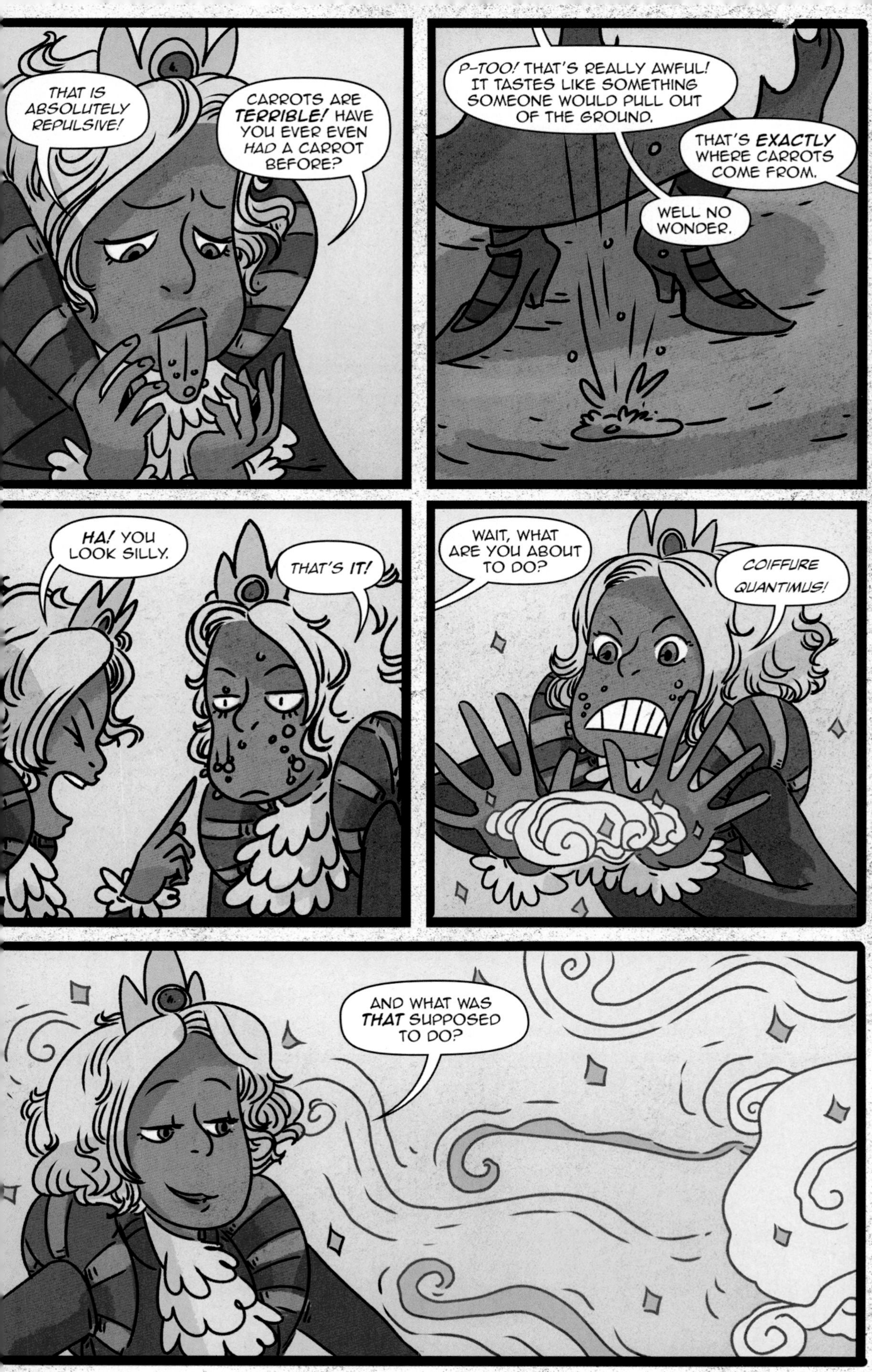
THAT IS ABSOLUTELY REPULSIVE!
CARROTS ARE TERRIBLE! HAVE YOU EVER EVEN HAD A CARROT BEFORE?
P-TOO! THAT'S REALLY AWFUL! IT TASTES LIKE SOMETHING SOMEONE WOULD PULL OUT OF THE GROUND.
THAT'S EXACTLY WHERE CARROTS COME FROM.
WELL NO WONDER.
HA! YOU LOOK SILLY.
THAT'S IT!
WAIT, WHAT ARE YOU ABOUT TO DO?
COIFFURE QUANTIMUS!
AND WHAT WAS THAT SUPPOSED TO DO?

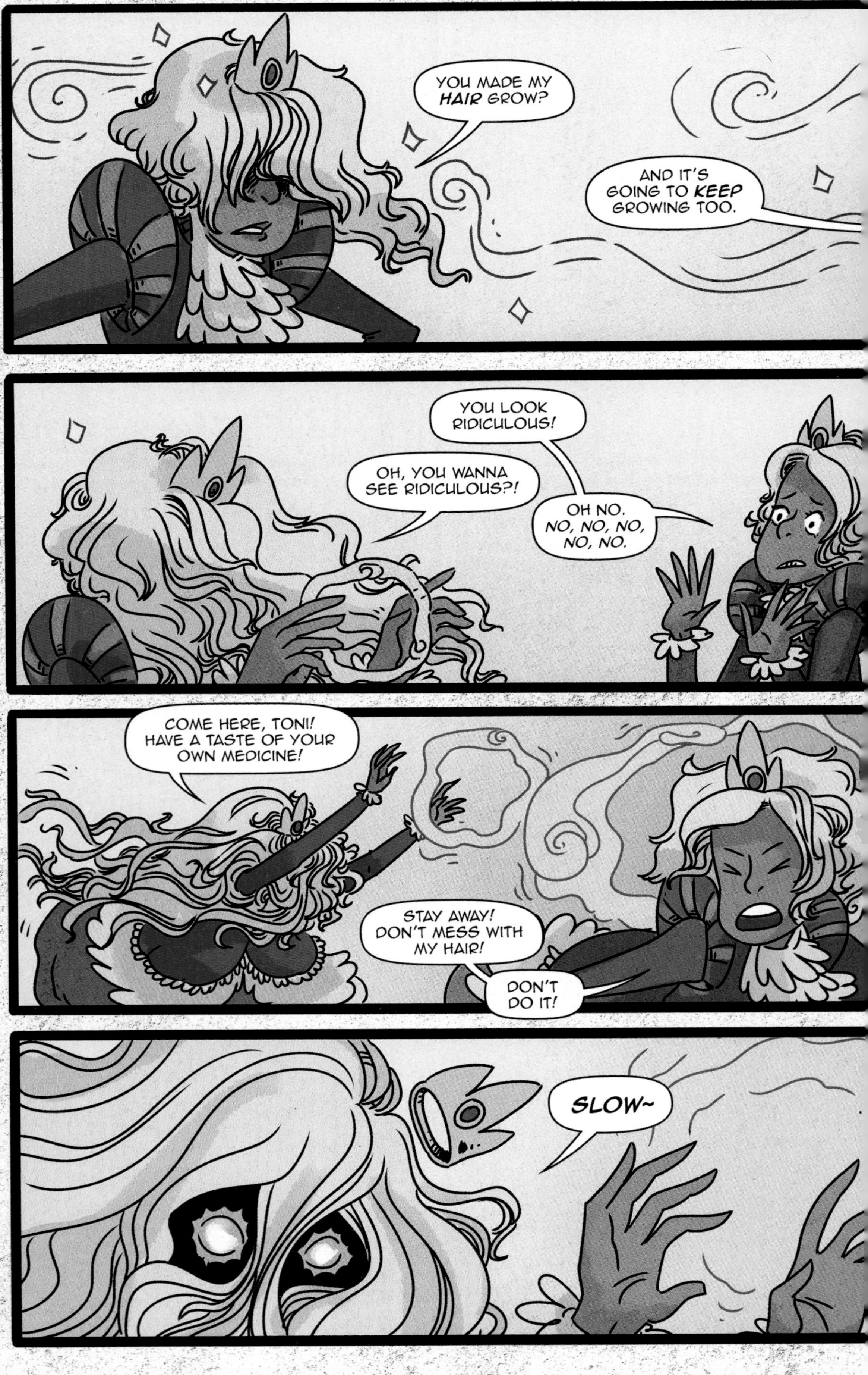
YOU MADE MY HAIR GROW?
AND IT'S GOING TO KEEP GROWING TOO.
YOU LOOK RIDICULOUS!
OH, YOU WANNA SEE RIDICULOUS?!
OH NO. NO, NO, NO, NO, NO.
COME HERE, TONI! HAVE A TASTE OF YOUR OWN MEDICINE!
STAY AWAY! DON'T MESS WITH MY HAIR!
DON'T DO IT!
SLOW~

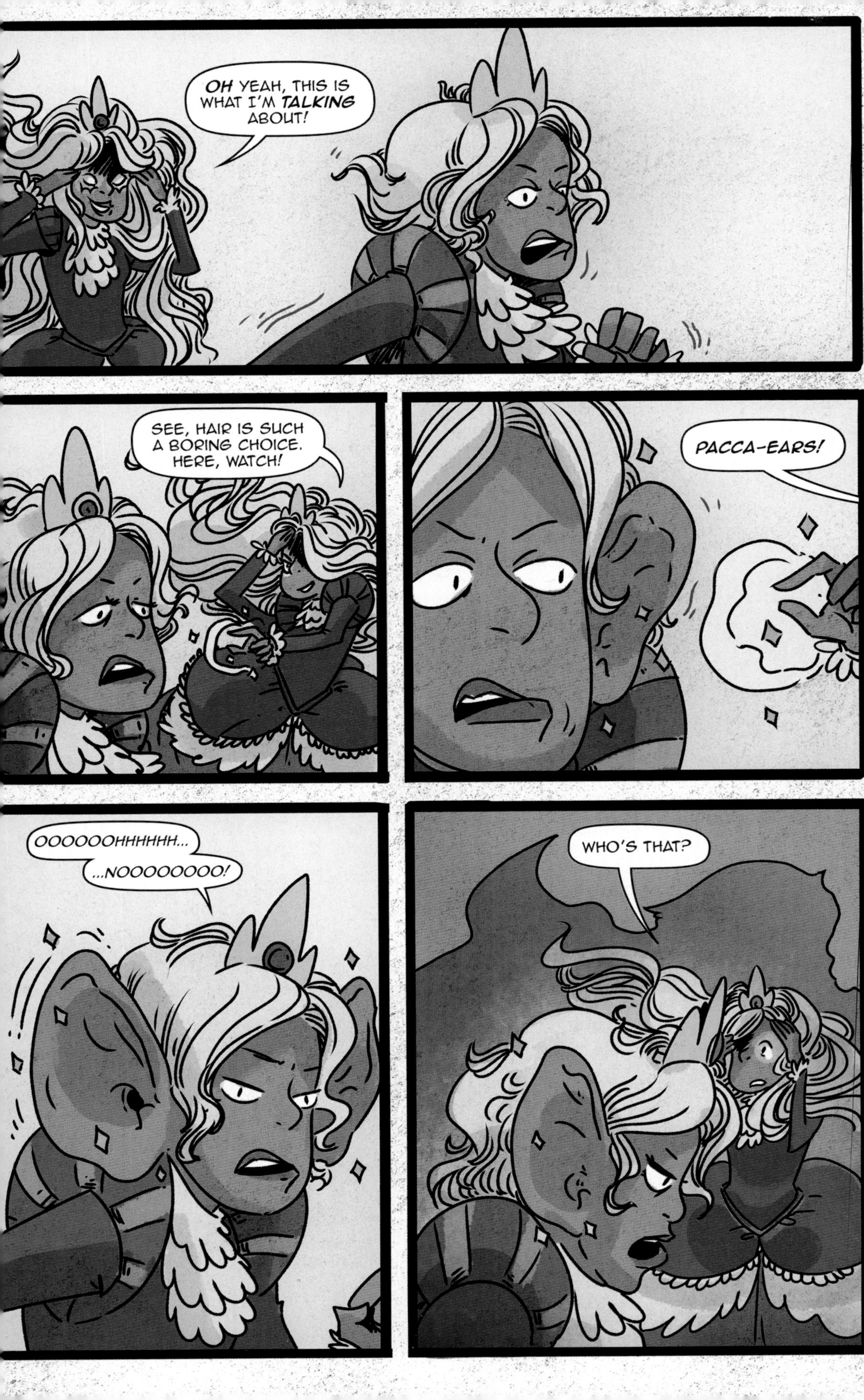
OH YEAH, THIS IS WHAT I'M TALKING ABOUT!
SEE, HAIR IS SUCH A BORING CHOICE. HERE, WATCH!
PACCA-EARS!
OOOOOOHHHHHH...
...NOOOOOOOO!
WHO'S THAT?

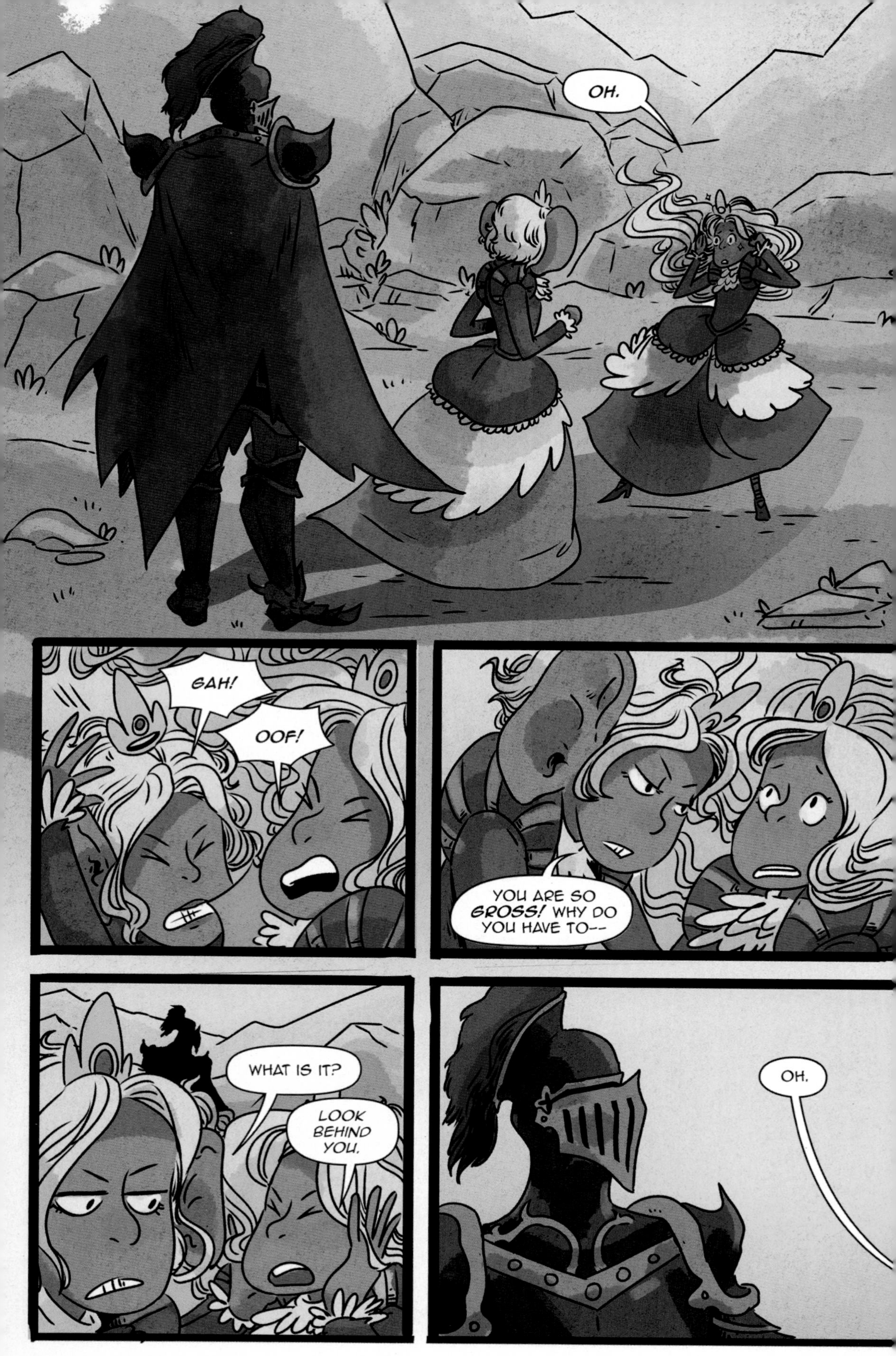
OH.
GAH!
OOF!
YOU ARE SO GROSS! WHY DO YOU HAVE TO--
WHAT IS IT?
LOOK BEHIND YOU.
OH.

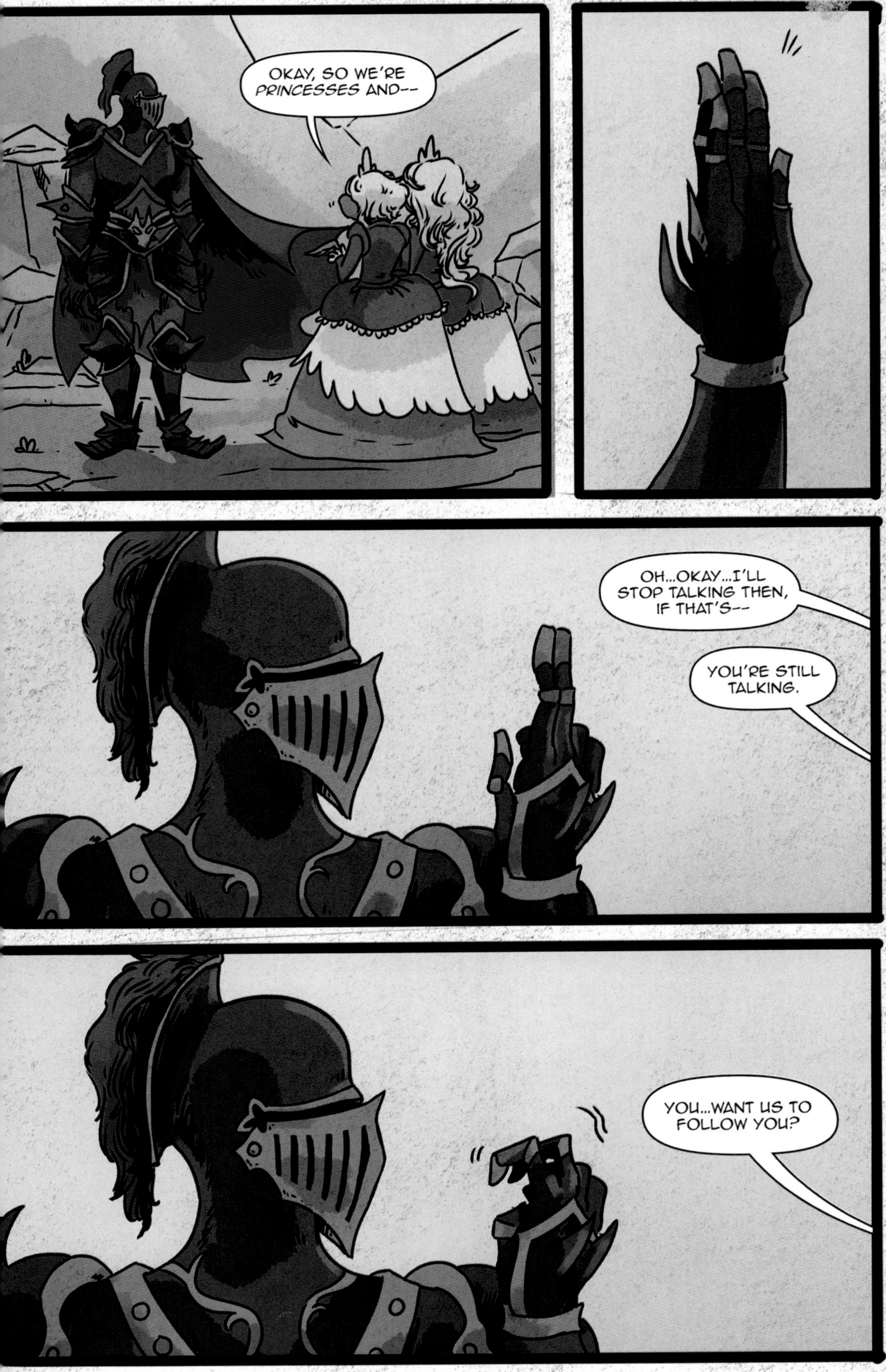
OKAY, SO WE'RE PRINCESSES AND--
OH...OKAY...I'LL STOP TALKING THEN, IF THAT'S--
YOU'RE STILL TALKING.
YOU...WANT US TO FOLLOW YOU?

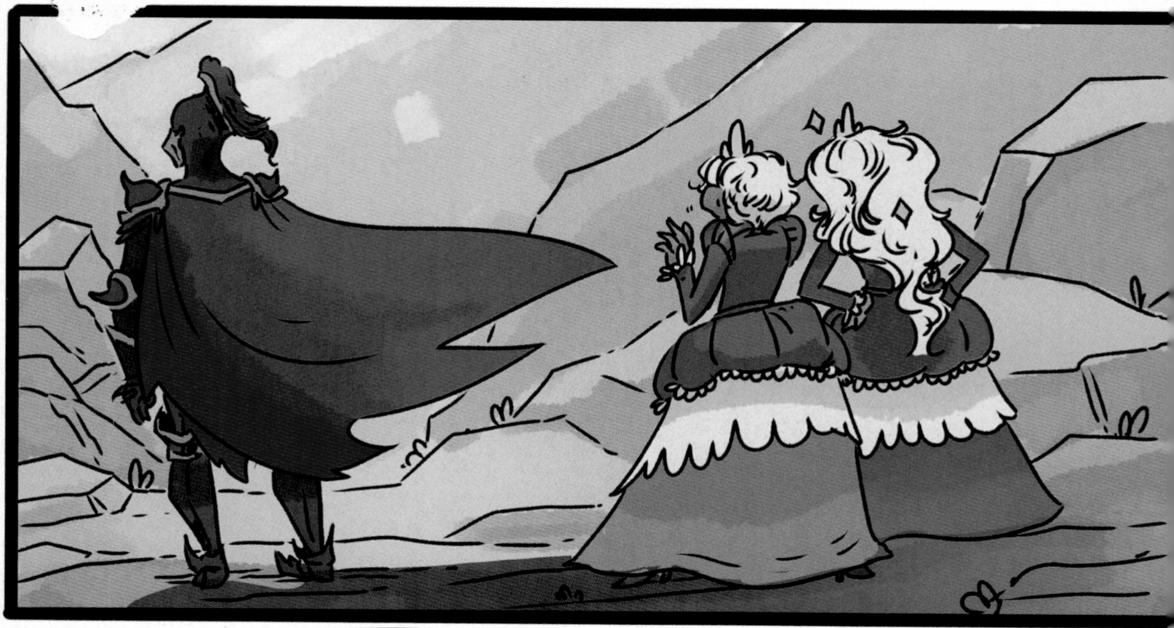

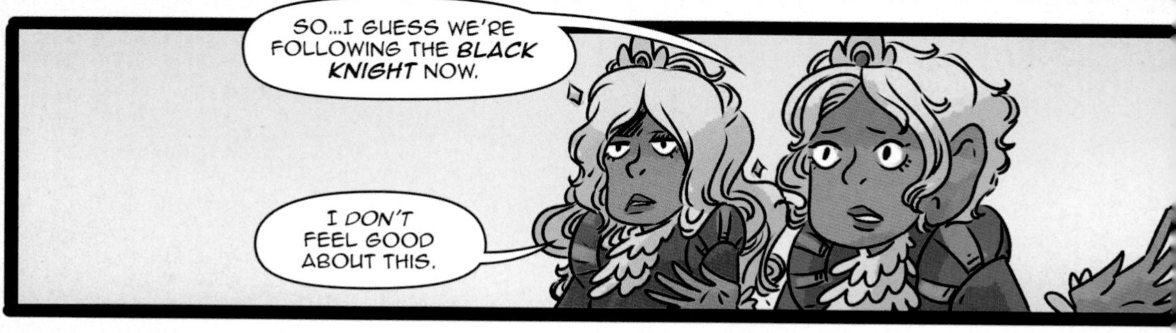
SO...I GUESS WE'RE FOLLOWING THE *BLACK KNIGHT* NOW.
I *DON'T* FEEL GOOD ABOUT THIS.

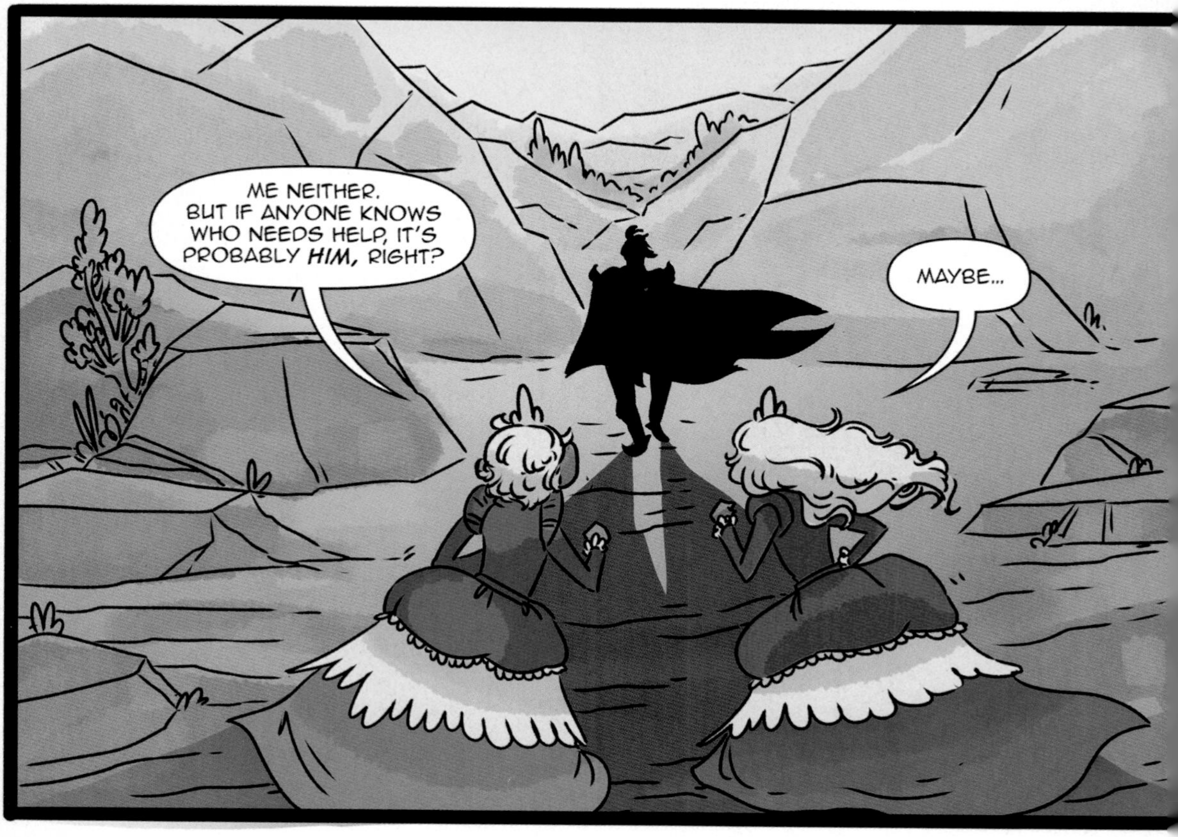
ME NEITHER. BUT IF ANYONE KNOWS WHO NEEDS HELP, IT'S PROBABLY *HIM,* RIGHT?
MAYBE...

# ISSUE #1 (Alize)

By Kaitlin Jann

## Page Two
## Inks & Colors

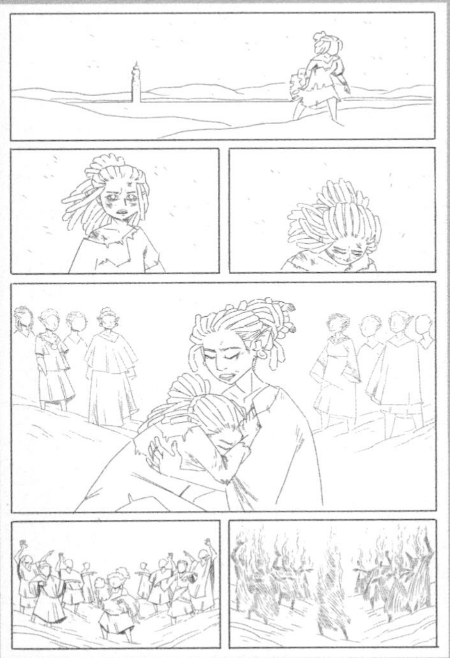

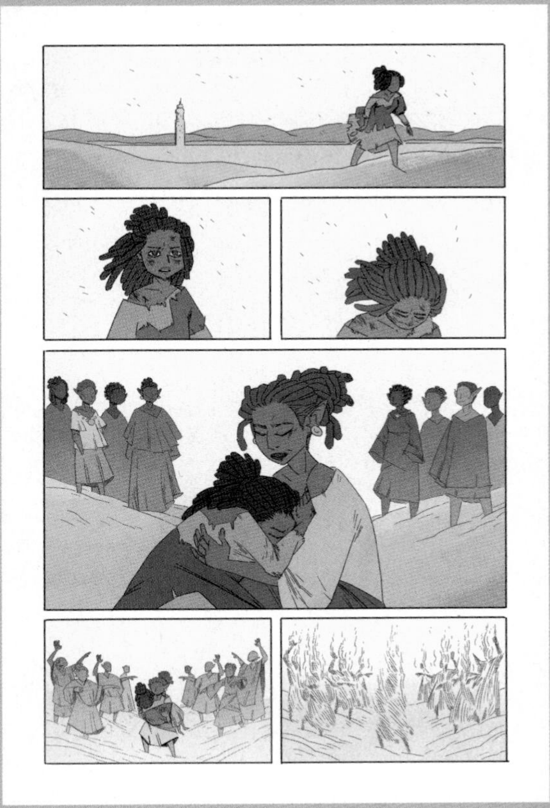

## Page Five
## Inks & Colors

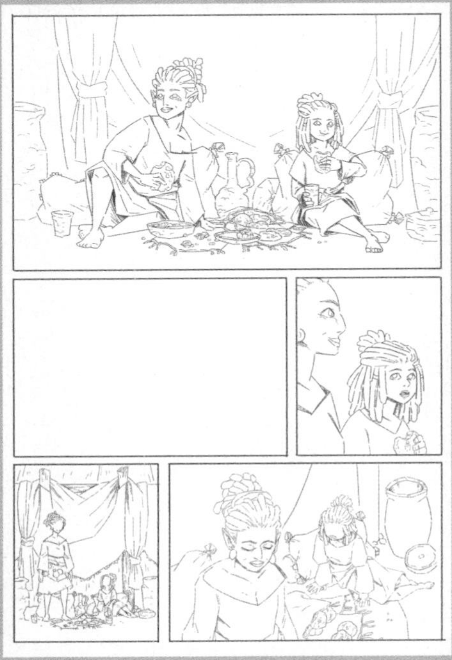

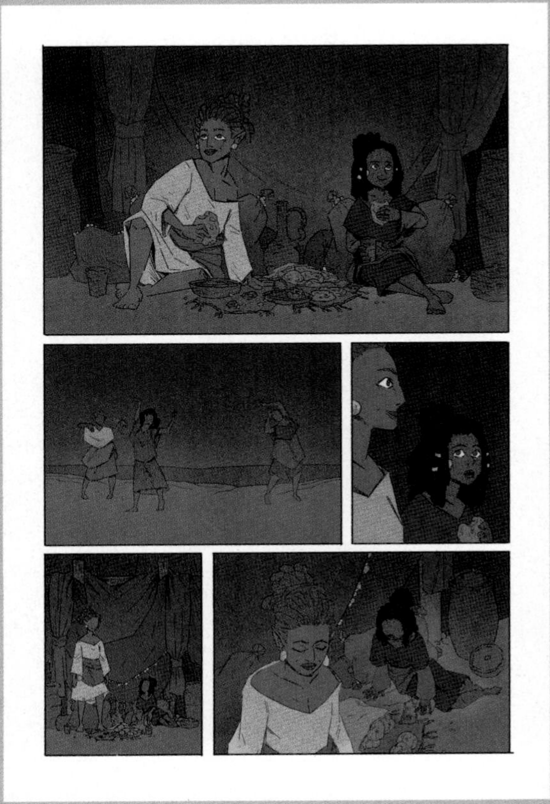

# ISSUE #1 (Alize)

By Kaitlin Jann

## Page Ten
## Inks & Colors

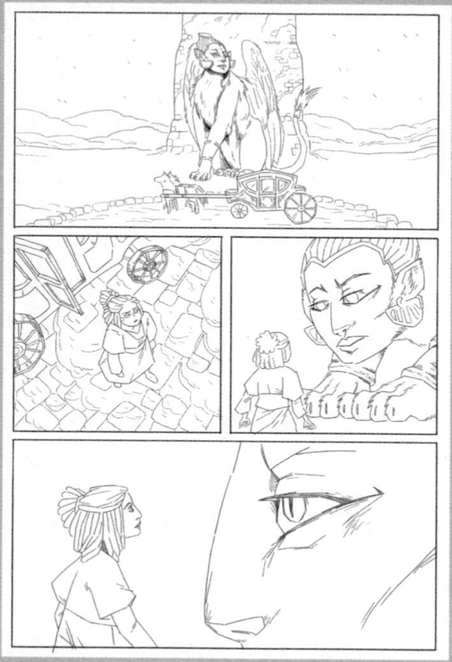

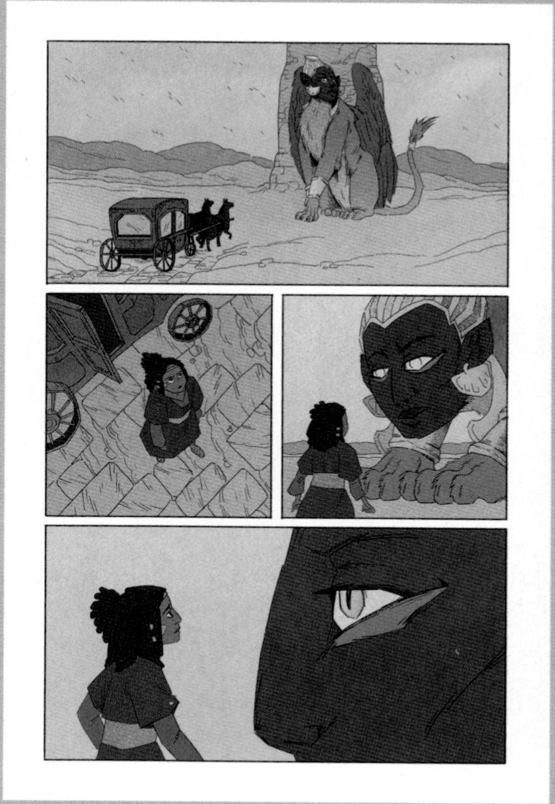

## Page Eleven
## Inks & Colors

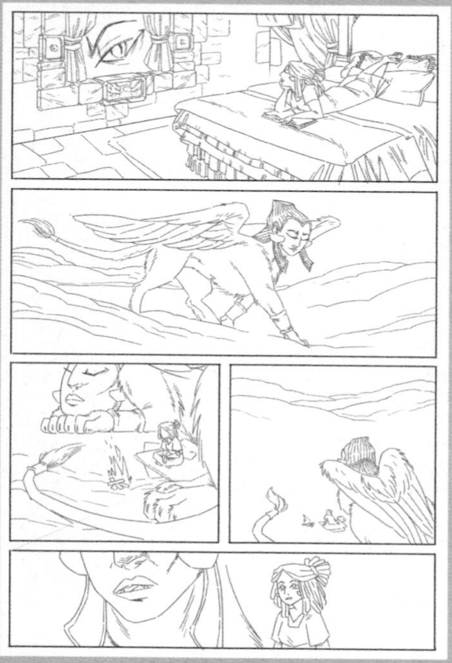

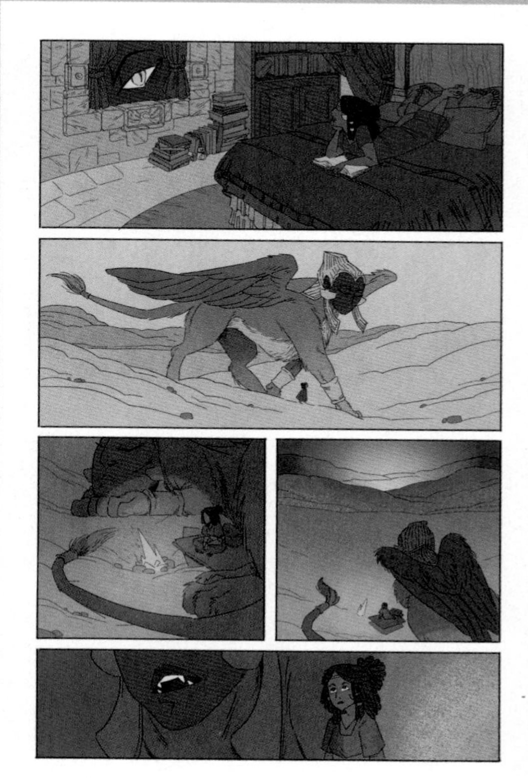

# ISSUE #1 (Alize)

By Kaitlin Jann

## Page Seventeen
## Inks & Colors

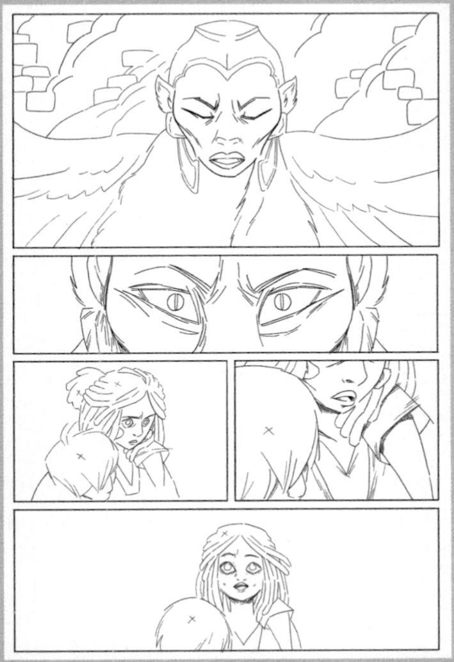

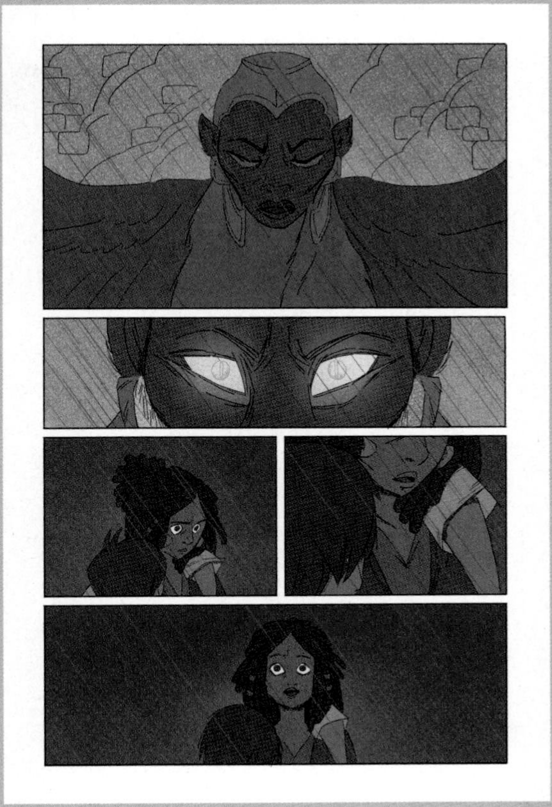

## Page Nineteen
## Inks & Colors

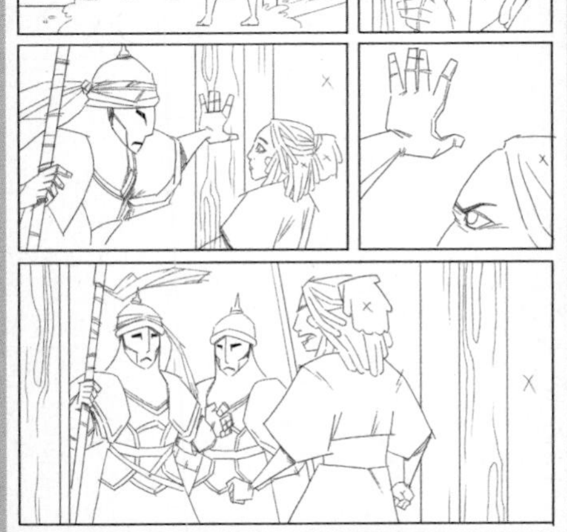

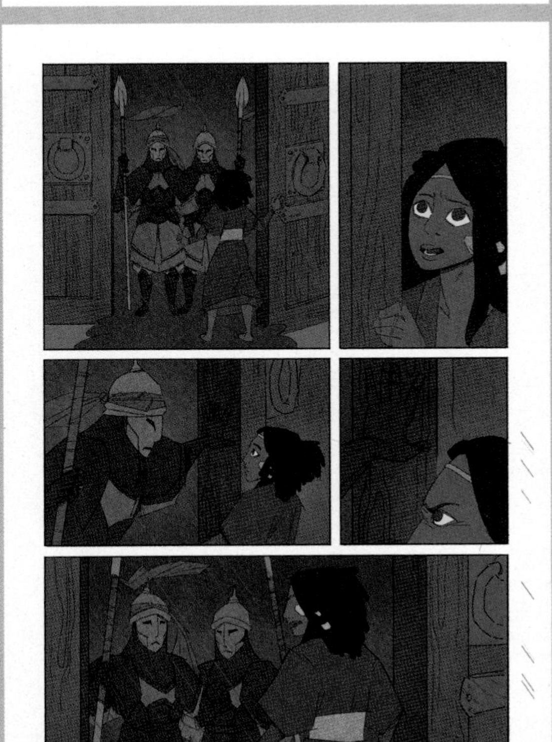

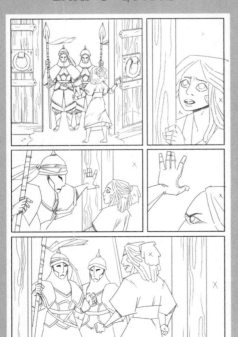

# ISSUE #2 (Angelica)

By Jackie Crofts

## Page One Inks & Colors

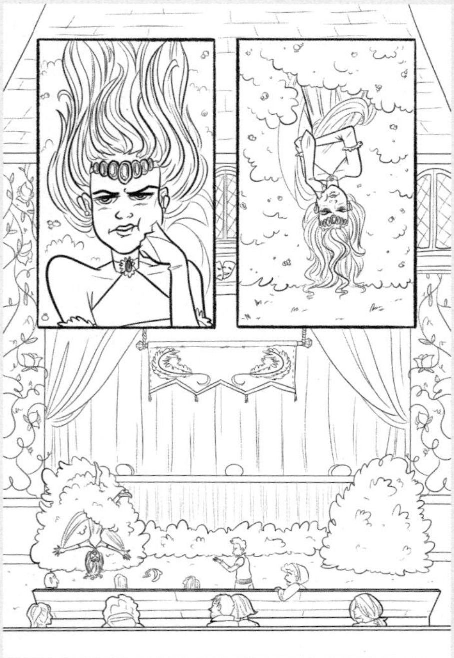

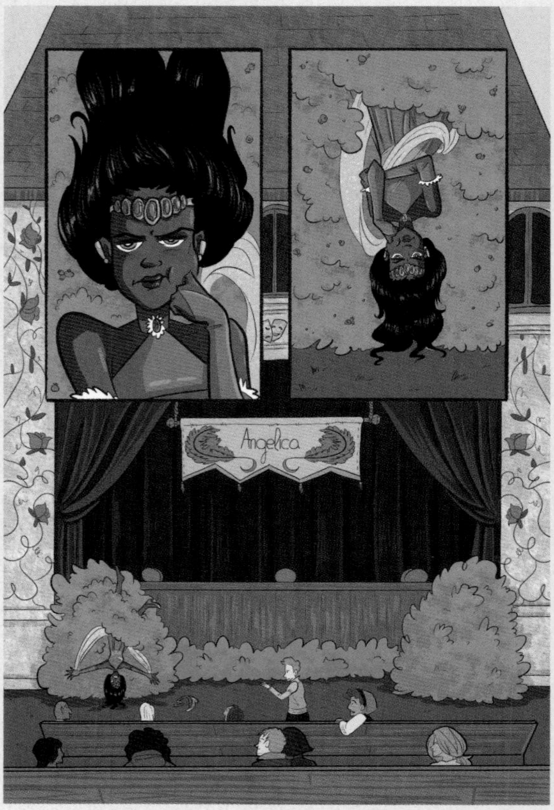
Angelica

## Page Four Inks & Colors

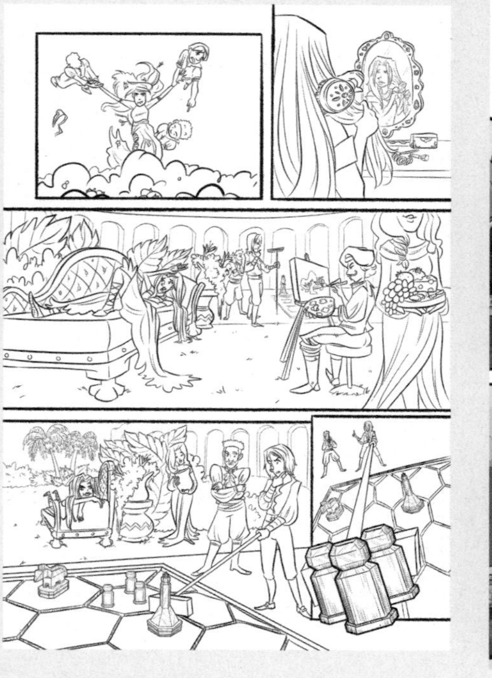

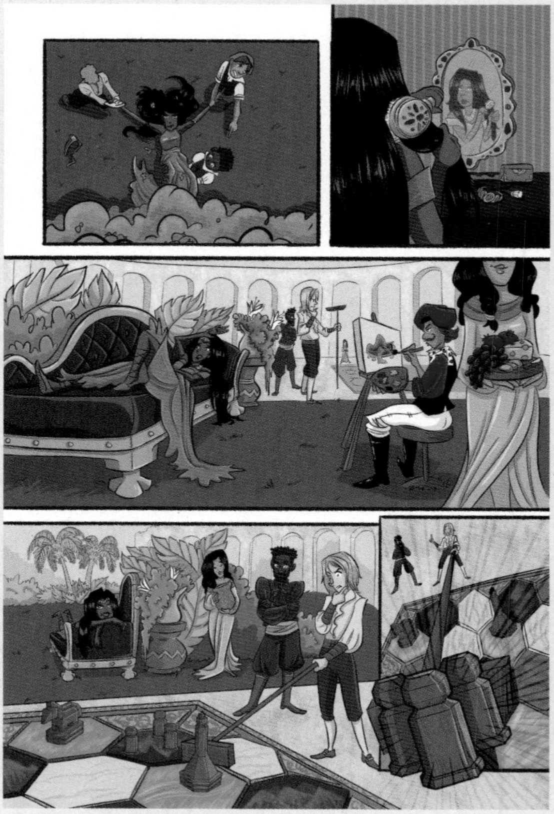

# ISSUE #2 (Angelica)

By Jackie Crofts

## Page Seventeen
## Inks & Colors

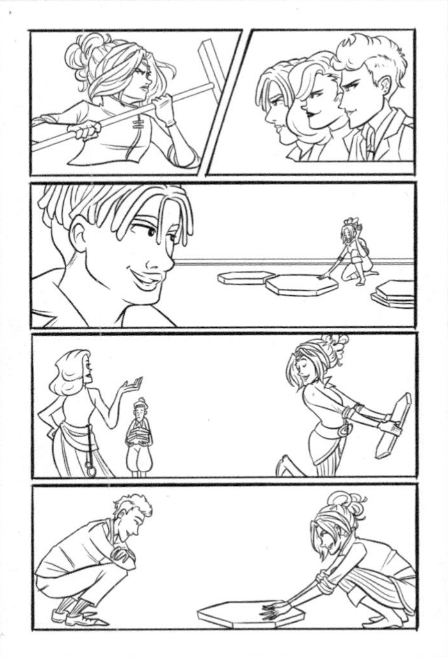

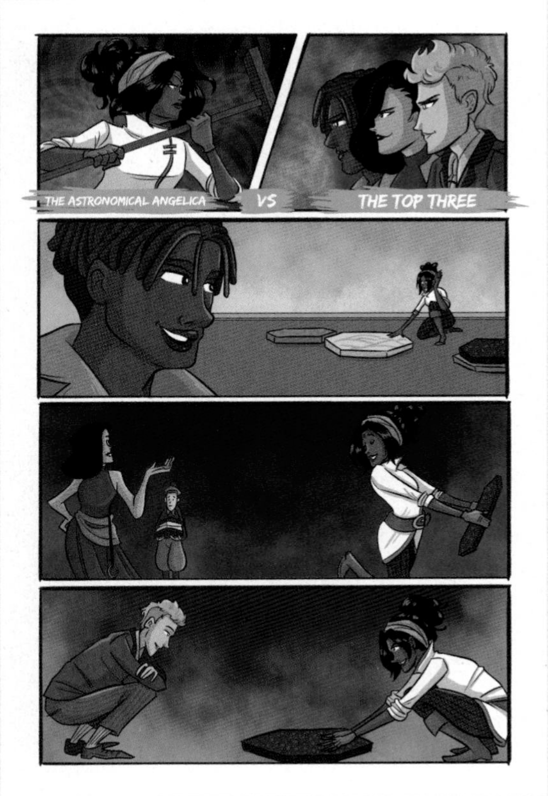
THE ASTRONOMICAL ANGELICA
VS
THE TOP THREE

# ISSUE #3 (Angoisse)

By Takeia Marie

Page One
Inks & Colors

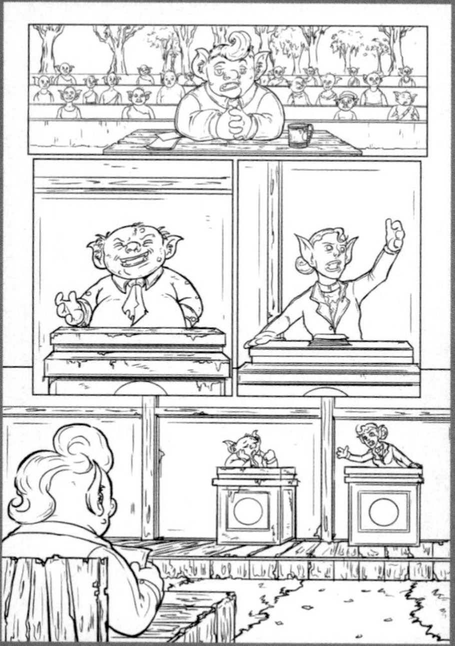

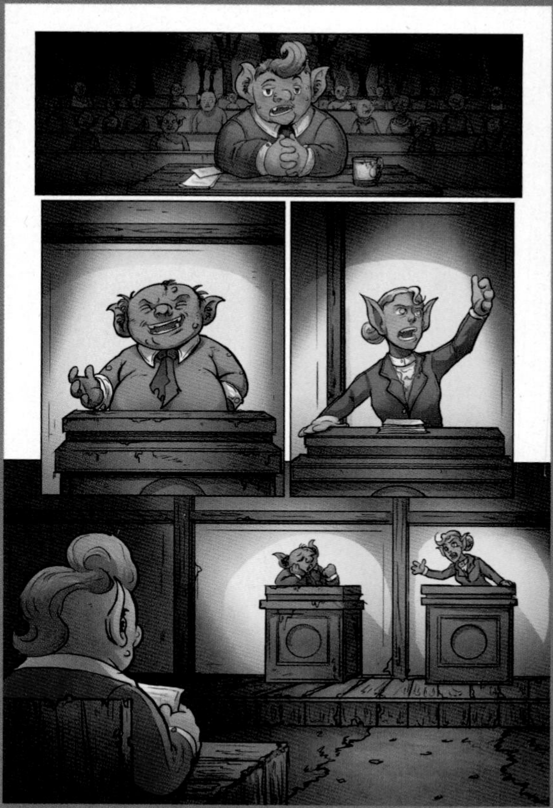

Page Three
Inks & Colors

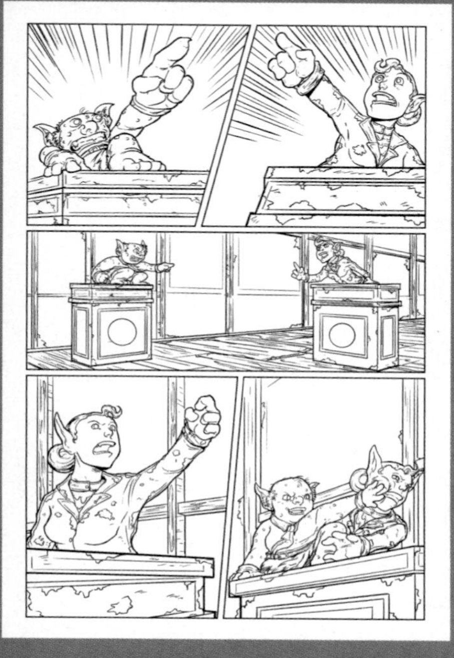

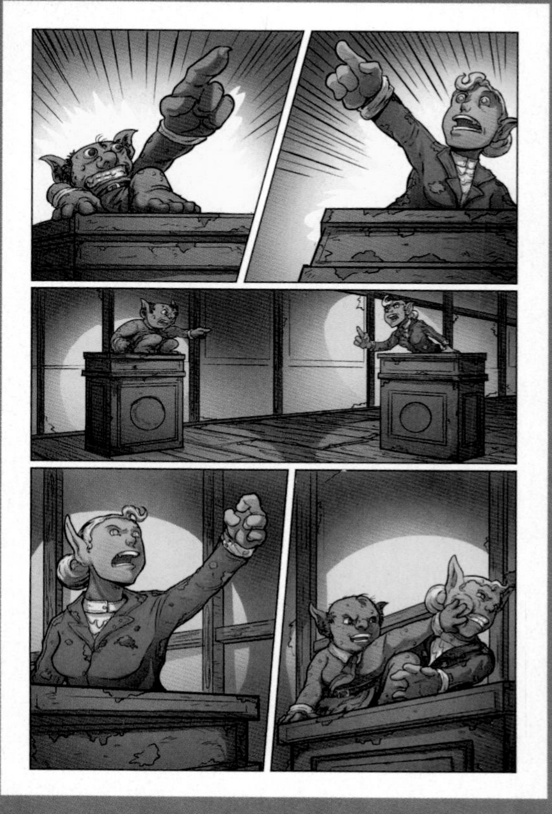

# ISSUE #3 (Angoisse)

By Takeia Marie

## Page Four
## Inks & Colors

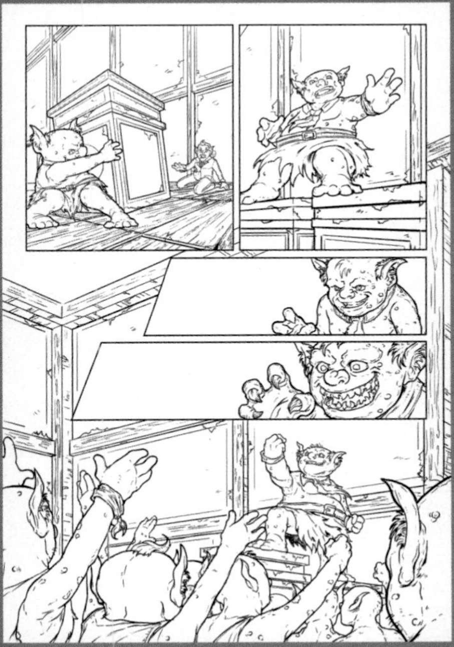

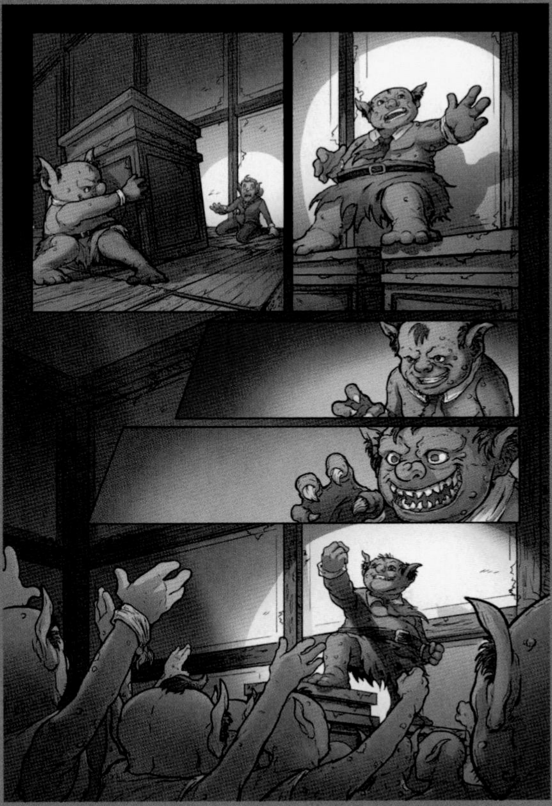

## Page Seven
## Inks & Colors

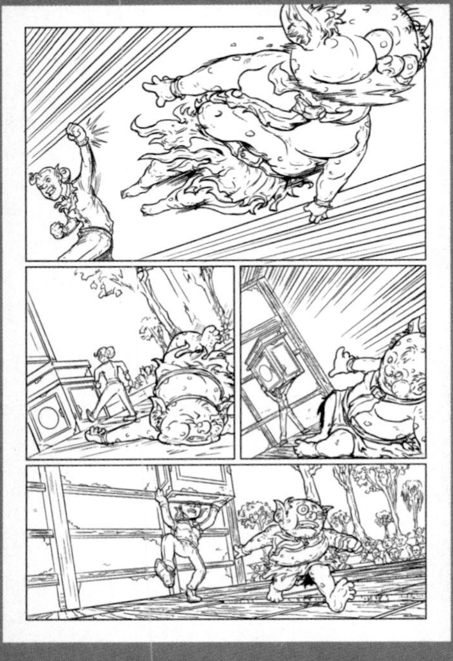

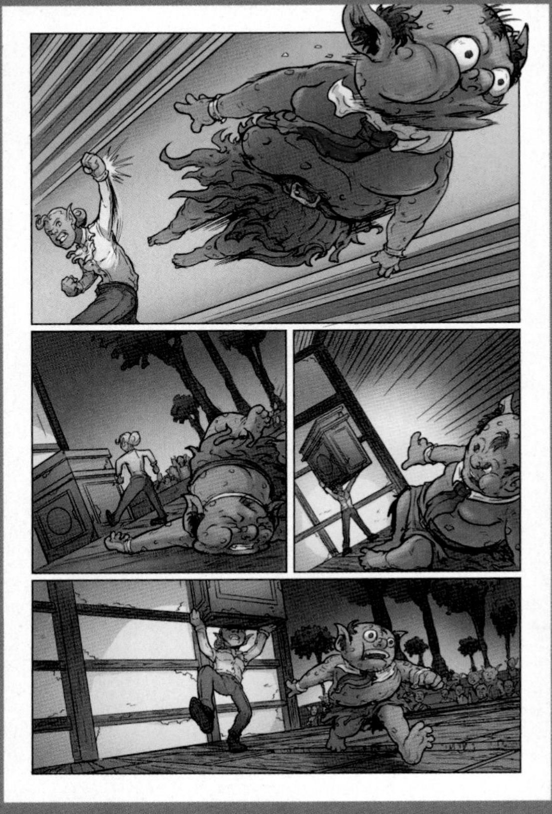

# ISSUE #4 (Antonia & Andrea)

By Robin Kaplan

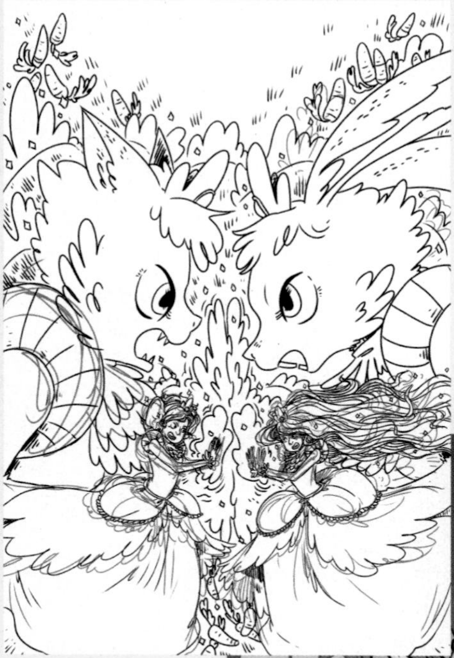

Cover
Inks & Colors

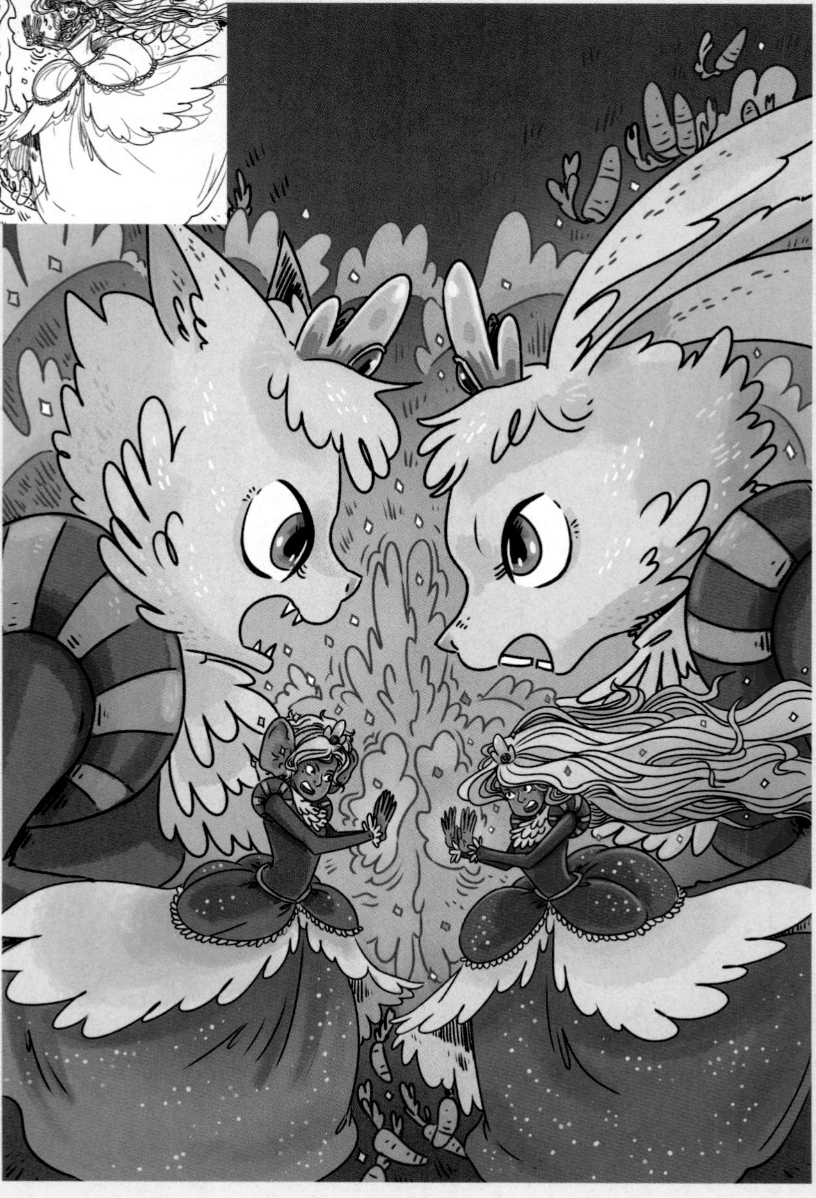

# ISSUE #4 (Antonia & Andrea)

By Robin Kaplan

## Page One Inks & Colors

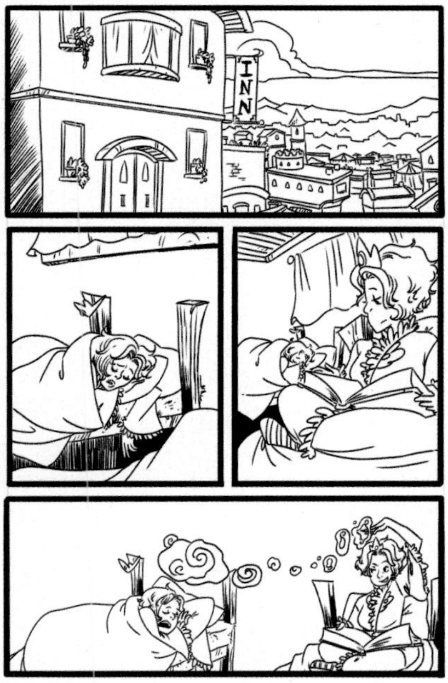
INN

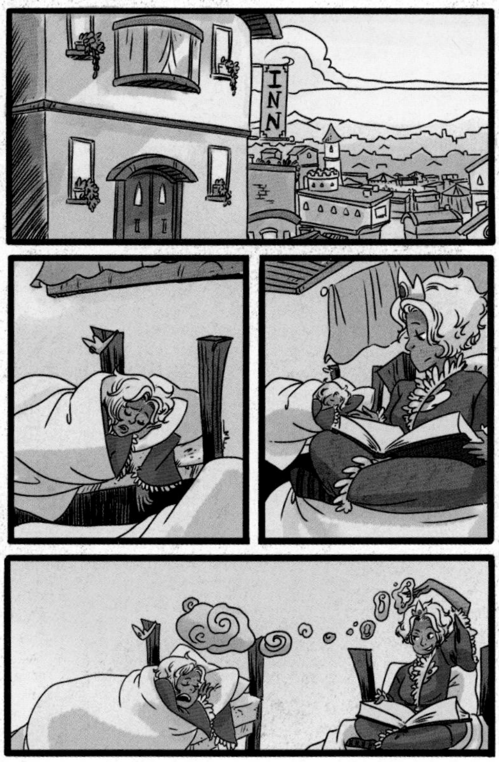
INN

## Page Three Inks & Colors

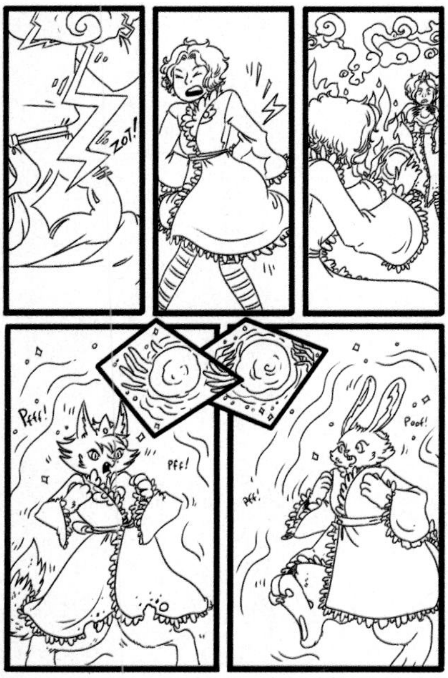
ZOT!
Pfff!
Pff!
Pff!
Poof!

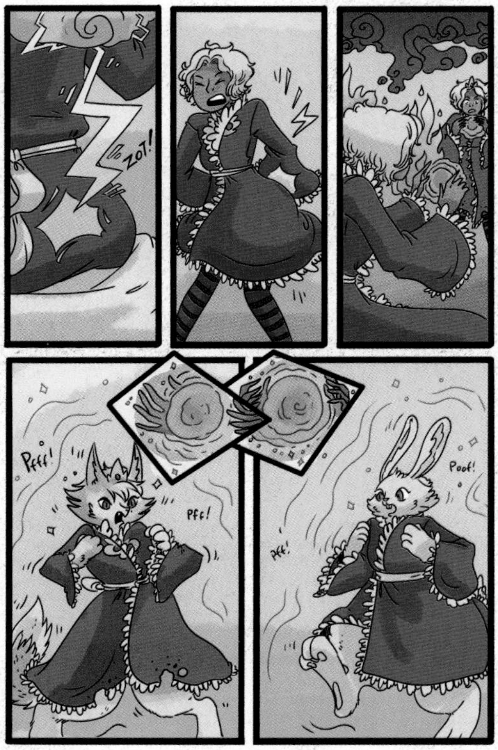
ZOT!
Pfff!
Pff!
Pff!
Poof!

# ISSUE #4 (Antonia & Andrea)

By Robin Kaplan

## Page Eight Inks & Colors

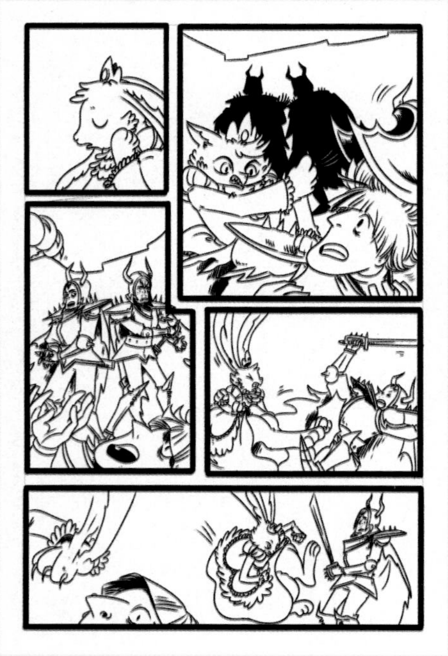

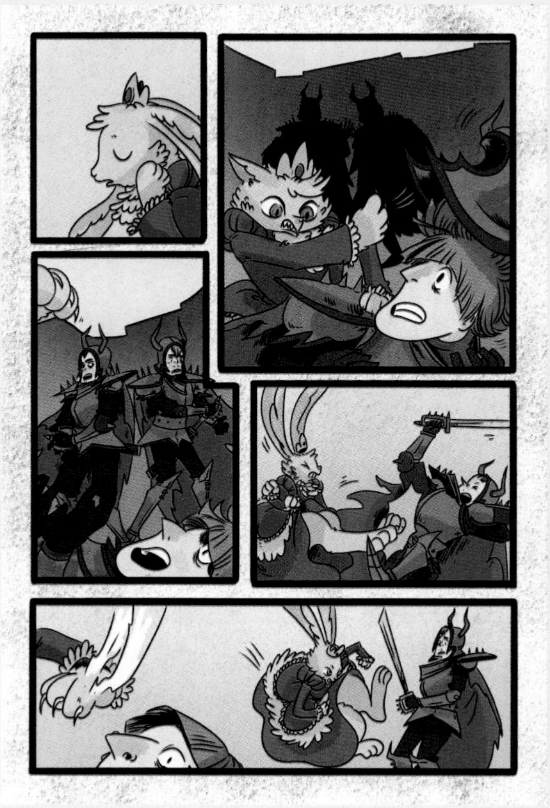

## Page Nine Inks & Colors

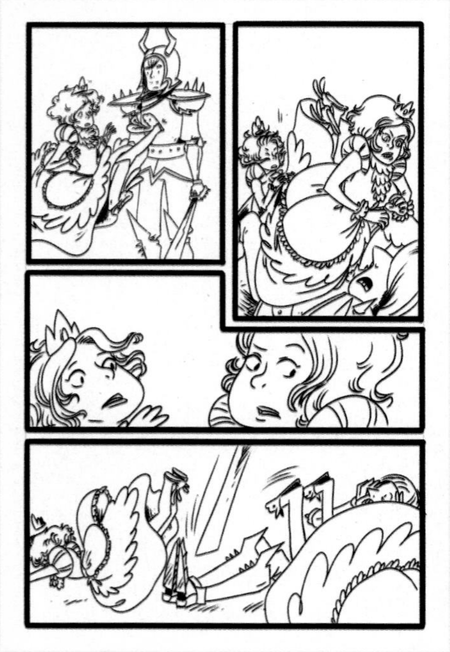

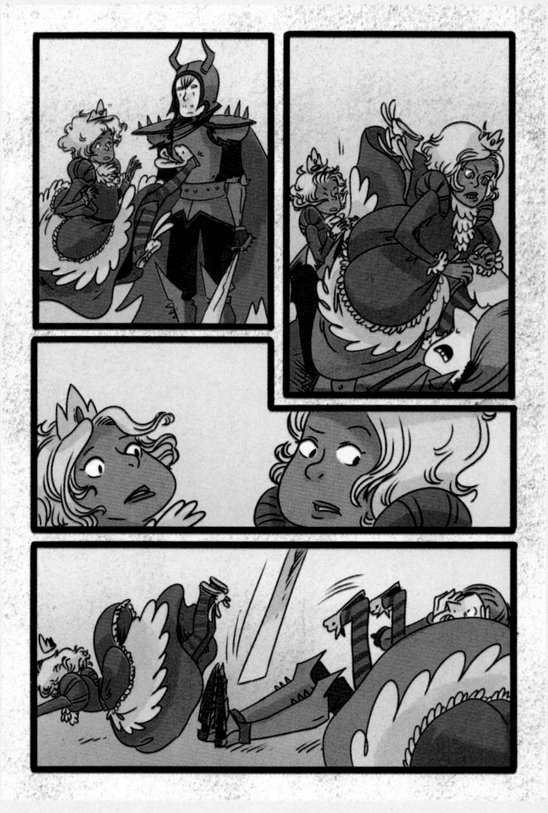

# ISSUE #4 (Antonia & Andrea)

By Robin Kaplan

## Page Eleven Inks & Colors

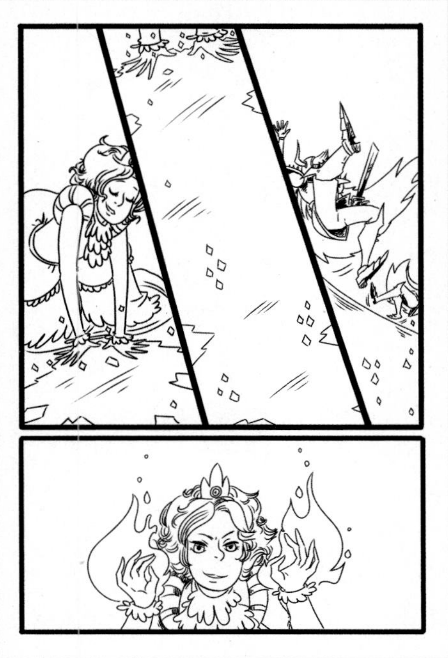

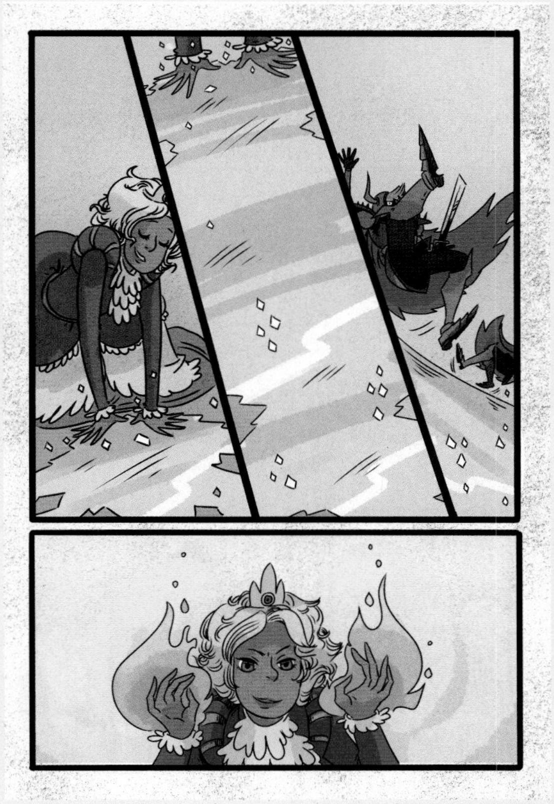

## Page Twelve Inks & Colors

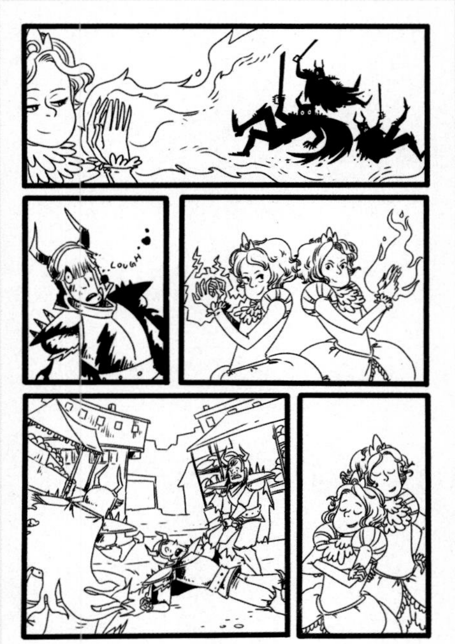
COUGH

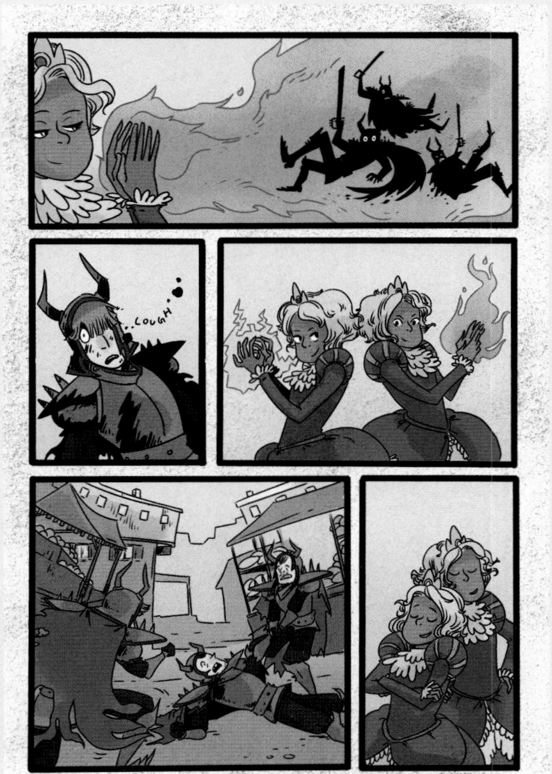
COUGH

# ISSUE #4 (Antonia & Andrea)

By Robin Kaplan

## Page Seventeen Inks & Colors

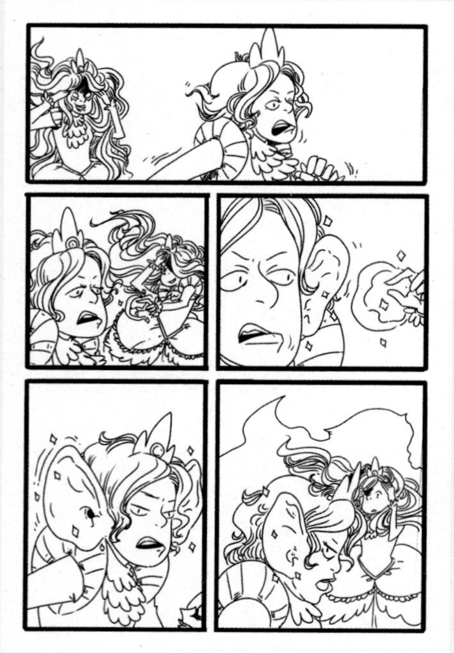

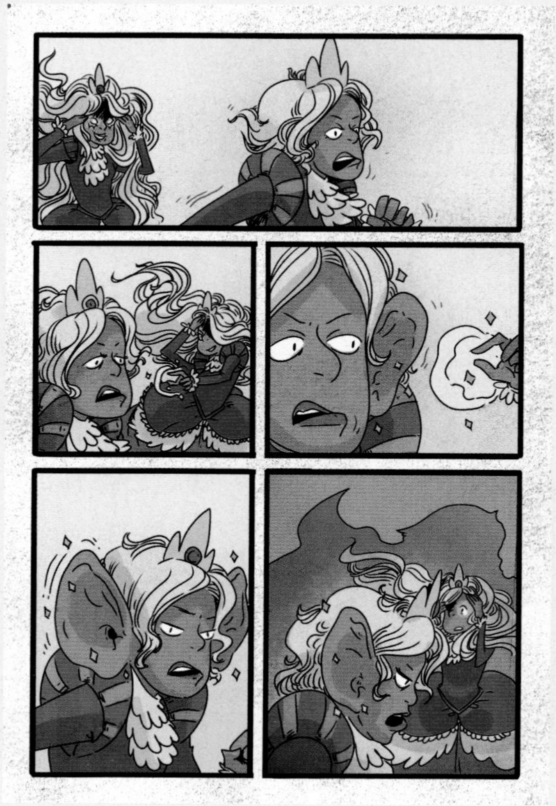

## Page Eighteen Inks & Colors

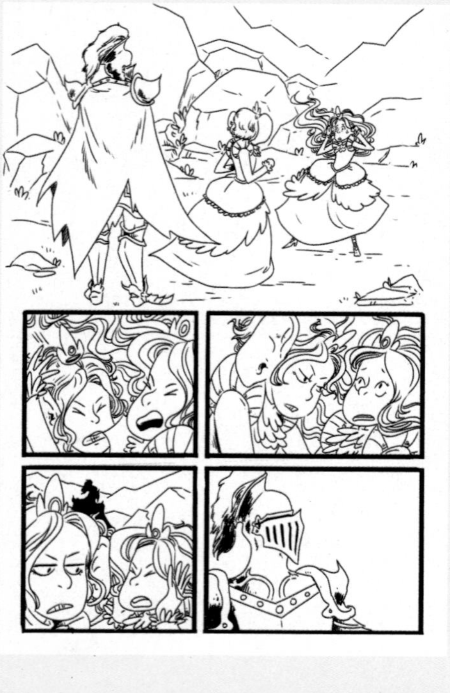

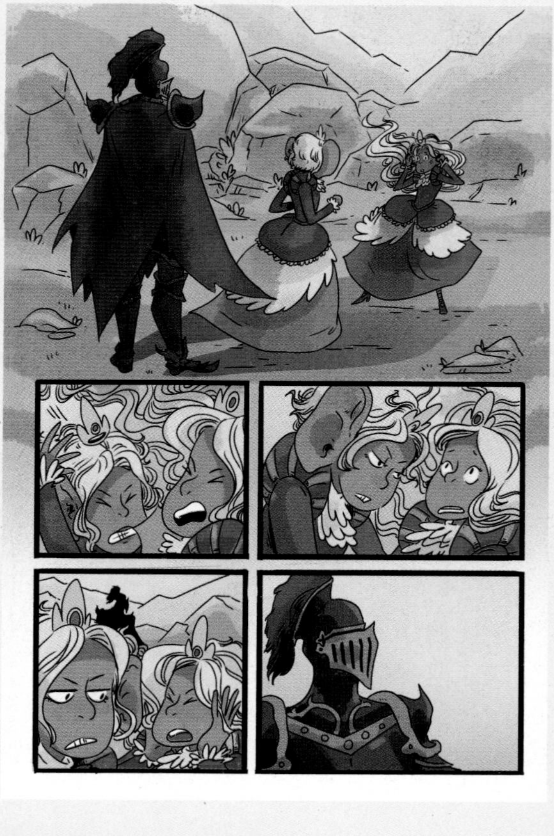